Who Cares?

Drew Kinayle

Best Wishes
Drew Kinayle
x

ᑫP.

U P Publications
2010, 2011

First published in Great Britain in 2010 by
U P Publications Ltd
25 Bedford Street, Peterborough, UK. PE1 4DN

Cover Design copyright © Richard Barnard 2011
Cover Artwork copyright © Sally Artz 2011

A CIP Catalogue record of this book is available from the British
Library

Originally released in the UK under ISBN 978-0-9557447-8-5

This Edition printed in England by Lightning Source UK Ltd

ISBN 978-1-908135-04-9

www.uppublications.ltd.uk
www.kinayle.com

Dedicated to my Children

First and foremost – Caron
For her dogged determination to make me finish – and the courage to tell me when I'd got it wrong.

Kelly – for providing me with half the story content and finding me a publisher!

Jaimee – for her attention to detail and for sending me her angels

Finally, Rhys – for being there!

One

What's the deal with good luck then? Why are some people always boasting about how lucky they are, whilst others live with a permanent run of bad luck? Why isn't there a number you can call to complain that your luck has run out and you'd like to renew it over the phone?

Perhaps there's an unwritten law that states if you don't use all your good luck by a certain time you lose it by default and sadly, company policy, it can't be carried over. If that's true then it would explain why I believe my luck well and truly ran out at the age of twenty-four!

But wait, let me clarify. After all, I wouldn't want to mislead anyone into thinking that the first twenty-four years of my life were filled with good fortune, blessed interventions, bounteous wealth and opportunities – far from it. No, my luck situation is akin to a game of snakes and ladders. Up I go, throwing double-sixes, racing my way up the board and then, just when I can see the end in sight, I trip on the huge anaconda and go tumbling down to square one again.

My first real memory of bad luck happened when I was just nine-years old and I suppose it's fair to say that up until that point I was unaware of my good fortune as I enjoyed the above-average, healthy life of the upper classes.

There are photographs of me winning numerous prizes at school, surrounded by lots of friends, both socks the same colour (I'll explain that one a bit later). Glorious holiday videos show me running around carefree; my sun-kissed, auburn hair flowing wild and unmanageable around my suntanned face. Even the freckles, that would plague my later years, complemented the amber of my eyes and always in shot were my proud grandparents making sand castles or paddling with me in the sea, whilst my parents sat sedately in their loungers, sipping Pimms and reading the Financial Times (yes even abroad)!

So up until the age of nine, my life was going pretty well but then without warning it all changed and, in true bad luck fashion, it just happened to be, Friday the thirteenth.

The school rang my mother to inform her I had a temperature and would she arrange for someone to fetch me immediately. Hillside School for Girls had a zero tolerance policy on illness, as well as lateness, absence, underachieving and…well most things actually.

It was this very bigoted elitism that made Hillside the coveted school of choice for the rich and famous and every child and their parents were subjected to the third degree before membership could be guaranteed.

It was a private school that took only children of a particular status. No scholarship could win you a place and no charitable organisation could pave your way, for it was known affectionately as the MCP policy: money, class and position and one out of three didn't cut it. Luckily my father, Milton Hall-Smyth was born into the upper classes and both he and my mother were barristers, earning six-figure salaries so, naturally, I was fully qualified!

Until, of course, Friday the thirteenth!

My mother, as was her way, was far too busy to actually come and collect me herself so she instructed my grandmother to come instead. I'm ashamed to say that just the thought of my grandmother's imminent arrival caused me to actually vomit. Well, not just vomit but projectile vomit, which travelled the length of the headmistress' room at about ninety-miles an hour, delivering a direct hit to her chest.

I thought she might pass out but she quickly recovered her composure and screamed for the nurse who practically threw me out of the room. I tried to tell her I was happy to call for a taxi and make my own way, because my poor grandmother was infirm, disabled and far too busy with her charitable works to fetch me, but the door was closed (well slammed), in my face.

You've never truly known fear until you're faced with the

prospect of your ancient, non-conformist, ex-showgirl, maternal grandmother on her way to pick you up in her old 'Moggy' Minor from one of the most exclusive, discriminatory and prejudiced schools in the country. My only hope was to make a dash for the entrance and try to head her off before she got inside. I started to make my move but was pulled back by the nurse.

"Miss Hall-Smyth, take a seat, I'm sure your grandmother will be here shortly."

As she said it, I felt something rise up in my throat and the nurse, having witnessed the state of the headmistress, took a quick step back giving me my chance to make a break for the door. "It's okay, I'll wait for her outside, she's only got one leg, she'll never make it all this way," I shouted, whilst dashing towards the main vestibule and its grand, marble entrance. I thought for one awful moment she might give chase but, luckily, at that moment the door to the office opened and a badly stained blouse was passed out.

Now, don't get me wrong, I love my grandmother but she is a tad eccentric. She and Granddad bought the old Morris Minor when he was alive and did it up to take it to Classic Car rallies. When he died she just couldn't part with it – which is lovely, except she still insisted on giving it a run out whenever she had the chance and, apparently, picking me up from school was the perfect opportunity.

Couple this with the fact that she had a penchant for dressing-up, it would be so like her to arrive wearing her big, straw hat tied under her chin, old Katherine Hepburn style glasses, tinted yellow with wings on the side big enough to hang your coat on and bright red lipstick that would give a post box a run for its money. You can understand why I had to head her off at the pass.

I waited twenty-minutes outside the main entrance and my grandmother still hadn't appeared. Then suddenly the door opened behind me and the nurse stood there with a haughty expression on her face.

"Miss Hall-Smyth, is your grandmother able to drive with only one leg?"

Who Cares?

"Oh yes Miss Pennington, she has a specially converted Mercedes she drives all the time, it's only walking she has a problem with."

"A specially converted Mercedes, has she? That's quite remarkable."

"It is, Miss Pennington, it's the only one in the country and brand new, cost an arm and a leg my dad said... well, in this case, perhaps just a leg."

"No, Miss Hall-Smyth, what's remarkable is a lady with two legs driving a Morris Minor just came to reception asking for you. Apparently she arrived at the wrong gate and has been wandering the corridors looking for you. She says she's your grandmother!"

"Oh, that grandmother," I said, contorting my neck to see around the nurse. I had to see where she was and what she was wearing. "The two-legged one!"

I begged the nurse to let me wait outside for her but she pulled me back in to collect my grandmother, hat and all, from the office and then made me walk the length of the school to the back entrance. As luck would have it, *bad* luck of course, it was lesson change-over and the corridors were crowded. For me, it was like the walk of shame, but for my grandmother it was a golden opportunity to sing songs from *West Side Story*, taking off her hat, dramatically, to reveal she'd left a curler in the back of her hair.

Laughter reverberated around me and I doubted I'd ever be more embarrassed in my entire life. But, boy was I wrong; Friday the thirteenth hadn't finished with me yet.

My grandmother was in high spirits on the way home, delighted by how many young people had enjoyed her rendition of *Maria* and *I Feel Pretty*. Are show-people so blind they don't understand the difference between applause and laughter? However, as I looked over at my grandmother I realised it didn't matter because she didn't care, she was happy in her world. Gran was the half-full type of person, always looking on the bright side, always ready for a challenge. She simply didn't care what other people thought of her.

If only I'd inherited her quirky qualities, how much simpler my life could have been. I looked over at her singing *Happy Talk* from *South Pacific* and I felt a well of love for her and as if, instinctively, she knew, she reached over and squeezed my hand.

The journey home was predictably slow, after all the Morris Minor didn't venture over thirty miles an hour even on a straight run and in some cases it would have been quicker to walk but it didn't matter; there was no hurry. Both my temperature and the sickness had subsided, and of course no one would be at home, my parents rarely came home before evening and even at that young age I felt the loneliness of working professional parents and an empty house.

As the ten minute journey stretched into half an hour we started on a joint rendition of *Happy Talk*, eyes squinted and imaginary chopsticks in our hands, which was quite scary given that Gran was driving at the time. As we approached home our journey culminated in our version of *There is Nothing like a Dame* and in true Grandmother fashion we carried on singing as we got out of the car and walked up the path, finishing on a crescendo as we burst through the door. However, the sight that greeted us shattered the illusion of *South Pacific* forever.

There, in what should have been an empty house, standing by the sink, marigolds on, washing up the breakfast things was a tall, slightly overweight woman with shoulder length, blonde hair, a silk see-through blouse and a black miniskirt topped off with black stockings and knee-high boots.

As she turned in surprise at our loud and excitable entrance, we could see that her face was heavily made up with green eye-shadow, a thick coating of honey coloured foundation and a rather too heavy splurge of blusher and bright red lipstick. Oh yes, it was fair to say that this was nothing like a dame and I felt my stomach rise up into my throat again as I heard my grandmother exclaim with delight, "Milton, don't you look stunning."

My father stood, torn between the pleasure that my grandmother liked his ensemble and horrified that I was there. I on the other hand, was just horrified! My tongue felt four sizes too big and the blood from my head started edging its way down towards my feet. My grandmother caught me before I fell and although I only passed out for a few seconds, when I came round I was blissfully unaware of what had caused me to faint in the first place, until I saw my worried father bending down in front of me holding my hand, calling my name, now minus the blonde wig, which somehow, unbelievably, made the whole look that much worse.

Of course my father tried to explain, but at nine-years old you don't want to hear about the longings and desires of a man in his thirties, you just want your father to be your father. He goes to work in a suit; comes home in a suit, does man-things and loves you.

My mother took it personally and seemed to be more concerned as to where he'd got the vulgar clothes from. She even remarked that she thought a man of his age would have dressed with more decorum and managed to turn it round as a personal insult, wondering loudly how a man who had lived with a woman of taste and discernment for so many years could ever dress like a two-bit whore.

As things got more heated, Gran took me off to her house for the night.

The following day we arrived home to find my father packing trunks into the back of his top of the range BMW. Inside, the house was quiet. My mother had gone to work as usual, even though she knew my father was leaving. The pile of offending clothes had been placed discreetly in a carrier bag, a Harrods bag of course, and had been deposited in the bin.

As my father picked up the last of his things he came gingerly over to sit next to me. He tried once more to explain. He tried to tell me that no matter what, he would always love me. He implored me to try and understand and not judge him too harshly but I sat stone-faced, coldly looking in the opposite direction. He tried to take my hand but I snatched it away and placed it with the other in my lap.

Out of the corner of my eye I saw him take a handkerchief out of his pocket and wipe his face but I would not be drawn. I remained calm, resolute, unfeeling and determined that this deviant man would not soil me.

Who Cares?

I was nine years old. What on earth did I know about deviants? I knew only what my mother had stressed upon me during her phone call the previous night. I did not understand about cross-dressing or the need to explore one's inner-self, but I did understand about shame and about how this would look to my class mates and peers, for my mother had explained it in full, glorious, detail.

My mother went on to divorce my father and she held nothing back. They'd both been high-profile barristers, handling big public cases of corruption in high circles and it was a dot on the cards that the press was going to have a field day. They liked nothing more than knocking someone off their self-appointed pedestal and it was soon obvious that my mother was well prepared to hand them the balls and in this case, they were my father's!

The papers were full of the exposure, literally. Every day the newspapers carried mock-ups of my father in his judicial wig and women's clothing and each day the outfits got worse and more scandalous, culminating in a rather scary photo of my father in, nothing more than, stockings, suspenders and a barrister's wig. Of course my father lost his job but worse, he lost his dignity and self-respect.

My mother, on the other hand became an overnight celebrity. Vivian Hall-Smyth, daytime television queen, she who pleads against injustice for women. First, *Woman's Hour* on the radio, then *The Dick and Julie Show*, satellite's equivalent to the more popular *Richard and Judy*! Then she was in talks with *Oprah*. It was, without doubt, the best thing that had ever happened to her.

Eventually, she went off to pursue her exciting new media career leaving me with a Venezuelan cook who didn't speak English, a matronly-type nanny who thought televisions were the curse of the modern-age and a chauffeur who, despite being married, was having an affair with the cook!

Hillside school for girls removed me from the register brutally quickly and equally as quickly I lost my, so-called, friends.

My mother soon bought out my father's share of the house with her new found wealth and I was put into a new private school. Within the space of a few months, my life had been turned upside down and everything I valued or held dear was gone. Fate had played its first hand and unbeknown to me, still held all the cards.

Queen Mary's House, yet another private school, resided on the other side of town and wasn't quite so particular about position and class, and I suspected it was secretly pleased to have a minor celebrity on board.

As for my father, strangely he never got back in contact. I fully expected that once the hurt was over I'd have a chance to forgive him and come to terms with the fact that our life as it was, was over. My father was not quite the person I thought he was, but after all, he was still my father. I thought we would find a way of rebuilding our relationship. But it just didn't happen, no birthday cards, no Christmas presents, no Father!

Every day I was filled with an illogical fear of what disasters the day may bring. I know people may have thought me a little odd but over time I clung to the things that I believed brought me good luck. The first time I realised a whole day had passed with no bad luck, I was wearing odd socks. A good omen like that couldn't be ignored, so from that day on, odd socks it was.

Queen Mary's School was nice enough but starting over again was hard and it wasn't easy making new friends. Gran, bless her, saw that I was struggling and tried in her tactful way to help me.

"I know it's been hard, darling. Starting again is always frightening but you can do it, you're strong, Remi." She moved a strand of hair from my face and held me close.

"They don't like me, Gran. They won't even talk to me."

"Give them time, when they get to know you they'll love you," she said, pulling me closer and snuggling me in to those pillow bosoms that Grans always have.

"But," she said, softly. "Perhaps the other children are a little put off by your appearance."

I sat up immediately. "Well if an odd sock, a rabbit's foot and a clove of garlic puts them off, who cares?" Straight away the jazz hands were out and I knew a song was right behind them.

Who Cares?

"Don't care was meant to care, Remi, come on," she said, getting up and pulling me to my feet. Soon we were dancing around her little sitting room and for the umpteenth time during my lifetime we were singing – forget your troubles – come on get happy. By the time we got to the shout hallelujah, we both had our hands waving in the air and broad smiles plastered to our faces.

Who needs friends, when you have Gran?

By the second year at Queen Mary's my mother was absent more than she was at home.

The chauffeur was now having a *ménage à trois* with the cook and the nanny, and I was rushed to hospital, Gran by my side, with what turned out to be a very serious case of hypochondria. Anyone who has ever suffered with hypochondria will know it's a very difficult condition to correctly diagnose as the symptoms are endless.

Mine started with headaches which, as everyone knows are the first signs of a brain tumour, even the doctor agreed it was all in my head.

Next, I noticed my arms and legs were of different lengths which may have been caused by an over-active growth hormone or possibly a calcium deficiency, both apparently known signs of hypochondria.

Then, whilst turning off all the lights in the house and shining a torch into my eyes to watch how quickly they dilated, I thought I could see the early signs of cataracts. I checked this out with the doctor first, then Gran took me to the opticians to get a second opinion but apparently my eyes were normal, although the rather rude optician said that looking at them in a darkened room with a torch, wasn't!

My next visit to the doctor was for acute breathlessness, which I discovered after cross-country running at school. It was really frightening, it took me ages to get my breath back and of course, I thought it could be the onset of heart disease or, worse still, a collapsed lung and yet the doctor wouldn't give me a letter to excuse me from double-games on a permanent basis.

Shortly after that I suffered badly with stomach pains. They were so excruciating I decided it was prudent to go straight to hospital to get checked out. The doctor, who was far too young to be properly qualified, tried to say it was gas and I should stop being ladylike and release it more often. Can you imagine being told that?

Of course, I knew what he meant. I'd read an article about spontaneous combustion only a few days before: people exploding in the middle of nowhere, nothing left but their boots. I was a little surprised that he didn't want to keep me in hospital overnight but I guess he knew I could've been putting the other patients in danger – what with me about to explode at any moment.

I travelled home on the bus that afternoon, expelling as much air as I could, frightened to sit near anyone with a lit cigarette in case I disappeared in a puff of smoke, which actually wasn't that hard as, amazingly, everyone got off at the next stop.

When I was sixteen I made, yet another, appointment to see my doctor, who I knew quite well by then and he welcomed me warmly as I hadn't been there for a few months.

"Remington! How lovely to see you. Are you well?"

"Well no," I said. "That's why I'm here."

"Tell me all about it then," he said, leaning back in his chair and taking hold of his mug of coffee and stretching his neck at the same time.

"Well," I faltered. "I've been getting a lot of nose bleeds lately and I have boils all over my body."

"Oh," he said, coming down with a bump. "Actual boils or have you got a rash from using a new washing powder again, like last time, when you thought you had scabies?"

It's irritating that he constantly brings up my previous complaints. If it's not that, then he's had the same as me but worse. Frankly, he worries me. I think he imagines most of his illnesses. Anyway, I persevered with what I was saying.

"No Doctor, these are boils," and I lifted my top to show him one that had formed under my armpit. He seemed a bit shocked and jumped off his chair to examine it, so I went on to show him the others. "I've had lots of nose bleeds as well," I continued, knowing that this must be a definite sign of something sinister.

"You have a scab up here," he said, after examining my nose.

"Yes."

"How long have you had it?"

"Forever, it just won't go away."

"Do you pick it?" he asked, heading back to his side of the desk.

"Sometimes," I said, mortified with embarrassment. "I can't help it. It feels like there's something stuck up there."

"And do the nose bleeds come after you've picked it?"

"Well they used to; now they come if I cough, sneeze, sometimes even when I just bend down." He started writing something down and then looked back at me.

"Roughly how long have you had it?"

"As I said before, Doctor, years. If you look in my notes you'll see when I first mentioned it."

Dr. Andrews picked up my folder with my notes in but I could see he was struggling with the weight of the whole thing. In fairness it did look like a double version of *War and Peace*. He gave up and reached into the drawer instead, taking out a swab and proceeded to stick it up my nose, which of course started yet another nose bleed. He told me to come back in seven days time, which I did.

"Well, I can tell you that the nose bleeds are caused by you constantly picking the scab. The skin around that area has grown thin and now pressure, such as sneezing and bending, will cause nose bleeds. Also, because you've picked it so much it has caused Staphylococcal bacteria, which normally lie dormant on the skin – or in your case up your nose, to enter the body causing the boils. In short, you either stop picking the scab or the boils will get worse and you may get other, more serious, complications."

In my mind I saw the final headlines...Daughter of cross-dresser, Milton Hall-Smyth; Remington Hall-Smyth died today. The first person in recorded history to die from picking her nose!

Dr. Andrews obviously anticipated my next question and handed me a prescription.

"Use this cream three times a day. Stop picking your nose and, hopefully, it'll clear up in a few weeks."

Who Cares?

As I passed through reception I looked over at the two snooty receptionists, who always seemed to have a smirk on their faces.

"I have a prescription," I said, holding it up for them to see. I walked out holding my head high.

Two

Eventually, after numerous visits to the doctor and many near death experiences, I left school just after my seventeenth birthday, with a clean bill of health, five GCSEs, two A-levels, and two best friends.

One of the two friends in question was Juliet Bradley, daughter of Mrs. Bradley, a psychiatrist and Mr. Bradley who, according to Juliet, was a professional wanker.

At the tender age of ten one doesn't ask how one becomes a professional wanker or how money is to be made from such an unspeakable act, but in time I came to realise what Juliet meant. Her father was in fact the headmaster at another senior school, who had cheated on her mother with numerous affairs and went on to have a very public affair with one of his pupils, who he subsequently married and she was henceforth known as the 'Teen-Bride'.

Poor Juliet was painfully thin with long, mousey hair, thick, tortoise-shell glasses and a dress-sense that was, quite frankly, appalling. I know I'm not one to speak but really… hers was outrageous, she looked like she stepped off the pages of a black and white 1940s magazine. As well as being outdated, everything she wore was much too large, too long, too wide and too old for her.

For the first six months after I joined the school I thought she'd lost both her hands in a horrendous accident, until one particularly hot day that summer when she took her cardigan off to reveal all her limbs intact.

Juliet and I first became friends out of pure necessity, mainly because no one else wanted us as friends but also because deep down (dress-sense excluded) we were very alike. Amongst other things we both had a pathological dislike of PE and once a week, when we had double period of games, we stood on the playing field like a pair of bookends waiting to be picked for one side or the other.

On more than one occasion one of the teams would offer the pair of us to the opposing side, saying that was all the advantage they needed. It wasn't our fault we were useless at physical activity, poor Juliet's socks were so long and her shoes so big, she fell over them all the time. I on the other hand was too frightened of getting hurt so I tried my hardest to stay clear of all the other players, which I suppose doesn't bode well when one is part of a team activity.

Norman joined our school half-way through a term, when we were twelve-years old. He was very shy, quite tall for his age and had an American accent, which singled him out immediately and I think Juliet and I sensed straight away that he was destined to be one of us.

Yet another victim of a dysfunctional family, Norman came with his own baggage, which, unfortunately in his case, included a teddy that he kept in his satchel, and even more unfortunately, was discovered, to his horror, by the school bully, Penny Brightman.

Penny Brightman was built like the proverbial brick ****house, with muscles like Arnold Schwarzenegger and she was absolutely terrifying. It was said she could knock a boy out with one punch and she had an entourage surrounding her that even Mariah Carey would be proud of. Juliet and I knew first-hand what it was like to suffer under Penny Brightman, first with name-calling, jostling in the corridors and on more than one occasion a good thumping when we refused to hand over money or food. We were, however, just two of many. Penny bullied anyone who was afraid to stand up to her and the more she bullied, the less people challenged her.

On the day Norman's teddy was discovered Juliet and I were sitting outside on the bench farthest away from the school yard eating our packed lunch and discussing fashion and health matters, as we always did.

"Do you think ponchos will ever come back in fashion?" Juliet asked, whilst browsing through old knitting patterns that showed a picture on the front of a lady and a little boy with a faraway look, sporting a cable-knit jumper. I looked over at her and then at the pattern book.

"Juliet, that little boy is probably in his fifties by now and as for ponchos coming back, I don't think so."

"But they're so stylish," she said, turning the page to look at a woman sporting one such poncho and blowing a dandelion into the wind. Her reverie on the knitted garment front was suddenly disturbed by shouts of pure excitement, like hyenas being called to the kill. There were whoops and cheers as the crowd started to congregate at the edge of the playing fields.

Juliet and I knew from experience that this meant trouble. The playing fields were just out of sight of the staffroom windows and at this time of day Mr. Mackie, the duty-teacher, would be off having a crafty cigarette behind the store room instead of keeping law and order in the school playground.

"What's happening?" Juliet asked, returning her gaze back to the double-breasted cardigans. I jumped onto the bench and strained my head to see.

"I think it's the new boy, Norman. They've crowded round him and Penny's holding something up in the air. Oh my God, I think it's a teddy bear." I looked down at Juliet as she looked up at me, we both knew what it was like to feel fear and we both felt it at that moment for Norman. Juliet closed her book and stood to her full-stance, which actually wasn't very much but I could see from her determined look that she had something in mind. We both looked at each other for a few seconds then without hesitation we both said together..."*Operation Goliath?*"

I felt a huge surge of excitement as Juliet joined me to stand on the bench, but that was quickly followed by a fear which gripped the very heart of me. What if this was to go wrong? We had discussed it many times but, as of yet, we hadn't practiced it once. Juliet touched my arm and said, "We have to do this Remi, it'll be alright." She reached into my open bag, pulled out the secretly placed slingshot and handed it to me. "Remember what your gran said, take a deep breath and hold it so your aim is true"

I looked over at the crowd. There was a big gap in the middle as the mob had moved out to leave enough area for ten-ton Penny to shove poor Norman around. I could see the teddy still in one hand and in the other she had something else. What was it? Something small and round, I couldn't quite see.

The crowd was chanting and clapping now and their voices were getting louder and louder. Penny decided to get up on a bench so she could play to her audience, it took two to pull her and three to push her fat arse up there but, eventually, she made it.

At last I could see more clearly. It was a lighter she had in her other hand and the crowd was shouting, "Torch the ted, torch the ted."

I looked down at Juliet and she smiled, encouragingly, up at me. I knew it was now or never. I brought the slingshot up to my cheek, pulled my right arm back, and then squinting my left eye, I took a deep breath. When I was sure I had her in my sights, I let go and watched as in slow motion, the lump of clay we had previously selected as our weapon of choice, flew through the air. It was a direct hit, straight into the side of her head and she toppled off the bench and fell to the floor.

The crowd drew back immediately unsure of what was happening, probably thinking it was a new ploy of Penny's. As they moved out I could see for myself what was going on. Penny was lying awkwardly on her back, dazed but still clutching the teddy. Her face was thunderous, her legs askew and her underwear on show to all who were brave enough – or stupid enough, to look.

At first there was a deathly silence, and then a few giggles which carried on building until they erupted into a crescendo of laughter as people started to laugh out loud at the flailing Penny. Her face turned a terrible shade of puce and she jumped to her feet, well as fast as anyone of eighteen stone with her skirt still caught up round her waist and a lump of clay still stuck to her head can do. She jumped up and rushed towards the crowd but that just seemed to make them laugh even more as they pointed towards the dishevelled skirt and the knickers on show.

"Oh dear," said Juliet, with more than a hint of sarcasm in her voice. "Fancy having her big knickers on... today of all days." Mr. Mackie, alerted by the commotion, soon made a hasty return and the crowd started to disperse, most of them still laughing. He ploughed his way through the remaining few and plucked the clay from Penny's head taking a clump of hair with it at the same time, to which Penny reacted instinctively by aiming a well-placed kick to his groin area. Mr. Mackie fell to the floor like a sack of potatoes and remained there until another teacher came running in answer to his extremely high, soprano cries of anguish.

The day just couldn't have got better. Penny Brightman was suspended. Mr. Mackie, still in the foetal position was taken off to hospital in an ambulance and due to lack of staff, as Mr. Mackie was the PE teacher, double-games was cancelled. Result!

I doubt anyone would ever have suspected that the piece of clay stuck to Penny's head had anything to do with Juliet or myself. But we remembered what Gran – God bless her, had said when she had initially shown us how to use the slingshot (although goodness knows how she learned to use it in the first place). Her parting advice was, "Remember, darling; always plan your escape before you go in."

So with that in mind, we drank the last of our tomato soup from my wide-mouthed flask and, discreetly, I picked the slingshot up and popped it in.

"What about these?" I said, picking up the remaining clay balls. "Should I put them in as well? There's only two left."

"I should," Juliet replied, matter of factly returning her eyes back to the knitting patterns again; "It's two more than Mr. Mackie's got at the moment." We both looked at each other and burst out laughing.

"One up to us," I said. We gave each other a low five.
Later that day Norman was handed back his teddy, which he deposited into his satchel and to my knowledge it was never seen again.

Although Norman wasn't in our form, when we got the chance we sought him out and invited him to sit with us, it wasn't long before he was, as we predicted, one of us.

Norman lived with his father, half-sister Bernice and

stepmother Jane, in Hampstead and, contrary to the old, wicked stepmother stories, it was obvious that he loved his stepmother very much. His father, however, had very little to do with any of them and worked away from home most of the time, which from what Norman said, was how they preferred it. His real mother had died in childbirth when he was born and I suppose Juliet's mother, the psychiatrist, would say that Norman's father blamed Norman for her death.

Unlike Juliet and me, his appearance had very little, if anything, to do with why he was bullied. He was in fact quite ordinary, with dark, curly hair and deep-brown, soulful eyes that lit up when he smiled, and his accent, which had singled him out in the first place, was subtle, soothing and soft as velvet. His clothes were fashionable and well-fitting. He had no hang-ups about luck or health, or anything else for that matter. He was generally well-rounded, healthy and no doubt, would have been good at sports had he been given the chance but, of course, he always ended up on the final line up with us.

To be bullied though, I guess you first have to be a victim and Norman, despite his very ordinary, outward appearance, was a victim just the same as us. With his quietly spoken voice and his impeccable politeness, his reticence was taken for timidity and it was these things that singled him out for special treatment, both from the teachers and the bullies and, in particular, Penny Brightman, who, after getting over her big knickers situation, reverted to being an even bigger bully than before. Mind you having KO'd Mr. Mackie helped in that department, boys in corridors covered their nether-regions for months after that particular event. The teachers inadvertently played their part in Norman's bullying, by either mothering him or commending him for his intelligence and good manners. Within days of being at the school he was called Yank, sissy, gay and teacher's pet. Regrettably, the die was cast.

We never let on to Norman what part we played in the knicker-day conquests. As Juliet and I revelled in the euphoria of our successful campaign, it was easy to make plans to stand-up to the bullies and defend the underdogs but, of course, it was all short lived. In reality we kept our heads down, kept out of

Who Cares?

Penny Brightman's way and over the years sadly allowed her to find other, more pathetic people to bully.

Eventually, after five more years of torment and numerous humiliations (although at the same time many wonderful hours spent with Juliet and Norman), the final days of school-life loomed. All exams had been taken and all thoughts of work were forgotten. The teachers started to act almost human as they realised that this particular year of moulding was almost over.

On the very last day of school Juliet, Norman and I were the first to arrive and we sat talking quietly in the classroom, excitedly looking forward to the day ahead. The last day was always a hectic one and this would be no different. There was going to be a big award-giving ceremony, which included big cash prizes and gifts such as spa days, helicopter flights and clothes vouchers. All this was to be followed by the notorious end of year dinner, prepared by the local cookery college, which was the real highlight of the day.

We sat huddled right at the back of the class so as not to draw any attention to ourselves and, as usual, Norman, who was not in our form, sat with us while we waited for the bell to ring to signal the beginning of the last day. We took the opportunity, before the school filled up and it was still quiet, to exchange a few parting gifts that we had bought for each other.

Norman had bought Juliet a hand knitted hat and scarf in the perfect colour to compliment her eyes and for me, he bought a home-testing blood pressure kit, which must have cost a fortune and was just what I'd always wanted.

Juliet bought Norman and me personalised writing-paper sets along with beautiful pens with our names engraved on them, all wrapped in hand-dyed paper and raffia-binding.

Finally, I handed over my presents. A locket for Juliet with *Best Friend* written on it and a picture of us, taken one day in Woolworths in one of our lunch-breaks, and a watch for Norman with *Love Always, Remi* inscribed on the back.

Juliet's eyes watered slightly and Norman's face had a pinky glow to it. "Come on you two, don't get all woozy on me, it's the last day and we, my friends, are going to enjoy ourselves."

In front of Norman were seven, deliciously wrapped identical boxes of mouth-watering, dark and light chocolates; full of fruit and fresh cream from Fortnum and Mason. It was so typical of Norman to bring presents for everyone. There was one for each of the teachers who had taught him throughout the year, each one neatly wrapped and addressed with a little thank you note.

He seemed a little jittery and I knew, because of the sort of person he was, he would be feeling a little self-conscious about handing them out, so Juliet and I offered to help take them round to the appropriate classes. But as we stood up a shadow fell on the room and a gloom descended on us immediately.

"What's this then Normy, bought us girls a little present have you?" Penny Brightman stood framed in the doorway – huge and ugly, with her little entourage right behind her. Her hair was pulled, dramatically, up on top of her head and she had enough make-up on to cover the entire cast in a remake of *Ben Hur*. She was wearing a low-cut top in an unflattering colour of bright green and her cleavage looked like one vast, big bosom. She was also sporting a ridiculously short miniskirt that was so high we could see where she had been sitting on the toilet that morning, as it had left a red ring round the top of her legs.

Any other time Juliet and I would have burst out laughing but the emotion was quickly suppressed as she made her way over to us with the most menacing and hateful look in her eyes.
As she waddled closer, she started to swing her hips in an awful parody of Marilyn Monroe and puckering up her big, red mouth in a grotesque pout, she headed towards Norman.

As I looked over at him, I saw the colour drain from his face. He shrank back in his chair, pulling his face as far away as he could. In the twinkling of an eye she had reached out and grabbed all the chocolates from the table, turning dramatically to show the haul to her followers.

Juliet jumped to her feet immediately. "Penny, leave his chocolates alone! His stepmother bought them for all the teachers as a thank-you."

Penny leaned forward into Juliet's face. "Well perhaps it's me he should be thanking, for not pummelling him into the ground every day for the past five years. Anyway I'm sure gay-boy Norman would be happy to know his chocs were going to a good home." With that she grabbed at the top box and ripped the Cellophane off.

Norman jumped toward her to retrieve the others but she had a firm grip of them and aimed a powerful blow towards his groin, which he only just avoided. As she stuffed the first half-dozen into her big, fat, red mouth, I was amazed but fearful to see tears in Norman's eyes. Penny caught sight of them too and even with chocolate dripping down from the corner of her mouth, she burst out laughing.

"Ah poor Normy, crying for his lost chocolates," and she hurled another four of five down her throat, without even checking to see what the flavours were. After, all but demolishing the first two boxes, she started almost immediately on the third and threw the others to the waiting hyenas behind, who split the boxes open, downing the ones they wanted and grinding the others into the floor.

I reached out to Norman but for the first time ever, he turned away from me. Then Juliet tried to talk to him, but with a small apology he got up and left the room. It was painful to see him so upset. It wasn't the start to the day we'd expected. By the time Mr. Mackie strolled into the classroom there wasn't a chocolate in sight. Norman was back in his own classroom and the register was called for the last time.

The big prize-giving began and the various gifts were allotted. Needless to say neither Juliet nor I received anything, which came as no surprise. We couldn't contain ourselves when Penny Brightman was called out for an award. *The Biggest Contribution to the School*!

Even the teachers looked a bit surprised. Mrs. Finch checked her list again but there was no mistake, it was there in black and white and she held out the shield as she had with all the others. Penny's face was a picture of pure delight as she jumped out of her seat to collect her prize. As she made her way to the front of the hall, the silence was deafening.

"A round of applause for Penny Brightman everyone," Mrs. Finch said, encouragingly, to the crowd and reluctantly a small trickle of clapping started.

"You fat, ugly, bleeding slapper," came a voice from the

Who Cares?

back of the crowd. "You're dead meat, fat-arse."

There was a gasp from the assembly and all eyes turned to the back of the room as a woman in her twenties, started racing towards the front where Penny was standing. Penny, who seemed temporarily stunned by either the initial verbal outburst or the sight of a demented woman running towards her, was momentarily pinned to the spot, her award-winning smile still plastered to her face and the shield still held high in the air.

The young, slim, attractive woman ran from the back of the hall up the full length of the aisle. Her dark hair was pulled up into an untidy, but stylish, knot at the back of her head and she was wearing an expensive, black Juicy Couture tracksuit and, what looked like, *Prada* trainers. As she reached Penny she made a desperate girlie-grab for Penny's hair.

Eventually, and not before time, Penny regained her senses, bringing down her arms and aiming the award towards the stranger's head. It made contact, causing the women in the *Prada* shoes to lose her footing and topple backwards. Within seconds the two of them were rolling about on the floor, spit, hair and blood flying freely. It felt like ages before two of the male teachers ventured forward to intervene and it took two teachers apiece to hold them away from each other and still they were swearing and cursing. The Juicy Couture tracksuit was torn into tatters and the woman's hair was stuck flat to her face with sweat and drying blood.

Penny's mouth was bleeding and a tooth was missing from the front row. She had tramlines across her face where the other girl's sharp nails had caught her and half her miniskirt was hanging off and was twisted the wrong way.

"Oh dear," Juliet said, quietly under her breath. "Today was not a good day to wear a thong was it?" I choked and let out a loud laugh and as I did, it set off a chain reaction and the once mesmerised and quiet hall suddenly erupted.

"That's enough," shouted Mrs. Finch, trying hard to raise her voice above the crowd. "This is not a laughing matter!"

"Well I think it's pretty funny," I said, taking Juliet's hand to my left and Norman's hand to my right and squeezing both.

Luckily someone had already called the police and they

arrived in good time, taking the pair of them, still kicking and screaming, off to the police station and finally leaving us all to enjoy the rest of the day. We were sent outside for a break whilst the head and the rest of the staff sorted out the mess in the hall and probably downed a few stiff drinks to boot.

Juliet, Norman and I took the opportunity to go outside and sit on the grass, away from the all others. The sun was high in the sky and there was a soft breeze which carried the scent of the beautiful flowers, which were planted around the borders.

"Well that went well, didn't it?" said Juliet, taking off her cardigan to reveal two, stick-thin arms which were the colour of milk bottles.

"I thought it was brilliant," said Norman, putting his arms behind his head. He stretched out on the grass, squinting as the sun blinded him.

"I suppose you had to feel a bit bad for Penny though," I said, picking up a blade of grass and looking over at the other two.

Suddenly, our faces lit up and smiles, as big as Broadway, beamed out as we all threw big high-fives up into the air. We'd waited the best part of five years for this day to finally arrive and it had been worth it. Operation *Penny Down* had been a massive success, bigger than we even dared dream about.

"I couldn't believe it when the 'Teen-Bride' made her entrance into the hall like that; she was like a Pit-Bull ready for a fight. Whatever did you say to her, Juliet?"

"Oh, I just told her that I saw Penny leaving our house the other night while she was out and that Penny had boasted that I would soon be calling *her* Mum and before long she would be moving in and Stacey, the 'Teen-Bride', would be moving out."

"Oh my goodness, what did she say to that?"

"Something about 'over my dead body' and 'no school-girl slut was getting all this after what she'd had to put up with.'"

"And all that from the original school-girl slut," Norman piped up, which made up both turn around instantly because it was so out of character for him to say something like that.

"Well it's true, isn't it?" said Norman, a little embarrassed that he'd spoken out.

"Absolutely," said Juliet, taking his hand and squeezing it. "In fact she was much worse. Look, I hate my dad with a passion but I did overhear him once saying that she'd been the one to come on to him, and of course the old fool had been flattered, until she went on to blackmail him. She threatened to testify that she had been underage when they started the affair if he didn't marry her. He managed to persuade her to wait until she left school so that he didn't lose his job and as it was the money she was obviously after, she agreed. She drains every penny out of him and would leave him now, if half the house wasn't in my mother's name."

"So she must've been livid when she thought she was being replaced." I said.

"Definitely! She was all for ripping her throat out, there and then. She asked me where Penny lived but I said I didn't know. I mentioned that she would be at school the next day and as an afterthought, I said that she might be receiving an award. The rest is history!" We sat open mouthed as Juliet described her Oscar-winning performance of the previous night.

"She asked me to describe her and when I mentioned she was about thirty stone and ugly, she went absolutely berserk and called her a scheming, little cow "

"So how did you get her to be here at the right time?"

"I told her to wait at the back of the hall until she saw her get up to collect her prize, then she would know who she was. I thought she'd wait until it was all finished and then corner her but no, she just went for it, there and then. It couldn't have been better!"

"Of course it was genius that Norman changed the award list," I said, grinning. "And put another prize on the award table. By the way, the *Biggest Contribution* award was priceless."

"It was brilliant and who would have reckoned on the red thong! Now that was just pure class," said Juliet, screwing up her face at the thought. Both Juliet and I rolled about laughing at the thought of that ridiculous miniskirt and the bright-red thong that hardly covered her dignity.

"Mind you, if some vigilant member of the public hadn't

rung the police when they did, the whole thing could've blown over with just a stiff warning from the headmaster," Juliet said, shaking her head.

"Yes, and didn't they come quickly!" retorted Norman.

"Well they would when a worried member of the Neighbourhood Watch thought they'd seen a hooded man running into the local school with a gun in his hand," I laughed. "And let's face it, it didn't take much to ensure that she stayed in the cells for the night."

"I know," said Juliet, laughing. "We saw your leg come out as that poor policeman tried to hurry her down the aisle and just as she started to fall she reached back and grabbed the only thing available."

"Don't," I said, feeling slightly ashamed. "I doubt he'll be fathering any children in the near future, but at least it got Penny a glorious stay at Her Majesty's for a while." We laughed again but noticed that Norman was unusually quiet.

"What's up Norman? Surely you're not regretting what we did today?" I said, ruffling his soft, brown hair.

"No," he said, eyes closed still facing up at the sky. Juliet and I both looked at each other and shrugged our shoulders, something was wrong but what it was? We had no idea. We sat up and looked at him.

"Come on Norman, something's wrong; why aren't you celebrating with us?" Norman sat up and looked at as both with a strange look on his face.

"The thing is I'm just tired, that's all."

"What? Tired of all the bullying, all the scheming and planning, or tired of us, Norman? For goodness sake, tell us what's wrong." Norman took my hand and one from Juliet and squeezed them.

"Of course I'm not tired of you two, you're the best thing that's happened to me at this rotten school and no, I'm not tired of planning our revenge, it's what got me through the past few months and I shall miss it all, now it's all over."

"Then what is it?" Juliet said, now taking hold of my hand as well so that the three of us made a circle.

"I just mean I'm tired," he said, looking us both in the eyes.

Who Cares?

"I mean *really* tired, due to the fact that I spent the whole night injecting laxative into seven boxes of Fortnum and Mason chocolates!"

It took a few seconds before we realised what he meant and Juliet's hand rushed up to her mouth, her eyes were wide open in disbelief. My mouth was just hanging open like some demented half-wit.

"You mean all those chocolates you brought in this morning were all spiked?" I said, at last.

"Afraid so," said Norman, playing with yet another blade of grass.

"No," said Juliet, tears now starting to form in her eyes where she was trying not to laugh. "She ate three boxes of those things."

"She did indeed," said Norman, his face breaking into a huge grin. That was it, we were gone. Juliet burst out laughing and the tears rolled freely down her face.

"But you were so upset," I said, hardly able to breath from laughing now.

"That's why I didn't tell you. If you had known then you wouldn't have jumped up and tried to defend me and save the chocolates, it was perfect. I just had to bite my tongue to stop myself from laughing and the pain of that, made it look like I was crying."

I didn't think it was possible to laugh anymore than we already had. My stomach ached and my sides felt like they had literally split and tears were running down everyone's faces. We all lay back and let the sun shine down on us in our moment of glory, each recalling and replaying different parts of the day and still laughing when something new was remembered and then again when we thought of Penny and her red thong, sitting on the bucket in her cell all evening.

"Mind you," said Norman, with a wicked glint in his eye. "This does put a different slant on a criminal being on the run, doesn't it?" We all rolled about laughing again.

Three

Despite all the career talks at school I still had no idea about what I was going to do when I left. I'd mentioned to the advisers that I'd like to work in show business so they fixed me with an interview at the local cinema!

It might even have worked out, had it not been for the fact that they were half-way through their foreign-film season and how is anyone supposed to stay awake through one of those films, for goodness sake?

Next, I chanced upon what would surely have been the ideal job for me. I was sitting in the doctor's surgery, waiting to have my eyebrows checked out – apparently eyebrows that meet in the middle are the first signs of madness. I know, it's probably not true but I always think it's best to get a second opinion on these things. I sat there quietly minding my own business, checking out the patients and making sure to sit clear of the ones that may have something contagious.

Time spent at the doctors can sometimes be a bit boring so I amuse myself by reading as many of the posters on the wall as possible. One poster that has been in the surgery for as long as I'd been going said, '*Do you really need an appointment? If it's not serious, stay at home. You may be taking the place needed by someone who is seriously ill*'. However, the doctor's waiting-room is still packed with people who obviously aren't that ill, half of them have probably only got a sniffle and the other half just want a certificate to stay off work. Whatever is the country coming to?

Then, by chance, I spotted it. It hadn't been there the previous week when I had visited, but it was definitely there now. Stuck up on the glass panel that separated the patients from the reception area was an advert for a part-time receptionist in the surgery. It was definitely my lucky day. I was more than qualified to do the job as I probably knew more about illnesses than the doctors themselves. In fact, I could probably help out by diagnosing the patients before they got to see the doctor, saving him stacks of time. All he'd have to do then is hand out the prescriptions.

I got up and started making my way over to take a closer look. As I did, one of the receptionists looked up and followed my gaze. Suddenly, she got out of her seat and started running out of the inner sanctum of the nurse area, sending patients flying as she ran past the queue, skidding as she turned the corner, just reaching the advert before me.

"Sorry, it's filled," she said, taking the piece of paper down and ripping into bits. She returned to the other side of the glass, where the other nurses patted her on the back and one woman actually threw her arms around her and kissed her on the cheek. I stood for a while, just staring through the glass in disbelief, and then… I saw it.

"Oh my God," I spluttered, bringing my hand up to my mouth. Even though it was hard to believe, it was true. The nurse, the one that had ripped the paper up…had a unibrow!

Eventually, my mother stepped into the breach and got me a job behind the scenes working on the *Dick and Julie Show*, better known to the viewing public as the cheap alternative to the *Richard and Judy Show*.

I can't tell you how many friends I had to text to let them know that I was now a minor celebrity and working on the TV. Well of course I can… it was just the three, Juliet, Norman and Gran but they were absolutely thrilled for me and promised to watch every day, just in case I wandered into shot.

My mother had been a regular legal-advisor on the show, both on camera and behinds the scenes, for many years by then. Of course she didn't have time to show me around, nor introduce me to anyone; she just dropped me off at the back entrance and, after parking her car in one of the reserved car spaces, sauntered through the main doors doing her lovey air-kisses to all and sundry.

Who Cares?

It was all very friendly though and my job title was officially listed as Refreshment Officer, which basically meant I was making teas and coffees all day long, and for the first five days I didn't even get to see the programme being made and not a sniff of Dick and Julie.

"I'll never be a star at this rate," I moaned to Juliet, over the phone, after the first week. "They won't even let me get near the couch and my mother hasn't so much as waved at me since I've been there."

"You'll just have to try and get yourself seen more and try to create a good impression somehow," advised Juliet, in that slightly annoying way she had of stating the obvious.

"And how am I supposed to do that when they won't even let me near anything that resembles a camera?" I said, slightly put out that Juliet couldn't come up with something a little better.

"All I'm saying is, if an opportunity comes along, make the most of it and perhaps try batting your eyes a bit for good effect."

As we talked Juliet reminded me that Norman was leaving that night to go back home to America. We'd known for a few weeks that it might happen; his father had been working back over there for a few months and had recently been offered a permanent position. Norman, Juliet and I had said our tearful farewells and, of course, we all promised to stay in touch by text, phone and emails, but it would never be the same again and I think we all knew that. I spent another hour on the phone saying, yet another, last goodbye to Norman and when I woke in the morning I knew that he was gone, back to the States, his other friends and the life he had before we all met.

It felt like a big cloud was hanging over me all day and I walked around the studio in a bit of trance, going through the motions and working on auto-pilot. One of the production staff was celebrating a big birthday and the team had bought a massive cake to be shared out. They put me in charge of cutting it up and distributing it to everyone on and behind the set, which meant, at last, I got my big chance to venture out to where all the action was taking place.

I should have been ecstatic, but I wasn't. All I could think about was poor Norman and all the good times we'd had over the years and wondering if his plane had touched down yet. I managed to deliver the cake to everyone except those who were doing the live recording, which included the camera men, production staff, Dick and Julie and my mum who was doing a slot on legal-advice for harassment in the workplace.

As I waited in the wings with plates of cake, I found myself wondering if Dick was the sort of person to sexually-harass people at work. Was he, for instance, the type of man to saunter up behind a young, nubile work-experience girl and offer her a job, if she plays *Julie* to his *Ali G*?

I hadn't realised it but I must have been staring at him because he caught my eye and remembering Juliet's advice, I batted my eyelids in a seductive manner, which he must have found quite alluring because he began to look away but then turned to look back at me, holding my stare for, what seemed like, an age.

As the legal-advice drew to a close, Julie took over and explained what would be happening after the break and, at last, I managed to attract my mother's attention and mime to her that she should come over to me when they cut for a break. I must admit I have always been good at charades; Gran and I played it all the time when I stayed over at her house and even Gran thought I would make a brilliant actress and she should know after all! I made a mental note to try harder to get myself seen.

When the break arrived I ran quickly over to D & J, proffering the cake, aware that they only had two minutes before the show was on air again. As I leaned over to give Julie hers, Dick jumped up and dashed at a fast pace towards the back of the set. I could see he was heading towards the toilets; poor thing must have been desperate because he looked quite flushed. I deliberated whether to just leave the cake where it was or wait for Dick to return, so that I could give it to him personally and perhaps get the chance to batter my eyes again.

Having never batted my eyes at anyone before I was suddenly overwhelmed with a desire to look in a mirror to see how it looked. Sometimes these things look better in the mind than in reality. Obviously Richard was impressed but I was

Who Cares?

desperate to see how I came across; did I look cute? Was it sexy or did I just smoulder with unsuppressed sex-appeal?

I noticed that the nearest camera was still trained on Julie, which was where they had left off, just before the break. Conveniently, underneath the camera was a small mirror, probably there in case Judy needed to check whether she had spinach or something stuck in her teeth.

If I could just make it to the camera and have a quick look, it wouldn't take a moment and besides everyone was so busy, touching up make-up, shouting orders into microphones and chatting amongst themselves, that I doubted anyone would even notice.

I put Dick's cup of coffee and slice of cake down on the table and, with a quick look to either side, I made my way round to the back of Julie's seat. As I suspected they were all far too busy to notice and I glanced over at the little mirror and tried the old batting the eyelids thing. Of course it's hard to see what ones face looks like when one is actually batting eyelids so I leaned a little closer so as to get a better look, trying hard not to disturb Julie's hair which was now right in front of me.

How professional am I? I thought. Even without training I'm aware of not disturbing hair; I was definitely born to be in show business, a chip off the old-block coming through.

Suddenly, it was all actions stations as shouts were heard, whistles blew and people rushed about, surely it couldn't have been two minutes already! I couldn't believe it – I know I'd never been on set before but I just assumed these people were more professional than that, for goodness sake. It looked more like a raid on Entebbe than the end of the break. What happened next was a little confusing...

I heard a man's voice shout out the name, "J U L I E," and when I looked up Dick was tearing across the studio, he suddenly leapt straight up into the air, cleared the cameraman, skidded across the table and collided with Julie, knocking her and her chair to the ground. I only just managed to step out of the way in time. My God what did the poor woman say this time to deserve treatment like that?

As I came to my senses, I tried to lean down and help poor

Julie up but was pulled back instantly by a pair of strong arms. I could see why they pulled me back, that Dick was mad. Who would ever believe this went on behind the scenes?

Then, suddenly, we were all surrounded by security men holding guns. Dick was crying and cradling the stunned and slightly winded Judy in his arms and when I looked around I noticed that the rest of the crew had also thrown themselves to the floor and the only person still standing was, in fact, me. Slowly it sunk in that all the guns were also trained on me and Dick was pointing an accusing finger in my direction.

"She's got a knife, guys!" he screamed, still holding the shocked Julie.

"No, no I don't have a knife," I said, holding open my hands. Unfortunately, at that moment my cardigan swung open to reveal a large chefs-knife hanging precariously out of my apron pocket. I must have inadvertently left it there after cutting up the cake. The security guards pounced once again, knocking me to the floor and holding my arms tightly behind my back whilst pushing my cheek firmly and none too flatteringly, into the ground.

As I tried to explain to Gran later, after she rang to say she had been watching *It's Morning* when they had announced that an attempt had been made on Julie's life, followed by some footage of me being escorted into a Black Maria van... IT HAD ALL BEEN A GHASTLY MISTAKE.

Dick, who prides himself on knowing everyone on the production team, had been surprised to see someone whom he didn't recognise pulling strange, maniacal faces from the back of the set. Seriously though, what was wrong with the man? Why couldn't he tell the difference between a flirty bat of the eyes and a Psycho's, *I'm going to kill you*, smile?

He then saw me make a sign of cutting someone's throat and then breaking some bones and as the break came he saw me rush over to where he and Julie were sitting. As I handed some cake to Julie, he saw the knife in my pocket and as he rushed to get help, he saw me creeping up behind Julie with a bizarre look on my face. It could have happened to anyone.

The outcome was, that the whole story was hushed up, after

all no-one wanted the facts to be published, especially Dick, seeing as though his observations were a little zealous, to say the least. The management had a fit when they realised that my mother was their legal-advisor and they ended up giving her three slots a week instead of just the two, and also promoting me to Wardrobe Assistant, with triple the salary I had started with, the week before. So, all in all, it was quite a good week. Mind you, Dick and Julie left a month later but I'm sure it didn't have anything to do with me!

The next few years were probably the best of my life; my confidence was on the increase and my trips to the doctor's surgery on the decline. There was that one occasion when some guy came onto the show with a vulture that absolutely refused to let me stroke him, not that I had wanted to anyway but they made such a big thing about me not wanting to, I felt compelled to have a go.

Anyway, the man said it was really unusual that the vulture wouldn't let me near him; but the doctor wasn't convinced that a vulture could smell impending death – only rotting flesh and suggested I change my usual perfume for something a little less overpowering.

The perks of the job were great; gifts of designer clothes and shoes which I spread liberally around the other members of staff, keeping, of course, any goodies I received from Dr. Mark, the resident TV doctor, for myself. You can have enough jumpers and shoes but, God knows, you can't have enough pills, potions, slings, bandages and body supports.

We were given tickets for film premieres and previews, which meant, every month or so, Juliet and I swanned along in all our finery to some big, red carpet event whilst acting like we were the main attraction and being snapped by the paparazzi.

On one or two occasions I took Gran and, needless to say, she stopped and tap-danced for the press and one time regaled them with a rendition of, *There's No Business like Show Business* from *Annie get your Gun*…Isn't she priceless?

Four

At twenty-two it finally felt like my bad luck was well and truly behind me. Four years doing a job I adored, I was promoted, yet again, which enabled me to finally rent a little place of my own, just five minutes' walk away from the studios. The added bonus to that meant I could leave the car at home, so saving me from sitting in traffic jams and breathing in life-threatening carbon monoxide fumes and dying an early death from lead poisoning!

Along with my promotion came extra money and that meant a long-overdue chance to revamp my wardrobe. Shopping at all the finest stores London had to offer, even those where you had to make an appointment to be let in! One of which made a big point of telling me how Victoria Beckham shopped there all the time to which I mentally checked out every face hidden behind sunglasses until the rather snooty shop-assistant went on to say that they always closed the shop for her.

Well, I pondered, maybe one day it'll be *her* nose pushed up against the window when the shop is closed for Remington Hall-Smyth-Mountbatten-Windsor. Or probably they'll just call me Mrs. Wales in a jovial, the next 'Queen of England' type of way! Well, a girl has to dream!

One morning at work, whilst doing one of the regular, weekly hair makeover features, everyone started to panic over a missing model. Mary, the new 'Julie', quickly suggested that one of the team should step into the breach and looked pointedly over towards me. It was fair to say my hair was in dire need of a makeover, certainly it was dull, lifeless and unmanageable to the point of scraggly, although having it done in front of millions of viewers wasn't the ideal way to sort it out… But as Gran would say *'The show must go on, darling,'* so I gave an assertive nod to Mary and boldly made my way over to the set.

Who Cares?

Fortunately, Mary and I were on nodding terms again by then after that regrettable business with me, her husband Mike and the Heimlich manoeuvre, had been sorted out. Unfortunately he thought I was choking when I was merely coughing to see if any blood came up after a tuberculosis special with Dr. Mark but, as he went to grab me from behind, I bent down and he grabbed two handfuls of ample bosom instead, just as Mary was passing.

As the hair special got underway and we were just about to go live, the overly flouncy, gay hairdresser revealed that shaven heads for women were all the fashion and in his opinion, very sexy.

He picked up the razor and leaned towards me to make a start. As good luck would have it, I chose that moment to have my second-ever faint, which caused me to slump forward, just missing the blade, and I slipped gracefully to the floor. The cameraman quickly diverted to another model and I was rushed off to the side to be attended by the ever so lovely bedside manner of Dr. Mark... Oh bliss!

It did occur to me at that point, that perhaps the rift between Mary and me wasn't as over as I thought it was! Anyway the upshot was that the hairdresser, who felt really bad that I hadn't been told about what exactly was going to happen, invited me to his salon where he gave me a brand new makeover of my own.

So perhaps it wasn't so surprising then, that with my auburn locks now sun-kissed again with the aid of highlights, and a beautiful, new, sophisticated style, face made-up with the finest products and tips taken from the weekly makeover shows and clothes good enough to don any magazine cover in the country, I started getting some very appreciative looks from the opposite sex. Not Mary's husband of course, once bitten twice shy and all that!

One particular look came my way in the shape of Michael Hayes, a regular outside broadcast reporter, whose flirtatious and funny banter with Mary had led him to be a real favourite with the viewers and in turn gave him a regular spot on the couch discussing holidays.

He had, it's fair to say, the whole package! He was unbearably handsome in a Colin Farrell sort of way. His dark hair had that 'just got out of bed' look about it, slightly tousled and sexily unruly. His mouth was full with a small smile that lingered permanently in the corners and his eyes were dark blue and shrouded in thick, black lashes. He was impeccably dressed, well heeled, owned a flat on the Embankment, drove a Porsche and had health insurance. He was Prince Charming and he was looking at me!

I checked discreetly to make sure there was nothing hanging from my nose, no sleep or gunge in my eyes and no wardrobe failure leaving me with one boob hanging out. He looked, he smiled and on one occasion, he winked at me, to which I felt myself go weak at the knees and for the first time in my life, I didn't think of rushing off to the doctor to have them checked out!

After a week of playful looks and accidental meetings in doorways, he finally asked me out for a drink. We went to a really trendy wine bar not far from where he lived and, if the car park was anything to go by, it was packed with the cream of London society. Many people stopped briefly to talk to Michael as we struggled through the heaving masses to find a seat and I noticed that I had become something of a talking point amongst the women.

Michael found us a seat and left me to go over to the bar and get our drinks. I opted for plain orange juice as I thought it wise to keep a clear head on our first date, especially, as I hadn't eaten much during the day, and the last time I drank on an empty stomach I had vague memories of dancing a lambada on a table, as Juliet hummed the tune.

As I sat down I took the opportunity to practice what I liked to call 'Safe Sacs' – air sacks that is – breathing in through my nose and out through my mouth. These may be the best of London's upper-class but they still carried germs the same as anyone else!

"Are you okay?" Michael asked, as he put the drinks down and squeezed up close to me on the already overcrowded seat. "I thought you may be having an asthma attack!"

"I'm fine, this is great," I said, picking my glass up and taking a sip. In reality, I wasn't fine at all. I felt totally out of my depth and very aware that I was completely under-dressed for a place like this. I could feel everyone's eyes on me and the self-confidence I had built up in recent weeks seemed to be slipping away from me.

Michael was older than me by about nine years and this was his local. It was obvious that he was completely relaxed and at ease, which somehow just seemed to make me feel and act worse; I could feel my cheeks starting to tingle, tiny beads of sweat trickling down my face and my hands were getting decidedly clammy.

I grabbed out for my drink and took what I wished had been a small dainty sip but in reality was a large, loud, lager-lout type gulp that half-missed my mouth and spilt straight down on to my chest and trickled its way down to my lap. I saw some of the women, who had been watching us when we had first came in, laugh out loud and whisper to each other and my cheeks began to burn. I was floundering and I knew it, so I did the only thing a person can do when there sinking... I dug a bigger hole and threw myself in!

I started talking louder and louder and mentioning every celebrity's name I could think of. Whenever Michael spoke I threw my head back and laughed as if we were having the best conversation in the world. I finished my drink off in two more unladylike gulps and I think I called Michael, 'Sweetie,' when I asked him to refresh our glasses. I was the world's worst date and I knew it but I couldn't stop myself.

Michael sat facing me for a moment and smiled, not a big smile, just a small smile that played on his mouth and teased in his eyes. I felt the magnetism of his smile begin to draw me back down to planet Earth and, at last, I could feel a calm descending upon me.

Then, just as I began to feel like some control was coming back into my life, I felt him rubbing up against my calf. He carried on smiling and the rubbing went further up to my thigh. Oh this was not on, this definitely was not on, I thought.

"What the hell do you think you're doing?" I tried to whisper discreetly but unfortunately it came out louder than I meant it too. He had the barefaced cheek to look a little taken back.

Who Cares?

"What do you mean?" he said, his smile slipping slightly.

"You know perfectly well what I mean," I replied, keeping my voice lower this time.

"I don't," he retorted, the smile back in place. My head started to spin a little and I felt decidedly light-headed.

"Oh… my… God," I said, trying to make sense of it all. My cheeks were on fire now and I could feel my hair starting to stick to my head. The beads of sweat that had once been on my face had now joined forces and were now sporting a salty, wet moustache on my upper lip.

"I've heard about things like this, you 'batard!' " He looked a little surprised and instantly I realised why. 'Batard' was one of Gran's polite, swear words. Ever since I was little she'd always use her own made up words instead of swear words.

"There's no need to be coarse, darling," she always said. "There are nicer words!" Mind you I could have kicked myself for using it, if ever I needed a real one it was then.

Despite the fact that he was still looking decidedly amused, I carried on with my tirade. "I know you've spiked my drink with some date-rape thing and now you think you can feel me up under the table and then probably take me home to your place and have your way with me." Instantly he pulled his hands out from under the table and put them out in front of me, which was very confusing because the rubbing of my thigh didn't stop and did, momentarily, make me wonder if he was double-jointed and was using his feet! He pulled the table away and there looking up at me, eyes wide with wonder, tail swishing with joy, was a big grey cat whose head started to resume its graceful rubbing of my thigh, purring with untold joy.

Why, oh why, is it that cats single out the one person in a room that absolutely hates them and then makes a beeline to be overly-friendly? I glared at the cat, who purred sweetly back and then I turned myself back to Michael.

"But my drink, that's definitely spiked!" I cried, although the accusative tone had now gone out of my voice, it was now more of a whine with a slight *I know I'm making a fool of myself but throw me a line here*, feel to it… "My head definitely feels woozy."

Who Cares?

"Not guilty again I'm afraid. You drank my double-vodka and orange, this is yours!" he said, holding up a full glass of untouched orange that was still left on the table.

"Then why didn't you tell me?" I mouthed, checking around to see if anyone was still listening. Everybody turned away at the same time, so fair to say they had all been listening.

"I didn't get the chance," he whispered. "You pretty much downed it in three and you didn't come up for air."

He took me home shortly after that and I never expected to hear from him again which was a real 'batard' because I really liked him. Unbelievably, two days later he asked me out for another first-date and I accepted.

Needless to say the second, first-date went much better than the first, first-date and the only slight mishap was when he stubbed his toe on the car door to which he shouted, "Buddy batard".

It was great being part of a couple, going out to dinner, the cinema and concerts, and on one occasion the hospital, after I had choked on a peanut and thought I was suffering from Anaphylactic shock.

At work we kept a distance between us and tried to keep it all very professional although everyone knew we were an item. We went on holidays together, we spent Christmas together and I introduced him to Gran, who insisted on showing him all my childhood photos and made him play charades until he dropped.

He knew my mother of course, although she made no attempt to socialise with us and he promised to take me to America one day to meet his family.

My life was in good order and running smoothly, little did I know what it was storing up for that fatal age of twenty-four!

Five

There was no particular running order to the things that happened over the next couple of years. There were good things and there were bad and sometimes life just jogged along without anything significant happening at all.

Then one morning in early January, after suffering the effects of all those overindulgent Christmas dinners and holiday goodies, all talk was of New Year resolutions and in particular dieting. We had experts in every diet under the sun on the programme telling us when to eat, what to eat and how to eat it. We had phone calls from viewers explaining how they lost weight and more from those who couldn't.

By the middle of the month we were running a competition to pick the best dieters, with the best stories. Michael was working away from home at the time so I volunteered to be part of the team to sift through all the letters and find some worthy winners.

We sat for two whole days, ploughing through hundreds of applicants finally whittling it down to the final five, who would appear on the show. I was the first to come across one, from a woman who had gone on a sponsored-diet, losing four stone, and gave all the money she made to the *Save the Children Fund*. She was our first finalist.

I slogged on further and came across a similar story where another slimmer had been sponsored, all donations going to a cat's home; needless to say I tore that one up and threw it in the bin.

Another member of the team found a young woman who lost ten stone in three years and went on to run a diet club to help others. She became the second contestant. Then there was the man who thought his wife was going to leave him so he went on a diet, lost lots of weight and started courting her again and they were set to renew their marriage vows. Lastly, a mum and daughter who between them had lost sixteen stone and had entered the London Marathon together.

Finally all the contestants were in place and my next job was to find clothes they could wear on the programme. They were all going to be treated to a makeover and the lucky overall winner would win five thousand pounds and a luxury holiday.

They arrived at the studio early on the day of the show and were sent to the Green Room where I was to meet them to go through the schedule and pick out the clothes I thought would suit them best. As the date of the program had been brought forward at the last moment, all I had to go on were their ages, sizes and rails of clothes I thought would look good.

Michael had arrived home late the night before and after a late supper, two bottles of wine and reunion sex in the morning I was in dire need of caffeine – intravenously being the preferred method.

As I passed a mirror, mug in hand, it occurred to me that I should get better lighting in the bedroom as nothing I was wearing had anything in common, least of all the colour. I stopped and pushed a hand through my unbrushed hair and rubbed away the overspill of eyeliner that had accumulated beneath both eyes.

As I opened the door to the Green Room, the bright light temporarily blinded me and I tripped over an ill-placed white-board and felt myself falling towards the floor. Suddenly I was aware of someone catching me.

"Are you alright, Remi?" Somebody was helping me to my feet and guiding me over to one of the sofas.

"Nothing an insurance claim couldn't rectify," I said, jovially, in a bid to save face and giving myself an extra few seconds to get my composure back at the same time. I dusted myself off, picked up my clipboard and, after thanking the woman who'd helped me, I made my way up to the front of the room to ask for a few minutes to go through my notes before we started the introductions.

They all walked over to the coffee machine and politely

chatted amongst themselves while I flicked through the file with all the names, sizes and photos. I had only seen one of the original letters before, the one I'd picked out myself so it was nice to be able to put a face to the name.

Martha was five feet, eleven inches with glorious red hair that fell into soft curls around her shoulders. Her face had that alabaster complexion which was the perfect accompaniment to that colour hair, and her hazel eyes were set off by her high cheekbones. Her only small imperfection was her mouth, thin lips that turned down at the corners, giving a slightly soured expression but despite that, she was gorgeous. Certainly a worthy contestant and a walking clothes horse as far as the outfits were concerned.

I knew instantly which of the outfits I had put together would be perfect for her and I asked my assistant to put it to the side whilst I perused the other files.

The mother and daughter choice was easy enough, I had three young outfits for Katie, the daughter, any of which would look amazing on her. I looked over at Mary, the mum. She was a surprisingly, pretty woman in her late thirties, whose face showed signs of, not only, weight loss but hard times. She wore a clean and tidy outfit that had obviously been worn many times before, and yet it was equally obvious that Katie's outfit was brand new.

I liked Mary. I knew instinctively that this was a woman who put others before herself; her face was full of pride, not for her own achievement but for that of Katie. For Mary it would be the Max Mara tailored-suit, coupled with a Betty Jackson blouse and... would I dare? Yes I would... Manolo Blahnik shoes. Oh my God! The accountants were going to go ballistic, but I didn't care.

All the contestants were allowed to keep their outfits and I wanted Mary to go home with something that would make her look a million dollars. With a smile still plastered to my face I turned to the next file but the smile was short-lived and so was my coffee if my stomach had anything to do with it, as it lurched dangerously towards my mouth.

Penny Brightman! Surely, it couldn't be the same Penny

Who Cares?

Brightman? I looked up quickly and searched the room, my heart was racing and my lips began to feel numb and I was sure my arm was starting to ache. Surely, I was too young for a heart attack.

All the contestants were still chatting by the coffee machine and I was relieved to see straight away that she wasn't there, so I hurriedly flipped open her file to check the details. Five feet eight inches, twenty-three years old, blonde hair and works as a dietician. Okay, that sounds innocent enough although, to be fair, you don't get many people stating 'professional bully' as a living.

I carried on reading, checking the door apprehensively in case she walked in. *Lives in Hertfordshire, runs camps for overweight kids in the summer and on the Board of Governors at her local school.* I checked the photo, a bit grainy but no way was it her. The more I read, the more I relaxed, this was no more the Penny Brightman I knew than I was the Queen of England!

"Hello Remington." – Oh God! Just call me Liz and hand me the crown. I hadn't even looked up but I knew, straight away, it was her.

As I lifted my head, I saw a beautiful, manicured hand extended towards me and as my eyes travelled upwards I noticed the delicate, understated, cream outfit she was wearing with a soft pink cashmere polo neck jumper beneath.

There she was, not the Penny Brightman I knew at school at all, but a new, stunningly beautiful, elegant creature, who was the epitome of style and composure.

I stood and tried to keep my tongue from lolling out of my gaping mouth. My eyes searched her face, trying to find something familiar but there was nothing. She must have taken my imbecilic stare as non-recognition because she took my hand with both of hers and held it gently as she spoke to me.

"We went to the same school Remington. I thought you might remember me." Still I said nothing. I just stared at the face in front of me. Her make-up was subtle and natural, no big eyes, no big red lips. Her eyes were like sapphires, so blue in fact that I was amazed that I hadn't noticed them at school. Her smile lit up her face and her voice was soft and sweet.

"You picked me up when I fell," I said, suddenly remembering the soft hands that picked me up and guided me to a seat. "You called me Remi!"

"I did, I'm sorry if it was wrong of me to be so familiar, I just didn't think," she said, releasing my hand. "Someone told me you worked here and I was just so excited about meeting you again and then you slipped!"

People were starting to make their way back to their seats and, after apologising once more, Penny sat down. My mind was all over the place. Penny Brightman was here at my work. A thought suddenly struck me, was she trying to intimidate me? Was she going to blackmail me to make sure she won the competition? If so, what did she have to blackmail me with?

For anyone who has never had to do this before, I can tell you it's very hard to be thinking one thing, whilst talking about something completely different at the same time. My mouth and one side of my brain was talking about where they would be taken to after leaving the Green Room and what would happen when they got there.

The other half of my brain was running through all the events at school trying to determine whether or not there was anything Penny could hold up against me.

Suddenly the two halves of my brain came together and I noticed that there was an uncomfortable silence hanging in the air. I looked around at the bemused faces and realised that I had no idea what I'd been saying.

"So! Any questions?" I said, hoping to get over this little hurdle and move on as quickly as possible.

"Just one," said Mary, looking a little nervously around the room. "Who exactly is wearing the big knickers and the red thong?"

Eventually everyone was dressed and had their makeover and I watched from the wings as they told their stories. They all had their *before* weight-loss photos and a sample of their big clothes and I sat, drawn and waiting for Penny to have her turn. I had tried to ring Juliet a million times and in the end just left her a message telling her to watch the show.

At last Penny was up, the photo was hideous and brought

Who Cares?

back memories I thought were long forgotten. She also brought in the old miniskirt that she wore on the last day of term and it was agreed that four *new* Pennys made one old one. She was asked how she lost the weight and she sat, confidently, back in her chair.

"Well, I tell this story to all my students at the diet clinic," she said, gently squeezing the miniskirt in her hands. "I was a terribly overweight child when I was young. The more people laughed at me the more I ate and the more I ate, the more they laughed." There was collective sigh from the team and I felt like screaming in outrage. Penny looked briefly over in my direction, reddened slightly and held up her hand, then continued.

"Please I don't deserve sympathy... I'm ashamed to say that I did what many children do when confronted by ridicule. I turned to violence and instead of being bullied, I became the bully." Everyone looked at her in disbelief, as if this sweet, beautiful woman could ever have done such a thing... It was laughable.

However, Penny carried on. "I made other people's lives a misery. I was mean, ruthless and violent and I know now just how much I hurt people and I'm deeply ashamed. Even on the last day of school I got into a fight and the police were called. I spent the night in the police cells, missing all the activities of the last day." She took a deep breath and composed herself, then continued. "While I was in the police station, I must have eaten something that disagreed with me and I was violently ill, so ill in fact that they called the ambulance and the next morning I was rushed to hospital." Suddenly it was *me* feeling sick, even my knees were knocking.

We'd never given a thought to what could happen to someone who ate three boxes of spiked chocolates. Penny continued, "I was in hospital for two weeks and when I came out, I was surprised to see that all my clothes were too big for me. I'd lost two stone. It felt so good that I decided it was time to find out how I could carry on losing the weight and I joined a club and a gym. It took me two years to lose another four stone and then out of the blue, the club I belonged to, closed down.

"I knew there were other people who, like me, relied on the

support of a club, so I started one of my own and, amazingly, people came. People looked up to me, respected me. They told me their stories and I realised how many of them had been bullied at school or work, even by their own families; how that bullying had destroyed their lives and their self-confidence.

"Over the next few years I sought out most of the people I bullied at school. I explained to them why I had become a bully and asked them to forgive me. I set up camps for children with weight problems and I joined the Board of Governors on both my local school and the one I used to attend and set up anti-bullying campaigns."

My mouth was hanging open again and I swallowed hard. Suddenly Penny looked straight at camera and said, "There are still people who I know suffered because of me, people who I've not been able to apologise to and I would like to take this opportunity to do so now." Her gaze went from camera and looked directly at me. "I'm truly sorry for any upset I caused. If I could take it back I would, I can tell you that I have changed and ask for your forgiveness."

Small tears started to run down her cheeks and she took a small, linen handkerchief out from her sleeve and dabbed her eyes. I was still reeling from the shock of it all when the programme came to an end. Everyone was clapping each other on the back and congratulating themselves on a record-rating show.

I just stood back and watched as Penny Brightman and the other contestants were ushered back to the Green Room. I saw her eyes glance quickly in my direction and I thought she tried to lift her hand, perhaps to wave goodbye, I wasn't sure.

The competition was won by Martha, the beautiful, redheaded woman I'd personally picked out. I should've taken some pride in that but I didn't. I felt sort of numb.

I wanted to speak to Juliet or Norman, people who would know how I was feeling but Juliet hadn't called me back and neither of us had any idea how to contact Norman. We'd kept in touch with him by email and texts for a while after he went back to the States but then when he went off to some college or other, we lost touch.

Who Cares?

One night in desperation Juliet and I had phoned his home number in the States and some grumpy, old guy had told us, in no uncertain terms, there was *no* Norman living there. Since then both Juliet and I had also moved house and changed phones.

Martha received her cash prize and her holiday of a lifetime and, in a lovely twist, the other contestants were surprised to find out that an online holiday company, who'd been watching the show, had offered to give each of them vouchers towards a holiday of their choice up to the sum of one thousand pounds, as long as Michael advised the contestants and covered the whole thing on the programme. It was a great ending to a great show and everyone involved pledged to do the same thing again the following year.

Six

Juliet hadn't watched the show, so I had a copy made and sent it to her. She watched it and rang me straight away.

"What do you think? Is she for real?" I asked, sinking into one of my comfy sofas at home. I pulled my feet up under me and sipped my hot chocolate, waiting for Juliet's reply.

"Well she certainly sounded convincing and she definitely looked amazing. I think if I'd never met her before, I would have believed her without a doubt." She was right of course.

Everyone on the production team had loved her and even Michael, who'd been advising her and the others on where to take their holidays, was sure she was the real thing.

As part of the ongoing programme he'd even been taken to one of the schools where she had set up the anti-bullying campaigns and where she was also in the process of opening an after-school, fitness club. He'd been very impressed by it all and the teachers and children were full of praise for her, apparently.

"I had an email from her asking if we could have coffee with her one day soon." I said, dipping a biscuit into the last of my hot chocolate. There was a small gasp from the other end of the phone.

"What did you say?"

"I said I'd ask you and get back to her. So what do you think, shall we go?"

"Of course," said Juliet, immediately. "I can't wait to see her for myself and see if she really is this new person. I'm off next weekend, what about you, can you make it then?"

"Yes, that's perfect for me; Michael is away that weekend, so you can stay here and we can have a girlie night in, or a wicked night out!"

Juliet laughed. "Email her tomorrow and let me know."

Who Cares?

Penny got back to me straight away saying that she was away that weekend but could meet up with us Friday evening or Monday morning. Juliet managed to get away early Friday night and we all met up in an exclusive, little coffee house in North London, near the boundary with Hertfordshire.

Neither Juliet nor I were driving, so we made a point of downing a few shorts before we left for our rendezvous, after all we needed some Dutch or, in this case, Scotch courage before we embarked on this little tryst. Penny was waiting for us when we arrived.

She looked beautiful sitting in a corner booth with only candle light reflecting on her face. Her make-up, as before, was light and natural-looking and her outfit, if I wasn't mistaken, was *Prada* in a gorgeous shade of teal that complimented her face and hair to perfection. Juliet and I were dressed more shabby-chic – well, actually more shabby than chic.

I had on a pair of *Guess* jeans with a plain, *Armani* T-shirt, topped off with a short, fitted, vintage, leather jacket I'd found in a charity shop. Juliet – who was the original, living-breathing, hippy-chick – was wearing a long, floaty boho-skirt with an equally loose-fitting ethnic top and a poncho that had appeared on last week's programme. I had nabbed it straight away and surprised her with it this evening.

Despite our three completely different images we fitted in with this trendy, little café quite well and as Juliet and I approached the table, Penny jumped out of her seat and ran round to meet us. She first threw her arms around me and kissed me twice on both cheeks and then took Juliet's hands, holding them out so she could get a better look at her.

"You look beautiful, just as I remember you." she said, taking Juliet into her arms and again doing the double-kiss. Juliet and I were always a little wary of strangers who kiss and I could see Juliet felt a bit awkward when we sat down and she pushed me into the seat nearest Penny. The first ten minutes were a little strained but, eventually, we all unbuttoned a little and, to my and Juliet's great surprise, we were soon chatting away and even reminiscing on some of the funnier events that happened at school which had no bad memories for any of us.

Who Cares?

After an hour we moved onto a wine bar and Juliet and I partook of the grape in our usual, over-indulgent fashion. Penny discreetly declined the wine, sticking instead to black coffee but kindly made no mention of the amount of calories she knew we were consuming with every glassful.

As Penny was going away for the weekend she was the first to break up the party but not before apologising once again to both Juliet and me, kissing us both in her usual fashion, to which we now responded with more enthusiasm. We all hugged and promised to stay in touch, she promised to email me the next week. I promised to send Norman's last known address before we lost touch, as apparently he was now the only person that she'd not made contact with and she wanted to try and track him down if she could.

On the way home Juliet pondered on the thought that perhaps Penny meant to *hunt* Norman down, as opposed to tracking him down.

"Perhaps she realised why she had such acute diarrhoea all those years ago and wants to take her revenge on 'Poor Normy'," she said, using Penny's own vernacular for Norman. In the cool light of day however, we felt that Penny had more to thank Norman for than anything else. Without him she would still be that overweight, hideous-looking, violent excuse for a human being, instead of the warm, loving, and beautiful woman they had met up with last night. It appeared that Penny was not the proverbial bad Penny returning, she was, it seems, a shiny new Penny and both Juliet and myself felt that she had genuinely changed for the better.

Over the next six months I got to see quite a lot of Penny and the other contestants as they drifted in and out of the studio. It was funny how they had all bonded so well together; it was almost if they had created their own 'buddy' system to keep each other on the right track and make sure no one started snacking in the middle of the night. They were all interviewed on the programme about where they had chosen to have their holidays and we did a special makeover, *Holiday Fashion doesn't have to be Expensive!* We were still paying for the Manolo Blahnik shoes.

Who Cares?

In truth, Penny was the most personable of all of them and the audience seemed to identify with her and her no-nonsense style of healthy eating. On one occasion she actually returned just to reply to letters that had been sent personally to her via the station. A couple of times after the show we went out and grabbed a meal together or a few drinks and it was at that point I realised that, despite myself, I really did like her.

It was the middle of the summer and it seemed that everyone and his uncle were busy, except me. Penny was running her fat camps, Juliet had been made Head Librarian where she worked and was busy alphabetically ordering or something, Gran had joined a new dance class and was learning to salsa and Michael was working flat-out. London is a great place to live when you're working there or shopping or indeed, if you have friends. But when you're on your own it can be very lonely.

One Sunday, at the end of August, I found myself, yet again, with nothing to do. The end of the month meant no money, so shopping was out; I'd watched all the good films at the cinema and had rented out all the good DVDs from the hire shop. I had slept in late and was planning an early night but that still left at least eight hours with nothing to do. I picked up the phone and rang Juliet and she answered on the first ring.

"Hi, fancy coming out to play? I'm bored," I said, glad that I had found her in for a change.

"I can't, I have a *told*," she said, in a creepy, raspy sort of voice.

"A told… What the hell's a told?"

"A told, not a told," she said, getting annoyed and sneezing into the receiver. "See a told!"

"Oh! A cold. Why didn't you say so?" I laughed and she tried to laugh too. After telling her to wrap up and take a hot toddy of whisky, hot water and honey (Gran's recipe) I promised to ring her the next day.

Next, I tried Michael but got the same answer I had for the past two days; the caller is unavailable, please try again later. I could only imagine that there was no service wherever he was. I knew Gran was out because she had asked me if I wanted to go to water aerobics with her, an invitation I'd gracefully declined, guessing that the pool would be filled with sixty and seventy year old crazy ladies like Gran, herself. Mind you, if I'd known how boring my day would turn out I might have donned one of her daisy covered swimming hats, put on some of her luminescent goggles and danced my way through... *Splish Splash I was Taking a Bath* with her and the other incontinent water-bathers anyway.

I tried Penny's number and even she wasn't there. I was getting desperate so I tried her mobile as well and she answered in a hushed voice.

"Are you okay to speak?" I asked, sensing that I had called at the wrong time.

"Hold on, I'll take it outside," she said, and I heard her put her hand over the receiver and after a few seconds she came back on. "Sorry about that, it's a bit awkward."

"Sorry. I was at a loose end and wondered if you fancied coming out somewhere for a bite to eat?"

"Oh Remi, I'm a bit tied up right now and by the time I get away from here it'll probably be too late." I heard myself give out an involuntary sigh and she must have too as she asked me to hold on a moment. When she came back on she said she thought she might be able to get away a bit earlier and perhaps we could meet in a couple of hours.

"Great, what if I come and pick you up?" I said, thinking that would take some of the time up and would save her getting a train into town.

"No," she almost spat down the phone and then composing herself quickly continued. "Don't be silly. I'll finish up here and I'll meet you at King's Cross at about one."

I spent a very happy hour on *ebay* looking for coloured swimming hats and salsa dresses, just in case next time I had to resort to spending an afternoon with Gran, I figured I may as well be prepared just in case.

At one o'clock Penny was waiting at the station, she kissed me on both cheeks and we raced off to find somewhere suitable to eat. Frankly, I could have eaten a stuffed horse I was that hungry but I was resigned to the fact that I would have to eat something sensible with mineral water and then grab a

Who Cares?

McDonalds on the way home. We found a little organic bistro that specialised in kelp and Penny sat gracefully nibbling away while I tried desperately not to think about whether to have the Big Mac or the triple-cheeseburger on the way home.

Our conversation was a little stilted at first and I couldn't help but wonder if Penny had something else on her mind. We talked about the weather and work. We talked about Juliet and her new job and Penny told me about the fat camps and how successful they had been but all the time I could feel she was distracted.

"How's your gran?" she asked, pushing her plate away and picking up the herbal tea she'd ordered.

"She's fine. She's at water aerobics today, probably learning how to tap dance under water, knowing Gran."

"And Michael...is he away this weekend?"

"When isn't he away lately?" I said. "I've only seen him four days in the last month, I'm beginning to feel like a work widow and I haven't even had the pleasure of the honeymoon yet!"

She looked up abruptly and stared at me for a moment. "Have you been talking about marriage then?" she said, stirring her tea once again and laying the spoon down on a napkin, so as not to dirty the table cloth.

"No not exactly, we used to talk about it sometimes but lately it's been all work and no play, if you know what I mean?" Apparently she did know because she flushed a little and I remembered, all too late, that this was not Juliet I was talking to.

Juliet and I could talk about anything and everything and we often sat up late into the night just doing that. Mind you even Gran had asked after my love-life the other day and when I told her off for asking she just replied, "If it's not earth moving, darling, then he's not the one!" Earth-moving! Who has earth-moving sex for goodness sake, dumper truck drivers? New-Age hippies? Maybe, people living on a seismic fault, quite possibly, but for the rest of us it's good but not earth moving.

"Why don't you join him on his trips then?"

I laughed. "I can't get that sort of time off, the studio would freak-out, besides he wouldn't want me dragging around after him all the time, we're not the sort of people that live in each other's pockets!" There was a small silence before she spoke again.

"So you've never considered moving in together?"

I shrugged my shoulders. "I suppose it never really came up. We see each other a few times a week when he's home and to be honest he's always been a bit funny about his own home, he's very tidy almost to the point of being anal," I laughed. "And I get the feeling that he wouldn't want any of my things cluttering up his space."

The conversation was starting to make me feel queasy. It suddenly occurred to me that although I could talk to Juliet about anything and everything, we never talked about Michael or my relationship with him. We laughed occasionally about his obsessive behaviour and the fact that he was the only man I knew who used doilies but other than that; Michael was taboo. Penny leaned back and looked at me, then coming forward again, she took my hand.

"Perhaps he's not the right man for you Remi. You deserve someone better, someone who will love you and will be there for you." I stared at her for a while, amazed that she had been so forthright. She hardly knew Michael for goodness sake, how did she feel she could make such judgments on our relationship. I pulled my hand away from hers and looked down at my shaking hands. I couldn't even describe how I was feeling. I was angry and hurt of course, but there was something else, something that was making my stomach do cartwheels, something that was tightening my intestines and threatening to make me throw up.

My eyes suddenly started to sting and I knew that tears were trembling on the threshold and just one word could send them spilling down my cheeks. Was she right? Ever since that second, first date, I'd thought he was the one, that he was the best thing that had ever happened to me. Was I wrong? I looked up still keeping my shaking hands firmly in my lap.

"I do deserve him," I said. "And he's perfect for me. He makes me laugh, he makes me feel secure. He worries about me, takes care of me, hell, he even comes over and cleans my flat!" The tears started to fall and I could taste the salt as they touched my lips. Penny reached over immediately and touched my arm.

"Sometimes we think it's the right person, we believe they are the right one, but sometimes we get it wrong. Perhaps it's better to see that now before it's too late."

Now I knew exactly what I was feeling. It was anger, pure and simple. How dare this woman who had terrorised my life for seven years feel she could tell me what to do yet again? This was the same old bullying but this time it was wrapped up in honey and designer clothing. I stood up so quickly the table rocked and knocked her herbal tea into her lap and she jumped up with a start.

"Michael and I are fine and I don't need you interfering in my life, now or ever. Now if you're ready I'll drop you back at the station." She stopped wiping the tea from her skirt and tried once again to reach out to me but I pulled away and went and paid the bill. We walked in silence to the car and I could see her deliberating whether or not to get in. Typical I thought, she'll probably say she'll walk or get a taxi back to the station and leave me to feel guilty about it. Well I wouldn't feel guilty; if she didn't get in, I wouldn't be losing any sleep over it... this was Penny Brightman after all!

She did get in the car and we drove in silence back to King's Cross. Before she got out, she looked over once more and I could see that she was deliberating about what to say. She did look terribly upset but what the hell... so was I.

Eventually she spoke. "I can understand that you wouldn't want to take advice from me, Remi. I can understand why you must feel I'm interfering in matters that don't concern me, but please understand they do concern me." She looked for a moment as if she was going to elaborate but reigned herself in and then after a few moments she said, "Despite our past relationship I have come to care about you and I don't want to see you get hurt anymore than you have too. Promise me that you will think about it, talk to Michael about your relationship and see where it's going; call me if you need me." With that she got out and without looking back she made her way through the hustle and bustle of the busy station.

I brooded on the conversation all the way home and, as soon as I got in, I rang Juliet and told her what had happened. She listened in silence as I went through the conversation word by word. Well she wasn't exactly silent – she sneezed once, blew her nose twice and then cleared her throat before she spoke.

"Well she does have a point," she said, eventually.

"WHAT?" I shouted down the phone. "What point, what you mean? That's absolute spit." I didn't need to explain spit to Juliet; she talked Gran's polite talk as well.

"It wasn't the most tactful way to put it, but surely even you must have wondered where it was all going, you hardly ever see him anymore, he's away most of the time and when he comes back… Well… Isn't it all reunion sex nowadays?"

I didn't like to admit that even the old reunion sex had lacked the passion it used to have and instead of getting off the plane and dashing home to seduce me wherever I stood, it was now sometimes a day or two before I even got to see him. There was yet another uneasy silence and then Juliet carried on. "What do you think she meant by, I don't want to see you get hurt anymore than you have to? It seems an odd thing to say, don't you think? I could understand her saying that she didn't want you to get hurt but why more than you have to. It sort of implies that you're going to get hurt anyway…"

"I don't know, perhaps she has psychic abilities and can see into the future," I said, feeling utterly miserable. "I wish I could have seen into the future when we started that competition, I would have ripped her 'buddy' application form into shreds because I'm telling you now Juliet, that woman has not changed, there is something not right about her."

"Don't you think you're being a bit harsh? She might be genuinely concerned about you or perhaps she was just having a bad day herself?"

"Well I may have interrupted something; it was obvious she didn't really want to come over today."

"You didn't do the big sigh thing, did you?"

"Of course not, what do you take me for?" I lied.

"Well perhaps it's time that you and Michael had a chat about things; clear the air so you know where you both stand."

"Maybe, I'll see how it goes when he comes home." We talked on for a few more minutes but, in truth, I was distracted. I felt sick and although I knew I should confront Michael, part of me wanted to ignore it all and just carry on as we were.

I put the phone down, tidied myself up and picked up my keys. If there was one person I could always rely on to tell me the truth, it was Gran. I guessed I'd have to brave a houseful of old biddies if I went to see her now, but it had to be done. If there was anything I hated more than animals, it was old people. I don't like to be mean, it's just with the exception of Gran, they're rude, mean, smelly and they harp on about the past all the time.

As I arrived, true to form, the last of the old moaners were on their way out of the door, grumbling about the weather and their hip replacements whilst leaving a trail of lavender and peppermints behind them. After they had all shuffled off, I told Gran I needed to talk to her and, as always, she sat me down and jollied off to the kitchen to make a pot of tea. Tea was Gran's all occasions' panacea; there was nothing so bad that it couldn't be cured by a nice cup of tea and today would be no exception.

She returned carrying a little tray and laid it on the coffee table in front of us. I knew there was no point in starting the conversation until the ritual of the tea-making was finished, so I just sat back and waited, as I had a million times before. The teapot was probably older than me because I had no recollection of it not being around. It was small and dainty and matched the two cups, the sugar bowl, the milk jug and the little plate filled with chocolate biscuits. The tea-set was white with a strawberry pattern emblazoned across. The handles were fluted and, with the exception of a small dint in the bottom of the sugar bowl, they were in perfect condition. There was something very warm and comforting about it all and by the time the tea had been poured into the cups, I already started to feel better about the whole Penny episode.

One sip of Gran's tea and a whole series of memories are instantly evoked. She is the only person I know who defies the modern intervention of the teabag. Gran continues to warm the pot and she only uses real tea leaves. Also, she insists on leaving the tea to brew for a least five minutes before a single drop is poured. The taste is always so perfect that you wallow in the flavour and the memories and before you know it, you're down to your last drop and gagging on the mouthful of leaves deposited at the bottom of the cup.

As I picked the last of the tea leaves off my tongue, she sat back and waited for me to begin. I told her about lunch and what Penny had insinuated, I told her that Juliet thought I should confront Michael about our relationship and for good measure I threw in about the doilies; I don't know why – perhaps I thought it might just be just another mystery Gran could clear up!

"Well, darling, he is very nice and very good looking but, perhaps, he's a bit too old and a little too set in his ways for you."

Damn, I wished I hadn't mentioned the doilies – that had obviously thrown Gran off the scent. At least I didn't tell her that he has all his CDs, DVDs and books in alphabetical order, all his underwear in separate compartments, his towels folded so no outside edges show and the toilet paper folded at the end like they do in hotels!

Just like Penny did, she leaned in and took hold of my hand. "Probably no one will ever be good enough for you in my eyes but only you know if he is the right man for you, darling." She fell silent for a moment and looked down at her tea, when she looked up she was smiling but her eyes were watery and wistful. "Does he make your heart race faster whenever you see him; does he give you goosebumps when he holds your hand and when he kisses you do you feel like there's nowhere else on earth you would rather be? If he doesn't, then perhaps Penny and Juliet are right. Never settle for second best Remi, I didn't and a life-time wasn't long enough."

I leaned over and cuddled her. It was easy to forget sometimes when she was always so cheery and upbeat, just how much she loved Gramps and how she must miss him. She kissed me on the forehead, wiped away a tear and set about pouring another booby-trapped cup of tea.

On my way home later that evening I was resolved to take the bull by the horns and talk to Michael as soon as he came home. We had been good together. No, we *are* good together! It was only recently that things had got a bit strained and that was down to spending too long apart.

It was two days later when Michael rang to say he was back and did I want to go out? He would pick me up in an hour. I dressed like a woman on a mission, picking out a stunning, black, Karen Millen dress which draped low and sexily over my boobs, pinching in at the waist and flowing out into a gypsy-like hem. I teamed it with a high pair of *Jimmy Choos* that tied with ribbons around the calf and made my legs look long and slim. I wore the gold bangle he'd bought me for Christmas and the diamond-stud earrings Gran had bought me for my twenty-first. As I looked at my reflection I knew I was 'smoking' and I felt a tingle run through me. This was going to be some home-coming. I popped my coat on over the whole ensemble and waited for him to hoot when he got outside.

I got into the car and he leaned over to kiss me. It was probably meant to be a small peck on the cheek or a light touch to the lips but as he leaned over I reached out and, taking his head, drew him into a long, sensuous kiss. He didn't respond with quite the same passion but he did stay with me and as I pulled away he stayed there, staring deep into my eyes. I was impressed; I was making quite the *femme fatale*; when I kissed 'em, they stay kissed, baby! It was only then that I realised he was struggling to disentangle himself from one of my earrings and his eyes were more glazed than adoring.

We engaged in small talk on the way over to the restaurant but inside I was buzzing with excitement. Occasionally I peeked over at him as he drove. His hair was tousled and sexy; his freshly-shaven face showed no lingering signs of a weary traveller and his clothes were, as always, designer and immaculate. He smelt divine and I couldn't wait to get to the restaurant so that I could slip off my coat.

We were shown to our table and the waiter stood behind and waited while Michael, ever the gentleman, helped me out of my coat. He pulled the seat out for me and I made an excuse to go the toilets; this outfit needed a big entrance and that was just what it was going to get. Once in the ladies toilets, I checked my make-up, made sure my dress was hanging correctly with no 'skirt in knickers' *faux pas*. I bent over and threw my sun-kissed locks back in a wild and carefree manner. After taking a deep breath I made my way back to our table. Damn he had his head buried in the menu.

I took my time, stopping to smell a flower arrangement on my way, which had no scent whatsoever as it was plastic, but was very dusty, causing me to sneeze loudly and inappropriately over the nearest table. I said loud, profuse apologies and was delighted to see that when I turned back Michaels eyes, and the rest of the restaurant, were upon me. I could feel a charge in the atmosphere as I sat down and, without looking at him, I took my own menu and studied it. I knew he was looking; I could feel, rather than see, the lascivious looks he was giving me and the heat racing through my own body was matched, I knew, by his. At last he spoke.

"You look sensational tonight," he said, leaning over to take my hand. I was going to say it was nothing special but I thought better of it. I was going for the *femme fatale* look; the quiet, sexy, full of my own sexual assurance approach and, tonight, I was smouldering... Enough said!

I spent the evening being outrageously flirty – encouraging admiring looks from other men and making sure Michael saw them too. He was hooked and I knew it, this was one fish that would not be swimming away tonight. Shivers of excitement passed through me in anticipation of what the night still had to hold. His phone rang and after checking it he turned it off.

"I'm off duty tonight," he said, raising his glass and refilling mine at the same time. "Tonight I'm all yours," and he was right. That night I was all his and he was definitely all mine. There was no hint of going through the motions of reunion sex; it was raw, unbridled and passionate.

The first time was quick, lustful and much needed but, after a few more glasses of wine, we made love again and this time it was sweet and gentle. We caressed and fondled, we explored in a way we hadn't since we first met. He looked me deep in the eyes and told me I was a very special person and that he loved me. I felt he wanted to say more but he drew back.

We slept soundly that night, cuddled up in each other's arms and in the morning he surprised me by wanting to start again.

Who Cares?

"'Buddy' hell," I said to myself. "That dress I wore last night should have a government warning on it."

We kissed deep and longingly and, if the phone hadn't rung, we would have made love for a third time. The phone call broke the mood and within minutes he was up, showered and on his way to a meeting but I didn't care, I had proved them all wrong. Michael loved me, of that I was certain.

I spent the day in a euphoric trance, filled with thoughts of our lovemaking and the possibility of more that evening, I hadn't forgotten how amorous he had been that morning and had it not been for the untimely phone call we would probably have both been late for work! Of course the late night lovemaking made for a few mistakes during the day. Calling Mr. Clitheroe Mr. Clitoris was one of the worst ones, compounded even further when I asked one of the guys in production to go down and find Mr. Clitoris. Apparently, he wanted to report me for sexual harassment!

After work I called in at the local supermarket and picked up some bread, cheese, olives and a good bottle of red wine. I then stopped off at the video shop to rent out a romantic comedy that I hadn't seen before – all the time wondering which outfit to wear to tempt Michael with that night.

Having laid out all the food and removed the cork from the wine to let it breathe, I showered; blow-dried my hair and went into the bedroom to try on some clothes. After much deliberation I settled on a Collette Dinnigan knee-length, cream, silk skirt and a delicate, georgette top – also in cream, which I had bought on one of my first-ever spending sprees in London. I added some coffee-coloured pearls and a matching bracelet and, having decided I didn't need shoes, I painted my toenails in soft, pearlescent beige. My make-up was light and I pulled my hair back and held it in place with a pearl clip, allowing a few tendrils to snake softly around my face. I felt beautiful, feminine and very sexy and my hand shook as I poured myself a glass of wine and sat back on the sofa, trying not to ruin any part of the effect.

I checked the time every half-hour. I checked the house phone and my mobile to make sure they were on, not on silent and that I hadn't missed Michael's call. I jumped up to look out of the window every time a car slowed down and nearly pounced on the pizza delivery guy who knocked on my door by mistake.

I phoned Michael after the first hour, then again after another half-hour, then every ten minutes after that, always with the same answer; the caller cannot take your call, please try again later. I must have fallen asleep at some point, as when I woke, it was in the early hours and still no sign of Michael. The next day was so unlike the day before. I was still in a trance except this time it was with worry, anger and self-doubt all over again.

It was much later that evening when Michael finally rang but there was no apology for not calling the day before, no excuses as to why he had been unavailable and no mention of the passion we had shared just days before. I almost held my breath as I heard the clipped rather brusque description of how busy he was and how he wouldn't be able to see me for a while.

"Michael," I said, feeling my heart thumping heavily inside my chest. "Why didn't you come round last night? How busy do you have to be not to pick up the phone and let me know?"

There was a small delay before he answered. "I don't remember saying I would be there last night."

"Well, perhaps, I just assumed you would come round, seeing as though I've hardly seen you lately and we are supposed to be a couple. I thought that's what couples did!"

"Don't go all high-pitched on me Remi, you know I hate that, you are a very special girl and I love you dearly, but…" This so didn't sound like it did the other day when we were making love, then it sounded like the start of something new, now it just sounded like the end of something. "Things are really hectic at the moment. I'm going away tomorrow to America for work and then travelling on to see my family. I think we need some time apart to see how we feel about each other. It's not fair to keep stringing you along like this Remi, it's time to start thinking about settling down and I need time to think about that and all it entails."

Suddenly I could hear my heart pounding in my ears, so loud that I was actually struggling to hear what he was saying. I heard him say again that he loved me, that he would ring me while he was away and then he said goodbye.

It was a week before I heard from him again; he rang in the middle of the night, which I guessed was early evening wherever he was. It was polite conversation, finishing with the timeless... "It's not you, it's me".

Once again I cried myself to sleep wondering, what I'd done wrong and why he was acting like that but, when I woke the next morning, I was resolved to see it for the better good. After all, perhaps it takes something like this before people can truly commit to each other, perhaps one day we would be telling the grandchildren the story of Granddad Michael running off to America to avoid Gran and then coming home and proposing. For the first time in many days I had a spring back in my step and positive thoughts in my head.

As I passed the chemist, Boots on the way to work I noticed they were offering a free diabetes test and couldn't resist nipping in. See, my luck was already on the up. Unfortunately this made me a bit late for work and as I rushed in, hanging my coat on the nearest chair, I could see the disapproving looks from the rest of the production team.

"Hey you lot, I'm only half an hour late, so sue me." I expected someone to give in and laugh but nothing; they just turned their backs and carried on with what they were doing. Someone handed me my worksheet and I rushed off onto the set just as they were about to go on air. 'Damn,' I thought. 'I must be later than half an hour.' I hadn't realised the time so I put my head down and got on with my work even though the looks continued on set.

During the break I could hear an argument ensuing from the sofas and I leaned forward trying to catch it. It was Mary talking and she was getting very heated with the director. "It's just not good enough. She'll have to be told." With that the director looked over in my direction and then turned back, trying to placate, the now livid, Mary.

Flipping heck! I thought Mary and I had been on a better footing in the past few years. Surely she wasn't after getting me the sack for being an hour or so late. With hindsight, perhaps I'd taken my job a little for granted. One thing was for sure, I was really starting to regret popping into Boots on the way to work; it was all getting out of hand.

I decided that in the lunch hour I would apologise to everyone and promise that it would never happen again. I nipped into the ladies so that nobody would catch up with me and sack me before I had a chance to grovel. Maybe I would offer to do overtime or something.

When I returned the programme was back on air, minus Mary. My heart was racing, if she was so angry with me that she'd walked off set then I would be sacked for sure. I looked around and finally caught sight of her coming out of the ladies toilets where I'd been just a few minutes before. She was still looking really angry and I stepped back into the shadows before she could catch sight of me.

The studio was live and I knew she wouldn't be able to come over or speak whilst the show was on so I relaxed slightly, knowing I had at least half an hour to buy some time and work out my strategy. Should I go on bended knees to Mary and beg her to forgive me or should I just say that I was called into the doctor's urgently with suspected diabetes? Well let's face it…that was nearly the truth!

The sound of the outside broadcast caught my attention. The studio was crossing live to Las Vegas and Michael was on the screen. I peered round from my hiding place, still hoping that Mary couldn't see me. Michael was looking really good. He was dressed in a beautifully-cut navy-blue suit, which, unless I was mistaken, was *Prada*. Underneath he wore a crisp, white shirt and a blue and gold, brocade waist-coat, all finished off with a gold, silk tie. I'd never seen that outfit before but it wasn't unusual for the film crew to hire clothes for him to wear to suit the occasion.

Even though the set was deathly quiet, I was struggling to hear clearly from where I was so I inched over a few more feet, aware that I had now put myself into view. I kept one eye on the television screen and the other on lookout for Mary.

"So Michael, we hear that Las Vegas is this year's top holiday destination?" Michael pointed out over the panoramic view of the city and the bright lights and I estimated that in Vegas it was the early hours of the morning and yet the place was still bright and alive.

"It certainly is," Michael continued. "There's something for everyone here. Of course there's the gambling, but you don't have to throw all your money away on that. The shows are worth a visit alone, everything from variety shows and circuses to Tom Jones and Celine Dion. Each one of the hotels has its own spectacular theme. You can walk through St. Mark's Square in The Venetian, complete with gondolas and singing gondoliers, or shop in the markets of Marrakech, complete with indoor rain storms, or even see all your favourite movie stars, dead or alive, at the MGM Grand. It's truly an action-packed place, full of energy and vitality; the casinos never close, there are no windows, the artificial skies are always sunny and there are no clocks to be seen. It is a city that, truly, never sleeps."

"It sounds great Michael, but isn't there something else it's quite famous for?" Michael laughed in that sexy way he had then looked down and shook his head.

"That is true, it's also known for its numerous wedding chapels, the Elvis Chapel, Cupid's Chapel, the Little White Chapel, to name but a few. There's even a drive through wedding chapel. Stars that have married here are also numerous; including the likes of Cary Grant, Elizabeth Taylor and Richard Burton, Bridgette Bardot, Paul Newman and Clint Eastwood."

"Ah, but a little bird tells us that someone else may be getting married there soon, is that right Michael?"

"It is," said Michael, holding his hands up.

"Are we right in thinking that you are marrying a certain young lady known to us here at the studios?"

Oh my God, oh my God… My heart was racing; it was the most romantic thing in the world. Michael was going to propose, then and there, in front of millions of viewers. To think I'd doubted him, questioned how much he loved me. Automatically my hand went up to my hair, smoothing it back behind my ears. I wished I'd had some notice, the cameras were sure to swing over in my direction. I wondered if I had enough time to run over to wardrobe and find an outfit, or at least get someone to make my face up. 'Sob' it, I didn't care, it was my big day.

As I watched the screen it went back to Michael and panned out for the bigger picture.

"Yes you're right. I am an extremely lucky man to have found such a wonderful woman and as you rightly said, you and the viewers will already know her."

In fairness the studio all knew me, but the audience... well not so much. There was that time I fainted whilst having the hair makeover and another time when I accidentally walked on to screen and looked up to see the director mouthing at me to get off. Luckily the old acting gene kicked in and I quickly adjusted Mary's hair – much to her surprise, picked some papers up off the table and made my way out to the side. But even that was only a few seconds of air time, hardly enough time for the viewers to know me. Probably, what he meant was that my name was on the credits that they would recognise the name, even if they didn't know the face. I mentally practiced my surprised and shocked face and then decided that perhaps surprise and tears would be a better look.

Michael continued again, looking as pleased as punch. I wondered if he would go down on one knee. "You will all know her from one of the programmes screened earlier in the year."

I thought for a moment, earlier in the year...Yes, yes I remembered then, that I'd been Fashion Adviser on one of the catwalk programmes; I hadn't done much, just handed over a few outfits when they were asked for but bless Michael for thinking everyone would remember.

"And what programme would that be?" the stand-in for Mary was asking, obviously trying to build up the excitement.

"It was our very successful diet competition, held earlier in the year. I met this wonderful woman when she consulted me about where to take her holiday, we met again to talk over her travel arrangements and I have to tell you, I fell hook, line and sinker and I am very proud to say she has consented to be my wife. By this time tomorrow we will be Mr. and Mrs. Michael Hayes.'

There was a small, polite round of applause and people started scouring the room. I knew they were looking for me and

Who Cares?

I slipped back into the anonymity of the shadows. My head was spinning, my thoughts were totally confused. Why, why was he doing this to me? If he had fallen in love with someone else why hadn't he told me? Only a couple of weeks ago we had been making mad, passionate love. He'd even rung me while he was away. Why didn't he tell me then and why, after all the things he said, would he leave me to face this alone? To be made a fool of, a laughing stock in front of everyone.

I continued to stare at the screen but my eyes were so full of tears I could hardly make out the figures on the screen. And yet, without seeing, I knew who was standing by Michael's side and who was about to become Mrs. Michael Hayes. How could I have been so blind? Wasn't it there under my nose all the time? Stupid, gullible Remi... of course it could be only one person.

Just then someone touched me on the shoulder and I turned to look into the familiar face of my junior assistant. She spoke but it was almost as if someone had pressed the mute button. She said it three times before I could make out the words. "Remi," she said, concern showing in her young face. "It's Penny."

I stood just looking into her face but my eyes were unseeing. My hands were shaking, my heart was racing and my stomach felt as if someone had reached in and squeezed it beyond endurance. How could I not have seen it? Was I so vain that I didn't see the signs, hadn't she tried to warn me?

"Of course it's Penny," I said, feeling the tears falling unchecked down my face and the pain of the most awful treachery tearing at my insides but when I looked up, there was Penny...

Penny was rushing along the side of the set, dodging cameras and production staff, her arms outstretched, tears falling down her own face. She would have reached me if it hadn't been for a small hand on my shoulder and, when I turned round, there was Mary with tears in her eyes. She pulled me to her and held me tightly and the floods unleashed.

"I'm so sorry," she said, kissing me lightly on the head. Over her shoulder I saw Michael kissing Martha, her glorious, red locks bouncing in happy anticipation of her big day.

Not my day. *Hers!*

Seven

I suppose many of us may have wondered, at some time or another, if it's really possible to die of a broken heart; however, in my case, an impromptu visit to the doctor confirmed that the probabilities were low and the doctor was able to assure me that, in time, my heart would heal.

I sat with my eyes closed and imagined my once plump, regularly pounding heart torn asunder and laid flat open, with blood and ventricles on show – not quite dead, not quite living. I could almost see the tiny scabs forming, trying desperately to pull this massive, life-giving organ back together, eventually I would be left with a big, patchwork heart, unable to expand to let anyone else in, just enough room left to allow blood to seep through and keep this useless body alive to suffer forever.

"Oh get over it Remi, it's been four months. Your heart's absolutely fine and if you're honest, the only real thing you're suffering from is humiliation at what that 'batard' did to you and the embarrassment that he chose that red parasite over you, but that's his problem not yours. Now snap out of it."

Juliet had been on an assertiveness course and I can't say that I liked the results very much; but I suppose, in my heart, I knew she was right. It was time to pull myself together. I just didn't know how, or even where, to begin.

After the fateful programme had aired, everyone and his cousin had taken me aside to commiserate. People I barely recognised took me by the hand, tears brimming, to tell me they felt my pain and if I ever needed someone to talk to, and yet when Michael returned with the gushing Belisha beacon by his side, they avoided me like the plague. I wouldn't have been able to find someone to tell them the building was on fire, let alone find a shoulder to cry on.

Who Cares?

In the end I knew the only way out was to leave but, of course, how embarrassing was that! I didn't want it to look like I was running away which, of course, I was. So I did the only thing a respectable, dumped in front of millions, girl can do and told them I had been headhunted by the BBC and that they had offered me a huge salary which I couldn't refuse plus the chance to work with some of the big stars. Whether they believed me or not I don't know. With hindsight, perhaps the big stars thing was a tad too far.

They asked me all sorts of questions; what type of job it was? Who else I would be working with? What programme would I be on? The trouble is once you've told a lie; you have to build a whole network of lies to cover it all up. I kept building and building, until, in the end, I actually believed it all myself. It came as quite a shock and, I have to say, a huge disappointment when I came to the end of my notice and realised that I was, in fact, unemployed and wouldn't, in reality, be hosting the new series of *Strictly Come Dancing* opposite our long-time, family friend, Bruce Forsyth!

I soon gave up the flat, not just because I wasn't earning, but also, because I began to hate my own company. I had thought my mother would come to the rescue and ask me to come home but she made no mention of it, except to say, that I had brought it all on myself and got what I deserved... Hardly the response you expect from a caring, loving mum, but then it was time to face up to the fact that she wasn't one.

Gran, God bless her, took me in and I duly repaid her with sullen looks, fits of screaming, colossal arguments and torrents of tears.

I knew I was wrong. I knew I was taking out all my unhappiness on the one person who had never let me down, but I just couldn't stop myself. My days swung from deep depression, where I didn't even get out of bed, to over-oxygenated euphoria, where I was determined to become famous and show them all that I was over it.

Unfortunately, the good days were well and truly overpowered by the bad, due to the fact that, as of yet, I hadn't found anything I was remotely good enough at, to make me famous.

"You need to get a job, Remi." Juliet said, without lifting her head from what she was reading. "Something that makes you get up in the morning." She lifted her head and looked over at me, then added … "And you need to wash!"

She had a point, there had been some scaling down in the hygiene department but I wasn't about to admit to it, that was for sure. I leaned over to see what she was embroiled in.

It's a Quiet Life, the in-house magazine for librarians, packed with exciting articles like 'How to Show Disapproval Without Raising Your Voice', 'Stranger Than Fiction' and 'The Man Who Stole Paperbacks by Rolling Them Up and Sticking Them in his False Leg!'

"I will get a job," I replied, indignantly. "As soon as I find something I really want to do."

"Well you could start by going to the Job Centre or an employment agency" said Juliet, flipping a page over with a bit more impatience than was polite. "As my dad used to say," and she made the sign of a cross in a derogatory fashion. "Jobs don't just come knocking on your door, you have to go out and find them,"

Uncannily, at that very moment there was a knock at the door and we both jumped at the same time. Naturally I sat there, not bothering to get up, a habit I had come to acquire as I knew Gran would go and answer it.

"Have faith, Juliet," I carried on." I just know something will turn up."

"But it won't Remi, you have to go out and get it. Jobs don't just land in your lap, you know!" Before she could finish, a small piece of paper fluttered down from above and landed face down in my lap. We both looked up in surprise to see Penny had come into the room. Turning the piece of paper over I could see it contained no more than a name and a telephone number. I turned it over again just in case I'd missed something.

"A friend of mine is looking for someone to help her out and I thought this might be just up your street, nothing too strenuous, no qualifications needed and just a few hours a day. I said you'd give her a ring and go over and have a chat." She put her beautifully manicured hand up and started making her way back to the door.

"No need to thank me, the pleasure is all mine. Anyway it's about time you started getting out and doing something useful, and this girl really needs some help" As she passed, she picked up a small lock of my hair and grimaced. "And, by the looks of it, so do you." With that she was out the door, apologising for the brief visit and promising to ring later. Juliet and I just looked at each other and then, with a shrug of her shoulders, she went back to *The Quiet Life*.

I looked at the small piece of paper again and couldn't help but laugh. Penny probably knew that this small piece of paper, without any details on other than a name and telephone number, would eventually intrigue me. Whereas, had she told me all about it, I probably would have dismissed it out of hand. The Penny we had known at school was truly gone, I knew that now. But in those few short moments when Michael said he was to marry someone from the diet programme, I was sure that Penny was the one.

The facts seemed to be screaming out at me. She had warned me off Michael and insinuated that I would get hurt. She was never available at the same time Michael was away, the hushed tones when she eventually answered the phone and, last but not least, buried deep in the recesses of my mind, I suppose I could not forget the old Penny, the Penny who had made our lives miserable for so long. Yet on that fateful day, there she was; the first person by my side.

Mary had insisted that I was taken home and Penny volunteered immediately. She took control, driving me home, calling both Gran and Juliet on the way, hands-free of course. She made me strong tea with plenty of sugar in it, which normally I wouldn't drink but, at that time, it was strangely soothing and I reasoned I would probably be safe from developing diabetes with just one cup!

Eventually, she sat me down and, amidst my tears and unreasonable ranting, took hold of my hands and tried to talk to me. "Remi, I hate that this has happened to you but seriously what future would you have had with that lying, cheating, scheming, cold-hearted bastard? If you ask me, that Martha has done you a favour."

I knew she was right. Sometime, somewhere, somehow, in the future, he would have done this, I knew in my heart he would have and I knew it was better that it happened now, rather than later, but knowing it didn't help, knowing it didn't take away the pain and knowing it didn't stop me being humiliated in front of millions of people on national television.

"Did you know about it, Penny?" I taunted her. "I expect you went out together in a cosy foursome? All had a good laugh at me, did you?" I shouted through tears of outrage, changing the focus of my anger from Michael to Penny, knowing, of course, I was hitting out at the wrong person but I didn't care. Penny looked visibly stunned and for a moment she drew back.

I wanted to say sorry. I knew I was being ungrateful and irrational but I was like a runaway train. She sat for a while, perhaps deciding whether to stay or not, maybe wondering if she should revert back to her bullying days and just hit me. I wouldn't have blamed her. *I* wanted to hit me. But after a while she put her arm round me, rubbed my back and stroked my hair until the crying subsided.

"I did know about them," she said, suddenly. I looked up in amazement. Even though I had accused her, I didn't expect it to be true. "But I only knew for sure the day before it all happened." I blew my nose and peered up at her through swollen eyes, I didn't speak, and I didn't need to.

"When the diet show finished we all kept in touch. Our plights were similar, we'd all been through the struggle of losing weight and along with that came other problems, problems that we didn't air in public but things we knew we could talk to each other about. So I suppose that we created a sort of support system between us. We were on the end of a telephone if anyone needed help. Then we got together again for the holiday programme. I think it's fair to say that I could see some sort of rapport going on between Martha and Michael. They seemed to hit it off straight away and there definitely seemed to be some flirting going on, but then Michael was very charming. I thought, perhaps, it was just his way. Anyway, at that time, I had no idea that you and Michael were an item. I didn't find that out until we went out for that first get together with Juliet. That was when you told me about Michael and frankly by the end of the evening you were in no state to understand anything."

I knew what she meant. I half-recalled Juliet and I doing a rendition of *Singing in the Rain* on the way home and one or the other of us, falling into the children's paddling pool in the park. No correction – it was both of us!

"Anyway," Penny carried on. "From then on Martha rang me a few times, always bubbly and happy. She told me the Save the Children Fund was so pleased with her and the publicity she had created, they had offered her a job. She'd also been offered modelling work and had done some more interviews for television and national newspapers. In truth it was nice to hear from her, she was happy and that was more that could be said for some of the other contestants. When all the euphoria and excitement of the television programme came to an end, it was hard for all of us. It was a huge anticlimax. Do you remember Mary and Katie, the mother and daughter?" she said, looking at me. I sniffed and nodded.

"Well, Mary rang me one night. She was really upset. She'd been shopping that day and, without thinking, had bought all the things she used to buy before losing the weight; pies, cakes, biscuits and fizzy drinks. She couldn't remember buying them, didn't know why she had, but when she got home and saw them all sitting there in front of her, she knew she would eat them.

I went over to her house straight away and threw the whole lot into a black bag and dumped it outside the house. That way, neither of us would be tempted. I made her a black coffee and we just sat and talked for a while. It turns out that Katie had managed the publicity really well; she had received stacks of invitations to parties and events and had been out pretty much every night, whereas Mary found that her nights were now spent alone. Without the comfort and strength of Katie she was fragile and somehow her mind had transferred her back to another time."

I sniffed again and looked at her. "Is she alright now?" I asked

"Yes," Penny said, turning back to me and smiling. "She's brilliant now. I offered her a job at one of my classes, advising others on losing weight. She took to it like a duck to water and has made lots of new friends."

"Good, I liked Mary, but carry on about Martha," I urged.

"Well, a few times I asked her if there was anyone special in her life and she just laughed and said there were lots of special people. After we had lunch that time and you said that Michael was away a lot and that things weren't great between you, I started to worry that perhaps something had developed between them. I phoned her when I got home but I couldn't get hold of her. She rang me the following week explaining that she'd been away and her phone had been turned off. I tried to draw her out and make light of it. I said she probably had a secret man in her life, that was why she was so happy, hoping that she would reveal something but she never said a word.

Then, the night before the programme aired, she phoned me. She reminded me about what I'd said about the secret man thing and then she giggled and said it was true. She wouldn't tell me who it was but she did say that I knew him and all would be revealed the next day. I tried to find out more but she just laughed and said she had to go and that she would see me when she got home. Before she hung up she giggled again and told me to watch the television in the morning, with that she was gone.

"The first thing I did was to ring the studio to find out if Michael was away. They said he was on location in Las Vegas. Alarm bells began to ring, so I contacted all the good hotels in Vegas and, eventually, found out that both he and Martha were staying at the same hotel.

"I tried to ring you but there was no answer. I raced over to your flat first thing in the morning but you'd already left. I got to the studio and you hadn't arrived, which made me panic, so I came back to the flat and got in touch with your landlord, Mr. Davison and made him open it up, just in case…

"After we had established that you weren't there, I rushed back to the studio just in time for the announcement. So you see,

I didn't really know, I just suspected, and by the time I was sure, it was too late."

"Why didn't I see it coming Penny; how could I have been so stupid?"

"You're not stupid Remi, he is. He didn't realise what a remarkable person he had in you and has now thrown away the best thing he's ever had in his life." Penny had cuddled up beside me and allowed me to cry freely, reassuring me that time was a great healer.

Over the next four months they tried to pull me out of my depression but wallowing in self-pity had become a way of life. However, Penny had been right about one thing, I wasn't stupid. I could see that their sympathy was beginning to wear thin. I looked over at Juliet, still engrossed in her magazine, and then looked back at myself. I stood up and walked over to the mirror.

I felt physically ashamed of how I'd let it get the better of me. I looked at my reflection in the mirror; the greasy hair, the bags under the eyes, the grubby pyjamas that I'd worn for a week, Gran's old cardie wrapped around me as if it were a straightjacket, the tatty slippers and the socks which I'd slept in.

I was a mess and it was time to do something about it. It was time to take back my life. As I looked over at Juliet, she turned quickly back to her magazine, a small smirk still lingering on her face. Was it just coincidence that she was reading *Reprimanding with Mind Control*?

When I was alone once more with Gran I looked again at the piece of paper. It yielded no more this time, than it had the last, but, somehow, it did offer something. It offered a challenge, a chance to get back with the living and, maybe, a chance to put the past, back in the past.

"Did she say what the job was?" Gran asked, watching me turn the paper over for the third time.

"No, she just said it would be right up my street."

"How intriguing," said Gran, putting down the newspaper, taking off her glasses and turning to face me. "Do you think it's something in fashion or television, maybe?"

"I doubt it Gran, not written on the back of an old envelope, hardly the sort of thing top execs at the BBC send out when they're headhunting for new presenters. Penny said it was a friend of hers and she needed someone to help her out. No qualifications needed and nothing too strenuous. Could be a temporary job, shop-assistant, possibly in fashion or a window-dresser, that sounds more like the sort of thing I would love, maybe a make-up demonstrator," I said, warming to the subject.

"Well if it's that good you'd better get in touch before she gives it to someone else." Gran smiled and returned to her paper.

I looked over at her, sitting there, so small in the armchair. Had she always been so small or had I just not noticed it before? She started riffling through the pages and I knew it was time for her to start the crossword. How many times in the past four months had I watched her as she started it, knowing that within minutes she would be asking me one of the clues? How many times had I, begrudgingly, dredged up an answer wondering why, if she couldn't do them anymore, she insisted on the daily ritual of trying?

How unmindful and selfish had I become that I couldn't see the one answer that was staring me in the face? She didn't need anything from me, she was perfectly capable of doing the crossword on her own; she wanted to keep me involved, keep me talking and make me think of things, other than myself. It was then that I knew, whatever this job turned out to be, I would take it, even if it was for just a few months. I would take it and start to pay Gran back everything I owed; starting with some money.

The next day I rang the number on the piece of paper Penny had given me. Someone called Lucy answered and she seemed ecstatic that I had rung. She asked me if I could start straight away and after quickly imparting her address, hung up, without giving me a chance to ask what the job entailed.

For the first time, in a very long time, I had to make a wardrobe decision and it turned out to be much harder than I thought. Naturally, I wanted to make a good impression and look smart but on the other hand I didn't want to seem over keen. Thankfully, Gran had hung some of the better clothes up in the wardrobe on the day I moved in, the rest were stored, none too tidily, in black plastic bags. I shifted a few about on the rail, trying to see if any tops matched bottoms or if indeed, any of them would even still fit. As Penny had, so rightly, pointed out, I had piled on the weight in the last few months. Lack of exercise and self-pity eating didn't do a lot for the old figure.

Eventually though, I settled on a beautifully tailored *Max Mara* suit in cream, a brown and cream blouse with a pussycat bow, some comfortable Faith heels and a cream coloured military style Mac which tied in the middle. It was a good look and Gran agreed that it set just the right impression, not too keen but that of a professional, single girl wanting to get back on the ladder again. She suggested I topped it off with one of her hats and I thought immediately of her straw bonnets with the ribbon ties, but she handed me a delicate cream beret and, I have to say, it was the icing on the cake.

Eight

Forty-nine, Old Park Road turned out to be a lovely old, detached house, in a quiet cul-de–sac, in a very pretty part of London. Its leafy avenue of trees and its close proximity to the park could almost make you forget there was a bustling city just a few minutes away. It was a little sanctuary of peace and tranquillity that could take even the seasoned Londoner by surprise.

The house was an old, Victorian building with large, stone, bay windows on either side of the door. The old wooden, sash windows sported brightly coloured swathes of material and there were small transfers of birds in flight, stuck onto the panes. The upper windows were similar, although it was obvious that one, at least, belonged to a child, as there was a cluster of teddies lined up against the inside. I counted six chimney pots on the roof suggesting that most of the rooms had fireplaces. I felt a tingle run through me, thinking of how cosy they would all be in the winter months, with their little lamps on and their dancing fireplaces.

Not for the first time I felt the familiar pull of bitter regret that I had not been part of a family that huddled by the fire, telling stories and eating marshmallows. Perhaps these didn't either, but I wouldn't mind guessing it was close.

The front door stood at the top of a small flight of stone steps protected by an old, stone porch with a red, tiled roof the same colour as the house. As I approached, it started to rain and I made my way quickly up the steps and into its welcome shelter. I was more than a bit relieved to have made it before the onslaught started. The clouds above looked like there might be quite a storm brewing. The door was bright red with an old-fashioned, black, door knocker and a matching letter box. To the side was an old doorbell with a pull handle. The house just oozed warmth and I couldn't wait to pull the handle and hear the old bell chime throughout the house.

I took a few moments to collect my thoughts and adjust my coat and as I did so I noticed, for the first time, the higgledy piggledy collection of boots, umbrellas, hats, coats and ornaments that lay around me. On the wall was a line of pegs and on each peg hung a coat, on each coat was a hat, and tucked on top of those, were gloves and mittens. In the corner stood a big pot filled with a mixture of umbrellas: small, coloured ones, a fashionable *Burberry* one (neatly packed in its sheath) and a no-nonsense, black one that stood proudly and almost separately from the others.

The floor was littered with an array of dog leads, brushes, balls and bags. Yet despite all the clutter and chaos, it was actually incredibly warm and homely. Even before entering the house, you felt you already knew the sort of people who lived there.

I pulled on the handle and the bell resounded through the house. It wasn't as majestic as I thought it would be but it soon brought on an absolute cacophony of sounds and activity. Children started screaming and dogs started barking. In fact, all mayhem was let loose. I could hear scraping on wooden floors, followed by scratching at the bottom of the door as little hands grappled with the door knob.

"Daisy, ask who it is before you open it." The letter box opened and two little hands curled around the corners but as I bent down all I could see was a pair of eyes.

"Who are you?" a little voice cried through the hole.

"My name's Remi, Mummy's expecting me," I said, still crouching down by the letter box. I tried to peer past the pair of eyes into the hallway but standing behind them was a big mouth with a big tongue and even bigger teeth which seemed to be bared in my direction.

'Great, just my luck, they've got a 'buddy' dog,' I thought, but before I could decide how to handle it, the door was thrown open and I was pushed backwards onto the floor with one child on top of me, another about to throw himself at me and a big, and I do mean big, dog drooling over the top, with saliva running from its big, open mouth in a long, dangling dewdrop aimed directly at my face. I shifted as fast as I could onto my side, narrowly missing the stream of drool but unfortunately catapulting both the children onto the floor, whereby they started to scream.

It occurred to me as I lay there prone and motionless on the floor, boots asunder, half the coats and hats on top of me along with two children crying for all they were worth, that this was not best start I'd ever had to an interview, but at least it couldn't get any worse... That was when the dog repositioned itself above me and the drool landed a direct hit into my stunned and gaping mouth!

Eventually, Lucy managed to sort out all the flailing bodies, pulling the children off me and banishing the dog to a side-room. As she pulled me up, I brushed myself down and turned to take a better look at her. She was petite, probably just over five feet and her small, lean frame was being supported by a crutch, stuck under her arm. On her leg was a big, pink, plaster cast which ran from ankle to thigh. As her black hair fell onto her face she struggled to let go of the crutch she was balancing on, to tie the loose strands back behind her ear. Her skin was pale and clear, showcasing her big, dark eyes, which sparkled with excitement. Her mouth was well proportioned and full and even without a stitch of make-up on, she looked as fresh-faced as a teenager, although she must have been in her twenties.

I tried to apologise but she wouldn't have any of it. Her face practically beamed as she squeezed my hand, ready to lead me through to the sitting-room.

"Remi, I'm so glad you came. Penny wasn't sure if you would, but I had a good feeling about you, I just know you'll be perfect for the job."

"Well I don't know about that," I started. "I don't even know what the job..." I didn't have a chance to finish my sentence as the 'buddy' dog suddenly emerged from the side-room again, missing Lucy by a hair's breadth and pinning me up against the door, which shut with a loud bang, frightening both me and the dog. For one terrible moment I had visions of him doing a 'Scooby Doo' and jumping up into my arms!

Ten minutes later and order was restored again. Another smaller dog was playing with the children in the garden whilst the big, drooly one sat by the window looking in and staring. As Lucy rattled away with cups and saucers in the kitchen, I stood up and looked around the beautifully decorated room. All the time the dog watched.

As I helped Lucy bring in the tea-tray she started to tell me how she had broken her leg, whilst skating at the local rink with the children. Out of the corner of my eye I could see the dog watching me intently, especially as I leaned forward and took a biscuit from the tray. His head tipped slightly with an enquiring pose as I held it in front of me. What was I going to do with the biscuit? Was I going to eat it? When Lucy turned to grab something from behind her, I made a show of moving the biscuit towards my mouth... and then, still facing him, I quickly popped it in with a satisfied... Remi: one... Dog: nothing, type of look.

The dog made a whimpering sort of sound and Lucy turned back and looked over at him and then at me.

"Oh Remi not them, they're Bailey's," she laughed and handed me a plate of expensive-looking, chocolate biscuits. I looked over at the window. Was it my imagination, or was the dog laughing? The smaller, terrier-type dog had joined him and was now busy jumping up at the window.

"Which one is Bailey?" I asked.

"The big one," Lucy replied, pouring tea into two lovely, little, china cups. "The little one is Bob." I could feel the remains of the dog biscuit in my teeth and suppressed the feeling to retch.

"So, do you like dogs Remi?" Lucy asked as she handed me some tea. I wanted to answer honestly but thought it prudent at this point, to remain dispassionate. I didn't want to blow my chances of getting the job, just because I detested dogs, and in particular hers.

"Who doesn't?" I said, looking fondly towards the window.

"Exactly," said Lucy. "How can you not love them? One

thing I've learnt over the years, Remi, is that people who dislike animals can't be trusted." A gulp of tea went down the wrong way and I started coughing causing Lucy to jump up, without crutches, to help me, thereby knocking over her own cup of tea. She was sure right, we can't be trusted!

The phone rang and she got up once more to hobble over and answer it. As she passed the window, she let out a huge doleful sigh. She asked the caller to hold on and covering the phone she whispered. "I think it's an enquiry about a job, would you do me a huge favour Remi? I hate to ask but it's just so difficult for me... would you carry Bailey in for me? He's absolutely covered in mud. There's a towel by the back door but *please* don't let him walk on the floor in the conservatory." She mouthed thank you, uncovered the mouthpiece, apologised for the delay and carried on talking whilst struggling back to the sofa.

The little conservatory was off to the side of the sitting-room and led out into the garden. By the side of the door was a small pile of fluffy towels. I looked out of the window and saw Bob and Bailey, now half-way down the garden, digging up the flower bed. I was going to get filthy bringing that great lump in. I looked round and noticed a dark blue overall hanging on the door, a bit greasy but perfectly functional. On the floor were some old, green wellies, turned down at the top, so that the cream material lining was showing. Perfect.

I changed quickly and opened the door. Four pairs of eyes turned to stare at me. The children quickly returned to what they were doing and the dogs started bounding around again at the bottom of the garden, in the very productive act of, chasing each other's tails! I could see this was not going to be easy. I had no idea what breed of dog Bailey was, only that he was big, very hairy, very dirty and seemed to be in no hurry to come in.

I crept towards him, holding out my hand in an offer of friendship. As I neared, he cocked his head to one side and slowly started to make his way over to me. The dog didn't know me after all, and he wasn't smiling or anything. As I took a few steps back it seemed to trigger something in Bailey, who started moving at a faster pace. I turned to run but as I looked back over my shoulder, I saw Bailey's huge form jumping at me, his tongue connecting with my face with enough saliva to stick a thousand envelopes.

I pushed him back down to the ground, pleased that I'd had the foresight to put on the overall, which was already filthy. Emboldened, I grabbed hold of his collar and started tugging him towards the house but the 'buddy' thing wouldn't budge. Just when I thought it was an impossible task, I noticed a wheelbarrow to the side. If I could get him in, it would just be a matter of pushing him up to the door. How hard could that be?

I dragged him to the barrow and managed to get the front paws in but no more. I pulled the wheelbarrow backwards with the dog half-in and half-out. He walked on his back legs for a few feet and then gave up and jumped out. I tried again but he was having none of it. I tried pulling his collar again but he just stayed put. Suddenly, I hit on a brain wave. It wasn't going to be easy but if I could pull it off…

There was a small hill in the middle of the garden and I managed to pull him to the top of it. Holding onto his collar I positioned myself at the bottom of the slope. I braced myself, bent my knees slightly and pulled the very surprised dog up onto my shoulders. I stood and steadied myself and then, carefully, made my way to the back door. Amazingly, the dog was very cooperative. I felt a huge sense of achievement. It hadn't been easy but, against the odds, I'd done it. Lucy would see for herself that I was the sort of person that, when I set my mind to something, I did it.

The children, seeing what had happening, trooped in laughing and giggling behind me, just as Lucy was finishing her call.

"Here he is. Where do you want him?" I beamed. The dog struggled a bit on my shoulders but I held firm. "Okay Bailey," I said, authoritatively. "Hold on boy and I'll have you down in a sec." The dog started to struggle again and I could feel my whole body trembling. It took all the energy I had to keep him there. My neck began to wilt, my back started to hunch and my knees were giving way under the strain. My face was burning and I could feel sweat rolling down my cheeks. On top of all this

Who Cares?

I could feel a small but persistent tug on the side of the muddy overalls. Tug, tug, tug... couldn't the child see I was busy?

The tugging persisted and, eventually, I managed to turn and look down into the sweet, beautiful, angelic face with big, blue, innocent eyes, the remainder of freckles not covered by mud, stark upon his pale skin.

"I'm Bailey," he said.

Nine

The noise of everyone laughing, everyone except me of course, obscured the fact that Roger, Lucy's husband, had arrived home. He also, didn't see the funny side of it all, especially after seeing his mud-caked boots and equally dirty overalls in a heap on the floor. After shooing the dogs back out into the garden, he waltzed the children off to the bathroom for a bath.

Lucy regained her composure and was suddenly galvanised into action, leading me out towards the hall and grabbing her coat, hat, umbrella and one boot.

"I'm sure Penny told you the basics of the job but I thought I'd run it by you again, step by step, as it were." She laughed at her own joke as we headed towards the door. Outside the house, offset to one side, was a small unmarked, black van with darkened windows. She made her way over to it, unlocking the doors as she walked, by pressing the central locking device on her key ring.

"You okay to drive?" she asked, hobbling towards the passenger side. "I would but I'm plastered," she laughed… probably not for the first time!

I squeezed into the driver's seat and tried to manoeuvre the seat backwards which resulted in dropping the seat so low that I could hardly see over the steering wheel. Another press of a lever and I was thrown backwards, my head hitting the metal partition that separated the front from the back.

"I can't thank you enough for this; it means so much to me," said Lucy, struggling to put on her safety belt. "I've tried so hard to get this going and ploughed so much of my own money into it. Roger's always been against it, said it was doomed from the start. I think he was almost pleased when I fell and broke my leg, hoping, I suppose, that I'd give up at last. Finding someone to help me, someone I could trust not to take it all from me, was a nightmare. I thought he'd finally won. Then Penny told me about you. She said you were warm-hearted, honest and getting over a broken heart and I just knew that you would be the one, and of course, now I've seen what you were like at home, I just know you will be perfect."

I could see tears in her eyes and knew that this business, whatever it was, meant a lot to her. I felt quite humbled by her thanks, and pleased frankly, that I was of help to anyone. She gave me an address to head for, giving me directions as we went. Suddenly all the doors locked and the radio started playing, it was something like a scene out of the Bone Collectors and I have to say my heart must have skipped a beat or two. I made a mental note to make an appointment at the doctor's and have the old heart checked out again.

"It's okay, it's just the van, she's a bit quirky," she said, wrinkling her nose and smiling apologetically. "Just turn the window wipers on and the radio will stop playing and the doors will unlock next time we go over a bump. It's easy when you get used to it," she said, taking out her diary and grabbing a pencil from her handbag.

Fifteen minutes later, we pulled up at the address she'd given me. I was a little surprised to see a pretty, end of terrace house with a little picket fence outside. Don't get me wrong, it was a lovely house but I'd assumed we were driving to her office or perhaps a small shop, even a lock-up. She produced a little box that had previously been sitting on top of the dash board. Inside was a selection of keys, all with brightly coloured key rings, with names written on them.

"It's all very easy," she said, pointing to the house that we were sitting outside. "This one is the key with the pink key ring, this pink key ring, is *precious*!"

"Right," I said. "The pink key ring is precious. Got it!" I couldn't help but wonder how 'precious' we were talking about, hundreds, thousands, millions? Amazingly, it just looked like plastic to me. She pulled up the crutch, opened the door and started to make her way out of the van.

"I'll come with you on this one, show you the ropes and then you can give the next one a try on your own." I got out and followed slowly, very slowly, after Lucy. Each step was such an effort, I was tempted to stick an arm under her other shoulder to speed her on.

When we reached the door, she unlocked it with the key with the 'precious' key ring, and let us both in. It was a gorgeous house, all dark-wood floors and designer furniture. There were rooms to both the left and right of the passage way, with an expansive stairway running through the middle and up to two further floors. I started to feel a tingle of excitement.

Why had I not seen this coming? Lucy was so wonderfully artistic. Obviously, she must be some sort of interior designer or something.

She looked in the first room, appraising it, probably checking to see where to place murals, Art Deco statues, modern pots and vases. I looked too. I definitely had an eye for this sort of thing, I put my finger to my mouth and nodded appreciatively at what they had already achieved, my brain racing with things they could do to improve the overall look. I was just about to say that a splash of bright colour placed strategically around the room would be my suggestion, when Lucy left the room and went on to the next one.

As she opened the door to the huge kitchen there was a familiar patter of clattering on the wooden floor and I stepped back out of the way, cowardly leaving Lucy to handle it. One animal was quite enough for one day.

"There you are, Precious," she said, getting down on her knees and grabbing hold of the little, rat-like creature by its neck and kissing its face, to which it reciprocated by licking her all over, wagging its tail profusely. "This is Precious, she's a Yorkshire terrier, isn't she gorgeous? Her lead is kept over there, the bags are in this cupboard and she has a ball that she likes to play with, which I just stick in my pocket for when the walk's over."

It was at this point that the penny didn't just drop, it felt like it had been catapulted off the top of a high-rise building and was about to bring impending death, which in truth, might've been preferable to taking this ugly, rabid, mangy, flea-bitten excuse for a dog, out for a walk. I felt like I was, literally, stuck rigid to the spot with terror.

"Are you okay, Remi? Here, you take her and I'll show you how I put her in the vehicle, then we'll be off to get the next one," she said, cheerily hopping off in the direction of the door, leaving me with the flea-ridden thing looking at me expectantly.

I held onto the lead and walked, stiltedly, towards the door, Precious constantly trying to get there before me. Lucy was waiting for me outside to show me how to lock up.

"Don't forget to make sure you have the key with you because the door locks automatically."

When she opened the back of the van, I saw, for the first time, that it was filled with wire cages, two at the top and two at the bottom. She opened one of the top ones and stood back. "There, just pick her up and pop her in," she said, expectantly. I bent down and tried to figure how one picks up a dog, it wasn't something one did every day and, goodness knows, something I didn't relish now.

I tried to pick it up by the head, thereby avoiding the area that does the dirty work, so to speak, but that didn't work, the dog just whimpered. I was going to grab hold of the tail but Lucy's sudden gasp made me rethink. Eventually, I just took the whole thing in my arms and heaved, throwing her quicker and, perhaps, a little more forcefully than I meant to, in to the back of the cage.

"Right," said Lucy, getting back into the van. "On to the next one!"

The next one turned out to be a Red Setter called Lord; apparently his registered name was Little Lord Fauntleroy, shortened to, the ever endearing, Lord! Lucy asked me to try this one on my own and, I have to say, had I been a burglar, not only could I have made off with the family heirlooms, I could have shown prospective buyers all over the house and sold the property from under them. Lord was definitely *not* the guarding type!

Lucy had described where I'd find the lead, the treats and the bags and having navigated my way round all the toys, balls and shoes on the floor, I made it back, in one piece, to the vehicle.

Who Cares?

As she opened the back of the van I was relieved to see one of the bottom cages open and once the command was given, Lord obligingly jumped in and settled down.

The third dog was a German Shepherd that growled at me as soon as I entered the house. Lucy had already armed me with a biscuit bone which I produced from my pocket. It proved to be a brilliant deterrent to being savaged. Once I'd attached the lead, he waltzed me up the garden path and flew into the back of the open van without a hitch.

"Don't worry about old Sergeant, he knows all the tricks, just make sure you always have a supply of biscuits on you and he'll be as good as gold."

I had hoped that Sergeant was the last of the dogs to be picked up, but Lucy directed me on to the other side of town. As we approached I realised where we were. Gran's house was just a block away from this address. I was almost home again and couldn't help but wonder if this was what Penny meant, when she'd said it was right up my street! I didn't know whether to laugh or cry.

Humphrey was the orange key ring and I let myself in, as per Lucy's instructions. Sitting in the back of the kitchen was an overweight Golden Labrador which didn't even bother to look up when I entered.

"Hello Humphrey, do you fancy coming for a little walk?" Nothing! No lift of the head, no grunt, not even a flicker of an ear. I picked up the lead which was sitting on the kitchen table and walked over and took hold of his collar. The poor dog literally jumped out of his skin making me jump back in fear. I realised, straight away, that the old boy was obviously as deaf as a post and hadn't heard me come in.

"I'm sorry Humphrey; I didn't mean to frighten you. I've come to take you for a lovely walk." I said, sounding much more enthusiastic than I really was.

Humphrey took one look at me, another at the lead and then theatrically, plonked himself back down onto his bed. I attached the lead and gave it a quick pull to spark Humphrey into action, but nothing. I gave a harder pull, still nothing and then I pulled with all my might but there was just no budging him.

Who Cares?

"If I have to do this, then so do you, you great 'buddy' lump," I said, now levering all my weight behind the lead. The collar was now pulling up around the top of his neck, his fur was all pushed upwards and his face now looked distorted as it all squashed together. Suddenly he relented and stood up which was exactly what I wanted and yet, somehow, I hadn't figured it into the equation. So as he stood up, I flew back, landing, bottom first, into his water bowl.

"Look what you've done, you stupid dog." Could this day get any worse? As always, when I dared to test fate… it got worse. My bottom was well and truly lodged in the water bowl and as I struggled to stand up, I felt water seeping through my clothing and making its way gradually down my legs.

Five minutes passed and, eventually, Lucy came looking for me. The bowl was still attached and the dog was back on his bed and, to add insult to injury, he was snoring. It took both of us to get him up again and both of us to get him into the back of the van but, eventually, we were all in.

"Well," said Lucy, merrily. "That's the easy bit done."

Ten

At the park all four dogs were unloaded from the van, each had on the correct lead and all were sitting patiently for the walk to begin.

"Right," said Lucy. "Humphrey can walk by your side, he doesn't need to be kept on a lead; he won't go anywhere. Precious won't go far as long as you keep her ball in sight, so that just leaves Lord and Sergeant. They need to be kept on leads at all times.

The dogs need about an hour's walk, which normally means two or three times round the park. There's a little café on the corner, so I'll just sit in there and wait for you, give me a shout if you have any problems." With that she handed me, what looked like, over-sized gloves, Precious' ball and some doggie treats.

"What do I need gloves for?" I said, taking everything off her.

"Oh Remi, you're such a scream, they're poop bags. When they stop and do their business, just pop on a glove, pick it up then turn the glove inside out and throw it in one of the doggie bins. Easy as that!"

I watched Lucy hobble off to the little café and finally plucked up the courage to take a few steps. Okay, that wasn't too bad, I thought, just another fifty-nine minutes to go and my ordeal will be over. I made my way along the muddy path that circumnavigated the park, trying to avoid pot holes and puddles, although the reverse plan seemed to be the intention of most of the dogs, with the exception of Precious, who tippy-toed through as though she were avoiding land mines.

As the black clouds loomed ominously above me, I started to pay less attention to the dogs and more to the people that I passed. Folks that partake of the park are a strange nation. There are some who jog or run the walkway, either ignoring you totally, or scowling at you because you're taking up too much room. Those who have children either drag their offspring hurriedly off to one side or, worse still, slow down encouraging their children to pat the dogs; thereby, allowing their sticky, little fingers to entangle themselves into the dog's coats, transferring all facial dirt and runny noses onto them.

Then there are the clusters of teenagers who, apparently, speak a completely different language from the rest of us. They crowd around one park bench, have mobile phones surgically attached to their heads and look at anyone over the age of twenty as pensioners. They communicate with odd hand-signals, which looks remarkably like, rock, paper, scissors, the game we played as kids and they call each other Homie, whatever that means!

Next, come the park wardens who, when not picking up litter with their long, pronged grabbers are doing wheelies round the sodden park lawns in their four by four, lawn mowers – leaving more mud than grass in their wake. They wear earmuffs and dark glasses and, similar to old paintings, their eyes seem to follow wherever you go.

Then we get the pot smokers (of course not one of us knows what they're doing)! This group likes to think of themselves as the non-conformist members of society, the ones that don't follow the trends, smoking their Class 'C' drugs, rebelling against the establishment. They probably couldn't conceive, that even in this day and age, the majority of the population have either smoked it or still smoke it, pensioners included! That wouldn't do much for the old image.

They all wear similar clothing, all have on backpacks and woollen hats and a certain type of music blaring, which only seems familiar because you'll hear it three or four times more as you pass similar little huddles around the park.

But, of all the groups that make up the patina of the park, the strangest must be the dog walkers themselves. There are those that just keep to themselves, hurrying through the park, not allowing their dogs to stop or sniff; a five minute brisk walk and nothing more. Then the ones that see everybody else's dog as a threat and either walk fifty feet to the left or see you coming and walk in a different direction. The 'macho' men have the biggest, most aggressive dogs, all wearing big studded collars with golden name tags... and that's just the owners!

Hidden amongst these are the genuine dog lovers. Some just nod in the conspiratorial way that a Mason might meet another Mason. Some make polite conversation whilst passing by but never really stopping to chat. And others stop and chat, enthusiastically, about the dogs, the park, the other groups and the best places to walk.

On my first, and possibly my last, day as a dog walker, I encountered all these groups. The teenagers laughed conspiratorially as I passed, speaking something in Swahili. The pot smokers huddled closer together and the 'macho' men stuck out their chests and flashed their teeth. The warden's four by four spewed mud all over my cream suit, grubby little hands touched both the dogs and my clothes, and timid dog walkers scattered in different directions before I approached, so avoiding the crazy, mud-splattered, sticky lady, with four dogs in tow. Oh how I wish one of the pot smokers had offered me a quick spliff!

Inevitably, the time came when one of the dogs started circling on a scrubby bit of grass. Lord sniffed and circled in one place, then moved on and sniffed and circled again. Eventually, having settled on his perfect spot he crouched and started. I had both him and Sergeant on leads, so I transferred them both to the same hand in order to retrieve a poop bag from my pocket. Precious and Humphrey realising that business was about to take place hurtled back for a front row view, noses down and tails a wagging. After a few minutes Lord relieved himself from the crouching position and started to merrily attack Humphrey, treading grass as he went.

I am, of course, a responsible dog walking person and am aware that people will probably be watching to see if the professionals do in fact, pick up their muck, which of course I do. Or will do, as soon as I stop heaving.

I lean down and place my shaking hand over the offending mess. As I remove my hand from the glove, I realise that I will need the other hand to turn the bag over properly and do it up.

Who Cares?

I carefully position the two leads under the heel of one of my shoes, thinking how inventive one can be when one needs to be. Now I can lean down, with both hands free to pick up the bag.

As I started to straighten up, the ball in my pocket became visible to Precious, who jumped at me with all her might. She retrieved the ball and ran with it... and so did the others. Suddenly, I was thrown backwards and I felt the heel of my shoe snap from underneath me. Unfortunately it wasn't the heel that was securing the leads; that heel stays doggedly, excuse the pun, in place. In fact, that heel, now in an upright position, has secured the leads even firmer and as the ball rolled out of Precious' mouth and started rolling down the hill, all the dogs leapt off in hot pursuit with me, literally, in tow.

As the momentum started to build, all I could see were trees racing past me, small glimpses of distressed faces, and hands reaching in my direction. Twigs and leaves slapped my face as I passed and I felt my skirt being hitched up, higher and higher, around my waist, the wet mud making it easy for the dogs to pull me along. Finally, at last, I felt them slow down a little and with complete clarity I realised that we were about to pass the small café on the corner, and there, warming her hands on a big mug of something steaming, was Lucy. As she turned to look out of the window, I instinctively raised my hand, which amazingly was still holding the poop bag. The cup dropped away from her mouth and liquid spilt into her lap. Hurriedly she brushed it away, whilst trying to grab hold of the crutch she'd laid against the table.

As she pushed her way through the crowd that had amalgamated by the entrance, she called out to me in a complete panic.

"It's okay," I said, as I passed by. "I'm alright." As the dogs slowed, I managed to lean forward and grab hold of both leads, putting them firmly into one hand. Gingerly, I lifted myself up onto my knees, the thick, squelchy mud desperately trying to claw me back down again. There wasn't a part of me that wasn't covered in the thick, glutinous sludge. I could feel it in my feet, on my legs, in my mouth and sliding through my fingers.

I shook my hand and rubbed the remaining mud down my,

already ruined, suit. Too late, as I realised the mud on my hands, wasn't mud at all but the spilled contents of the poop bag.

I felt the first spits of rain as Lucy approached, crutch under one arm, umbrella in the other. By the time she reached me, it was pouring akin to a monsoon. She just stared at me for a moment, taking in the wet, tear-stained face with large chucks of hair plastered to my head. The beret, no longer cream nor positioned in a jaunty manor. The broken shoe, the dirty, dishevelled Mac, the ripped and filthy suit and the hands covered in dog mess. I wanted to say something but I just couldn't find the words. Lucy popped two of the poop bags onto her hands and took hold of the filthy leads.

"Come on," she said. "There's twenty minutes left, enough time to clean off all the leads, make the dogs presentable and take them all home to their rightful owners. You, on the other hand, may take a little longer to clean up," she said, laughing and turning me back towards the van.

Lucy's husband dropped me off at home but not before spreading newspaper all over his seats and in the foot-well. As she opened the door, Gran burst out laughing.

"I'm guessing it wasn't a window-dressing job then!" she laughed, reaching out to take the beret from my head. She listened to my full account of what happened and then promised to make me a nice hot cup of tea after I'd cleaned myself off. As I took my shoes, correction shoe, off and threw it in the bin, I heard her running the bath and, in true Gran fashion, she was singing away, her own adapted version of a song from the musical *Sweet Charity*.

"What a mess up. Holy cow! They'd never believe it. If my friends could see you now!"

Eleven

I promised Lucy that I would give it to the end of the week before deciding whether I would be able to carry on or not. So the next morning, after a hearty breakfast, I made a plan of attack. Four dogs at the same time: far too hard and doomed to failure. I figured that the best plan was to pick up the nearest two dogs and walk them somewhere close by. Then after taking them home, collect the other two, who were both on the other side of town, next to the park and walk them. I worked it out that, without having to travel across town twice and by choosing a nearer park, it would only take fifteen minutes more to do it my way.

That sorted, it was time to work out what to wear. Out of the black bag I pulled a pair of dark-coloured, jogging trousers, a black, polo-neck jumper, an old pair of trainers and a *Nike* jacket, which used to be a little too large but was now a perfect fit. I pulled my hair back into a tight ponytail and dug out an old pair of gloves from Gran's coat cupboard.

The day was clear and bright and as I pulled into Lucy's street, I could see the door to the house was already open and Lucy was waiting with an anxious look on her face. Her face lit up as I pulled over and got out of my car and she ran, as fast as a person on crutches can, to meet me.

"I wasn't sure if you'd come. I know yesterday didn't go very well," she said, sheepishly. "But look on the bright side, it can't get any…"

"Don't say it Lucy, please, please, don't say it. Whenever I say it can't get worse, invariably it does. Fate has a strange way of interfering in my life, on a regular basis, and it never seems to bring good luck with it."

"Rubbish Remi. Life's what you make it; fate's just nature's way of turning your life in a different direction." I wasn't going to disagree with her; she obviously had a blessed and beautiful life and could never understand what it was like to be plagued with bad luck. Still, she was right about one thing, things were definitely on the up, as I looked around I was relieved to see that the big, hairy, slavering dog, she affectionately called Blue, was nowhere to be seen.

I jumped into the van before he had a chance to venture out and promised Lucy that today would be far more organised, she was not to worry and that I would be back home at the appointed hour. I waved a confident goodbye and offered up a small prayer that what I'd told her was true.

Naturally the CD player came on – unasked, half-way along the first road and, of course, the doors locked and unlocked on a regular basis but other than that the journey was blissfully uneventful.

I pulled up outside Precious' house, picked up her key and went in. It was apparent from the moment I entered the house that it was not empty. There was a heady aroma of expensive perfume combined with foreign cigarettes. Sitting at the dining room table were two women, both thin as rakes, both had long hair tied up in extraordinary, decorative devices and both sat crossed-legged sipping at a glass of something cold and white.

They both looked up as I entered and gave only a passing interest to the T-shirt that Lucy had made me put on over my clothes. On the front it sported the very natty slogan; *Your Dog's Business is our Business,* and in big letters on the back, *Pet Walkers* along with Lucy's telephone number.

One of the women, the nearest one to me, lifted her hand. The cigarette between her fingers dispatching ash onto the kitchen floor, as she jerked it in the direction of the corner of the room where Precious was asleep.

"Please don't frighten her; she's still asleep. Poor thing's been very sickly all night."

"Well would you rather I left her today?" I said, thinking how much better the new plan would work with one dog down.

"No, no," she shouted back quickly. "I've got appointments all morning, I couldn't possibly take her out myself, darling," she said, her clipped, pronounced, upper-class accent already grating on my nerves.

"I've an Indian head-massage booked. That's in thirty minutes time, then a manicure, a pedicure, a complete body scrub and then a *St. Tropez* all-over tan. Oh my God, darling, where could I possibly fit in walking little Precious? No," she said, puffing on her cigarette and throwing her head back to exhale. "That's why I employ people like you," she said, giving me a quick up and down. "As you so rightly say, darling – doggy business is your business!"

She laughed at her own joke, downed her glass and stared at me with a withering, condescending smirk that made me feel about two inches high, while the other woman got up and headed for the refrigerator.

"More champers, Marianne?" She held up a half-empty bottle of *Dom Perignon* and tottered over to the table to refresh their glasses. Marianne, who I now took to be the owner of the equally delightful Precious, took the bottle and poured a small amount into the dog bowl then turned back to me, bottle still in hand.

"Oh, sorry darling, would you…?"

"Oh no, thank you," I said, anticipating her question and smiling broadly. "Unfortunately I'm driving."

"No, darling," she said, her eyes glittering with untold amusement. "What I was going to say was, would you mind cleaning the mess up that's just outside the back door before you set off? Poor Precious has had such an upset tummy and I'm afraid I've just been too busy to clear it up."

I felt the flush come up all the way from my toes as I made my way over to the back door and took a quick look out. There was a veritable minefield of dog poo outside, Precious hadn't ventured very far, but she sure had been busy. As I prepared myself for the task ahead I wondered if this was part of the job description. As I toyed with the idea of ringing and checking with Lucy, I heard the high-pitched tone of Marianne calling me back from the kitchen.

"Darling. Sorry, darling, I'm afraid I don't know your name… I've only ever dealt with that Linda woman who runs it."

"It's Remi," I said, through gritted teeth.

"Remi," she mused. "How unusual... Anyway, darling, I suddenly thought this is a bit over and above your normal duties, so please take this for your trouble."

I perked up a bit, smiled and thanked her, anticipating the crisp twenty pound note about to come my way. Then I realised she was pointing to a tall dustpan with a brush attached.

"It's a pooper scooper, darling, it'll save you lots of time" As she turned away I could hear the two of them giggling under their breath, she really was a nasty piece of work.

The smell outside was unbearable, I wondered what Precious had eaten but if the champagne was anything to go by, who knows? I heaved and gagged my way through the whole ordeal but, finally, managed to clear it all up. When my back was turned, a door opened and a pail of hot water, a bottle of disinfectant and a stiff, yard broom were placed unceremoniously on the step. I stepped over them on my way in, kicking the yard broom to the floor and waited for her to say something.

I liked Lucy and really wanted to help her out but one word from this anorexic, snooty bitch and her sidekick friend and I was out of there. Perhaps sensing my anger, she said nothing.

I picked up the bags and the ball, and then attached the lead to Precious' collar. Reluctantly, Precious stood up in her bed. She looked tired and bedraggled; her tail managed one small wag before shooting back down between her legs. Slowly she started to move but let out a small whimper as we reached the door.

Just as we were about to go out, Marianne called me back. "Darling, did you say your name was Remi?" I just nodded; I couldn't bring myself to converse with this woman, I wouldn't be able to trust myself. "It's just, that we," she pointed to the other, equally detestable, woman and back again, "used to know a Remi when we were at school."

My stomach lurched as I waited for her to continue. "Terrible business, darling, she had to leave quite suddenly." Marianne's face started to quiver slightly with suppressed laughter. "Due to a family crisis." Her eyes sparkled and her lips grew thin, she was so obviously enjoying this. The other woman hid behind her, her shoulders shaking. "Her dad was some sort of paedophile or pervert, as I recall. That couldn't be you, could it, darling? Surely things haven't got this bad that you have to clean poo for a living?"

She should've been an actress; she was certainly doing a good job. She had reined in her amusement and was now doing a remarkable impression of someone who was caring and concerned. Part of me wanted to run straight out the door, the other part wanted to run over and pull that stupid contraption out of her hair and punch her in her high and mighty face. In reality though, I just stood rooted to the spot, totally unable to move, unable to think of anything to say, just staring.

It was then that I was reminded of what Lucy had said; fate was just a way of taking you in a different direction. I smiled – here, but for the grace of God and the hand of fate, could have been me. I could have been this stuck-up bitch, looking for nothing else to do but to humiliate someone else in-between tanning sessions. Perhaps that terrible day and all the fallout that came with it, wasn't bad luck after all.

Suddenly I rushed up to Marianne, catching her off guard, and grabbed hold of her hand with both of mine.

"It was me," I enthused. "It was me and I never realised just how lucky I'd been, until now. Thank you," I said, shaking her hands again. "Thank you."

With that I turned and made my way back to the door, stopping only briefly to look back over my shoulder to see the other woman's quizzical face and Marianne appearing near-faint, as she looked down at her hands.

"Damn! I should have taken those dirty gloves off first," I said aloud, to myself. Then off we went. I practically danced back to the van. I had experienced an epiphany. My life, fate, bad luck, all the things I thought had been working against me; I could see them now for what they really were. I realised that Lucy was right; life was what you made it. From now on things could only get better. I opened the back of the van door and there staring out at me was Blue, the hairy monster. Oh well, I

Who Cares?

thought, one step at a time.

Despite the rocky start, the day went really well. All the dogs had a good run and each of them was returned safely. Thankfully, when I returned Precious home, Marianne and her friend were gone. However there was slight hiccup before I left. Precious, thirsty from her walk, slurped at the champagne in her bowl and was immediately sick on the kitchen floor. I had no intention of clearing it up and decided that Marianne would have more than enough time on her beautifully manicured hands, to take care of it when she returned.

However, one thing she didn't have on her hands was the big, sparkling, sapphire ring that she must have taken off in anticipation of the *St. Tropez* tan. It was laying on the edge of the kitchen table and as I passed by, my coat must have, somehow, caught hold of it and catapulted it across the room, where it bounced back off the wall and landed slap-bang in the middle of the kitchen. Poor Marianne... It's a well known fact that fate sometimes throws a spanner in the works but who would guess that, on this occasion, it would throw a ring in the spew?

Twelve

The week flew by with, thankfully, very few mishaps and by Friday, I was feeling quite proficient, even looking forward to the challenge and exercise the day had to offer. I felt invigorated and full of purpose as I pulled up outside Lucy's door and I wasn't even distressed when I saw Blue jumping up into the back of the van.

The journey went off without incident and I soon found myself outside the first house to pick up Precious. I sat for a few moments before getting out, firstly to collect myself, just in case the wicked witch was at home and, secondly, to take in the sheer beauty of the place. It sat at the end of the *cul-de-sac* with only trees as a backdrop. Probably built in the thirties, it was attached to an identical one by a large roof, the apex of which was high in the middle of the two properties. The walls were whitewashed and the wooden windows were pale-blue – a common sight on older houses in this area.

Around the door was a plant I knew well as it had bloomed each year around my own home, when I was younger. Not yet in flower, the Wisteria sat, regally, awaiting the spring so it could release its blooms. Entwined around the door and over the windows, I could almost visualise the explosion of lilac-coloured flowers that would drape, like bunches of grapes, all over the brickwork.

The original door was probably ledge and brace but had been replaced with a more modern, sturdier door for reasons of security. The small garden at the front looked slightly dishevelled and in need of some attention, but I could see flowers I recognised: wild ones that would bloom with gay abandon, spreading their seeds in a bid to cause even more mayhem for the following year. I thought of Gran and how she would love to don her gardening gloves and make her way through this jungle of fauna and flora. This was the sort of garden she described as a butterfly's paradise.

I got out and made my way to the door but before I could even unlock it and let myself in, I could hear heavy footfalls from upstairs and a man's angry voice. I couldn't hear exactly what he was shouting but he was swearing and throwing things about. Suddenly there was a high-pitched yelp and Precious came running down the stairs, followed closely by a boot of some description and the slamming of a door.

I crept along the hallway, barely able to breathe and made my way into the kitchen, which was where I'd last seen Precious disappear. Despite the experience, she seemed none the worse for wear, so I slipped the lead on, grabbed her things and we crept back through the hall. I was willing her to keep quiet; the confrontation with Marianne earlier in the week was quite enough. I didn't need a repeat situation with the grumpy guy upstairs…

We stopped off to get Lord and then made our way on foot to the nearby park. It wasn't as big as the other park that I went to with Sergeant and Humphrey but it was secluded and pleasant and the people who frequented it were friendly. Lord was the only dog that needed to be kept on a lead, so I let Precious and Blue off so they could play together. I walked, as I had become accustomed, at a brisk rate and the dogs kept pace with me. All week it had been fresh and fairly sunny but today was overcast and, I suspected, that was why it was so quiet. After two fast laps around the park we slowed to a walking pace, which gave the dogs a chance to catch up on all the dogs who had visited the park before us.

It amazed me how many times they stopped to mark their territory and where on earth all that water came from. No wonder they were always thirsty when I took them home. Lord dilly-dallied over everything, sniffing each and every bench, pushing his nose into every bin and pushing his head in-between the bushes and shrubberies, coming up with an array of papers, packets and condoms.

As I searched the park for people I might recognise, I noticed someone loitering, about a hundred-foot ahead of us. It was probably quite innocent but, as there were so few people around, I decided to be cautious, change track and go back in the opposite direction. We all bounced off back the way we came and when I looked back again the man was gone.

Juliet always said I was a bit of a 'wuss' and I must admit that, perhaps, I may have slightly over-reacted. Let's face it; I did have three dogs in tow – who would want to take us all on? We did another turn round the park and when I looked at my watch I could see that our time was nearly up. I wasn't sorry, it was turning quite chilly. I decided to take a shortcut across the park.

Precious had joined Lord and me, and was walking contentedly by my side, but Blue was nowhere to be seen. I doubled-back, calling as I went. The dogs, realising something was amiss, perked up, tails wagging and heads in the air. I wasn't a big fan of Blue but I couldn't go home without him… Could I?

As I stepped out of the clearing and back onto the path I was glad to see that the park was getting busier. Half of me was calling out for Blue and scouring the undergrowth, whilst the other, slightly less, functioning side of my brain was taking in where we were and what was happening around us. Lord and Precious, oblivious to the missing Blue, carried on as if nothing had happened.

"Blue, come on boy," I shouted, standing for a moment, whistling and then scouring the park to one side of me. The other half of my brain noticed a guy walking in front, swinging a lead; probably he had a far more obedient dog than Blue with him.

"Here, Blue… Come on Blue," I shouted again, slightly more panicky. The man in front paid no attention to me whatsoever, and just kept on walking.

"Here Bluey, Bluey, Bluey," I tried again, wondering at what point I should ring Lucy. It was strange though that the man in front didn't even turn round. Well you do – don't you? If you hear someone shout, it's human nature to look and see what's going on, or if someone's searching on the floor or looking up in the sky, we all stop and take a look. Let's face it; we're a very nosy species. But not the man in front, apparently...

"BLUE!"... I shouted even louder, determined now that both Blue and the man in front should hear me. Still neither any sign of Blue, nor a reaction from the deaf guy in front. It was possible, I pondered, that he was in heavy talks on his mobile phone, closing a multi-million pound deal but then, surely, he would turn and glare at me for making all the noise.

The coat he was wearing was certainly not a cheap one. If I wasn't mistaken and of course I rarely was, it looked like a *Burberry*, classic, beige raincoat, easier to tell from the inside with the distinctive plaid design lining.

"Here, Blue." I shouted, adding a whistle as an afterthought. The guy in front slowed slightly and bent down to tie his laces. His shoes were classic brogues and more than a bit scuffed, not the sort of shoes a top executive would wear, especially without socks on!

"Blue!"... I turned back quickly. No socks on – that was bad enough, but no trousers – that couldn't be good. Before I could think anything else, he had turned round. The lead he had in his hand turned out to be his belt. He had a hand on either side of his coat and was holding it wide open. Under the coat, he had, not a stitch on. And all I could think, at that crucial moment in time, was... I was right – it *was Burberry*!

The man stood still in front of me. His expression was manic, his eyes bright and frenzied, his mouth sneering and yet, strangely, my eyes were magnetically drawn, not to his rather sorry, flaccid member that he was so keen to show me but to the all-over tan he was sporting. At this time of year, it had to be fake, didn't it?

I gave a gasp and put my hand to my mouth. He seemed overjoyed that, at last, I had grasped the object of this exercise but he couldn't have been further from the truth. Despite the obvious seriousness of the situation, I couldn't suppress a snigger... the flaccid penis, the all-over tan and now, the final straw, the chest hair which was starting to fall off... the flasher was wearing fake chest hair!

Needless to say, my laughing got his gander up, which was

still more than he could say for his private parts. He started towards me and I realised, all too late, the potential danger I was in. His long, greying hair flew back behind him, his eyes blazed and his teeth bared... No! Wrong side of the brain, again. His teeth didn't bare, that was to the side of him... For there, standing just a few feet away, was Blue! His ears pricked and alert, his head slightly down. His eyes bright and fixed firmly on the flasher. His lips were drawn back and his fangs were showing, as he bared his teeth. He growled louder and I could see the hackles on his neck standing up. He took one step forward, his tail drawn closely between his legs. The flasher took one step back.

"Call him off," he shouted at me, but Blue took another step. "Call him off," he shouted again, frantically looking from the dog to me and back again.

Precious, who up until then had been quiet, suddenly stepped from my side and, tucking herself behind my legs, began to snarl as well. Lord, I noticed, had fallen asleep. But Blue didn't falter, he took no notice of Precious, he was oblivious to Lord, he kept his gaze steady and focused on the flasher. As he took another step closer, the flasher pulled his coat tight around himself and tried to tie it all up with the belt. The flasher took another step in the opposite direction, but his eyes never left Blue. He took another step, then another and then suddenly ran, with all his might, into the wooded area to one side.

Blue leapt into the air, covering the space between them in a second. His teeth flashed as he jumped high and came down with a resounding bite on the flasher's backside. Precious pulled on the lead to get free, but I held her back, remembering what happened last time she saw a ball coming out of a coat pocket!

I stood for a few moments, unable to move, listening for any indication of what might be happening. Should I try and help the flasher? Should I ring the police? Then, strutting through the trees, I saw the triumphant Blue, returning with his spoils. In his mouth he carried the flasher's coat, which he laid down in front of me and in the distance, running through the undergrowth, I saw the flasher, naked with only his hands covering his embarrassment, being chased by one of the wardens on his

Who Cares?

souped-up lawn mower.

I looked down at Blue, who was sitting quietly and patiently by my side, and I felt something akin to admiration and fondness for Blue. I leaned down and hugged him close and he nestled into my neck and licked my hand.

"Thank you Blue, you were a real star," I said, not really knowing what one says to a dog that's, possibly, just saved your life! He looked at me and turned his head from side to side, as if weighing me up, and then gave a small bark.

"Friends?" I asked, holding out my hand. He gave me his paw and I shook it. I felt a small constriction in the back of the throat and sniffed away tears that were bubbling to the surface. Could it be because I'd been confronted by a crazed, albeit rather obtuse, vain flasher or that I'd faced danger squarely in the face? Yet, I felt sure that the strange sensation I was feeling was the old, patchwork heart expanding to let someone else in...

Who'd have thought that that someone would be a dog?

Thirteen

Apparently, the park warden caught up with the flasher who was surreptitiously whisked away to the local police station. I, on the other hand, was so pumped full of adrenaline, I could have run the London Marathon, but settled for another two laps round the park before dropping Precious and Lord off home and making my way over to the other side of town. Blue was a little surprised when, instead of throwing him in the back with the other dogs, I decided such a hero, should sit up front with me.

By the time we picked up Sergeant and Humphrey it was much later than usual. The teenagers were obviously back in school or college; the pot smokers were probably packing out McDonald's. There was no sign of the 'macho' men but in their place were a group of about ten women jogging merrily around the park. They were all happily chatting, all in tracksuits with hair and boobs bouncing. They took up most of the parkway then separated as the dogs and I approached, shouting out a pleasant 'hello'.

I suppose that the adrenaline was still running merrily around my system as I felt a huge camaraderie for these ladies and an, almost, primal urge to join them. It was fairly obvious that Sergeant was also of a like-mind as he pulled vigorously on his lead to give chase. Humphrey, on the other hand, took full advantage of all the commotion to grab a few minutes sit-down. With much effort, I managed to get Humphrey going again and we started back off round the park.

Inspired by the ladies I decided to try jogging round, good for me, good for the dogs and perhaps I'd even shed a few pounds! Unfortunately Humphrey only did two speeds and that was slow or not at all.

The second time the ladies passed us by they all shouted out their 'hellos' as they tripped happily along and by the third time, they all stopped to take a few minutes break and pat the dogs. I supposed their ages ranged from early forties to late sixties. Collectively they were known as 'The Empty Nesters'.

Barbara, one of the smaller, more effervescent characters of the group, explained that they met every afternoon during the week. When they'd first met and formed the club, the only participants were older ladies whose families had all flown the coop, hence the 'Empty Nesters'!

"Now," she went on to explain, "we're delighted to welcome anyone."

Mostly they ran in the park, sometimes they played tennis or croquet and on Friday afternoons, during the summer, they had self-defence lessons in the hall which was situated at the back of the park.

"Join us," said Barbara, pulling up her socks and adjusting her baggy tracksuit bottoms. "We're a friendly lot, everyone's welcome." I explained that Humphrey was the sticking point – literally – but she suggested that I still give it a try.

"Nothing too quick, we don't want the old boy to keel over." Barbara laughed.

"That goes for the rest of us as well Barb," said one of the older women, who introduced herself as Hilda. "We've already lost one on the way round today and I'd like to stay around to see my next birthday, if that's alright with you." They all laughed and asked if the Queen would be writing to her on the next birthday, to which she replied by sending a well-aimed water bottle hurtling across, hitting one of the others on the backside.

"Come on girls, onwards and upwards," shouted Barbara. "No pain, no gain"

"That's the problem Barb, I get the pain but I still get the gain. I put on two pounds last week!"

"That's not the pain Gwen, that's the cream teas we all sat down to last Friday after the session. If I'm right, didn't you have two giant, fresh cream, Belgium buns?" Gwen looked a little sheepish and one of the others added,

"Big buns make for big bums, Gwen!" They laughed again,

jogged on the spot for a few moments and then started off up the path, calling for me to tag on the end.

I gave Humphrey a tug and pulled him off in their direction. He started with a stumble, progressed to a plod and then, stubbornly, slowed to a walk, which had a sort of 'John Wayne' swagger about it. It was obvious that we weren't going to catch up and some of the girls looked back over their shoulders and waved.

The adrenaline had well and truly run out by now and I could feel myself slipping into a real downer – thanks to Humphrey. I was about to tug hard on the lead again when I noticed that he'd progressed to a small trot. So small, in fact, that I had hardly noticed but it was there. He had tried to catch up with the runners, he'd understood what I was trying to do but he just didn't have it in him. His breath was coming fast and his tongue was hanging to one side and his eyes looked up at me imploringly.

I stopped and looked down at him, realising the huge effort he'd tried to make. I bent down and cuddled him and he was relieved to plonk himself down for a while. The rest of the walk was taken at a more leisurely pace, stopping frequently to let Humphrey get his breath back.

We stopped again by the lake so the dogs could have a quick drink and I looked out over the magical scene. The trees were just starting to blossom; the sun was shimmering and dancing on the water and the air smelt sweet and fresh. Swans were gliding ethereally across and ducks and moorhens played merrily without care. All those months of being cooped up at home sulking and brooding, wasting time. If only I'd taken the time to walk out into the park which was just a stone's throw away from Gran's house, taken in this glorious scenery and filled my lungs with this incredible life-giving air, surely my heart would have healed much quicker. Who needs drugs, when you have this?

As I looked across the water, my eye was caught by someone sitting on the opposite side. She was too far away to see her in detail, but she did look familiar. I vaguely remembered someone of her size and build amongst the group of ladies. Perhaps, this was the one they lost along the way. Her head was bent and she had something on her lap. Her fingers pinched the top of her nose and I suspected she was crying. It made me realise that all the people I pass; the ladies, the teenagers and the dog walkers, all seem on an even keel on the walkway of the park and yet we all go home to our own lives and our own problems.

She looked over the water and saw me staring. I felt slightly ashamed at my obvious voyeurism and was about to turn away when she waved – a small pitiful wave, but still a wave. I was slightly surprised that she had recognised me from earlier but then I'd forgotten I still had my two hairy, unforgettable friends who were still playing by the waterside.

As I called Sergeant out of the water, I noticed the other ladies had rounded the corner and were calling to the lady by the lake to rejoin them. She stood up, popped something into her pocket and brushed herself down. She looked over and waved once more before setting off in time with the others. My last sighting of them that day was running around the lake, arms waving frantically in the air, as if dancing to some boogie tune. Tomorrow, I decided, I would get the dogs done earlier and see if I could join the ladies on their afternoon excursion.

As I was about to leave the park, I saw the ladies swing by for one last lap. Most of them were slightly red in the face, some were puffing heavily and others were swilling on water canisters as they ran. I shouted out to Barbara that I'd like to join her the next day.

"We meet at the water fountain at two o'clock," she shouted, "See you there" and sprinted off to catch up with the others.

I looked over and watched them all file past. The woman who'd been sitting at the lake was in the middle of the grouping and, although taller than most of them, was inconspicuous in her outfit and kept herself slightly detached from the others. Her brunette hair was pulled back and tied discreetly at the nape. She didn't look over or wave and was soon disappearing around the corner with the others.

When I got home I relayed the day to Gran, who looked on in horror as I relived the whole flasher thing and softened as I told her how Blue had been the hero. I fully expected some sort of song to come tripping from her but she was unusually subdued. Even, the ladies in the park story didn't bring her round; she just kept twiddling with her hanky and looking distractedly at the phone.

"Is there something wrong, Gran?" I said, turning to give her my full attention.

"No dear, not wrong exactly…"

"Well," I said, apprehensively. "What is it?"

Gran looked once more at the phone and then at me. "I've done something I shouldn't have done, Remi. I've got myself in a bit of a pickle and I don't know what to do." She looked at me, her eyes almost imploring but still she didn't explain.

"Gran," I said, taking hold of her and drawing her close. "Who's always telling me that nothing's so bad, we can't fix it?" Gran nodded her head in understanding but was still unforthcoming with her problem. I sat her down in her big chair and sat beside her.

"What have you done, Gran? Tell me all about it." She looked at me again and took hold of my hand.

"After the big Michael thing, when you were really unhappy and had no job, I was so worried for you, Remi; I applied for a job in your name. Today they phoned and said that you'd been accepted and could you come along to arrange a start date. I never expected it to go so far or so quickly. I thought they'd check you out and perhaps ask you to come for an interview or something. Then when I didn't hear from them, I forgot all about it. Then you got this job with Lucy and I was really pleased that you'd worked it out for yourself."

"Okay," I said, trying to take it in. "It was a really nice thing you did, trying to get me a job and it's nice to know that they accepted me, so why would I be angry with you?" She was about to answer, when the phone rang and she looked paralysed for a moment.

"That's them," she said, in a small voice. Gran made no attempt to answer the phone or to carry on with her explanation so, cautiously, I picked up the receiver.

"May I speak to Remington Hall-Smyth, please?" a voice asked.

"Speaking," I replied, looking over at Gran who had turned away and was walking towards the window.

"Hello, this is Miranda from Equality Healthcare; you applied for a position with us?"

"Erm, that's correct," I said, looking over at Gran. Had she applied for me to take a position as a brain surgeon or something? Was that why she was so worried? Well I could probably fake my way through if need be, after all, how difficult could that be?

"We're delighted to tell you that you've been accepted and wondered if we could set a date for you to come into the office for an interview before we send you out to shadow someone."

"Shadow someone? What like tail them?" I retorted.

"Well," she hesitated. "I suppose so, in a manner of speaking."

"O...kay, would you mind holding the line a moment." I covered the mouthpiece and whispered to Gran. "Am I tracking down disability fraud or something? They want me to go out and shadow people." Gran shook her head; her guilty expression was still worrying me. What job could be so bad that she was frightened to tell me what it was? After all, I was now working with dogs, how much worse could it get? I took my hand away from the mouth piece and was just about to say something when a thought, a horrible thought, came into my head. I covered it with my hand again and whispered more urgently now.

"Gran, this doesn't involve old people, does it?" Gran's hand shot to her mouth.

"No! Not old people, Gran. How could you do this to me?" In my ear I could hear someone calling me.

"Hello," I said. "Sorry to be so long, My Gran had a small memory lapse and I just had to remind her of something." I said, glaring in her direction.

"Ah yes, we have all that down here in your application."

"You do?" I said.

"Yes indeed, for someone of your age to take your aged grandmother into your home and take care of her, as you do, cooking, cleaning, all her personal care, it's quite amazing. We knew straight away you were right for this job."

She had, of course, listed all the things Gran did for me – had always done for me. I immediately regretted how she'd upset herself about applying for this job. She was, without doubt, the most upstanding, caring and honest person I'd ever known in my life.

"Especially with her disability," I heard the voice say from the other end of the phone.

"Sorry," I said. "Disability?"

"Yes, it says here, she only has one leg?" I tried not to laugh as I looked over at Gran walking stiltedly across the room, doing her peg-leg impression.

"Oh," I said. "That Gran, the one-legged one!"

Fourteen

I'd been laughing so much I wasn't capable of turning the job down and somehow managed to mumble out an agreement to meet up with them the next morning. When I arrived at their offices I was welcomed warmly by everyone, which only made me worry about how desperate they must be.

After going through a few preliminaries, the job didn't seem that bad at all. Good money, working at my own pace, make a few cups of tea... and Bob's your uncle. So we arranged that I would go out and shadow someone the following night. Which unfortunately had nothing to do with spying, it only meant that I would be observing whilst someone else made their calls.

After leaving Equality Healthcare I made my way swiftly across town to pick up Precious. I was grateful that there was no shouting from upstairs and no smell of perfume as I entered. However, on the table was a note, written completely in bold, capital letters and underlined twice. *THE NEXT TIME I FIND THAT MUTT IN MY BED, I WON'T BE RESPONSIBLE FOR MY ACTIONS.* It was signed *JAMES.*

So, I thought angrily, James is the grumpy guy from upstairs and this must have been why poor Precious had a boot thrown down the stairs after her the other day. I wasn't a big fan of the odious Marianne but what on earth was she doing with such a brute, who was obviously unemployed, to be spending so much time in bed? There but the grace of God and the hand of fate, I thought.

After collecting Lord we made off to the park, which, surprisingly, went without incident. We all had a great walk and I felt quite limbered up for my date with the ladies later. As I opened the door to take Precious back, I heard someone, presumably that James guy, talking upstairs on the phone. My blood chilled as I overheard him say that he would be taking the knife to her in the afternoon, if she didn't improve. My God, I thought, you hear these stories but you just can't believe there really are such people in the world.

I tippy-toed into the kitchen, wondering what on earth I should do. Should I take Precious home with me and explain to Lucy? No, knowing my luck he'd sue me for stealing the 'buddy' thing. I spotted a dog cage in the corner of the room, very much like the ones we used in the van. I popped Precious in and rifled through the cupboards to find something for her to eat and then threw in some toys, which hopefully would keep her amused for the rest of the day. I didn't want the poor thing to whimper and end up being cut up.

I couldn't stop thinking about Precious as I walked Sergeant and Humphrey around the park. Part of me questioned if I should have taken her home and the other part wondered what sort of a person talks about knifing a little Yorkshire terrier? Next time I would report him to the RSPCA or the police, he was obviously a psycho!

Sergeant stopped to crouch and I pulled out my bag. I'd become quite adept at the doggy bag thing and didn't heave half as much as I used to. I noticed a group of people stopping to chat on the path not far from us. They looked over in disgust as Sergeant balanced dangerously close to the rose bushes.

I made a big point of holding the bag out so they could see that I was going to clear it up. There was nothing more annoying than irresponsible dog owners who allowed their dogs to mess and then walked away, leaving others to tread in it. I understood their grievance; I felt exactly the same myself. Sergeant finished and I turned back to see where he had been… There it was, and there it was, and also there, and there. Sergeant, obviously, had a bad case of the runs and he had deposited a fluid version of his, usual, huge dump, randomly all over the place.

I felt the heat rising up my neck. How does one collect a runny poo in a doggy bag exactly? Well, here's a professional tip! You lean over, doggy bag in full view, you shout out 'good boy'. You bend and scrape away in the area where the dog was crouching. Stand up, make a big deal of tying the bag up, walk over to the designated doggy deposit bin and throw in the empty bag. Then get away as quickly as you can before they see that you haven't picked up a thing.

By two o'clock I was standing by the water fountain, excited and slightly nervous about joining the group. Barbara was already there and made me feel incredibly welcome. One by one, the others arrived. We all had a quick warm-up and off we set. It felt really good running alongside these women; they were all so kind and we chatted so much, the time just flew by.

After three laps round the park we all stopped outside the little café that Lucy had been drinking at, the first day I came. It was a, refreshingly, bright day and the exercise had warmed us all up. Most sat outside sipping on coffees and juices, some needing no more than a few puffs on their cigarettes to refresh them. From the outside looking in, these were just a bunch of, slightly overweight, middle-aged women jogging around the park but, from the inside, it was a completely different story.

As I listened to some of their stories, I started to understand what this group meant to each of them. For all the same reasons, I knew it would be important to me. Barbara had been the founder member. She'd advertised for other like-minded women to join her, a year after she'd discovered she had breast cancer. She confided that, after having a mastectomy, she felt uncertain of herself, lacked confidence and no longer felt like a complete woman. This, unfortunately, was compounded when she found out her husband was having sex with his secretary on the actual days she was having chemotherapy.

"You must have wanted to kill him," I said, feeling heat rising up in me for the second time that day.

"Of course I did," she said. "I would have happily carried out a penectomy without the aid of anaesthetic at the time, but over the months I came to realise that he had suffered too. He was frightened of losing me. When he tried to talk to me, I pushed him away, too worried about myself to take his fears on-board."

"Please," I said, disbelievingly. "How can you excuse him so easily? He didn't have to go and have an affair and he, definitely, didn't have to do it on the very days you were suffering the most."

Who Cares?

"Ah, but he did Remi, don't you see? Those were the days he was hurting the most. It was on those days that I pushed him away. It was on those days he needed someone to hold him and make him feel needed."

I looked at Barbara. Her blonde hair, short and elfin-like, sat neatly around her heart-shaped face. Her bright, blue eyes shone with confidence in a way that, only someone who had faced adversity and battled through, could. Her trim, petite figure would be the envy of any woman. I noticed that her left hand still sported both an engagement and a wedding ring. She saw me looking and rubbed it affectionately. She lifted her head slightly and through dark lashes, smiled at me.

"We're back together again," she said. "We want to renew our vows at the end of this year, if the news is good," she added.

"Hopefully the news will be good Barbara, but if it isn't, what then?" I wanted to go further; I wanted to ask her, what if the news was bad. Would her good-for-nothing husband desert her in her time of need, again? Was his secretary waiting in the wings, just in case he needed reassurance in the future? I guess she knew what I was thinking because she took my hand and squeezed it.

"To forgive someone Remi, especially someone you love, can be very liberating. It gives us a freedom to love again. Forgiveness really is a two-way gift."

Briefly, I told her about Michael and that final day at the television studio but I felt such a fraud having listened to her own story. My humiliation was nothing compared to what she'd been through. My heartbreak was no more than an inconvenience, compared to the pain she'd endured. Bizarrely, talking to Barbara, a stranger up until the previous day, was amazingly cathartic.

I heard myself utter things like, unloved and betrayed, lost and afraid, all emotions that had evolved within me, long before Michael had come onto the scene. Feelings I had suppressed and hidden over the years were now tumbling out in a rampant and virulent tirade and you know what? It felt good.

Barbara looked at me for a few moments as if weighing me up. "It feels good to let it go, doesn't it?" she said, mirroring my own thoughts. "It's such a waste of energy to carry all that baggage around with us every day. When the club first formed, I wondered how we would get people to join us, or even if anyone would. But do you know what Remi? The club is like a magnet, it attracts people. People that have problems, people, like yourself, who just need to talk and people who have nowhere else to turn." She threw open her arms and gestured towards the rest of the women.

"All of these women have had their share of problems. Hilda, over there, was a young mother who found she couldn't cope with the responsibilities that entailed. Her husband left her and she turned to drink. Just cooking-sherry at night when she felt lonely, but soon it became an addiction.

"In the end she would drink anything she could afford. Her children were taken away from her, her family disowned her. She lost her house and ended up sleeping on the streets."

I looked over at Hilda, sipping on a fruit juice, laughing in the sunshine. Her face was lined and the grey in her hair made it hard to guess her original colour, or even her age. But she looked happy and strangely contented.

"How is she now?" I asked.

"You can see her, how does she look?"

"She looks great," I replied. "How did she do it?"

"One day she helped out in a soup kitchen, saw people worse off than herself and decided it was time to change. She went to church; they listened to her story and gave her a job. They contacted her family and children and set up a meeting. She hasn't touched a drop since.

"She joined our club a year ago and she runs with us every day. She's a shining light Remi, an inspiration to us all; she makes me believe anything is possible."

The old throat was beginning to restrict again and I searched round the rest of the group to avoid facing Barbara.

"There was a woman, the other day, down by the lake; she was crying... she's not here today."

Barbara looked up at me, sadness or something similar registering in her face. "Mary," she said, quietly.

"Is she alright?" I said, feeling that, perhaps, I'd overstepped the mark by encroaching on someone else's misery in a bid to ease my own embarrassment.

"I'm sure she will be," she said, looking slightly uncomfortable. Being compulsively nosey was a curse, I thought.

"It's just," I babbled, "I thought she looked vaguely familiar."

"Really?" said Barbara, who was on the verge of getting up and now sat down again.

"Well, only vaguely," I said, knowing that I had deliberately overstated the truth. Barbara looked out over the park to where the brunette had been sitting, only the day before.

"Mary does have a few problems it's true, but time's the best healer." Suddenly she jumped up out of the seat. "Come on everyone, time to get going again." She leaned over and squeezed my hand. It's all part of the patina of life, Remi, the problems that don't kill us, serve to make us stronger." Had she put that into song, I would have sworn she was Gran!

One of the other women overheard Barbara's pet talk and, as we set off, she shouted out, "Alright girls, it's time for inspirational sayings as we jog along. I'll start us off with: You're never too old to set another goal or dream another dream. Over to you Babs."

"Least said, soonest mended," shouted out Barbara.

"A miss is as good as a mile," spurred on another.

"Stupid is as stupid does," shouted Gwen. I was desperately trying to think of something inspirational to shout out, when I slipped on a poop that some irresponsible person had left lying around on the path near a rose bush, and I went crashing to the floor. As I picked myself up, both bum and ego bruised, all I could come up with was, "What goes around comes around!"

Fifteen

The next day Gran had to, literally, raise me from the dead and I've got to tell you, it wasn't easy. The previous day's events had left me exhausted, mentally and physically. From the view point of the bed, the day ahead also looked pretty daunting, four dogs to walk, running with the ladies and then shadowing someone tonight. I threw the covers back over my head, contemplating a few more minutes. This 'turning over a new leaf' and getting on with life was killing me, which reminded me, I was well overdue a visit to the doctor. I rummaged through one of Gran's old drawers and found some multivitamins and some iron tablets; I took a few of each, guessing they would do until I could make an appointment.

When I reached Wisteria Cottage, there was a car sitting out on the drive. It was one of those large four by four types in a smoky shade of blue with dark windows and, what looked like, real leather upholstery inside. The number plate was personalised and the bumper sticker boasted that his other car was a Porsche.

What a jerk this man was, I thought; threatening small dogs, driving along in his oversized car with the hideous, stick insect Marianne by his side.

Tentatively, I put the key in the lock, opening the door as quietly as I could. Standing by the sink, looking out at the garden with his back to me, was a man with short, blonde hair, gelled up in a modern style, who I assumed must be James, the grumpy guy from upstairs. His trousers were well-cut in a dark hue of blue; he had on a striped banker's shirt and a navy-coloured, cashmere jumper, wrapped round his shoulders. Strapped to his ear was (surprise, surprise) a mobile phone, which he was talking into animatedly.

Who Cares?

I realised I may have put myself in a slightly awkward position by entering the house, surreptitiously as I had. If I made a noise now, it would seem odd and he would probably freak out and start shouting at me and if I said nothing until he came off the phone then he might think I was eavesdropping on his conversation... and start shouting at me! Well, if I was going to get shouted at either way, I thought, I may as well listen – purely, you understand, in a witness-type of way. Let's face it, if he could kill a dog, who knows what else he could do? I stood rigid to the spot, breathing as shallowly as I could.

"Yes, I'm here and I got your note but like I said before, I'm doing everything I can. I've been digging around where she was last seen but unearthing her isn't going to be easy."

My hand shot to my mouth and my heart missed a beat, what had I done? This guy obviously worked for the Mob, or whatever the modern day equivalent of the Mob was, and I was standing in his house, eavesdropping on his conversation about someone who was dead. Somehow though, this all made sense. Marianne with her long nails, champagne and all-over tan; she was a gangster's moll!

I put my hand backwards and wondered if I could make it back to the door. Perhaps, I could slip back outside and then come back in again loudly, as I normally would, without knowing anything about bodies or hit men or anything. I took one step back and there was a small squeak as my foot left the floorboards. To my relief James hadn't heard it; in fact he was suddenly transfixed by something he'd seen through the window.

I took another step backwards and held my breath as it creaked again. Thankfully, I was nearly there and James was still totally engrossed in looking out of the window. At last I felt my hand on the door knob and silently inched back towards it. James was so intent on looking out of the window he even shifted his position in a bid to see better.

What on earth could he be looking at that was so interesting? I heard his phone click shut and I could just make out his reflection in the window. He was smiling at something, probably sadistically thinking about the body buried in the garden. Was it just my imagination or was he now waving at someone out there?

"Are you coming or going?" he suddenly said. Was he talking to me? I pointed to myself and he nodded.

"Hi," I said, raising my hand in a friendly, *'I've not been here long and I definitely didn't hear anything'* sort of wave. "I'm …," I went to give him my name and then thinking on my feet, changed my mind. Best not to give my real name away to a Godfather, better to have a pen name… Is it pen name, or is it pseudonym? No…

"It's an alias," I blurted out.

"Analias?" he repeated back.

"Spanish for Alice," I said. "Is Precious ready?"

"Isn't the Spanish for Alice, Alicia?"

"Possibly, in some parts but from where my grandfather came from it was Analias!"

"Oh," he said, looking puzzled.

"Anyway, I'm running late, so I'll grab Precious and go, shall I?" He leaned to one side and gestured the way. I grabbed the lead, the ball and the bags, trying not to make it obvious that I was looking over my back just in case a well-aimed shovel came my way.

"So Analias, do you have anyone to go home to?" I could feel the lead shaking in my hands and the hairs rising on my neck, I knew what this meant.

"Yes I have a huge family, who would really miss me if I didn't come home and I've got lots of friends, who ring me all the time, to make sure I'm okay… and alive," I added.

"That's great, but what I meant was, do you have a boyfriend?"

"Yes, thank you very much, I have a wonderful boyfriend. He's a policeman who does kick-boxing." He raised his eyebrow. "He's in homicide." I said, hoping they had that in the MET and wasn't specific to *CSI: Vegas*. I pulled Precious towards the front door, counting down the feet to freedom. As I put her in the back of the van and got in the front seat, I felt close to fainting. I only just managed to pick the phone up to ring Juliet to tell her all about it.

Who Cares?

"Who'd you think he's looking for?" she gasped.

"I don't know Juliet but he's a nasty piece of work, which is a real shame because his trousers were *Armani* and I'm sure I glimpsed Calvin's underneath!"

"How long since you've seen Marianne?" Juliet said, returning to the theme. "Perhaps she's buried in the garden and they want to remove her in case the dog digs her up."

It was a good point but I didn't have time to reply as a door slammed behind me and James came out of the house carrying, what looked like, a tennis racket in a case but would, of course, be the perfect place to hide a gun or a spade!

I whispered to Juliet that I'd ring her later and backed the van out of the drive. James pulled away in the same direction behind me. As I headed towards Lord's house, I kept watch in the rear-view mirror, praying that he wasn't following me. I was so relieved when he turned off and headed towards the city that I went through a red light and ended up with half a dozen motorists screaming and beeping their horns at me.

The walk was fine. The dogs enjoyed the run and I enjoyed being alive, a prospect that had seemed short-lived only that morning. I felt in a strange mood actually, on a high for having escaped death, yet again and strangely, on a low, not unlike a junkie looking for another thrill. As we neared the end of our walk, the dogs started digging around in the bushes. They were playing happily, or so I thought, so I pulled out my phone to ring Juliet back. Without warning Lord and Precious pulled back out of the roses and something shot past me towards the walkway. And then... all hell was let loose.

The dogs strained at the lead to get to the path and I had a job to pull them back. When I managed to get them under control, I took in the scene. A lady dog-owner was screaming at her Jack Russell, the Jack Russell was ragging a squirrel and the squirrel was screaming like a banshee. There was no one else around and I felt duty-bound, as a patron of the park, to help out, especially when I knew that it had been my dogs that had sent the flaming thing out there in the first place, but what could I do? The Jack Russell had the squirrel round the stomach and the squirrel was trying to bite the dogs face. The woman, dressed in a tweed skirt and cable-knit jumper was turning a terrible shade of puce as she shouted at her dog to let go.

Eventually, after what seemed like hours but was in truth a few moments, the dog stopped shaking its quarry and the squirrel stayed still; alive but, obviously, seriously injured. No amount of cajoling would encourage the dog to put it down and the woman looked imploringly at me.

"If I could take Jacky over there behind the tree, he might lose interest in it and drop it," she said, pain and anguish all over her face. "Would you mind taking Buster for a minute?" she asked, holding out a grey hound on a lead. ,

I took the lead she proffered and immediately regretted my actions. Lord and Buster took an instant dislike to each other and started snapping and snarling. Despite the previous disaster with the leads under my foot, I had no choice but to do the same again, except this time I made sure that it was the ball of my foot on the leads and not the heel. With the other hand I held onto Buster, who, now that he couldn't get to Lord, was pulling towards his owner. I prayed that this would all be over soon; I was being stretched in so many different directions, it was like being on a medieval rack.

From behind the tree emerged a terribly distressed 'Tweedy' and a gleeful Jack Russell. She walked over slowly, head bowed, her eyes darting from left to right.

"I'm just glad there were no children here to see it," she said. "A terrible business, just terrible."

"Is it dead?" I asked, hosting my most sympathetic face and leaning in slightly, in a conspiratorial fashion.

She looked up at me, her face contorted with agony as she whispered, "No."

"Oh," I said.

"Well I didn't know what to do," she whispered again. "Even though it was in a bad way, it was still trying to bite me. What should I do?" she pleaded.

"Look, this isn't your fault. Jacky was just doing what comes naturally to him and there was nothing you could have done to prevent it," I said, guiltily. "But it will die a long, slow, painful death if you don't put it out of its misery." She winced at every adjective I used and wrung her hands in desperation at what she knew she must do.

Without looking up she nodded and, handing me both Buster and Jacky, she walked back towards the tree. It was quite a few minutes later before she emerged again, still looking anxious.

"Is it done?" I asked as kindly as I could muster and she nodded. "Are you okay?" She nodded again. "It's for the best, you know, it was the right thing to do."

"I know," she said, taking the leads and nodding fervently. I looked over, reverently, towards the tree, realising how hard this must have been for her. As I did, I heard a rustle and into view came the bloodied squirrel. 'Tweedy' looked at me, her hands twiddling frantically, her eyes wide with fright. She didn't say a thing, just handed me back the leads and walked back to her 'Alamo'.

A few more minutes passed and I stretched my neck to see if I could see her. She was obviously offering up a little service to the late and departed squirrel and I could see a little tear slip down her face.

Sombrely, she came back and took the leads once more. How does one offer solace at a time like this? I reached over and touched the back of her hand.

"Is it definitely done this time?" I said, but her resigned face told me that it was. "I know it was hard but you have done the right and decent thing, you saved that little animal from further pain. There are lots of squirrels in this park, far more than it can sustain, it won't have upset the balance and the Park Warden told me once, that they sometimes attack other wildlife and can be very vicious."

She relaxed a little, composed herself and after thanking me for my help gathered in the dogs, especially Jacky and set off, back on the path. Her shoulders were slumped as she walked slowly away, giving only a passing glance at the big oak, which would forever hold bad memories for her.

I popped my dogs into the back of the van and made my way round the side of the park back to the main thoroughfare. This had certainly been an adrenaline-filled day; I could still feel the rush coursing through my veins.

Who Cares?

I pulled round to the side of the park in the van and ahead of me I could see the sweet natured 'Tweedy' trudging, despondently, along the road. Downtrodden and dejected, she crossed the road and walked off, miserably, towards home.

As I drew level and looked over at her, I felt duty-bound to shout out some sort of encouragement, to relieve her of the shame she carried with her. After all, I was the only person who knew. I rolled down the blackened window just a fraction and leaned forward. But in that moment between the good intention and the action, a terrible thing happened and try as I might, I couldn't stop myself. Just as I passed by I heard myself shout out, "SQUIRREL KILLER!"

Sixteen

No one could have felt worse about my actions than me. I mean, it just wasn't in my nature to be so cruel, I felt spurred on by an unknown force. Could it have been all the vitamins and iron I had taken that morning? I could see in my rear-view mirror that 'Tweedy' had no idea where the voice had come from. She was still pirouetting on the spot as I got to the end of the road, but to be safe, I thought, I'd better park further away next time.

Thankfully, the Godfather was out when I returned Precious home, so I nipped in and out, pausing only to have a swift look out of the window to see if there were any signs of disturbance and to close the laptop that was Googling the Spanish translation of Alice. Can you believe he even looked it up? There's just no trust in the world anymore!

I was late when I picked up Sergeant and later still by the time I got to Humphrey's house. The door was open and Humphrey was barking at the door.

"Good boy Humphrey, thank goodness you didn't wander out." I gave him a cuddle and ruffled his head, but he carried on barking. Now this is the sort of neglect that should be reported, far worse than inadvertently shouting out 'Squirrel Killer', whilst overdosed on multivits!

Humphrey was now tugging at my sleeve and, because I had watched many a Lassie film when I was younger, I knew that Humphrey either wanted to show me something, or there was a good chance someone had fallen off a cliff.

In the kitchen, lying on the floor was an old man who seemed to be only semi-conscious.

Okay, I thought, don't panic, you were nearly a doctor's receptionist once, you can do this.

His breathing was shallow and his colour was very pale and

he kept calling me Humphrey and patting my head! I grabbed my mobile and dialled nine-nine-nine. The operator asked me who I was, what number I was calling from. As I answered, I looked down at the old man and felt frantic with worry for all this delay. I described the symptoms and they asked me to look for a medical tag, I did. He was diabetic.

The ambulance was there within minutes and a man and woman in big coats followed my directions into the kitchen. I took Humphrey into the other room as instructed and waited for someone to come and see me. When they did come, it was with good news. Henry was diabetic and because he'd been unwell and slept most of the day, he hadn't eaten enough and had become hypoglycaemic. They'd dosed him up with glucose and his signs were all looking good.

While they finished checking him over I took Sergeant and Humphrey for a quick walk around the park. It was gone three o'clock and I could see the ladies running round the other side of the park. As they went by, Barbara peeled off and signalled the others to carry on. I explained why I was late, leaving out the *Mafia* and the whole squirrel thing – just cutting straight to Henry.

"You must be really proud of yourself, helping Henry like that; he could have died you know?" I really wanted to be proud of myself but the 'Tweedy' thing soured it for me. Of all the days to overdose on medication, it had to be on a day when I go and save someone's life.

"I see Mary's back on the team again," I said, pointing to the ladies disappearing in the distance, the height of the brunette standing her out amongst the others. Barbara sighed.

"Yes, it's good to have her back but I don't think she'll be staying. Life's hard for her at the moment, but I keep her in my prayers." She turned to look at me and added belatedly, "You as well, of course."

I let her get off and promised that I would try and make it back the next day. I dropped Sergeant home and made my way back to Henry and the paramedics. They were just getting ready to leave and thanked me for acting promptly. In the kitchen, Henry sat in his old chair, a blanket over his legs and a little, three-bar electric fire burning just in front. He still looked a bit pale but was vastly improved on the last time I saw him. I explained who I was and sat down opposite him. Humphrey, tired from the day's excitement and all the barking, waited for a quick rub on the head from Henry before making his way over to his basket and throwing himself in.

I didn't know exactly how old Henry was but I was guessing over eighty. He was immaculately dressed in pressed trousers, a check shirt and V-neck sweater. His white hair was sparse but neatly cut and gelled down at the sides and I noticed a comb and hankie inside his top pocket. He sipped on a cup of something the paramedics had made him and listened as I explained how Humphrey had been barking when I arrived. He nodded but remained quiet, looking dolefully into his cup. As I went to say something else he glanced up; looking me straight in the face with the clearest, brightest, blue eyes I had ever seen.

"It ain't much of a life, is it?" he said, sadly. His sad remark took me back and I looked at him for a long moment before asking him what he meant.

"What 'ave I got to look forward too? You shoulda left me gel." I pulled my chair up closer and took hold of his frail hand. His skin was paper thin and so transparent I could see the veins beneath.

"Henry, can I be frank with you?" He looked a bit perplexed but nodded. "This morning I did one of the meanest, nastiest things I've ever done in my life. It's fair to say, that if there is a thing called Karma, then I was well on my way to hell and damnation... But you, Henry," I said, patting his hand, "have changed that. By saving you, I may just have turned this whole thing around."

He looked at me and then asked. "What was it you did this morning?" It was tortuous explaining it all to another human being, it sounded even worse when it was said out loud.

"...I wound down the window and shouted Squirrel Killer," I finished. His bright-blue eyes were now like saucers as he stared at me, not a flicker crossing his face. Suddenly he burst out laughing, he couldn't stop and I was really worried that it would trigger off another attack. He tried to wipe away the tears with his hankie and, breathlessly, looked me straight in the face and took hold of my hand.

"I'm sorry darlin', I ain't enough to save you; you're still goin' ta hell!" he said and burst out laughing again.

On Henry's request, I made myself a cup of tea and sat down beside him. We talked about him and we talked about me. He remembered things from so far back and so clearly. He talked about his brothers and sisters, his parents and the things he used to get up to.

I told him about my childhood, leaving out my father and skipping straight to my school days. When I looked at my watch it was getting late. I made quick apologies and told him I'd see him the next day.

When I got home I told Gran all about the day. As I got to the part about Henry she clasped her hands, dramatically, to her face and closed her eyes, goodness knows what she'd have done if she'd heard the unexpurgated version of the squirrel story.

"Remi, I'm so proud of you, darling. Saving poor Henry like that. If it hadn't been for your timely arrival, who knows what could have happened to him." And there it was again. At last I have the opportunity to make Gran proud of me and what pops into my head? 'Tweedy's face! Life is cruel.

I had an hour before Samantha would be calling for me. Samantha was from Equality Healthcare and had already dropped some overalls, gloves and aprons in for me, which Gran had laid neatly on my bed. I put on strong, sensible shoes in black, as was the requirement and black, Betty Jackson trousers which were smart in a classic-cut.

I pulled my hair back and tied it in a scrunchy. If ever there was a time for a scrunchy, I reasoned, this was surely it. Finally, I put my overall on. It was white with burgundy piping around the collar and pockets with *Equality Healthcare* embroidered on it. It had a zip that went the full length of the jacket and I couldn't help but wonder if it was there for the sole purpose of a quick get-away. They had provided me with a name tag that hung on a burgundy ribbon which I popped over my head. I turned to face the mirror and take in the full effect.

To my surprise, I actually looked quite good, like a nurse in fact and really official. I headed off down the stairs and did a quick twirl for Gran. She looked at me with her tearful, proud face…Damn that 'Tweedy'!

When Samantha called, I had finished the outfit off with the plastic gloves and apron. She looked at me with a bemused look.

"You're supposed to put them on when you get there," she said, laughing. She opened her folder to check who the first client was and, without further ado, we zoomed away as if we were just about to do a few laps round Brands Hatch.

We pulled up outside a small house where the garden was overgrown and the outside of the house was sadly neglected. When we stepped inside, it was a similar story; frayed carpets and worn furniture. The only luxury being the heat; it was like a furnace. Within seconds I could feel sweat running down my cleavage. Samantha looked at me and laughed.

"You get used to it," she said. "All the houses are really warm; they feel the cold a lot more when they're older."

I followed Sam into the living room and she introduced me to June.

"June, this is Remi, she's helping me today," Sam shouted at the little old lady sitting in the corner of the room. June turned to look at me and then turned back towards the television without saying a word.

The television was probably well above the legal decibel level and I wondered if I should book up for an audio test just to make sure I hadn't damaged anything. Sam scuttled off beckoning me to follow. She showed me the record book, which, she explained, each client had. It itemised the medicines that each client needed to be given and a page where everything about the visit had to be documented. I watched as Sam carefully and respectfully washed and undressed June, putting her into a nightdress. At no time did June take her eyes off the television. Her medicines were given, the book written up and we left.

The next call was Dulcie. She sat in a room, which again was incredibly warm, but this time the cosiness was palpable. Sam introduced me in the same manner as she had before but the response was completely different.

Who Cares?

"Darling, how wonderful, come over here and let me take a look at you." I went closer and Sam laughed as she watched Dulcie appraise me. "Beautiful bone structure, darling, high cheekbones, rising forehead. Let me hear you speak, darling." I looked over to Sam for help, what does one say when one is asked just to speak? Sam just laughed and tripped off to the kitchen to fetch the record book.

"Come on, darling, speak up."

"My name's Remi and this is my first day working with Equality Healthcare."

"Project Remi, you must project your voice, how will the people at the back of the auditorium hear you if you don't project?" she shouted, annunciating every syllable. I was just about to try harder when Sam poked her head around the door.

"I need to take Remi with me for a moment Dulcie; she'll be back in a minute." She grabbed my hand and pulled me out of the room.

"Okay, darling but I have lots of hopefuls waiting in the wings; I can't keep the part open for long."

Once in the kitchen, Sam pulled open the record book and started writing.

"Don't worry about Dulcie, she has short-term memory loss, although sometimes I can't help but wonder if she just makes all this up for fun."

Getting Dulcie undressed was 'Oscar' winning. She quoted from Shakespeare and flung her arms round in gay abandon. When, finally, she was in her nightdress, she took a bow and asked where her flowers were. I was truly sad to leave her house; there was a similarity to Gran that I absolutely loved and looked forward to seeing her again.

We were nearly at the end of the round when we pulled up outside a house I knew.

"Is Henry on your list?" I asked

"Mr. Harper, yes, do you know him?"

"I only met him today but he's lovely."

"Yeah, all of the carers love him. He's a real old gentleman."
We went inside and Henry did a double-take when he saw me.

"You ain't letting her undress me are you Sam? She's a real

mean 'un,"

Sam turned to look at me, obviously confused. I shrugged my shoulders and stared back at Henry with a pathetic 'please don't say anything' look. Henry laughed and gave me a knowing wink. He took my hand and kissed it.

"Only joking, she's a life-saver and I should know!"

Once again, I was on a complete high when I left Sam at Gran's front door. The evening had been far better than I'd expected and seeing Henry was the icing on the cake. Gran sat in her big armchair and listened as I rattled on about the night.

"So did you get any numbers for me?" she laughed.

"Gran, they were far too old for you, even my lovely Henry. What you need Gran is a toy boy!" She laughed and I watched her as she got up and went into the kitchen to make hot chocolate for the both of us.

The only downside of the evening, I thought, was that you realise that people are vulnerable. They lead productive and full lives and then, all of a sudden, they need someone to come into their homes and care for them. Well that would never be the case for Gran, I vowed, tears welling up as I thought of her, I would always be there to care for her.

"Is that coffee done yet Gran, you've been ages?" From the kitchen I heard the cups rattling, the kettle humming and Gran singing away, as usual, with her own version of a popular song. She opened the door and waved her jazz hands at me, as she reached the climax and belted out "When I'm ninety four!"

"Shouldn't that be sixty-four, Gran?" I said, laughing.

"Darling," she said, throwing her arms wide. "Haven't you heard? Ninety-four is the new sixty-four!"

Seventeen

Generally speaking, the next few days went quite well. There was the small mishap at Precious' house which, at most, could only be classed as an oversight. In fact, the day had been going really well and having dropped the first two dogs off home, I went on to pick up Sergeant and Humphrey.

After our walk, I sat, as I had become accustomed, with Henry and enjoyed a cup of tea. I had an hour to spare before meeting up with the ladies and it was always nice to sit and relax with him and chat about the old days. But, as we chatted, something kept prodding at my subconscious. Somewhere in the back of my mind something felt wrong. I dismissed it on more than one occasion but still, the feeling kept drifting back into my head.

"You alright, Gel? You don't seem your usual self."

I laughed. "My usual self, Henry, what's that then?"

"Well, I suppose," Henry said, with a twinkle in his eye, "a bit batty!"

"You say the nicest things Henry, do you know that?" His face took on a slightly worried demeanour and he leaned forward and touched my hand.

"I didn't mean that in a bad way, darlin'. You're a lovely girl and I'm real glad you come and see me an' all, you know that but, you are a bit of a fruit cake. Normally when you leave, I have to take a nap, 'cos I'm tired out... But today, well you just haven't got that sparkle."

"I know what you mean Henry, it's just that I've got a horrible feeling that something's not quite right, but I just don't know why."

"Do you think it's a premonition, or is it something you've done?" I thought about it for a bit. Had I done something wrong?

139

Who Cares?

Forgotten someone's birthday, driven through a red light? I tracked back through the mornings events. No problems picking up Precious and Lord, no problems at the park. I dropped Precious home with no hiccups and Lord was easy enough, I just opened the door and he ran off into the house: all very uncomplicated and headache-free.

So why did I keep getting that feeling of impending doom and why did I keep seeing an image of Lord turning, frantically, in his little wicker basket? Why could I see him trying to tuck his tail in and lay his front legs down but finding that his bottom wouldn't fit? I could see him trying again, this time pushing his bottom in and having to settle for the front paws hanging over the side. I vaguely remembered seeing him stretch his neck to eat from the little silver salver, but what was wrong with that picture?

"Oh my God," I shouted, jumping to my feet, scaring Henry and causing Humphrey to give a loud grunt of disapproval. "I've left the first two dogs at the wrong houses."

I started running towards the door with Henry shouting after me not to panic, but how could I not? He didn't know what happened to people in Wisteria Cottage when they upset the 'Don'. On the other hand, neither did I, but today was not a day to find out.

I tore through the traffic, using as many shortcuts as I could remember, arriving at the house within ten minutes of leaving Henry. As I pulled up outside I was devastated to see the big blue car outside. There was nothing to be done, I knew I would just have to go in and face the music. Given my last experience with James, I opened the door loudly and flew into the kitchen like a whirlwind. I had on my best *'Oh my God, oh my God, I'm so sorry'* face and was totally prepared to take what was coming to me.

What I wasn't prepared for was James sitting calmly at the table, reading, whilst Lord sat in the wicker basket, bolt upright, hardly daring to breathe or make eye contact in case anyone realised he shouldn't be in there and threw him out.

"Analias, how lovely to see you." He looked at his watch," You're a bit late this morning aren't you?"

"Sorry?" I said, displaying my award-winning, village idiot face.

"I expected you ages ago, poor Precious must be cross-legged by now," he said, laughing at his own joke.

O...kay, so he hasn't noticed the big, red dog sitting in the corner of the room, it could happen! Or maybe... this was some sort of psychological mind game that the *Mafioso* plays. I laugh along with him and then he slams me up against the wall and threatens to kill me next time. Slowly I walked towards Lord and pulled at his collar. He resisted, pulling his head back and staying his ground. The dog was unbelievable, he lets all and sundry into his own house and now he wants to defect to another house just because they've got .... 'Buddy' hell, fillet steak in the food bowl!

James got up from the table and came round to the side of me.

"Is she playing hard to get?" he said, patting Lord on the head. I stepped back and stared at him, dumfounded. How does one answer a question like that? I watched as he ruffled Lord's head again and thought, perhaps, he'd had some sort of mental breakdown.

Right, I figured, I could either come clean, apologise profusely and promise it'll never happen again or I could just pull that 'buddy' dog out of that wicker basket and high-tail it for the door and never mention it again. Decision made, I grabbed the lead, attached it to the collar and yanked it as hard as I could. James did look a little surprised as Lord came hurtling out of the basket but still he never mentioned the fact that it was the wrong dog.

I waltzed Lord towards the front door and as I struggled with the temperamental lock, I felt James come up behind me. I swung round, hands up in front of my face, assuming a black-belt karate position, which was a bit of a surprise, seeing as though I don't even own a black-belt, let alone one in any sort of paper-folding. James laughed and took on a defensive pose. In his hand were the doggy bags and the ball.

"Don't forget these," he said, leaning in overly close to give them to me.

Who Cares?

"Oh right, thanks," I said, bringing my hands back down into a less dangerous stance. James leaned one hand on the door frame, effectively cornering me into the wall and whispered seductively into my ear. "Perhaps we could have dinner one night?"

"That would, of course, be very nice but I couldn't possibly," I said. "My boyfriend...the kick-boxer, would be very upset."

"Then don't tell him," he said, turning to face me head on. I was trying to remember if I'd given this imaginary boyfriend a name and if I didn't, what sort of a name would a big, butch, kick-boxer in the vice squad have? Before I could reply, he leaned in again, this time, brushing my cheek with his mouth as he said. "You keep quiet about dinner and I'll keep quiet about you being late for Precious," he looked down and patted Lord's head.

"I have to go," I said, pushing as hard as I could to release myself. He stepped back and laughed as I made a hasty retreat out of the door. My heart was racing and my knees were weak as I threw the confused Lord into the front seat with me.

I used the speaker phone in the van to phone Juliet as I travelled to Lord's house.

"I just don't know what to do Juliet, if I refuse, Lucy will have no choice but to let me go and then she may lose her business."

"You've more to worry about than Lucy," said Juliet, excitedly. "If you refuse, you may find a dog's head in your bed in the morning and if you give in and go out with him, you could end up in bed with the Mob!"

"You're not taking this seriously Juliet, it was very frightening! I can still smell his *Vera Wang* aftershave on my clothing from where he was pushed up against me so tight."

"Sorry Remi, you're right, but you do have a tendency sometimes to over exaggerate things a bit."

"Juliet, believe me, I'm not exaggerating. It definitely was *Vera Wang!*" Why Juliet was still laughing as she put the phone down was beyond me. I made a mental note never to ring her again when my life was is in danger!

Luckily no one had been home at Lord's house to see

Who Cares?

Precious rolling about on the bed in the master bedroom, so I deposited the ungrateful Lord and made my way back to take Precious back home. Relief swept over me as I pulled into the little cul-de-sac and saw that the car was gone. I ran her through to the kitchen, settled her into the basket and made to leave.

Now I wouldn't say that I was a nosy person by nature but I do have an enquiring mind, so as I passed the table in the dining room and saw the telephone directory lying open, my eyes did, inadvertently, stray to see where James had been looking.

My heart started racing as I looked down at the page. Was it just coincidence that the page was open on the letter H, or to be more accurate, on the page showing the name Hall? Well to be fair there were loads of them, pages and pages in fact. I noticed small ink marks on the margins where James must have doodled while he was looking. They were all situated further along the page, not in the halls at all. What a relief, it was more likely that he was looking for someone like.... I looked down the page... Hallam, Halliwell, Halliday. As I went further down the page, my heart started to speed up again as I got to Hall-Jones, Hall-Patch and lastly Hall-Smyth. Why was he looking me up and how on earth did he know my name?

Of course, I remembered. Marianne! Hadn't she said that first day that she remembered me, she may not have recalled my surname but it wouldn't have been hard to have looked back through the papers at the time and find out? But why would she have told the lecherous James my name and why was he looking up my address? Well he'd come unstuck, hadn't he; there were no Hall-Smyths in the directory at all. My mother had kept the name but was ex-directory. My father, to my knowledge didn't even live in the country and my paternal grandparents had emigrated years ago, preferring the warmer climes of Spain. I, being a child of the modern age, had always favoured the mobile phone; it's always accessible, small and compact and has the added bonus of being non-regional with no directory, therefore, no one can track you down. Yeah for technology!

I really wanted to slam the book shut, so he knew I'd seen it but I knew I mustn't forget that this was a dangerous man we were talking about. My eyes wandered again and I noticed a memo stuck to the table, it was signed by James and addressed to someone called Tony.

'Tony,

Barty is finally being released today. Could you pick him up for me and bring him home. Get him anything he needs. If he needs to go!!! Use the garden...

James'

Well this was as obvious as the pimple on my face. Tony, also known as, 'Italian Tony', was part of the *Mafioso* and was picking up Barty, who was obviously some sort of hit-man being released from prison. Tony had orders to pick him and take him home. If he's a liability or has squealed to the police, Tony has to 'do away with him' and bury him in the garden. Probably this time he'll put some sort of cross or shrub on him, so he can remember where this one is. I reversed my earlier decision and slammed the directory shut, after all, I reasoned, out of sight, out of mind!

I decided against ringing Juliet on this one, she'd probably have some plausible explanation for it all and, unfortunately, Penny was away, so I'd try her later. It was quite sad to realise that in this time of extreme danger I had so few friends to call upon. I couldn't tell Lucy, as it was her client although I was resolved that if anything else should happen, she must be told.

Melancholy set in as I travelled across town to meet the ladies, and Norman became the subject of my depression. It was terrible how we'd all lost touch like that. Why had Norman moved house without telling anyone? He could at least have given the awful man who moved in there a forwarding address. I decided to ask Penny if she'd had any more luck tracking him down. What would he look like now? I pondered. Quiet, unassuming Norman, with his big, brown eyes, no friends to speak of, probably working somewhere in the States, stuck behind a computer, perhaps still buying chocolates for all the ladies at Christmas. I stifled a small laugh at the prospect of all the ladies running off to the toilets at the same time. No, he was too nice to ever do anything like that again. Unlike the men that lived here, I thought. Laxative in chocolates was child's play to them; murder was more to their liking.

Who Cares?

When I met up with the ladies, I spilled out the whole story of James, the note I found on the table and the hit-man being released from jail. My theory being that the more people that knew the safer I was, after all he couldn't kill all of us, could he?

"Are you sure it was *Vera Wang*?" said Hilda, as she came up by my side. "It's very expensive you know."

"The aftershave he was wearing was not the point Hilda; he was blackmailing me which *was* the important thing."

"I know, but all the same, if someone's going to squeeze up against you and whisper in your ear like that, you'd be pleased that they smelt nice, wouldn't you? I mean, you wouldn't want him to smell of fish or something."

"No, no, that's true" said Gwen. "I think if someone had been pressing up against me, smelling all sweet with *Vera Wang*, I might've given in and gone out to dinner with him." The others started laughing.

"You'd have given in if he was wearing an old sock round his neck and offering you a bag of chips, Gwen." Gwen blushed but waved us all off in her good natured way.

"So you think this Barty is some sort of criminal just out of jail then, Remi?"

"What else could it be Barbara?"

"Well I suppose he could be an old uncle released from some mental institution or something, it may be quite innocent, you know."

"Barbara," I said, authoritatively, "you don't know these people like I do. I know for a fact that he was going to kill the dog if it kept barking. There's definitely some sort of body hidden in the garden and Marianne has so obviously got all the trappings of a gangster's moll."

"Well if they've trapped a mole," said Dolly, as she passed by, "then I'm sure that's against the law. Aren't they protected or something Babs?" I wanted to explain her mistake, that one was a rodent-like creature, with poky, little eyes which caused destruction everywhere it went, and the other was a sweet, little, furry creature, whose only crime was to make molehills in the garden, but by the time I had thought of my witty repartee, she'd swung past and was on her way to the smaller group in front.

Who Cares?

When we sat down at the little café to have a quick break I explained how Juliet had not been forthcoming with her concern and had even insinuated that I exaggerated the truth. Babs smiled.

"Perhaps you don't always see the whole picture Remi. Perhaps the old expression, can't see the wood for the trees, applies sometimes."

"No Barbara," I said. "I pride myself on how astute and observant I am, it's what I do best."

"Okay," said Barbara. "Without looking, tell me how many people were running today." I smiled, closed my eyes and counted.

"Right there was seven ladies running today," I said, opening my eyes. "Two of them had their hair tied up, one was wearing a Nike tracksuit, one was wearing pink separates and a five-bar bracelet, Hilda was wearing a *Burberry* polo-shirt and Gwen, a big, baggy T-shirt and you," I said, looking directly at Barbara's face, "are wearing *D&G* trainers to die for, Missy!" Barbara laughed and put her hands up.

"That's not bad Remi, but you did get the number of runners wrong."

"Did I?" I said, looking around the group and counting up again. She was right there were nine ladies sitting around; I must have missed two who were hanging around at the back.

"Okay, Okay, so I missed two but the clothing was pretty impressive, don't you think?"

"It really was Remi, but that's what I mean about half the picture. Just because a couple of the ladies were straggling at the back and weren't wearing designer clothes, you failed to see them, even though we were all together at the start. It's not just you Remi, we all do it." I guess she had a point about the runners but not about the *Mafia* boss and his crew, them, I was sure, I had completely right.

"And it was three you missed Remi."

"Really?" I said, rechecking the group.

"Yes, "she said, sadly. "Mary was running earlier but she's gone home now."

Who Cares?

The next day, when I let myself into Wisteria Cottage, I came upon a sight I had not expected! He was laid out on the floor, his eyes were wide open and not moving, his tongue was lolling out of his mouth. I hardly dared move, I had no idea if I was in danger or not. I scanned the area but couldn't see anyone else around – just Precious in her basket, so I took one tentative step towards the kitchen. Suddenly, he leapt from the floor and ran towards me, he was on me in a minute, licking my face and pushing his head up to my hand so I'd pat his big, old, thick, woolly head.

Now everyone knows I'm not a big dog lover, but he was gorgeous. He had a thick, brown coat and huge, brown eyes, I didn't know what breed he was, but I loved him. He followed me up the hall and waited patiently whilst I got Precious ready. His tail wagged in anticipation as he rolled over on his back, waiting for me to rub his belly. I wondered if I was supposed to take him out with Precious on our walk. I looked to where the leads were kept but there was nothing there and nothing where the treats and balls were kept.

As I passed the table I saw another memo stuck on the top. It was addressed to Marianne and it was signed by Tony. As I started to read it, I felt a cold clammy sweat form on my brow.

'Marianne, James had to go to the police station this morning, I don't know what it's about but I've gone to pick him up, can you make sure that Barty is let out into the garden to do his business, thanks Tony.'

Now…This can't be my fault entirely, can it? I may have, possibly, had something to do with it, but the police don't usually act on the ramblings of an anonymous, slightly inebriated, demented woman, calling in the middle of the night, do they? My stomach clenched and I could feel butterflies making their way up to my throat. For goodness sake, I thought, calming myself; they've probably had the man under surveillance for ages; it just needed a small prod from a law-abiding, upstanding member of society to give them the impetus they needed to make an arrest.

Hardly my fault, don't shoot the messenger and all that. The man, obviously, had something to do with the underworld; I had merely been doing my civic duty. I wouldn't lose another moment's sleep about it, I decided. I would just let Barty out into the garden to do his business and then I'd take Precious out for her walk, as normal. I felt my legs go a little weak at the knees.

"Oh my goodness, you're Barty!" I said, aloud. When he heard his name, he came running, skidding onto his back before he'd reached my feet. The old stomach cramps were returning. Not a hit-man or a lunatic, just a cuddly, friendly, big teddy bear-like woofer. Oh what have I done? I let Barty out into the garden and tried to work out a plan.

Plan A: I could go down to the police station and just explain what had happened. I'm sure they'd understand. I'd laugh as I give details of how I'd been rehearsing a play and hadn't realised that I'd accidentally hit the speed-dial button for the police station; on hearing about the misunderstanding this morning, I'd rushed immediately to clear it all up. The policeman would probably laugh as well, bringing in his colleagues, so they could all have a good chuckle. No doubt they'd say they wished they had more people like me dropping in to cheer up their day and they'd offer me a cup of tea then send me on my way, with a bit of a ticking off for wasting their time... and then they'd all laugh again and wave me off. Yep, that could work.

Or...Plan B: I could run home, pack my bags and get the next plane to Honduras, I believe that's where people run too when they're avoiding arrest, or maybe it was Honolulu. Well anyway, I could make a quick getaway and live off my savings until I could get a job, under a false name. I felt in my pocket, Three pounds, twenty six pence.... Scrub plan B.

Before I could even think of a plan C, I heard a car pulling into the drive. Why, why, why, does this sort of thing always happen to me? There was no time to bring Barty back in and besides he was far too busy trying to get to Australia via the garden route. I grabbed Precious, tucked her under my arm and ran into the little sitting-room, which was the room nearest to the front door and hid behind the sofa. I would make a run for it as soon as the coast was clear. I heard two people come in and head towards the kitchen.

"Analias," I heard James shout out. "Are you here?" I reached into my pocket and gave Precious a small chew to keep her quiet, then closed my eyes and held by breath. "She's probably taken the dog around the corner and left the van here." I heard him say again. "Don't worry, we'll find out who's responsible for this." I heard a fist slam down onto the table. "I bet it was Marianne, you're gonna have to do something about her."

I heard another, calmer voice now. "I will, I will, but in my own time, just make me a coffee, while I make a few calls."

Well, we all know what making a few calls meant but, luckily, before he could start, he must have caught sight of Barty, the canine pot-holer out of the window because both men ran out of the back door. I knew that this might be my only chance of a getting away, so I crept out of my hiding place, checked the coast was clear and tip-toed towards the door. I nearly made it but then I heard the back door open and I spun round to see James looking at me.

"Hi, you're back early, had a good walk?"

"Yes, yes, a great walk, on foot... feet," I corrected, looking at Precious. "I just took her to the local park as I've got a dentist appointment this morning. Oops," I said, looking at my watch, "I'm already running late."

He was pretty calm considering he'd just spent the morning, if not the night, in the cells. I popped Precious back into the basket and chanced a quick glimpse out of the window. Barty was running around the garden playing with someone, who I guessed must be Tony. Tony was throwing a ball and Barty was in his element running after it. Each time the ball was returned, Tony snuggled down into the dog's fur and hugged him hard. Actually it was hard to tell where one stopped and the other started, they were so similar in colouring.

"Barty's a lovely dog, what breed is he?" I said, turning back towards James. He just shrugged his shoulders.

"A big, brown one," he smirked. I looked at him in amazement and he held his hands up. "I've no idea and to be honest, I'm more interested in the dog walker, than the dog...

Have you thought any more about coming out to dinner with me?" He took a step towards me and I took a step back, straight into Precious' water bowl.

"Have you no shame?" I said, shaking out my wet foot. "What about Marianne?" His face showed no sign of remorse at all.

"What about Marianne?"

"Well, what would she think about you chatting up the dog walker in her own home?" He smiled leeringly again and side-stepping the water bowl, took another step towards me.

"I don't know what she'd think and, frankly, I don't care, it's got nothing to do with her. Anyway, this won't be her home for much longer."

I held my watch up and tapped it. "Must go," I said and side-stepping his wandering hands and made, yet another dash, to the front door.

It wasn't until I got home that night and sat down with Gran and Juliet on speaker-phone, that I realised the gravity of it all.

"He sounds like a real sleaze ball," said Juliet, angrily down the phone.

"I know," I said. "He is, and Marianne is hateful but I just feel as though this may be my fault. Not only is he chatting me up behind her back but, also, he thinks it was her that tipped-off the police, and now he's throwing her out."

"Serves her right, if you ask me. She deserves all she gets."

"You don't think I should tell him it was me that phoned the police then?"

"Definitely not," Juliet shouted down the phone. "Anyway don't forget he was going to take the knife to the dog for making a noise, who knows what he would do to you if he knew you were a grass."

Gran looked worried and I took her hand. I said my goodbyes to Juliet and snuggled down with Gran and two steaming mugs of hot chocolate.

"So what do you think I should do Gran?"

"Darling. I think you should just let sleeping dogs lie," and then added, "but, preferably next time, in their right homes!"

Eighteen

I followed Gran's advice and made sure the next day that all the dogs were delivered home to the correct addresses. Luckily there was no need for a confession as the first person I spoke to all morning was Henry.

The weather had taken a turn for the worse, so we sat huddled up in his little kitchen in front of the fire, supping on tea and digestive biscuits and trying to be heard over the snoring that was coming from Humphrey's basket. Henry was a great storyteller and painted pictures from his past with such colourful phrases and detail to names and places, that were a true testament to a life, well lived. How many times had I catalogued all old people together, mainly under the heading of lavender and peppermint? Never giving a thought to the lives they'd lived, the struggles they'd endured, the wars, the poverty and hard times. Perhaps Barbara was right when she said I only ever saw half the story.

Henry leaned back in his chair and fell into a sort of reverie as he talked about his childhood. "Me old Mam, God bless 'er," he said, looking up into my face. "She were a good woman, she worked real 'ard all 'er life. On the day I was born, me Da was down the pub, wetting me 'ead, or so he said. It was left to me elder sister, Rose to 'elp me Mam give birth. Rose tells me later that it were a real struggle and me Mam were in a lot a pain, she thought we might both die.

"The next day me Da comes home, heavy wiv the drink, shouting around, not a care for the pain me Mam had been through and 'e tells me Mam I'm to be called Arthur, after me Granddad." He stopped and looked directly at me, a twinkle in his eye. "Now me old Mam, she knew when not to rile the old bugger up but she tells our Rose quietly on the side, that I ain't

151

to be named after a drunken bully of a man like me Granddad an that she'll chose the name for this un, meaning me. At the time everyone were talking about the Titanic, which sunk on the same day I were born. Me Mam, she listened to the stories of the people who died and the ones that survived. She read the newspaper accounts and then she sees it. There were a man called Harper who had survived, and his name were Henry. Not only, she tells me later, did he escape wiv 'is life, but he also escaped wiv 'is little dog."

My eyes were wide in amazement. Could it possibly be true? We all knew the stories of the sinking of the Titanic, in which so many people died, many not making it into the life boats, women and children first and here was a man who even got his dog on board.

"Me Ma says," Henry continued, "that 'e were on one of the first life boats and at that point, people didn't really think it would sink. The women wouldn't leave without their men and the men were still drinking and playing cards. Those first few life boats pushed off with lots of room still on em. Anyway, me Ma said that Henry Harper 'ad survived a terrible death and I 'ad survived a terrible birth …So Henry it was."

I took Henry's hand and squeezed it. "I can't believe you were born in …" I thought for a moment. "Wasn't it 1912 when the Titanic sunk?"

"It were my girl, April 15th, 1912."

"You really are a survivor Henry, aren't you?" He gave me that look that started with a twinkle in his eyes and then lingered on his thinning lips.

"Do yer reckon if I were twenty years younger then, you and I would 'ave made a good couple?"

"Twenty years younger," I laughed, "and I might have fixed you up with my gran." I looked over at the old, black and white photo of Henry as a child. His blonde hair, unruly and windswept, his beautifully sculptured cheekbones and those eyes, even in this black and white photo, I could see how they must have shone. The young Henry must have been quite a catch.

I finished my tea, washed up and said my goodbyes. "It's not

Who Cares?

for long Henry, it's my first day as a care worker on my own tonight and you're on my list, so I'll see you later."

By the time I got outside it was pouring with rain. I pulled the hood up on my jacket and pulled my scarf tight round my neck. The park, where I ran with the ladies, wasn't far from Henry's, so I left my car parked outside and started running towards the park. A few of the ladies were already there when I arrived and a couple more jogged up as I caught my breath. Even with hoods tied tight around their faces it was not impossible to work out who was who. Hilda, a big fan of *Burberry* had the familiar plaid sported on her trainers. Gwen, with her big T-shirts was well padded and looked more like the *Michelin Man* than the dainty, little thing she really was. Barbara had a scarf wrapped, well and truly, around her face and looked like an extra from the *Mummy,* but still sported her *D&G* trainers.

At the back was the tallest of the runners, her auburn hair covered by a woolly hat and the hood from her jacket, topped off with a scarf wrapped round her face to keep her nose warm. Tentatively I put a hand up to wave to Mary but before she lifted her own hand in response, she checked behind, presumably to see if I was waving at someone else. She actually seemed pleased when she realised that it was, in fact, her that I had been waving to and returned my wave enthusiastically.

As I turned, I caught Barbara watching our little exchange. She smiled and nodded, perhaps appreciating that I was trying to see the whole picture for a change. Moments later we were on our way, jogging merrily round the park despite the cold wind and the persistent rain. By the time we stopped for coffee, most of us had shed some layers and sweat was the new precipitation. I grabbed some bottled water and plonked myself down next to Mary and Gwen, both of whom still had more layers on than an onion.

In front of Gwen was a big, cream bun which she was trying to shield from the other's view. She pulled small bits off at a time and I could see the pure enjoyment on her face. Mary, on the other hand, sat looking down into a black coffee, her face still covered by the brightly covered scarf. She picked up the coffee in her gloved hands and cupped it for warmth. Neither of them was in much of a conversational mood so, predictably, I felt duty-bound to break the ice.

"It's a good turnout for such a rainy day, don't you think?" I said, aiming at no one in particular. Gwen licked her fingers enthusiastically and nodded, whole-heartedly, in agreement. Mary looked round at the crowd, as if counting before agreeing.

"I'm Remi, by the way, we haven't actually been introduced but we did wave to each other the first day I joined." Mary looked over her scarf towards me, slightly bewildered until I explained that she had been sitting by the lake.

"Yes, I remember," she said, her voice muffled by the scarf.

"I had Sergeant and Humphrey with me. Humphrey didn't want to join in, so I had to take him home. Are you feeling better now, you were very upset that day?"

Mary looked away for a moment. When she looked back, she wiped away a tear and then turned her head again. I could have kicked myself for being so tactless.

"I'm sorry," I said, reaching out to touch her hand. "It's nothing to do with me, I was wrong to bring it up." As my hand touched hers the tears flowed freely down her face and she reached under her glasses to wipe them away.

"Thank you"… she paused for a moment…"Remi." She turned towards the rest of the group but carried on talking. I strained to hear her and just caught the last line. "It was a hard day for me but it was one of many and as Barbara is always telling me… take one day at a time… and that's what I'm trying to do"

"Well, Barbara is an amazing woman," I agreed. "She told me to try and see the whole picture, try and see the wood and not just the trees which, in a park with thousands of trees, is not an easy thing, I can tell you!" Mary remained quiet, her face still averted but Gwen laughed and leaned over to give me a hug.

"I'm sure you'll see that wood soon Remi, but there are all sorts of trees, perhaps it would help to know which one you are looking for." I returned Gwen's well-meant hug but couldn't help wondering if she was a little short of wood herself, like a plank, maybe! We did a few more laps and then I made my excuses explaining that tonight was my first night alone as a care worker and I had to get off and get ready. They all wished me good luck and one, possibly Barbara, even shouted out that she was proud of me, which made me feel all warm inside.

I went through the whole donning of the uniform again, which Gran had washed and starched since I last went out with Sam. I did the twirl and she gave me the thumbs up sign of approval. Nervously, I left the house and got into my car, checking I had everything. List, phone, pens, gloves and aprons were all on board. The office had said, to break me in, they were giving me an easy round to start off with. I had four tea calls and six bed calls which, on leaving, seemed like a mountain to climb.

The tea calls were actually quite pleasant, three ladies and one man, all of whom said they weren't hungry. I managed to cajole them all into eating something and each one was furnished with a cup of tea. I checked the record book to see what each of them should have done and what medication they should have.

I wrote up an account of what I'd done on each visit, signed it and, after saying my goodbyes, left, making sure they were all locked in safely. After the third visit, my knees started to stop shaking and I began to feel a little confidence creeping in. My fourth, and last, tea call was June, who was watching the television when I entered.

"Hello June, how are you today?" June glanced up from the television screen and then looked back, without answering.

"What can I get you to eat today, June?" Still there was no reply so I made my way to the kitchen and looked at what was available in the fridge. I checked the book to make sure there was no special requirement, which there wasn't. I memorised what was in the fridge and what I thought I could make in the time allotted and made my way back to inform June. June was on the phone, so I waited patiently for her to finish.

"I don't care how short-staffed you are, I don't want her here. She doesn't know what I have to eat, she hasn't made me a cup of tea and she hasn't emptied the commode, she's bloody useless and I want someone else"

Who Cares?

I felt heat of embarrassment rise in my face and the sweat from the overheated room running in the opposite direction. I'd only been here a few minutes, I hadn't even had a chance to show June what I could do and she hadn't spoken a word to me, how the hell could I have got it so wrong?

I jumped as the phone was slammed down and my own phone started to ring. I saw the name of Equality Healthcare come up and jumped into the kitchen to take the call.

"Hello Remi, did you hear all that?"

"Yes I did, but I don't understand it, she hasn't said a word to me yet. I said hello and asked her what she wanted to eat and when I came back she'd phoned you."

"Don't worry about it Remi, she's like that sometimes, just doesn't like new people, it takes her time to adjust. We should have sent someone in there with you for a few more calls. Just make her a toasted, cheese sandwich, a piece of cake and a cup of tea. Empty her commode and just try and talk to her about something, so she remembers you better next time."

"She's on my list of bed calls later, what will I do, if she doesn't want me here again?"

"She'll be alright; I'll phone her in-between and tell her that she has to accept you because there's no one else. Just read up on what you have to do on her bed call before you go, so you're prepared."

As I'd been asked, I made the toasted cheese sandwich and cup of tea and took it through to June, placing it on a small table to the side of her. I looked around and found the commode and took the bucket to the toilet. The dog walking and, in particular, the pooper scooping had put me in good stead with commode emptying!

I struggled for a good few minutes trying to put the bucket back in its position in the commode.

It occurred to me that doing a Rubik's cube might have been easier task but at last I managed to fit it back in. I had no idea what to talk to June about. Her eyes were still glued to the television and other than a snort of dissatisfaction over the cheese toasty, she hadn't said a word.

"Is this *Neighbours*?" I said, lamely

Who Cares?

"Does it look like *Neighbours*?" she returned.

"I don't know, I never watch *Neighbours* but it sounded like an Australian accent," I volleyed.

"So if it's Australian, it has to be *Neighbours* does it?" She returned my serve.

"No," I hesitated, "not necessarily but I just thought it used to be on about this time of night." Phew, only just made that one over the net.

"So, if it's Australian and it's on at this time of the night, it's got be *Neighbours*, has it?" Oh she's good... she just scraped that one off the floor and smashed it to the back line.

"Ah," I said, pointing my finger at the television. I could feel excitement rising, "I bet it's *Home and Away*." Oh yes, I'd slammed it back and reclaimed the game.

"Nope, it is *Neighbours*..." Game, set and match to June.

"Okay then June, I'll see you later for the bed call."

"I'll look forward to it," she said, looking in my direction and smiling.

Nineteen

With half an hour to spare between tea and bed calls, I drove down to the side of the lake and unwrapped the sandwiches Gran had made up for me. As I carefully undid the greaseproof paper that held them, a little note with a smiley face on it slipped out. *All things new must be treated as adventures Remi, life is all about the learning. Gran x*

I smiled, as I always smiled, but I was not surprised. All my life these little notes had accompanied everything I did. At my first ballet class there was one in my shoe. At my new school, there was one in my rucksack. Even when I'd had a tooth out at the dentist, the nurse gave me Gran's note just before they put me out. On the night that Michael had revealed he was to marry Martha, there was one on my pillow and to this day, I had no idea how she got it there.

I tucked the little note carefully inside my pocket. It would join all the others that I had collected over the years, in the shoebox under my bed. I couldn't throw them away, they were so much a part of my life and I suppose somewhere, hidden in the depths of my subconscious, I knew that if ever Gran was not around, I'd have to recycle them just to get me through.

The sandwiches were a welcome break, cheese and Branston pickle, a nice little filler to keep me marching merrily on my way. Gran had promised me her legendary sweet-chilli chicken to be ready when I returned home that evening, so feeling refreshed, I checked my list and made off to my next address. Six calls, three hours to go and with a bit of luck I should be eating chilli chicken by half-past nine.

The next two calls were fairly straightforward. Fred was eighty-two and lived on a warden-assisted complex and it appeared he had two or three ladies all vying for his attention.

He was quick to tell me that they all wittered on too much but it was also plain to see that he quite enjoyed all the fussing they administered him. When we were alone, I checked Fred's book. Medication, a cup of tea with a slice of toast and a chat was all that was needed and we conversed easily, as I made the small supper. As I left I could see one of the ladies eagerly awaiting my departure. She was a petite lady with a great figure for her age and a liberal splattering of red in her, now greying but perfectly coiffed, hair.

"Hello dear, is he alright?"

"Perfectly well," I said, hoping I hadn't broken any Equality Healthcare rules by answering.

"He can be a bit grumpy sometimes but deep down he's a lovely man," she said, blushing at her own forthrightness. "It's just so nice to have an unattached man on the complex for a change, most of them have lady friends off-site, you know. Beryl, who was here earlier, has set her sights on him, thinks he'll be husband number four." She turned to look over her shoulder and then whispered back conspiratorially, "But she doesn't know he's been sleeping with me for months," she said, touching her nose and winking.

"Really," I said, checking that I'd closed my mouth. Who would believe all this was going on this little, sleepy, pensioner's compound?

"Oh yes dear, we have an understanding, you know. I bake all his special cakes and puddings that he's very fond of and he, well he takes care of my needs," she blushed again. "If you know what I mean?" Unfortunately I did.

Quickly, I said my goodbyes and wished her a good evening, immediately wishing I'd paraphrased that differently. She smiled sweetly and as I got in my car, I saw the door of Fred's flat shut behind her. On the other side of the road I saw curtains twitching and wondered how long it would be before Beryl joined them.

Jenny was next, a beautiful lady with snow-white hair and a demeanour as sweet and innocent as a child. She thanked me profusely for every small thing I did and apologised that she couldn't do them herself at the moment. She'd suffered a fall and hurt her hip, which made movement difficult. Social Services wouldn't allow her to go home until she agreed to have home-help check on her twice a day. After assisting to wash her, I helped her out of her clothes and into her nightclothes. I tucked her up onto the sofa and made her a cup of Horlicks. Before I left, she took my hand and pulled me softly towards her. She kissed me gently on the cheek and thanked me for coming. I left with a lump in my throat and tears not far from reaching my eyes.

Next, it was June. Part of me dreaded the encounter, part of me relished the challenge but ultimately I was wearying and hoped that it would be straightforward getting her ready for bed, having a friendly chat and saying goodbye. But as Gran was often heard to say, hope is the springboard to which we fly or fall, and I was about to take a dive.

Naturally I shouted a big hello on entering and naturally she did not reply. I asked her if she was okay, to which she grunted something unintelligible and carried on watching the T.V.

"Shall I get you a Horlicks or something June?" Surprisingly, she turned and smiled at me.

"That would be nice," she answered, and then returned to her viewing. Hurray, I was making headway at last. I'd managed to do something that pleased her. I scoured through every cupboard and searched the pantry, I even riffled through the fridge but there was no Ovaltine, no Horlicks, not even an own brand, no malt or milk-based drinks anywhere. I sighed heavily and walked back to the lounge.

"You don't seem to have any June."

"No," she said, without raising her eyebrows.

"Why didn't you say?" I said, fuming but trying to keep calm and in control.

"You didn't ask if I had any, you asked if I wanted some and I do" she said. Before I said anything else, I went out to the kitchen checked what was available and checked the record book again. I returned with a cup of tea and a few biscuits on a plate and placed it next to her.

I turned to go into the bedroom to collect her night things when it occurred to me that the television was not up as high as the other night when I came with Sam. In fact, I now realised, she wasn't actually watching it at all; she was keeping her eye on me. I grabbed the nightdress and the wash things and made my way back.

"Are you ready then June?"

"Do I have a choice?"

"Of course you have a choice, If you feel you can do it yourself, I'll leave you to do it later."

"Well now you're here, you might as well do it," she said, grumpily.

I thought back to what I'd read in the record book. It stated that June was to be taken through to the bathroom to wash her hands and face, something I knew Sam hadn't done and I also knew why; June would miss her beloved television.

"Shall I take you through to the bathroom to get you washed, June?" A look of horror showed on her face.

"Why would you do that? All the other girls wash me here."

"Sorry June, it says in the book to take you through… but if you'd rather, I suppose," I hesitated, "I could do it here." She looked at me for a moment. There was a glint in her eyes but not on her mouth.

"Yes," she said, eventually. "I would rather it be done here. Thank you." Oh yes, oh yes, game, set and match to Miss Hall-Smyth! I stood well back to the back of June and did my little victory dance… it felt good.

"I can see you dancing." Damn! When will I learn that people can see reflected images in glass?

"Sorry," I said, realising that I was probably going to be reported on my first day. But when I looked over towards the T.V screen, the only image I could see… was June smiling!

Lovely Henry was my next port of call and although I was running late, he convinced me to stop and have a cup of tea with him. It was already nine o'clock and I still had two more calls to do after him but this was one person I definitely could not, and would not, short change. I guess Henry was one of the only stable men in my life at the moment.

Gramps had been unbelievably special but he had been gone

a long time. I hadn't seen my dad since I was nine, after the night of the *South Pacific* escapade. Michael – well, who knew what Michael was all about? He wasn't my concern now, he belonged to another woman.

Even Norman, lovely, gorgeous Norman, even he had forgotten me.

It surprised me that I'd come to think of him as gorgeous and lovely. When we were friends at school, it had always been a bit difficult, what with the three of us always being together and yet, if I'm honest, there were lots of occasions when our hands touched accidentally, or our eyes met over our sandwiches. Times when I dreamt he might lean over one day and kiss me. I'd even wondered what those kisses might have been like but, somehow, I knew that they would've been gentle, passionate and deep whilst beautifully sweet and loving because that was what Norman was like.

The sudden silence made me realise that Henry had stopped talking to me and was watching me.

"So, what do yer think?" he said, looking at me enquiringly. He was holding out a shirt and I had to surmise that he was asking an opinion on it.

"It's great Henry."

"Really? Oh that's wonderful darlin', you've made me day." He shook his head from side to side and tears welled in his beautiful, blue eyes. Oh dear, I had a feeling, that maybe, I'd missed something!

It turned out that Henry had been invited to a British Legion event where they were honouring some of the old local soldiers who'd been involved in various conflicts.

Apparently, Henry was a bit of a hero and I'd just agreed to be his escort for the night. I asked for the date and wrote it down in my pocket book, I'd have to make sure that I wasn't working that night. Well, after all, I hadn't had a date for a while, who knows this might be the making of me!

From Henry I moved onto Dulcie, who was on fine form. She made me recite lines from *Romeo and Juliet*, as I attempted to wash and undress her. "Put more heart into it, darling, you're supposed to be talking about the man you love," she shouted, as she pushed me away to do up the little silk-covered buttons on her dressing gown or her *robe-de-chambre*, as she called it. She looked up and started to act out the line herself. "What's in a name? That which we call a rose by any other name would smell as sweet." I leaned down and pulled off her socks and she hit me squarely on the head.

"Remi, have you never been in love, do you have no romance in your soul? Where's the passion in young people today? By your age I'd been proposed to three times and refused them all," she said, with a flourish.

"Why did you refuse them Dulcie?" I said, half-heartedly. I was, regrettably, thinking more of my stomach at this point than my heart. It was rumbling and I could practically smell Gran's chicken, which was making my mouth salivate.

"I refused them, darling, because none of them," she repeated it again for emphasis, "not one of them was the love of my life. I knew he was out there somewhere, and I was prepared to wait."

I laid her clothes in a pile by her bed and looked at her again. "And did he come along?" She gave a huge sigh and then looked at me. Her eyes flashed with a defiance and radiance that cut through the years that lined her face. She beamed and her smile transformed her. I could almost see the young woman she'd once been.

"Oh yes, darling, he came and with that first kiss he changed me from a girl into a woman; he showed me how to love and how to be loved. His love was so great and so powerful, it carried me through nearly seven decades." She put her hands together as if praying and a single tear rolled down her face onto them. "He was the one, he is the one and he will always be the one," she said. "We may only have had a short time together, but it was enough to keep me loved for a whole lifetime."

I was beginning to get cramp in my foot but I was too frightened to move and break the spell; I wanted to know who this great love had been, what had happened to them and where he was now? But the moment was gone and Dulcie was reciting Shakespeare again, only this time, it was *Macbeth* and that damned spot.

Dulcie asked to be put into bed but as I left, I worried that I'd stirred up memories that would leave her sad and lonely during the long night. As I opened the door, she shouted behind me to be here at nine in the morning, sharp, for rehearsals, so I sort of guessed she'd probably be okay.

Only one last call but, unfortunately, the bad weather had made the sky an inky-black and a fog was starting to descend. Although I was fairly sure where Green Road was, actually getting onto the estate where Mrs Bretherwitz lived turned out to be a nightmare. It was a full half-hour before I actually stepped through the door and my slightly dishevelled state was not lost on her.

"You're late," she said, looking at her watch. Then looking back up at me she continued, "And you're dripping all over my carpet."

"I'm really sorry Mrs..." I tried to look down at my sheet, desperate to recall her name.

"Well move backwards, you're making a puddle." I wasn't of course, my hair was dripping a bit and my shoes were a bit damp but I'd given them a good wipe before coming into the front room.

"I'm really sorry I'm late, I couldn't find the address in the dark and then it started to rain again and then to top it off I had to walk right around the block because they've closed the road off, due to a burst water pipe." I looked back down again at the sheet again but still nothing.

"Moaner," she shouted out. That was it! I was wet, tired and suffering from every emotion possible but I didn't have to take that.

"I can assure you that I am not giving to moaning about anything, Mrs," I gave the sheet one last look and hey presto, "Mrs Bretherwitz," I blurted out. "But this has been my first night and I have been working for eight hours solid without a break and trying to do my very best for everyone I have visited." She didn't say a word she just looked at me. Okay, I think I handled that quite well, I hadn't been rude and she was waiting for me to say something so... "So Mrs Bretherwitz, my name is Remi, what would you like me to call you?"

"I told you once... Mona."

Who Cares?

I arrived home at nearly twelve midnight and Gran was waiting, worriedly, by the door. As I sat down in the chair she handed me a mug of hot chocolate and started to undo my shoes. I mumbled something about not being able to eat and she guided me up the stairs and into my room. Somehow I managed to undress and get into bed.

The last thing I remembered was Gran kissing me on the forehead and tip-toeing out the door.

The last thing that is, until my mobile phone rang in the middle of the night. The clock was saying two-thirty-five and I fumbled with the phone until I managed to get it to my ear.

"Who the hell is this?" I said.

"Remi, it's me, Michael. I'm sorry it's so late but... I think I've made a terrible mistake!"

Twenty

Well, there's nothing like an ex-boyfriend who forgot to tell you that he was running away to get married, before he dumped you publicly in front of millions of people, ringing in the middle of the night to tell you that he's made a huge mistake and that he now realises that he loves you after all, to wake you up and then keep you tossing and turning for hours.

So when, eventually, I did fall asleep again at about eight-twenty-nine, the alarm, oblivious to the fact that I'd been awake all night, went off merrily at eight-thirty. My eyes felt as though they'd been super-glued together. In fact, if Balenciaga made handbags in skin tone, it would've looked like I had a matching pair under my eyes. I grappled around on the floor hoping that something to wear would come to hand, which might explain why I arrived downstairs in black leggings, a baggy, brown T-shirt and a blue cardigan. I may even have got away with, if I'd remembered to take my pyjamas off first!

Gran ran me a bath, picked up my mismatched tangle of clothes and came back downstairs again with a suitable ensemble for taking the dogs out for a walk. She made me eat breakfast and sat with me for a few moments, while I pushed an egg round the plate.

"What's wrong, Remi?" I didn't answer. I knew if I did, it would all pour out and I needed to keep it to myself for a while. I knew Gran, Juliet and Penny would be furious that I'd even given him a chance to explain, let alone agree to go out to dinner with him. Gran wasn't giving up though.

"A thought aired, is a thought spared," she said, in her all knowing way. I looked up at her, unable to work out if she was just a wealth of phrases and sayings or whether she just made them up as she went along.

Who Cares?

"I'm fine, just a bit tired that's all. I'll get over it once I get out walking with the dogs." Lying to Gran was as bad as it got and I knew it, but the last thing I wanted this morning was one of her disapproving looks; I needed to have some time to work this out.

I was a bit late picking up the van and Lucy was waiting with the keys in her hand. "Hi, sorry I'm a bit late; it's been a bit hectic the last few days."

"That's okay, Penny said you'd got a new job. I was half expecting you not to turn up at all," she said, looking worriedly at me.

"Lucy," I said, grabbing hold of her hand, "I won't let you down, I said I'd do the job until you were on your feet again and I meant it. If it all gets too much, I'll have to cut down on something else."

Lucy was visibly relieved as she handed over the keys and it gave me a chance to ask about *El Mafioso* at Wisteria Cottage.

"What do you know about the people who own Precious, Lucy? They seem a bit of an odd bunch."

"Do they?" Lucy looked a bit surprised. "They seemed okay to me. She's a bit stuck-up but the guy, James I think it is, was lovely." She reddened slightly, checked behind and looked at me again. "I mean, REALLY lovely…"

"What, James?" I said, incredulous that Lucy would even look twice at someone like him. He wasn't that good looking, even though he obviously thought he was, and when it came to sleaze balls, he was world class.

"Perhaps that's where you're going wrong Remi, how can you not think he's gorgeous? Those gorgeous, sexy eyes, that hair, a body to die for and so unassuming and charming! He's what we like to call, on our girl's night out, the whole package!"

I just couldn't get my head round it. I mean, Roger, Lucy's husband, wasn't my type but I could appreciate that he was good looking and quite a catch, in a sort of, lots of money, slightly rugged, control freak, type of way, but James? No, not getting that one at all.

"Perhaps, it's the job thing," said Lucy, still dreaming.

"What, *Mafia* boss?" Surely Lucy wasn't attracted to the

powerful, dangerous type; she hardly fitted the definition of gangster's moll.

"Remi, whatever are you talking about? He's a doctor at Great Ormond Street Hospital."

I couldn't help but laugh.

"Is that what he told you?" I said. "You couldn't be further from the truth, Lucy. I honestly believe the man murders people for a living, I even heard him say as much."

I desperately wanted to go on and tell Lucy the whole story but she had collapsed into fits of laughing, tears were streaming down her face and she was bent double.

"Remi, you're such a scream, Penny said you were funny but I never believed you were this funny and so dry, you don't even crack a smile." She waved goodbye and headed back to the house, still laughing and wiping away tears.

I sat for a few moments, before pulling away. There was no way James was a doctor. That was one thing I would have recognised straight away. Hadn't I, after all, nearly become a doctor's assistant or a receptionist thingy? No, he was just much cleverer than I'd given him credit for. He had smooth-talked Lucy into believing he was an upstanding member of the community and the worst thing was, he had used the disguise of a doctor! It was unforgivable; there must be someone to report him too!

Despite Juliet's attitude last time I spoke to her about James, I decided to give her another go, while I made my way over there.

"So what do you think, don't you think it's terrible that he passed himself off as a doctor? Do you think I should report him?"

"Perhaps you should Remi. It's a very serious matter. I think I may have a listing on the internet of someone you could complain too." I thought for a moment that I heard her laugh but then she coughed and I figured it must have been that. "Yep, here it is," she said. "The HAU are the people you need to report it to."

"Oh that's great Juliet, is that some sort of Hospital Association or something?" There was a short pause and I could hear suppressed laughter before she said.

"No, it's 'Hoods are Us.' "

She was still laughing when I lost the signal and I definitely wasn't in the mood to talk to her after that. They could all laugh now but they wouldn't be laughing when my dead body was found, limp and bloated, after being cut up and thrown in the River Thames, would they?

My worst fears were realised when I got to the door of Wisteria Cottage. Inside I could hear blood-curdling screams. It sounded like Marianne and she was distraught.

"Get off... you bastard," I heard her shout. Things were being smashed, furniture was being overturned and her screams were changing to cries of panic. I charged through the door, looking for something to hit him with as I went. I picked up a *Jimmy Choo* which lay by the door as it had a four inch stiletto heel. It would do the job. Nice guy, Doctor at Great Ormond Street, my foot, I thought.

As I barged through the half-closed door of the sitting-room, the sight stopped me dead in my tracks. Marianne was still screaming, except now she was screaming at me to help her.

On the sofa, feet propped up on the arm rest... was Precious. Also on the sofa, propped up tightly behind Precious...was Barty. Marianne was behind the pair of them hitting Barty with all her might. The dogs were locked together and poor Precious' back legs were suspended high in the air, unable to touch down. She was struggling to get away whilst Barty was just looking around, completely dumfounded, ducking his head each time Marianne made contact with him.

"Don't just stand there, do something," she screamed at me, but all I could do was just shrug my shoulders. What the hell does someone do in a situation like that? "Get some water," she yelled again, smashing Barty over the head with a vase.

I dashed as fast as I could out into the kitchen and filled up a pot full of water. I ran back and threw it as hard as I could over the dogs. Unfortunately, I never was any good at sports and most of it was directed at Marianne's shocked face, but it must have done something because all of a sudden Precious was jumping off the end of the sofa, tail between her legs and Barty was on his back in a submissive pose.

It made no difference to Marianne who was now on the sofa, soaking wet and hitting Barty for all she was worth. I tried to pull her off and then she started on me too. Just then Precious made an appearance, shivering and frightened, at the door and Marianne suddenly turned and ran towards her.

"Poor, poor baby, what has that monster done to you?" she said, blubbering and sniffling all over Precious. Precious whined and shivered uncontrollably and Marianne was too stupid to see that it was because of her and her reaction, not what Barty had done. "Get that dog out of here now." she screamed. "Get him out or I'll have him put down."

I didn't know which way to move or what to do, so I stayed grounded where I was. She moved her face close up towards me. "Do you hear me?" she snarled. "Get him out or, I swear to God, I will have him destroyed this afternoon."

I wanted to ask if she should talk to James about it first but I was too frightened that she would carry out her threat and have poor Barty put down, so I grabbed him by the collar and dragged him towards the door.

Barty, totally forgetting that he'd ever been in disgrace, saw this as a great, new game and jumped around ahead of me, tail wagging nineteen to the dozen. When I opened the front door of the van to grab a cloth, he leapt into the passenger seat and sat there looking straight ahead. No amount of pulling him was going to shift him from this prime position. He sat his ground and I had to accept that he was there for the duration, or at least until we got to Lord's house.

I hadn't asked Marianne about taking Precious with us; I reckoned there'd probably been too much trauma for one day, and anyway, Marianne was already on the phone to the vet as I left, asking for the morning-after pill for Precious. I ruffled Barty's thick, old head, while he stared proudly in front.

"For what it's worth Barty, I think you would have produced beautiful babies, even with a little rat, like Precious." He gave me a quick sideways glance as if to say thanks, and then stared rigidly out the front window again.

Who Cares?

We made our way to Lord's house, stopping only briefly to pick up a collar and lead from the pet shop on our way. Barty had the most wonderful time in the park with Lord. The pair of them ran round like loonies, enjoying every plant, tree, puddle and dog. As they were both on leads, I had a pretty good run myself. At the end of it they both collapsed in the van. This time Barty put up no objection to jumping in the back with Lord although, for my part, I kind of missed him.

It was a similar experience out with Sergeant and Humphrey. Luckily, there was an area in the park which was totally enclosed, so I slipped them off their leads and let them run loose. Humphrey and I both looked on from a seated position; neither of us having enough energy to join them. Barty was completely spent, in more ways than one. After his run with Sergeant he only just made the jump back into the van. By the time I'd dropped Sergeant off and made my way back to Henry's, he was snoring soundly in the back.

I made Henry a cup of tea and cut him off a slice of cake I'd brought with me, it was a heavy, ginger cake with a sticky topping which I knew he was very partial to. I told him all about the Precious and Barty situation and he nearly fell off his chair laughing. By the time I got to the water over Marianne part, he could hardly breathe.

"Darlin', why does it always happen to you?" he said, reaching out for his cake.

"I have no idea Henry, I don't look for it, you know, it just finds me." Henry munched happily on his cake and I thought about my other dilemma, phone calls in the middle of the night were hardly the norm either. I really wanted to speak to someone about it but Henry looked tired and he didn't need me burdening him with any more of my woes. No, I needed some sympathetic souls who were fond of a bit of gossip and always up for giving advice, so I said my goodbyes and made my way off to meet the ladies.

Barty was wide awake by the time I got back to the park and ready for a new adventure, so I picked up his lead, let him out and we jogged off to the lake. It was a nice day and the ladies were out in full strength, all warming up on the spot before the run began. They all made a fuss of Barty, who wallowed in all the attention, laying on his back at every given chance. The dog was an out and out hussy.

As we started the run I found myself in the company of Gwen and Dolly, who were on fine form, chatting merrily about dieting and the clothes they were going to buy.

"Are you ladies off somewhere special then?"

"We are," they shouted in unison. "We've been invited to a very prestigious charity ball and it's only a few weeks away," continued Dolly.

"We need to lose a few pounds before then," said Gwen, already looking wistfully over towards the café where we would be stopping later and where she normally partook of a big, cream cake.

"Speak for yourself," retorted Dolly. "I'm quite happy with the way I am, I won't be losing weight just to impress a few men."

I couldn't help but laugh. It didn't seem to matter what age we were, it was always about impressing the men, no matter what Dolly might say. As they chatted on about what they were going to wear and how they were going to get there, they started to slow up and I found myself catching up with Barbara, who was exactly who I wanted to speak to.

As I gained on Barbara, her companions dispersed and I was pleased to see we would be alone. After exchanging polite conversation for a few moments, I was just about to tell her all about my night-time call, when I saw Mary making pace on us. Childishly, I felt disappointed that I couldn't get Barbara alone. It wasn't that I didn't like Mary, I didn't really know her, but she had problems of her own and if anyone could give me the answer I was looking for, it would be Barbara, who'd gone through a similar thing herself.

Selfishly, I stepped up the pace a little and Barbara kept up with me. Mary, perhaps realising what I'd done, kept a few steps behind us. Of course I felt bad that I'd excluded her like that but I desperately needed to speak to someone and who else did I have?

"I need some advice Barbara," I said, slowing up a little

because it wasn't easy to speak jogging along at such a rate. "Do you remember I told you about Michael, the guy I used to go out with?"

"The one who told everyone he was going to marry someone else on national television, without having the decency to tell you first?" she replied.

"Err yes," I mumbled. It wasn't quite the answer I'd been expecting but I carried on "Well he phoned me last night, to say that he'd made a terrible mistake and that he was really sorry and that it was me he loved all along."

"I hope you gave him short shrift," she said, without even turning her head.

"Well, to be honest, I didn't. It was the early hours of the morning and for a while I didn't even know what was going on, then when he started to explain it all, I sort of felt sorry for him. I mean, you said it yourself Barbara, everyone deserves a second chance, don't they?"

"Well perhaps I should have said *most* people deserve a second chance, Remi. People who are genuinely good people but have made a mistake, or people who, through difficult circumstance, have chosen the wrong path or even people who just weren't brave enough to stand up to their own problems." I guessed she was talking about her own husband who hadn't been able to face the thought of being without Barbara when she was diagnosed with cancer. Mary drew level with us and I decided to hold-fire and catch Barbara again a bit later on.

"Have you spoken to your gran about this Remi, or your friends?" Barbara continued, despite the fact that we were no longer alone.

"Not yet, Gran would only be worried and I didn't want to put her through that again, until I know where I stood with it all."

"Perhaps you were hoping that, given my own situation, I'd tell you that you had done the right thing. Maybe you weren't looking for advice at all," she said, looking at me for a moment. "Perhaps, just someone to agree with what you already think."

Okay, this wasn't going quite like I thought it would, but she did have a point, maybe I didn't really want advice, just someone to talk to about it.

"What do you think Mary, should Remi go back to a man who publicly humiliated her on national television or should she look for someone who would love her properly, like she deserves?"

Mary must have heard the question but she didn't answer, in fact she even started to speed up and soon pulled ahead of us. "I think I may have upset her earlier," I said. "When I pulled away from her to try and catch you on your own."

Barbara was beginning to look a bit strained, probably from the running but as we carried on she leaned over and took my hand. "I don't think Mary's angry in the least, it's not in her nature but one thing is for sure, no one could give you better advice about your situation than her." Before she could say anymore Gwen and Dolly pulled up beside us, still chatting merrily about their charity ball.

When it was obvious that they were there for the duration, I mouthed my thanks to Barbara and decided to step up the pace once more. What could it hurt, after all, to ask Mary for some advice, but as I rounded the corner I saw Mary speeding off ahead and finally paring off in another direction out of the park. Obviously, Barbara thought a lot of her but she was a little too anomalous for my liking, always making dramatic exits and such like. No, I thought, like it or lump it, this was my problem and a decision I'd have to make on my own but if I was truthful, hadn't I already made it?

On the way home I phoned ahead to let Gran know I was bringing someone home with me. She flustered a bit about what they were going to eat but I told her it was all in hand. I stopped at the pet shop again and took advice about what to get this giant of a dog to eat, if only advice for me flowed as easy!

As we pulled up outside I tried to explain to Barty that it might be a bumpy ride, neither Gran nor I had much time for animals and a dog the size of a small cow would come as a shock to most people. The plan was to tippy-toe in and when Barty was sitting quietly I would explain the whole story. That was the plan... but in reality?

I opened the door, Barty smelt food. He pulled the lead out of my hand and thundered through to the kitchen. The next thing I heard was Gran shouting for help.

I sat her down with a nice cup of tea and told her the whole story of that morning's events, occasionally we both looked at Barty, which he took as a signal to come over and cover us in wet kisses.

"The thing is Gran, Marianne is a hateful cow, she would have carried out her threat to have Barty put down, I know she would. What else I could I do?"

"Couldn't you take him to a rescue centre?" she said, quietly, so Barty wouldn't hear.

I knew she was right, I could and perhaps I should've but something inside was stopping me. I really liked Barty, even on that first day; his big, woolly head and deep-brown eyes were just adorable and taking him to a shelter seemed wrong, somehow.

"Gran, I promise I'll sort something out. The chances are she'll be asking for him back tomorrow but while he's here I'll make sure he keeps out of your way." Gran nodded and Barty plonked his huge head into her lap and, reluctantly, she gave it a little ruffle. We sat for a little while watching the television together; Barty's head still on Gran's lap and her little fingers weaving in and out of his fur. When I turned around, they were both asleep.

Twenty-one

The next day was a real dilemma, should I take Barty with me and risk Marianne's vengeance or should I leave him at home and risk upsetting Gran? In the end it was Gran who made the decision for me.

"Leave him with me, if I have any problems I'll give you a call."

"Are you sure Gran, I feel terrible lumbering him with you but if it all goes okay today with Marianne, then in future," I checked myself, remembering that I was supposed to take him to the shelter or something, "or until I've sorted him out a new home, I'll take him with me." In the rear-view mirror I saw them both standing in the doorway, Gran waving, Barty, tail wagging.

As I pulled up outside Precious' house, Marianne was waiting for me as I had feared. Damn I knew I should have brought him back with me. She was standing by the front door with Precious enfolded in her arms. She made no effort to come towards me. As I approached, ready to explain why I hadn't brought Barty back, she extended her arms and handed over Precious, her ball and lead, and walked in without a word. I don't know what I was expecting but it certainly wasn't that, she hadn't even asked after Barty.

I collected Lord, as usual, and we went for our walk. It was surprisingly boring without Barty. He had only come the once but what a hole he'd left, the only consolation being that he would be there when I got home.

Once again when I got to Precious' house, Marianne was at the door before I could even knock.

"Good walk?" she said, not waiting for an answer and before I could say anything the door was closed in my face.

"Yeah, a great walk. How lovely of you to ask!" I said out

loud, as I walked back to the van. Exchanging pleasantries with Marianne was what made the day that bit sweeter....*Not.*

I stopped for my usual tea and biscuits with Henry after I'd walked the dogs and, despite my knock back with Barbara, I told him all about Michael and the phone call.

"Sounds like a rum 'en to me, girl," he said, in his usual, no holds-barred, way.

"But if he's made a mistake Henry, doesn't he deserve a chance to explain it to me?"

"Some sort a mistake, darlin', not telling you he was seeing someone else, then marrying her without letting you know and worst of all, letting you find out the way you did. They ain't mistakes, darlin', they're down-right lies, and the bugger needs stringing up."

Henry had old-fashioned standards and no amount of talking or explaining it to him would make him see the situation differently. So I nodded in all the right places, said goodbye and decided to try Juliet. I couldn't go home and call her so I pulled over into a side-road and phoned her on my mobile.

"Are you crazy? Have you taken leave of your senses? Take a reality check Remi, the man's a complete 'batard'. You know that, I know that, Gran knows that, the whole damn world probably knows that. Why ever would you even consider meeting up with him? Why didn't you just tell him to explain his mistake to his wife who, incidentally, was probably in the next room?"

"So you don't think I should meet up with him just to let him say sorry and explain?"

"I don't think you should meet up with him if he was offering you a free trip of a lifetime, all expenses paid and a makeover thrown in for good measure. The man is a sleaze ball, keep away from him Remi, please," she added, imploringly.

I told her I wouldn't do anything irrational, then we talked for a few minutes about her coming to London for the weekend soon and said goodbye. I sat for a while pondering over what Juliet had said. Perhaps it was just that we had grown apart, our ideas that had been so similar, were now stratospheres apart. After all, wasn't I the one that had been hurt by all of this? Yet I was prepared to listen to what he had to say. Didn't I deserve another chance at happiness? I began to feel angry at Juliet's short sightedness, angry at all the people who couldn't see that this was the best thing to happen to me.

My eyes filled with tears and, as I looked out of the window, I blinked them away. I felt so alone. There was no one who really understood me, or how miserable I felt. Other than Gran, who did I really have? Was it so wrong of me to grab at this little chance of happiness? Through the misty haze of tears and condensation running down the inside of the car, I could see someone I recognised coming out from one of the small mews-type houses opposite.

It was Mary. She had on a lovely, navy-blue, jogging suit, a matching padded jacket and a jumper, tied around her waist. As she closed the door behind her she adjusted her hat and scarf, pulling tendrils of auburn hair around her face. As she made her way up the garden path, she stopped for a moment; she looked out into the distance then turned and made her way back towards the house. With only a fraction of hesitation, she opened it and went in. I sat for a few moments more and looked at my watch. It was coming up to two o'clock, the ladies would already be meeting at the park, was Mary going to go or not?

Before I had a chance to decide whether I should knock and offer her a lift, my mobile rang. I assumed it was Juliet ringing back to apologise. Having had time to think about it, she probably realised that I was right all along. It came as a bit of a surprise then, when I answered and heard Gran's voice, high pitched and irate, at the other end of the phone.

"Gran, you keep breaking up, speak slowly."

"Barty," I heard her say, and then it crackled again. "Trouble." The crackling continued, "Police." I heard enough.

"Gran, don't call the police, I'll come home straight away, please don't call the police, I'll take him to Battersea Dog's Home tonight, I promise."

It was too late, the line had gone dead. I threw the phone into my bag and dashed off, as fast as I could, to take the van back to Lucy and pick up my car. When I had time, Lucy and I would often stop and have a natter but, on this occasion, I just shouted that I'd got an emergency at home, jumped into my own car and sped off down the road.

As I pulled up outside Gran's house, I realised I was too late. Damn, I should have come straight here and returned the van later. It was a strange, but true, fact that every male that came into my life left sooner, rather than later and Barty, it appeared, would be no exception. The door was open and with a heavy heart, I walked in. I was greeted by a policeman, who was far too young to be confiscating dogs, and a police woman who was too beautiful to be in the house at all.

"Is that you, Remi?" I heard Gran call out. The police woman confirmed that it was and I made my way through to the lounge where she was sitting. Okay …slight surprise to see Barty not only still here, but sitting tucked up on the sofa, head tightly ensconced in Gran's lap. When he saw me he jumped off the sofa and ran towards me, nearly knocking me flying. I grabbed hold of his big woolly head and looked into his deep-brown eyes. A tear fell from my own eye and as it hit my hand, so Barty licked it off.

"Oh Remi, what a day, I don't know where to start," said Gran, getting up and coming towards me.

"Okay Gran, well I'm home now," I said, grabbing hold of Barty's collar. "I can take care of him now." I turned to the policeman who was standing behind me. "I'm sorry that you've had to come out but I can assure you that it'll never happen again."

"I should hope not," said the policeman, putting his hat back on his head. He didn't have to say what he was thinking, I could see it in his face. Boy was he annoyed!

"A poor pensioner like this, it makes me really mad." Hold on there, that's a bit steep, I thought, she's hardly your average, old-age pensioner: this tap-dancing, synchronise-swimming, lime-light grabbing, tornado of a woman. How dare he take such an upper-hand with me when he didn't know all the facts?

"If it hadn't been for the dog," he said, looking over at Gran again.

"Yes, yes, I know, like I said, it'll never happen again. I'm taking him too Battersea Dog's Home tonight, I've already rung them to make sure they can take him in."

Gran's hands flew up to her face and the policeman looked as though I'd just said I eat little children for dinner.

"Remi," Gran shouted, grabbing Barty's collar out of my hand. "You'll do no such thing!"

"But Gran, how can he stay when he's caused all this trouble? I thought that's what you wanted me to do." Barty suddenly worried about all the shouting stood his ground and started barking.

"See what you've done now, you've upset him," said Gran, getting down on all fours and cuddling up to him

"Okay Gran. Obviously, I must be missing something here. Did you ring to tell me that Barty had caused lots of trouble and that you were calling the police?" They all looked at each other as if I'd escaped from the local mental institution.

"No, I rang to say there had been some trouble and that Barty had saved the day, and the police were on their way." The policewoman, realising what had happened, sat me down and helped Gran to her feet.

"Miss Hall-Smyth, the problem has not been with the dog at all." She looked down at her note book. "Today at about twelve-noon, two gentlemen called at the house saying they were from the Water Board. As you may know we've had problems with the water in the area so it was not unfeasible that agents from the Water Board would call." I nodded; remembering that not too far from here, outside Mona's house, the road was up because of a water leak.

"Your gran followed the correct procedure. She saw no Water Board van outside so she asked to see their identification, which they showed her.

"These were not amateurs Miss Hall-Smyth. They have pulled off a string of similar offences over the last two days. Unfortunately, by the time reports started coming in we had no time to get warnings out to the residents we thought might be in danger. It seems their intended victims were elderly people, living alone, in good neighbourhoods."

I looked over at Gran, who at this moment looked nothing like a victim, more like Emily Pankhurst on a protest day.

Who Cares?

"Anyway, after letting them in, they started to check the water pipes, both upstairs and down. Your gran, not thinking anything was amiss was busy in the kitchen... the one place they did not bother to look!" Gran did have the decency to look a bit embarrassed, let's face it; most of the water pipes were in the kitchen! "Anyway, they explained that everything had been checked and no problems had been found. They apologised for disturbing her and went to leave."

This was where Gran jumped in with the rest of the story.

"You wouldn't believe it Remi; I had no idea that anything was wrong. They hadn't been here very long; they didn't make any noise or mess, so I thanked them and went to show them out.

"When I turned round Barty was standing there with his teeth showing, growling quietly under his breath. I was petrified. At first, I thought he was growling at me.

"The workmen started to get nervous and asked me to put the dog away which, of course, I couldn't – I was just as frightened as they were.

"Barty started walking forward which, in turn, made us all walk backwards. Then," she said, looking indignant, "they called me 'Old Woman'. Remi, can you believe that? They said put the dog away 'Old Woman', or else someone will get hurt! That's when it struck me that the Water Board would never hire people who called valued customers 'Old Woman'.

"But as I turned back to look at them, Barty nipped past me and started growling even more. Now Barty and I were on one side and the men were pinned up against this wall." She pointed to the wall and Barty wagged his tail in agreement.

"That's when I knew that this was serious and that those men were not nice." Gran turned her back to the police and mouthed to me, "Real 'batards'." She turned back to her audience, "So I grabbed the phone and called the police," she said, proudly.

I waited for her to continue but she looked to the policewoman to carry on. "We had a patrol car in the area and as we'd had so many reports about these guys, we came straight away."

"They were here in minutes," Gran said, excitedly. "I let

them in!"

"When we came in, Barty here pulled back and we took over. The satchel they were carrying, supposedly full of tools, was filled with jewellery, money, documents, not just from your gran's house, but from a few other jobs they'd done previously."

I looked over at Gran, who put her hand into her cardigan pocket and pulled out a gold watch, tears filled her eyes.

"It was Gramp's watch; they took it Remi, can you believe it? Thank goodness for Barty."

Barty, recognising praise when he heard it, nuzzled his head under her arm and she kissed him on the head.

Half an hour later we were sitting alone, with just Barty the hero, for company.

"You're always saying that fate fights against you Remi but if things hadn't transpired the way they did yesterday and you hadn't come home with Barty, who knows where we would be now? I may even have realised that something was wrong and tackled them about it."

"Don't even say that Gran," I said, reaching for her hand. "Thank goodness he was here and thank goodness you're alright."

As the excitement started to die down, Gran started to get tired and before I left for work she was asleep on the sofa. I looked at Barty tucked up by her feet and knew that she would be okay.

Perhaps Gran was right though. Perhaps fate had a plan and I should just sit back and wait for it all to happen. Let's face it, who would ever imagine, after everything that had transpired, that Michael would come back into my life? Maybe, just maybe, fate had a plan for me after all.

Twenty-two

It was a busy night but I didn't care, the only thing I could think about was the following day and my date with Michael. Tea calls were fine, no particular problems. June and I played a round or two, naturally June won hands down, which pleased her immensely. Dulcie gave me lessons on deportment and explained how important it was that people saw me dressed and standing correctly at all times.

When I arrived at Fred's it was to catch him in flagrante with Beryl, in the bedroom with the door wide open, which I can tell you was not a pleasant sight. Fred, for his part, did have the decency to look shocked and embarrassed, whereas Beryl seemed positively ecstatic to have been in caught in the act.

"Oh pet you mustn't mind us," she said, pulling a wrap around herself and adjusting her hair. "It's so hard to find time for ourselves lately, without people popping in all the time." She checked herself when she realised I was about to say something. "Not you, of course, although you are a little early this evening," she said, looking down at her watch as she picked it up from the dressing table. She came out into the sitting-room, closing the bedroom door behind her and, in a conspiratorial fashion, ushered me over towards the window. "It's Mavis, you see. She comes over here all the time, interfering and trying to do jobs for Fred and he's just too polite to send her on her way."

"Is Mavis the lady with the red hair?" I asked, knowing it must be the lady I ran into last time I left Fred's house

"Well, we called it ginger in my day, pet," she said, her hand going up instinctively to her own hair as she spoke. "Most of it comes out of a bottle nowadays anyway," she said, pulling the curtain to one side to look back down the street. "She can't have that much real colour left, she's older than me, you know."

Who Cares?

"Really" I said with, perhaps, a little too much surprise in my voice. "That is, I would have guessed you were about the same," I said, desperately trying to backtrack a little.

"Good gracious no," said Beryl, throwing the curtain back and checking that Fred hadn't come into the room. "She's at least two years older than me. Perhaps you haven't looked at her close up."

At that moment the door to the bedroom opened and the rather sheepish Fred stepped out, supported by his Zimmer frame. I offered to make him a sandwich and a cup of tea but Beryl was having none of it, practically shooing me out and making it quite clear that she was more than capable of seeing to all Fred's needs. I stood on the doorstep and looked back.

"Capable?" I said out loud. "We called it downright bossy in my day, pet." As I turned, it was to see the tear-stained face of Mavis, smiling sadly.

"She's got her hooks in him good and proper, hasn't she?" A small tear fell down her pretty face. "I thought we had something good between us," she said, as she wiped the tear away with a delicate, little, embroidered hanky which she pulled from her sleeve. "He's the first one." She looked up at me, her face a deep shade of pink. "You know, since my husband passed away ten years ago. He gave me something to look forward to, a reason to get up in the morning but now I dread getting up. I hate walking past here or talking to the other residents. Beryl's made no bones about what they get up to and everyone is talking about it." She sniffed again and I reached out and put my arm around her.

I wanted to say that he couldn't possibly prefer the domineering, viper-tongued Beryl over her, but what did I know about what men wanted? My relationship with Michael hardly made me Agony Aunt of the year and I guess I never gave Dad the chance to say what he wanted from a woman – or even from himself, for that matter.

When I returned home, Gran was still tucked up on the sofa with Barty, who hardly lifted his head in response to my key in the door and only gave a small unenergetic wag of his tail as I laid my clipboard on the chair opposite.

"So much for the old guard dog," I whispered under my breath, as I made my way to the kitchen.

"That's because he knows you're friend not foe," said Gran, without opening her eyes. I laughed at the pair of them, as I had to make my own Horlicks and take off my own shoes. "I've been usurped by a dog," I said, as I laid back into Gran's big chair.

I had little sleep that night and what I did have was scattered with weird and fanciful dreams. The worst one being Michael picking me up and taking me to a top-class restaurant and when the waiter showed us to our table, there was Beryl, already sitting at the table in her wrap and a red wig. When I turned back to Michael, he was dressed, head to toes, in women's clothing and the band was singing, *There's Nothing like a Dame!*

I woke in a cold sweat on more than one occasion and eventually abandoned any further thought of sleep for a hot shower and a good rummage through my wardrobe to decide on an outfit for that night. I decide to keep the ensemble low-key, after all a lot of water had passed under the bridge since my *femme fatale* night and what a disaster that had turned out to be. I opted for a black, cashmere polo-neck jumper, a short, pleated skirt from *Next*, which I had picked up in the sales and a pair of *Chie Mihara* boots I had bought on *ebay* and were my only concession to shopping during my depression over the whole, Michael leaving period.

Was this fate at her best again? The very boots that I bought to drown my sorrows are the first thing I choose to wear when Michael steps back into my life again.

I tossed up whether to go running with the ladies that day. Part of me wanted to go as it always made me feel good about myself and, of course, there was always the chance I might drop another pound or two before the evening. On the other hand things had been a little strained after I brought up the subject of Michael the other day and I didn't need a repeat of that today.

Despite myself, I got in the car and made my way over there. As I pulled the car over to the side of the park, I could see the ladies all huddled together ready to start. Barbara and Mary

Who Cares?

seemed to be in deep conversation and Mary, who was head and shoulders above the others, was looking around, as if looking for something. As I pulled away, it suddenly occurred to me that I didn't have to run there, I could go and have a run somewhere else. The park where I took Precious and Lord would be an ideal place and it was only a ten minute drive away.

When I arrived all the parking spaces around the park were full, so I turned off and parked down a side-street. I did a couple of warm-up exercises, much to the amusement of some of the residents and then made my way off at a leisurely pace. I was glad I'd had the foresight to pop my mp3 in my pocket. Soon I was off, running and singing merrily along to all my favourite tunes.

The usual suspects were out in force, the dog walkers, the pot smokers and more medallion men than you count at a Jimmy Saville convention, but once on the track and in the mode, everything else blended into obscurity. That was until I passed a guy putting something up on a notice board. There was definitely something about him that looked vaguely familiar but I couldn't quite put my finger on it. It felt invigorating to be running free, music in my ears and the excitement of the evening to look forward too. It's strange how we soon forget that the whole world isn't party to the music selection blaring through our headphones, we don't even take on board the odd glances they give us as we pass or the sniggers when they realise what we're singing along too.

So that's how it was when, for the second time, I came upon the guy putting the posters up on the trees. My head was thinking *'What a cheek putting up your rave posters on these lovely old trees that have been here for hundreds of years'*, unfortunately my mouth was singing its own take on; *Don't Break my Heart, my Achy, Breaky Heart.*

As I passed he turned and for one split-second, he looked me squarely in the face. He turned back to hammer yet another nail into the tree and I carried on past. Suddenly, his face started ringing alarm bells in my head. I glanced briefly over my shoulder to take another look. At the exact same time he stopped what he was doing to look over towards me.

Who Cares?

I hadn't had a good enough look at him to be sure who he was, but something in the way he looked at me started my heart pumping with fear. He dropped the papers he was holding down onto the floor and spat the nails out of his mouth and started waving his hands at me.

"BUDDY HELL," I shouted.

As I checked behind I saw he'd started chasing after me. I stepped up the pace, first to a run, then a dash, then to a full, out and out pelt. The man was clearly a maniac and he was closing in. He was shouting something, but all I could hear was Billy Ray Cyrus singing in my ear and my own heavy breathing.

My only advantage was I knew the park like the back of my hand. I hauled myself through the bushes and darted off into a little copse of trees. Without looking behind me I took the shortcut past the public toilets, past the tennis courts, through the memorial gardens and found myself fifty yards from one of the main gates. I thought I was home and dry but as I looked behind me I could just make him out standing in the gardens looking all around. If I ran for the gate, he would definitely see me but I couldn't just stand there.

Decision made, I jumped head first into the wide expanse of bushes that ran parallel to the park and right up to the entrance. Luckily, the park was in full-bloom and as I ducked down I knew I would not be seen from the pathway. I yanked the headphones out of my ears and kept my head down out of sight. Within seconds I heard running which then stopped just a few feet from where I crouched. I couldn't see his face only his feet but I heard the anger in his voice.

"Damn, damn, damn," he cursed, as he walked up towards the gate. As I peaked over the top of the bush I saw him scouring the roads outside the park. I was glad I'd parked my car further out. I sat down abruptly, as he turned on his heels and headed back. He grabbed something out of his pocket, presumably his phone and started to shout. "She was here, God damn it, I saw her. I can't believe it. She was here and I let her get away." My heart was pounding so hard I was sure he would hear it. "I'm positive it was her, I just know it. You've got to find her. I don't care what it costs; she's got to be found."

Who Cares?

I could feel myself hyperventilating and grabbed a doggy bag out of my pocket to breathe into.

"She was jogging, for goodness sake; she can't live that far away. I don't care if you have to knock on every door in the neighbourhood, I want her found."

In, out, in, out, I tried desperately to concentrate on breathing in the bag, the last thing I wanted now, was to pass out and have my would-be attacker slay me all the easier. Over the top of the bag and through the heavy density of the bush, I watched as he turned and walked away. When I could no longer see him, I relaxed back with a huge sigh of relief.

"Hey man that looks like good stuff, wanna swap some for a bit a da weed?" I jumped back in shock, sure that the maniac had doubled-back behind me but there, huddled up behind the bushes and half-hidden behind the tree, were what looked like two teenage boys. Caps on and hoods pulled up over them, they sat with their knees up, cradling a shared joint in their cupped hands, looking eagerly at the bag in mine.

Now, I didn't want them to cause a scene and start shouting so I decided a bit of the old acting was in order and I was going to have to handle this carefully. I can't say that I've been party to many pot smokers in my life but I have watched *Ali G* and felt sure that having escaped the clutches of the *Mafia*, these two shouldn't be too difficult. I checked cautiously around and when I was sure the area was safe, I started to my feet.

"I is sorry homies," I drooled in my best, 'East Side' – 'West Side', voice. "I's only got enough fa da one 'erbal remedy, yous knows wot I mean? I catch yous next time bruvvers." I gave them the V for peace sign and left while they were still stunned, or should that be stoned?

I dashed for the entrance but as I did, something caught my eye. It was Barty. There was a poster pinned to the gate with his picture and name on it. The guy chasing me through the park must have been Tony. I ripped the poster down and ran. I didn't look at it again until I was safely back in the car. As I drove through London, negotiating taxis, buses and white-van drivers, my head was in a spin. Apparently, James was offering a five-hundred pounds reward for the safe return of Barty, the

Who Cares?

Newfoundland. What the hell was going on? Had Marianne not told him that she practically threw him at me and threatened to have him put down? More to the point what was I going to do now?

As I looked over at the clock, I knew there was nothing that could be done then. There was only two and a half hours before I met Michael and I would need every minute of that to get ready. This would have to wait until the morning.

When I arrived home both Gran and Barty gave me a hearty welcome. Gran was skipping around the kitchen like a woman half her age, fussing over Barty, getting him something to eat and singing one of her songs from the musicals. How could we both have taken to Barty so quickly? I knew it was going to break Gran's heart to take him away but that was something I'd have to deal with tomorrow – for tonight I would be seeing Michael. Downstairs I could hear Gran singing one of her old music hall songs to Barty and I remembered how she used to sing the same song to Gramps when he was alive...

"You better love him in the morning, kiss him every night, give him plenty of loving, treat him right, because a good man nowadays is hard to find."

So true, I thought!

Twenty-three

I took a long, leisurely shower, covered myself in Aromatics body wash and wrapped my hair in a towel. After drying, I rubbed Aromatics body lotion all over the top half of my body and then powdered liberally with talc. Then sitting on the little, wicker chair in the bathroom I grabbed the razor and began the odious task of de-furring my, well overdue, legs. They were, by any standards, hideously man-like and wouldn't look out of place on a football field. Still not for long, I thought, as I made positive strokes towards the first leg.

Startled by the mobile phone ringing, I put a small nick in my leg which started to bleed. When I saw it was Michael I was glad I'd had the foresight to bring it into the bathroom with me.

"Hello," I said, offhandedly. No point letting let him know his number was still stored on my phone.

"Hey gorgeous, it's Michael." Was it just my imagination or was he whispering? "Are we still on for tonight?"

"Tonight...? Yes, of course. I'm out at the moment but I should be back on time, I only need to change into a more comfortable pair of shoes and I'll be away." I hoped that sounded noncommittal enough in a, I'm trying to fit you into my busy schedule; it's no big deal, type of a way.

"Oh right... it's just that I'm in town now and wondered if you could make it a bit earlier?"

"Erm, well I suppose I could get away with these shoes, if you don't mind me coming as I am."

"Shall we say half an hour at the wine bar then?"

"Yep see you there." I closed the phone, sat for two seconds then threw everything on to the floor. Pulling at the towel on my head I rubbed it dry, and then hung my head upside down and rough dried it with the hairdryer. The static I'd caused made it stand on end and I had to dampen it down with wax. My clothes for the evening were all hanging on the back of the door and as I grabbed frantically at them, they dropped to the floor.

"No, I don't believe it," I shouted in frustration. The black, cashmere jumper and the short skirt were covered in white patches from the talc that littered the floor. With no time to change what I was wearing, I pulled them on and patted them down. As I pulled the polo-neck over my head, my hair stood on end and a bit of paper that had got swept up with the clothes stuck to my hand. As I removed it with the other hand, so it stuck to that, eventually making the leap to my jumper. Damn, I'd brush it down when I was ready to go. I'd planned to wear black, woollen tights but the talc marks were so bad I plumped at the last moment for flesh coloured Lycra.

As I pulled my boots on, I quickly glanced at the time. Only ten minutes left and it would take all of that to get me through traffic. I grabbed my phone, coat and handbag then dashed out of the bathroom, with just a quick glance in the mirror. With a flimsy excuse for my departure to Gran, I hurried towards the car, checking only to see if I'd popped my make-up bag in my handbag. With just five minutes to go, I darted across town. I'd never been to this particular wine bar before but I was fairly sure I knew where it was.

As it happens my memory has suffered with lapses recently, probably a return bout of Alzheimer's which may also have affected my directional skills because I ended up detouring five miles wide of the wine bar before, eventually, settling on a parking space several hundred yards away from the front door. Even though I was fifteen minutes late, I took a deep breath to calm myself and despite the poor lighting, I managed to make up my face.

I locked up and started walking towards the wine bar. Trepidation in every step… not because I was nervous about our first meeting but because this was the first time I'd worn my Chie Mihara boots out and began to realise why they were being sold so quickly and cheaply on *ebay*. The right heel was rocking beneath me and every footfall was veering more and more to the right. I had to make it, I just had too. I started taking more of the weight onto the left foot and quickened my pace.

At last I was outside Bon Nuit. I took, yet another, deep breath and entered. The hat and coat stand was to my right and I took my time taking off my coat and hanging it up. A pep talk was in order and I was just the girl to give it. Okay Remi, keep this cool. All the odds are in your favour. Don't forget it was him who asked you to come here tonight. It's him who needs to impress you. All you need to do is keep it calm, look beautiful and simper sex appeal... How hard can that be?

The foyer of the wine bar was brightly lit with big spotlights and, as I stepped back from the hat stand, I stared straight into one. As I passed through into the more subdued lighting, all I could see were big orange circles in front of my eyes. I tried to see past the spots to see where Michael was sitting but wherever I turned the spots came with me. I heard my name being called and turned in that direction and could just make out Michael sitting at the bar, on a high stool.

I turned and strode, confidently, towards the bar and I very nearly made it, if it hadn't been for fate and her friend, bad luck, stepping in. Three paces before I reached Michael, I passed underneath a balloon archway, the static in my hair attracted the lowest ones which stuck to my head. As I reached up to get the balloons off, the heel came off my boot, my ankle turned and in slow motion, I felt myself crashing to the floor.

Michael jumped up to save me and in doing so, threw his drink all over my dress. He apologised profusely and made to pat it down, coming away with the paper that I hadn't removed from my skirt. As luck would have it, it was only the outer cover of a tampax, so no embarrassment there!

He tucked the paper quickly into his trouser pocket and turned back to order fresh drinks at the bar. A couple of girls looked over and started to giggle. The orange spots had started to dissipate and as I looked down I could see that the strobe lighting had picked up the talc on my black clothes. I looked as though I'd just finished a day in the bakery.

As I started rubbing the white marks away I realised what else they were looking at. There were little lights dancing all over my legs, I tried to brush them away and, to my horror, realised that they weren't lights at all but big, thick, coarse, blonde hairs poking out through my flesh coloured tights. They giggled as they turned back to the bar.

All I could think about now were the hairy legs, the broken heel, the dirty clothing, the tampon wrapper and the balloons, one of which was still stuck to my back. Thankfully, Michael suggested we move to a quieter spot and I couldn't get there fast enough. He looked sexy and he smelt gorgeous, his dark eyes smouldered as they stared unflinchingly into mine.

"You look wonderful" he said, leaning across to kiss my hand. "I've missed you so much."

"Really?" I said, pulling my hand away. "I would've thought you'd had your hands full!"

He had the decency to look embarrassed but still held my gaze. "Remi, it was a mistake, a terrible mistake. The studio thought it would be a good publicity stunt and I agreed to go along with it. Before I knew it she was talking about getting hitched for real and the next thing I know, the chapel's booked, the I do's are said and the book's signed. Babe," he said, grabbing hold again of my hand. "I've made a mistake and I've paid the price. There hasn't been a moment when I wasn't thinking of you – wishing I could turn the clocks back, wishing it had been you and me in Vegas."

I searched his eyes for the truth and looked deep into his face for a sign but as I did, something caught my eye over his shoulder. Sitting in the cubicle behind him and staring right at me was Penny. I jumped back in my seat and yanked my hand out of his. I felt the colour rise in my face and a sweat form on my brow. What was she doing here? I downed my drink in one and asked Michael to get me another while I went to the ladies. As he got up, I jumped out of the cubicle, grabbed hold of Penny's hand and manoeuvred her off to the toilets. "What are you doing here?" I said, when we were alone.

"I could ask you the same thing," she countered.

"Have you followed me here? Did Gran put you up to this? Are you spying on me?"

"Hold on, hold on, let's start with number one," she put a beautifully, manicured finger up into the air. "Am I following you? No. Did your Gran put me up to this?" She shrugged her shoulders, "Why would she? Number three," she started to sway. "What was number three?"

"Are you drunk?" I asked, incredulously.

"Ah yes, number three, am I drunk? Yes. Yes, I think I can categorically say, that yes, I think I am drunk."

I stared at her for a moment. Talk about the seven faces of Eve. First the overweight bully who had made my former years a misery, then the slim, beautiful, transformed queen of style and glamour and now this but what was this?

"Penny what's happened, why are you like this?"

"Is this question four and five?" she queried. I walked her over to one of the empty toilet cubicles and sat her down.

"Penny, are you alright? I've never seen you like before?"

"Haven't you?" she said, brightening up, "but I'm always like this." She hung her head for a while and when she lifted it, there were tears in her eyes. "I'm a drunk Remi, a drunk, always have been, always will be." She squeezed my hand and I smelt the drink on her breath. If I hadn't seen it for myself I would never have believed it.

"Why now Penny, when everything's going so well for you? Your business, the T.V work, the diet and health clubs. You have everything."

"Poor Remi, when do you ever see the whole picture?" she said, sadly. "Yes, I have all those things but I don't have anyone to love me, no one to hold on to, snuggle up at night with, someone to tell me they love me. I want to belong to someone, Remi."

"You do belong Penny and you're beautiful, so beautiful. Any man would be lucky to have you as a girlfriend; you could take your pick."

"Ah, but what about the Penny you knew at school. Was she beautiful, would any man be lucky enough to have her as a girlfriend?"

I stared at her in disbelief. "But you're not that girl anymore Penny, that girl's gone."

"That's just it Remi, that girl hasn't gone, she's here." She stabbed at her chest and the tears rolled freely down her face.

"She's here Remi, She's still inside here. On the outside there may be successful Penny, beautiful Penny but on the inside I still feel like fat, ugly Penny. When men talk to me, I shy away because I know they're making fun of me. When I get dressed up to go out, I look at the mirror and feel good but by the time I get to where I'm going the only image I can see in my mind is the other Penny and then I drink to get rid of that image. Then I drink too much."

I took my friend in my arms and held her tight.

"I love you Penny. I have more reason to dislike you than most but I don't, I love you. The old Penny is gone, gone for good." I lifted her to her feet and took her over to the basins. "This is the only Penny, this is the beautiful, inside and out Penny, this is the Penny I love." She looked at her own image and then threw her arms around me and cried like a baby. As I walked her back to the toilet to sit her down, the contents of her bag fell on the floor. I picked it all up and was left with a card in my hand. It was an AA card and on it was a name and telephone number.

I clicked open my mobile, dialled the number and a man answered. I explained who I was and where I'd got the card. He asked me where I was and told me to stay there, he would be there shortly. I sat Penny gently back against the cistern and poked my head out of the door. A waitress was passing and I grabbed hold of her hand.

"Would you please tell the man sitting in the cubicle over there, that I'm feeling a little unwell and that I'll be with him shortly?" She looked me up and down, her eyes resting a few uncomfortable seconds on the forested area of my legs, and then she nodded and left.

I put my arm round Penny's shoulders and held her close to me. She was barely conscious as I kissed her head and handed her over to Lawrence, her AA buddy. He thanked me and told me to stay, saying I could be of no further help.

"She just needs to sleep this one off," he explained. "This is the first one for a long time, she was doing so well but she gets lonely." It was like a knife in my heart to hear those words, my friend was so lonely, she had to go and drink in the company of strangers.

I sat for a few minutes more after they'd left, and then made my way back to Michael.

"Are you okay?" he said, pushing my drink towards me.

"Actually no, I really don't feel too good at all, would you mind if I went home?" I could tell by his face that he did mind and his voice and tone became quite abrupt, as he ushered me towards the exit.

"Could I see you again?" he said, as we stood to take our different routes back to our separate cars.

"I'd like that," I said. "I'm sorry about tonight." He pulled me towards him and kissed me gently.

"You can make it up to me next time," he said, a smile lingering on those dangerously, full lips.

He held me close and as I wallowed in the safety of his embrace, I looked up at the stars and wondered, not for the first time, if this was fate. As he released his hold, my eyes strayed fleetingly across the road. Two people were walking slowly and furtively along the street. Two people wrapped up in warm coats, hats and scarves. Two people who were looking directly at me, one of whom I recognised instantly and yet the other one also looked familiar but I couldn't quite place why. As I pulled back to take a closer look they hurried away without looking back.

Twenty-four

After yet another sleepless, dream-filled, night I woke to the recognition that it was the weekend. No dogs to walk and no Equality Healthcare. Don't get me wrong, I love visiting everyone on my round but the thought of having a Remi-filled day with no ties and no responsibilities, was an invigorating thought.

For a few moments I lay blissfully unaware of what the day held or the problems that the previous day had brought. But as my thoughts turned to Michael, so the whole fiasco of the evening before came into plain view.

I looked at the alarm clock and noted, with surprise, that it was already past nine o'clock. I picked up my phone and rang Michael's number. The phone was switched off. After thinking for a moment, I rang Juliet; she was the only other person who would understand about Penny and how we could help her.

"I don't believe it. Was she alright when you left her, did you take her home?" I explained about the buddy system and about Lawrence. I didn't explain why I didn't take her home myself or about Michael but, thankfully, she was too worried about Penny to pick me up on it.

"I'm coming down; I can be there in a couple of hours. If nothing else, we can talk it through with Penny, make her realise that we care about her and that she is beautiful and the old Penny has definitely gone."

There was a short silence and then Juliet came back on the line. "I'm bringing someone with me, is that okay?"

"Sure," I said, but before I could ask who, she said goodbye and the phone went dead.

Downstairs Gran was waiting for me. Her face was solemn and she was unusually quiet, which was always a bad sign.

Who Cares?

Somehow, she must have found out about my date with Michael. I should have known she would of course; she always had a way of second guessing me. I sat myself down on the sofa with Barty and prepared for the worst. A few minutes passed before she came into the sitting-room, cup of coffee in one hand and the leaflet with the picture of Barty on, in the other.

"What's this all about Remi? Are they going to take Barty away from us?" At that moment I almost wished she was quizzing me about Michael, after all that would've been easier than this. She sat on the arm of the sofa and stroked Barty's thick fur.

"Does this man, James think you've stolen the dog?"

"Gran, I just don't know. I saw a man sticking up posters in the park yesterday and when I looked, this was on them."

"Was the man in the park, James?" she asked.

"No, I think it was one of his henchmen, a guy called Tony." I noted Gran's surprise at the term henchmen but that story was far too long to explain now.

"I'll go over and see them this morning, see if I can clear this up." I squeezed her hand. "But I think we might have to accept that Barty may have to be returned to his owner."

I had a few hours to kill before Juliet arrived, so I threw on some old clothes and made my way over to Precious' house. There were no cars out front, I wasn't sure if that was good news or bad. I pressed the bell and waited... nothing. I pressed the bell a second time and heard a small, moaning noise coming from inside. What now? Was someone tied up in there, unable to shout out for help or come to the door? I peeked through the letter box. I'd give it a few more seconds. I thought, and then I'd ring the police.

Suddenly, the door opened a crack and a hideous apparition came into view. Marianne without make-up, her hair in disarray and a silk wrap pulled ridiculously tight around her skinny waist... Truly a sight to behold!

"What the hell do you want?" she said, in her beautifully articulated fashion. "It's the weekend."

"I know but I needed to speak to you. Is James here?" She looked at me with such contempt, I felt like I'd just asked the

Queen where she got her toenails clipped. Without answering she turned and walked back into the kitchen. Grabbing a cup, she proceeded to make a coffee, needless to say, she didn't offer me one.

"It's about Barty. You told me to take him away then yesterday I see these posters up in the park, what's this all about?" Still she said nothing; she poured the water into the cup, grabbed a couple of tablets, threw her head back and swallowed them, chasing it off with a mouthful of the newly-made, scorching coffee.

"That's better, I'm not human until I've had coffee in the morning," she said, grabbing a cigarette from the packet and lighting it. I didn't feel I was the one to inform her, that from my view point, she was hardly human with or without the caffeine.

I waved the poster in front of her again but she just turned and flicked ash into the ashtray.

"It's a mistake, darling," she said, in her dismissive tone. "James put them out there ages ago, when poor, old Barty got lost, he was back in a couple of hours but trust James to go over the top with it all."

"But I saw Tony putting them out yesterday." She looked a bit confused.

"No, darling, you must have seen Tony taking them *down*, we keep getting crank calls, plebs after the reward, darling and you know how these people can be." She flicked her ash again and looked down her nose, before adding, "Don't you?"

I was so relieved that Barty wouldn't be leaving us I completely forgot to mention the fact that Tony had chased me half-way across the park.

"Anyway, darling, you'll have no need to come here much longer. Tony has a little place across town and Precious and I are going to live with him." She must have caught my surprise, as she bit her lower lip slightly and dragged hard on the cigarette again.

"I thought you and James were together," I said, hardly believing that I was even contemplating conversing with the Queen of Mean. She looked wistfully at me for a moment through the cloud of smoke she expelled from her mouth. Her eyebrows rose in consentaneous agreement, her mouth remained pursed.

"Well that was the plan, darling. He has the connections and the money and, of course, this lovely house. As my tutor always used to say; 'Love grants in a moment, what toil can hardly achieve in an age'." She laughed at my confusion. "Marry for money, darling; it's a lot less work."

"Have you fallen out?" My 'inquiring nature' was getting the better of me.

"Hardly, darling. We never fell in, if you know what I mean. I was renting this house from an agency when all of a sudden they gave me six weeks to find somewhere else, apparently the owner wished to take up residency and he didn't want a sitting tenant. Well I tried, darling but you know what finding a good property in London is like, virtually impossible. So a friend said, sit tight, what can he do? After six weeks he turned up and I gave him the sob story, flashed my beautifully, coiffed eyelashes at him and, reluctantly, he agreed to let me stay on for a while until I could find something suitable."

She took another long draw on the cigarette and then stubbed it out into the ashtray. The smoke spewed out of her mouth as she spoke. "Anyway for a while it was okay. He moaned about poor, little Precious and I had to keep her out of his way, but generally he was decent enough. Then he goes on and on about someone else, never gives her name but he makes it quite clear that he loves her."

I felt a pang of guilt run through me. James may not have taken to Marianne and who could blame him, but hadn't he pursued me from that very first day? I was the other woman! A small tingle of excitement filled me. Under no circumstances did I find James attractive in that way but I did accept that he had good taste.

I made it back to Gran's with just minutes to spare before Juliet's expected arrival. Before I went in I rang Michael once more, but his phone was still off. I explained the whole Barty, James, Marianne and Tony situation to Gran, who was visibly relieved and gave Barty a huge hug. Knowing that Juliet would be there at any moment, I went on to tell her the story of the night before, tactically missing out any reference to Michael.

Gran's face was a picture of shock and genuine pity for Penny. "Ring Penny now and get her over here, we really need to sit her down and talk to her."

"But Gran, she's a grown women, I can't tell her to come over and expect her to drop everything to get here."

"Then tell her I asked her to come," said Gran, smiling.

"Why don't you ring her then Gran and ask her yourself?" Gran didn't answer straight away; she was too busy sorting out her hat and coat. She took off her slippers and placed them, tidily, under her big chair, putting on her day shoes. She slipped the lead onto Barty, the hat on her head and the coat over her arm and made towards the door.

"Where are you going?" I asked.

"To church, of course," she said, touching her nose in a conspiratorial way. My mouth was still open as I watched her disappear through the door. Gran was a very spiritual person and often attended the small, local church on a Sunday but I always thought it was more to do with meeting all her old cronies and partaking of the tea and cake that was served afterwards. To see her rush off on a Saturday, presumably to pray for Penny, was a bit of an eye-opener.

Luckily, I didn't have long to think about it. After ringing Penny and conveying Gran's request, a car pulled up outside and Juliet stepped out of the passenger side. Her hair was long and flowing but instead of the mousy colour she'd always sported, it was bright red! Not red, as in Beryl's defamation of ginger, but bright, pillar box red.

Her clothes were still outdated and unusual but the bright colours she now wore, strangely brought them into fashion. Over her arm she carried the poncho I'd given her years ago and I breathed a sigh of relief for some semblance of normality. As I got up to open the door, she flounced through it and we hugged, as we always did. Her face had a sort of radiance about it, no longer the mousy Juliet; I wondered briefly if a Romeo had put this smile on Juliet's face. As we released she turned back towards the door.

Who Cares?

"Becky, this is my oldest and best friend, Remi." As I offered my greetings, Juliet slipped behind me and when I caught her again; she was holding Becky's hand and glowing with untold joy. "Remi, this is Becky, Becky is my partner!" and with that she leaned over and kissed her cheek.

Twenty-five

Now we live in a multicultural, cosmopolitan society. London itself is awash with gay shops and clubs. I myself have many homosexual friends, many of which I'd met during my years at the studios. Nobody could ever say I was narrow-minded or homophobic, so why did I find it so hard to take on board what my best friend was saying? How, for instance, had I never noticed or picked up on any of the signs? More to the point, what was wrong with me? She'd never shown any of those feelings towards me, what was wrong with me? In lesbian terms, was I a bit of a minger, how would one know after all?

Juliet's arm detached from Becky's shoulder and she came over and hugged me again.

"Are you alright, you're not shocked are you?"

"Of course not Juliet, I can read the signs you know," I said, indignantly. "Just surprised you never said anything before."

"I wanted to come over and introduce Becky to you but I've been busy and you've been busy, there just didn't seem to be the right moment but I'm here now and it's time for us to get all the skeletons out the cupboard."

Juliet busied herself making tea, as comfortable as I was in Gran's kitchen. Becky made small talk, telling me how they first met.

As I listened, I felt myself wondering what Penny could remember about the night before and would she remember that I was with Michael? That was one skeleton that needed to stay firmly in the cupboard until I had a chance to work it out for myself. I returned to the conversation just as Becky was explaining how she asked Juliet out.

"I thought she'd never get round to it" said Juliet, returning with the tray of tea and biscuits. She perched herself on the arm next to Becky and started handing around cups.

"So how long do you think Penny's had this drinking problem then?" she said, dunking a Bath Oliver into her tea.

"I don't know," I said, shaking my head. "It was such a shock to see her and then when I realised she'd been drinking, I couldn't believe it."

"What were you doing there, who were you with?" said Juliet, picking up another biscuit. At that moment my mobile rang and I jumped out of my seat.

"I'll have to take that, be back in a mo." I ran to the bathroom and ducked inside, checking that Juliet hadn't followed behind me.

"Hi," I whispered.

"Hi gorgeous, are you feeling better this morning?" He purred down the phone.

"Oh yes, lots better, I've already been out for a run," I lied. "Fit as a fiddle today, thanks. I did try to ring you this morning to apologise but your phone was turned off."

There was only a short delay before he answered. "Had a meeting first thing this morning, some of us have to start early, darling," he laughed. "Anyway I'd like to see you again, preferably for a bit longer next time." I could still hear the chuckle in his voice and relaxed, pleased to know that lasts night debacle hadn't ruined our renewed friendship.

"I'd like to see you too," I said, realising, all too late, that I had dropped the pretence of indifference.

"How about today?"

"I can't today; I've got the girls round, what about tomorrow?" His voice was less jovial as he said he was tied up for the next few days.

"I've got a cocktail party to go to next Friday, a new company I'm trying to impress, how about you coming as my guest?" My stomach, unashamedly, did somersaults and instinctively I licked my dry lips.

"That would be lovely."

"Shall I pick you up at the flat?" I was surprised that he thought I still lived at the flat; had he not checked on me at all?

"No, I'll be out most of the day, meet me at Bernie's."

Who Cares?

Bernie's was a little restaurant we used to go to all the time right in the central part of London. It wasn't called Bernie's, that was just a nickname we'd given it and it stuck. There was a small, yet distinctive, silence before he answered.

"Save both of us parking, what about I meet you outside?" I felt a small pang of disappointment, it would have been great to have seen Marcus, who ran it, I hadn't been in there since the split but perhaps I was rushing things.

"Okay, see you there, what time?"

"Eight, suit you?" I clicked the phone off, washed my face in cold water and made my way back. Juliet stared at me, probably waiting for me to reveal all but I side-stepped her and started chatting to Becky which I knew, instantly, was the wrong move because Juliet seemed even more suspicious. Luckily, at that moment we heard a car pull up outside and Juliet jumped up to see who it was.

"It's Penny," she whispered.

"What are you whispering for?" I whispered.

"I don't want her to think we were talking about her."

"But we are talking about her"

"I know, but she doesn't need to know that, does she," said Juliet, brusquely.

I jumped up and opened the door. Penny was immaculately dressed, as always, her hands manicured, her hair perfection; the only addition to her normal, well-presented self was a pair of dark glasses. She stood for a full moment; then stepped forward and hugged me.

"I'm sorry," she said, tears rolling down her beautifully made-up face. "I'm sorry you had to find out," she paused again, "to find out the way you did." I took her hand and lead her into the sitting-room. If Penny was surprised to see Juliet she didn't show it. Neither did she bat an eyelid when Juliet introduced Becky in the same fashion as she had me.

"You're not surprised about me and Becky?" Juliet asked Penny.

"Of course not," Penny said, smiling and taking Juliet's hand. "It was fairly obvious at school where your interests lay."

"Really?" said Juliet, covering her mouth in surprise, yet

despite that her eyes shone with pleasure. "I thought I kept it well covered, especially from you Penny, no offence, but you were the last person I wanted to get hold of something like that." Penny nodded her head grabbing a tissue out of her sleeve and dabbed her eyes. Juliet jumped up immediately and hugged her.

"I'm sorry; I shouldn't have brought that up, it's water under the bridge. I'm so sorry," she said, affectionately stroking Penny's head and moving a strand of hair away from her face. I watched Becky move uncomfortably in her seat, but she said nothing.

"The thing is," Penny said, collecting her composure and straightening up, "it's still a problem for me, it's not water under the bridge, and it's still very much a part of my life. I don't know if Remi told you?" She looked over towards me and I nodded. "I'm an alcoholic!"

"Come on Penny a few drinks doesn't make you an alcoholic," I said, reaching for her hand. Penny shook her head and pulled her hand back into her lap.

"That's the thing Remi, it's not a few drinks. It's a lot of drink, every day."

"But how? You run all your businesses, you always look immaculate, you help other people with problems, and I've never even smelt drink on you."

Penny laughed an uncomfortable and bitter laugh. "Drunks are very clever people Remi, we cover our tracks really well and probably if we didn't drink we'd all be millionaires." Before we could reach out to her again, she stood up and made her way across the room, tears flowing freely now.

"How long?" asked Juliet.

Penny looked out of the window, perhaps wondering how much to tell us but, eventually, when she turned around, we knew that she was going to tell us everything.

"Even when I was at school," she said, moving back towards us.

She sat herself down on the arm of the chair and looked at us all, before starting. "When I was on *This Morning,* you might remember that I said I was overweight at a young age, that when other people laughed at me, it just made me eat more." We both

Who Cares?

nodded.

She paused, we knew what this was taking to tell us.

"When I was only six years old I was sexually abused by my uncle. I was only a child," her shaking hand dabbed at her tears again. "I didn't know what was happening; I only knew that it was wrong and painful. It was my mother's brother, so I went to my mother and told her about it. She hit me and told me I was a vicious, spiteful child and God would punish me for telling such lies. She hit me every day from that day onwards."

Penny paused and Juliet and I wiped our faces with the back of our sleeves.

"Both my mother and father drank, both were alcoholics. They spent every night down the pub and came back after closing time. It was then that my uncle came back, time and time again to abuse me. I tried to hide out of the way, once I even locked the door and wouldn't let him in but he broke a window and got in anyway, I got the blame for the broken window. I had no friends, no other family I could stay over with. I was alone.

"My life was empty, the only joy I had was when I ate. Then one day my uncle hit me and said I was getting fat and ugly, that no man would want me if I was fat. That was when I started to really eat and sure enough, when I was big enough, my uncle stopped coming to our house. The children at school started to laugh at me and call me names and I started using the only thing I had... and I hit back. My life was a mess, I had no real friends, only people who were frightened of me and those who just enjoyed seeing me make other people's lives a misery."

She looked over at us and mouthed sorry, her voice not being able to say the words aloud. I passed her and Juliet a tissue. My own throat was taut and painful from trying to hold back the tears and for yet another time, I had to wonder at how much I missed of other people's lives. Was I so self-absorbed, that other people's misery just passed me by?

Penny collected herself once more and carried on.

"I started to have a little drink at night when I came home from school and felt better about myself. Then I started to have a drink before I went to school and that gave me confidence, it got to a point where I had a bottle on me at all times. When I left school and lost all the weight, I wanted desperately to change everything, the drink included. After the initial loss of weight I did join a club, as I told everyone on the programme, but the weight didn't come off quickly enough for me. I wanted a big change, I saw it as my salvation, but I'd had years of eating, it was hard to change. So I started binge eating and being sick.

"I didn't know I had an eating disorder, I just thought I was being clever, eating everything I wanted but not allowing the calories to put weight on. When I realised the effect the Bulimia was having on me, I got help but started to drink again. I set up the clinics and felt good that I was able to help other people. I got to grips with the eating, the more I helped others the better I got. Finally I realised that the drinking was as big a problem as the eating and I went along to an AA meeting. When we met up again I'd been attending the meetings for two years and hadn't taken a drink in all that time."

"That's right," said Juliet. "When we went out together that first time, you didn't have one drink. Remi and I thought it was part of your diet thing, we never thought it was part of something bigger."

"So if you're going to meetings," I said, "why last night?"

Penny sniffed and looked up at us. "Celebrity is a two-way sword," she said. "It was lovely being recognised, the clinics started to fill, people came to me for advice, I felt great, totally able to handle everything life offered. Or so I thought. I met a lovely guy and he asked me out, we started dating and it was wonderful. Then one day the inevitable happened. We'd been out, had a lovely night, he came back to mine and wanted to make love. I tried."

She pulled the hankie back out from her sleeve and wiped away the spilling tears again.

"I really tried to put the past behind me but my body stiffened... and it all went wrong. He was understanding and said we could take it gently but it happened again and he started to get frustrated with me. Eventually he stopped calling and I went back to hide in a wine bottle, it seemed the safest place. I made sure that I was always smart and tidy so no one would suspect. I covered myself in everything I did, even my mother, had she lived to see me successful, wouldn't have known."

With that Penny broke down again and Juliet and I both jumped up to hug her.

As Juliet held her, I went to the kitchen to make more tea. I set out a tray with the matching strawberry teapot, sugar bowl and milk jug and placing the four teacups on, I took them through to the sitting-room. Juliet was perched back on the sofa with Becky and Penny had remade her face up. I sat down the tray and poured the tea. There was a small silence in the room broken by Penny.

"Anyway, after last night, you'll be pleased to know, I'll be rejoining the AA programme again, thanks to you Remi. I know I need help. Lawrence, the guy you called, took me home and wouldn't go until I'd sobered up this morning and I've given him a solemn promise to come to the next meeting, which just happens to be today."

"Now that we know," said Juliet, leaning forward, "you must let us help. The past is just that, the past. You're our friend, our very good friend and we love you." With that we all started to bawl again and finally ended up laughing together, through our tears.

"From now on, from this day forward," Juliet giggled, "we will have no more skeletons in cupboards, from now on we tell all; deal?" She put her hand out and one by one we slapped it in confirmation, even Becky jumped off the sofa to be part of our pledge. We laughed and hugged again but as we pulled away Penny's gaze settled on me and, in that instant, I knew that she remembered everything.

Twenty-six

"I can't believe you knew about me at school Penny, and never said anything," Juliet said as we settled down again with another cup of tea.

"It wasn't rocket science, I may have been an overweight bully but I wasn't blind; I always thought you had a bit of a crush on Miss Bevis, the English teacher, although what you saw in her, heaven knows." Juliet looked a little embarrassed and snuck a quick look at Becky who laughed out loud. Apparently, Juliet had confessed her first crush but was positive that no one suspected.

"And what about Remi and Norman, what was that all about?" said Penny, looking towards me, shrugging her shoulders, palms up, as she queried it.

"What do you mean, me and Norman? There was nothing going on between me and Norman," I replied, tartly.

"Oh Remi, of course there was something going on between you but you were always too busy with other things to see it," laughed Juliet, trying to pick out the dunked biscuit that had sunk to the bottom of her cup.

"But there wasn't anything between us," I protested. "Surely I would have noticed!"

"Goodness sake Remi, don't tell me you never noticed how he looked at you, how his big, brown, doleful eyes followed you around. I just naturally assumed that you were an item or something." Penny looked across at Juliet for confirmation. Juliet picked up the baton and started to run.

"Remi do you remember that time when he reached across the table to grab a pen and you went to do the same thing and he grabbed your hand?" I nodded my head. "Do you remember how red he went, how embarrassed he was? I just tried to make light of it but you just took hold of the pen and started writing, I don't think you even realised."

I tried to think back to see if anything stuck out but other than a few, small, similar incidents, there was nothing. Could he really have liked me and I hadn't noticed. "I was quite poorly at that time if you remember, Juliet?"

"Remi, you were *never* really poorly. Margaret Jones, who broke her leg in the gym, was poorly, Bryan Whatsisname who got pneumonia, now he was really poorly but Remi all your ailments were in your head."

"I know," I said. "That's what the doctor said; I think he thought I had a tumour or something. Anyway, perhaps I did notice something and maybe I did quite like Norman but I couldn't have done anything about it, I wouldn't have wanted it to come between us all."

"Why would it have?" Penny asked.

"Well because Juliet probably liked him too, it would have been awkward." There was a bit of an uneasy silence where both Juliet and Penny stared at me.

"What have I said?"

"Remi how long have you known I was gay?"

"Ages," I said, flatly.

"How long, really? Remi, tell the truth."

"Okay, not that long."

"How long?" she said again, this time raising her eyebrows

"Okay, okay," I said, quietly. "Today. I'm sorry. I'm sorry I didn't know, I never read the signs, I had no idea about you, no idea about Norman and, apparently, never see the wood for the trees, I'm sorry."

Suddenly Penny laughed. "What a lot we are all sitting here with our secrets. But still, now that were letting it all out, is there anything else anyone wants to get off their chest?" There was a small silence and I knew Penny was watching me and willing me to say something. The word, 'YES', suddenly broke the silence.

"I had a boob job when I was nineteen, these aren't my real boobs." We all turned to look at Becky, who was still pointing at her, amazingly, perky boobs and burst out laughing.

Who Cares?

At that moment Gran arrived home, Barty in tow. She made a beeline for Penny giving her a big hug and Juliet jumped up to receive her cuddle. Gran looked over at Becky, then giving Juliet a little squeeze she smiled and said. "I was wondering when you'd get around to bringing someone to meet us."

Juliet's smile was dazzling as she said. "Gran, this is Becky. Becky, this is Gran," Suddenly we were startled by a small polite cough from behind us and we all turned round to look. There was a man standing in the doorway. He had fair hair, spiked up in a modern, windswept style – blue eyes which stood out on a rather pale complexion and a generous mouth. He was wearing a modern, check, buttoned-down shirt, tucked into faded blue denims and brown loafers on his feet. All in all, he looked pretty damn cool.

"Oh excuse me Vicar; I should have introduced you to everyone." As she made the introductions, all I could think was, how can this be a vicar and where was he when I was going through my traumas? How come Gran didn't nip off and bring one of these home for me?

When she got to Penny, she linked her arm though hers and patted her hand. "This is Penny, Stephen. I hope you don't mind Penny but I did explain your small problem with Stephen, he runs a very good clinic at the church and everybody raves about him."

Stephen looked positively uncomfortable with Gran's profuse praise and turned quickly to talk to Penny. "The thing is, we run a number of clinics within the parish, one of which may be of help to you," he said, tactfully. "But we also have a couple of life-style classes, where we encourage people to keep active and lose weight and Gran explained to me that was your forte. I was hoping that, perhaps we could help each other in some way."

Now I may be wrong, and apparently it seems I often am, but are Vicars allowed to look sexy, are they permitted to have winning smiles and isn't it against some Deadly Sins rule book for a man of the cloth to proposition someone with the strong possibility of a double-entendre hidden in its depths? Whatever the answer, it didn't matter. Penny seemed delighted and made arrangements to meet Stephen the following day, after service, to check out the parish and to talk to him in private.

Before long everyone was making their excuses, promising to meet up again soon and heading off out the door. I sat back down on the sofa and Barty came and sat with me.

"What's wrong with me Barty, why is it I don't see things that are right under my nose?" Barty didn't have an answer exactly just a friendly lick to let me know he understood. Gran brought in two cups of something hot and frothy and sat down on the sofa with me.

"Did you know about Juliet?" I asked.

"Yes. For quite some time," Gran said, candidly.

"Why didn't you say anything to me?"

"I just assumed that you knew," she said, looking at me in surprise.

"Is there anything you don't know?" I said, sarcastically.

"Well let me see. I knew Juliet was gay; I had my suspicions about Penny, I always knew that Norman had a bit of a crush on you. Oh and between you and me," she said, leaning over and whispering, "I think them boobs of Becky's are falsies."

"GRAN…" I said, laughing and turning around in shock, to look at her. "I can't believe you just said that." She just shrugged her shoulders. "Anything else?" I said, shaking my head.

"Yes," she said, suddenly serious. "I know that you went out with Michael last night and if you're not careful, you're going to get hurt again."

Years of experience had taught me that the only way to handle Gran when she had a bee in her bonnet was to take the attacking position. Of course, so far I had never had a situation where I was right and she was wrong…until now.

"Gran for goodness sake, I'm a grown woman capable of making my own decisions. I wasn't hiding the fact that I had a date with Michael," I lied. "I just knew it would cause an argument and I really didn't need to get into all that." I crossed my arms and sat back in the chair waiting for Gran to respond. She didn't, she just agreed I was old enough to make my own *mistakes* and picked up the paper to get on with the crossword.

There was nothing more annoying than Gran, when she

thought she was right, I hadn't missed the emphasis on mistakes, which she'd made.

"Anyway, it was just a drink, nothing more than that." I couldn't help adding.

"That's alright then," she countered. Oh I knew her game, trying to get me to spill the beans, well it wasn't happening, no sir…ee, it ain't happening… Less than a minute passed and all I heard was the biro scribbling on the newspaper.

"Anyhow, he knows he made a big mistake, he said as much, he just wanted to explain how it all happened."

"That's good."

"Well yes, actually, it was good."

"Good." There was no winning with this woman when she was in this sort of mood; I was better off just leaving it alone. I heard the pen scratch again.

"Anyway now that he's getting a divorce, I'll probably be seeing more of him."

"He said that, did he?" she said, looking over the top of her reading glasses.

"Well not in so many words but if he's made a mistake, that would surely be his next course of action."

"You'd think."

You'd think, can you believe she said that? Where does a seventy-something woman get the turn of phrase, you'd think? I blame the television; there should be some sort of parental control, or channel blocking for pensioners!

"Look Gran, it wasn't a big deal, just a drink with a friend which got cut short because I bumped into Penny. He was really great about it and I said we would meet up another time." I ended up telling her the whole story, anything to stop her going on about it all the time! I left out the bit where we cuddled in the street, where he held me tight, where I felt safe in his arms. After Gran had warned me yet again and reminded me of what a mess I was in when it ended last time, I kissed her gently on the cheek, reassured her I'd be careful and went off to take a relaxing bath.

The thing about taking a bath is, once you lay yourself down and relax into the water, your mind starts going through all the events of the last few days. You find yourself rewinding and replaying everything, changing the bits you didn't like, wondering what would have happened if you'd done something different, or said something different.

So that's how it was then. Whilst relaxing gently in the bath, I started running through the events of the night before. Editing it slightly, so that no balloons stuck to my head, no wrappers attacked my skirt, where Penny didn't interrupt us and where Michael held my hand, romantically, over the table and whispered sweet nothings.

I started to think how it might have been had we not parted outside, if he'd whisked me off to a hotel for a night of passion. I tried to imagine the hotel suite and how he would slowly undress me and how I'd turn out to be this uninhibited sexual goddess but, despite my furtive imagination, something kept pulling me backwards; back to the last few moments outside the wine bar. I couldn't help but wonder if my subconscious was trying to tell me something. What was I missing?

I remembered looking over Michael's shoulder and seeing two people across the road, the two people who were looking at me, one of whom I recognised as Barbara. Was it just coincidence she was there, at that time? I didn't know where she lived; perhaps she lived close by and was taking an evening stroll. Why then, did she not wave and say hello?

The warm water swirled around me and I felt myself slipping back still further. I thought back to all the conversations I'd had with Barbara, had I told her where I would be meeting Michael? No.

I replayed every detail in my mind, every look, every word. My mind, as always gravitated towards clothing. Somehow clothing always said something about people that they weren't prepared to tell you themselves. There was Gran with her quirky hats and glasses, Juliet with her outdated clothes, Penny with her immaculate collections. My mind strayed again to other clothing I'd seen.

Slowly I sat up in the bath. I'd had, what is described, as a Eureka moment but I wasn't ecstatic, I wasn't jumping up and punching the air, my Eureka moment was sobering and I felt goose-bumps stand up all over my body. I dragged myself out, trying desperately not to think about all the obvious signs that I'd totally missed. The clothes had said it all and I hadn't seen it. I dressed slowly; I was in no hurry to do what I had to do. My appearance must have been odd because Gran called out to me.

"Not now Gran, there's something I have to do."

"Remi wait, what is it, shall I come with you?"

"No thanks, Gran." I said, grabbing hold of my coat and putting it on. "This is something I have to do alone." I went over and kissed her, reassuring her there was nothing to worry about. "It's okay Gran; at long last, I can finally see the wood for the trees."

I got in the car and started the engine; I wasn't sure how to go about this, I just knew I owed it to myself and others to carry it through. I turned the engine off again and got out; the walk would do me good. I pulled my coat up around my neck and tugged my gloves out of the pocket. I walked for about fifteen minutes, not much more, if I'd ran I would have made it in half the time.

I stood outside for a while. There was a light in the window and I saw shadows moving inside. There was no point rehearsing, better just to get on with it. I walked down the little path lined with pretty flowers, their petals closed now that night had fallen and stood listening for a moment before lifting the knocker. I took a deep breath and rapped on the door. A curtain moved in the window to the side of me and then I heard footsteps. The door opened and Mary stood there looking at me, still in her running clothes, still head and shoulders above the rest, her brunette hair pulled back from her face, the sadness still etched on her face.

I took a moment to study her properly for the first time before saying, "Hello, Dad."

Twenty-seven

For a few moments we just stood and looked at each other until the pain of the receding years overtook us both. As I burst into tears, so my father stepped forwards and took hold of me. As he held me close, I felt his hands shake and his heavy, laboured breathing, told me that, he too, was crying.

It seemed like an eternity before we broke apart. He held my face in his large hands and gently removed the wet strands of hair from my face. As he tried to say something the words caught in his throat and he heaved me to him again. Without warning my mood changed and anger rose up in me like a torrent. I pushed him away and screamed furiously him.

"Why did you leave? Why didn't you come back?" He tried to grab hold of me again but I pulled away. I cupped my hands to my mouth, tears spilling down my face and in a quieter voice I asked. "Why didn't you take me with you?

I was aware that someone else had taken hold of me. I heard her soft voice trying to calm me as she led me over to a small chair and sat me down. As she leaned down next to me and took my hands down from my face I looked at Barbara and wondered how she had succeeded where my mother and I had failed. She took a tissue out from a pretty, porcelain box and handed it to me.

"Remi, you're father never left you, he left your house. He was made to leave the house but he never left you. He tried to talk to you but your mother stopped him, he sent you letters but he knows you never got them." I stopped crying and blew my nose, trying to take it all in.

"What do you mean, what did my mother do?" Barbara started to explain but my father's hand went to her shoulder and she stepped back. He sat on the chair opposite, his eyes red and sore, not just from this encounter, I suspected, but from years of sorrow.

"After I left home that night, I stayed at my parents for a few days. I didn't explain what had happened and they never asked. I tried to contact your mother, to talk to her, to explain, but she wouldn't pick up my calls.

Within days the press was searching for me, they hounded me everywhere I went; they set up a camp outside my parent's house... Naturally enough, my father asked me to leave."

Barbara's hand went to his and he squeezed it. I thought back and remembered the men, with their cameras, standing outside our house.

I recalled my mother chatting merrily on the phone and then rubbing her eyes, making them red and painful before she stepped out onto the street, to be snapped by the waiting pressmen. I remembered that she pulled hard on my hand causing my coat to chaff my arm, making me cry, I remembered how pleased she looked.

My father continued. "I didn't know how bad it was going to get or how Vivienne was going to milk it. I thought a few months or a year, and it would all die down... Instead the divorce was huge, I had no family to help me, my friends turned away and there was an injunction to stop me seeing you. In short, I had no reason to live."

He lifted his bowed head and looked me straight in the eyes. "I didn't want to live." Barbara was sitting by his side now, holding his arm and reassuring him. He looked at her then turned back. "That's when I met Barb," he said, affectionately.

"Your father tried to take his own life, Remi," she said, her voice controlled and clear. My father hung his head again and I saw a tear drop onto his lap.

"He felt it was the only way out. Your mother had told him the publicity was making you ill, that you'd had to change schools and that you hated your father for what he'd done to you." My head was spinning, my thoughts clouding into one jumble and yet, when I reached back and thought of those dark days, had I ever said I hated my father? No.

"Your father was staying in a refuge centre and took an

overdose. When he was admitted to hospital, the next of kin were informed but nobody came. I was working as an auxiliary nurse at the time and sat with your father. When no one came to visit him I sat with him after work as well. When your father eventually came round, he talked to me about his problems, about you," she said, looking over at me, "and why he came to end up in hospital."

I looked at my father. "Are you saying my mother was informed that you might die and she never went to see you and she never told me about it?" I got up and started pacing the room. "All these years and you could have been dead and she would never have said anything to me?"

"She had her reasons Remi, I let her down, and I ruined her life."

"Ruined her life," I spat out. "Don't make me laugh; you didn't ruin her life you made it." My mother had long abandoned the cold winters and unstable summers of the British climes, for the glamorous and suntanned lifestyle of Los Angeles and the heady heights of *Good Morning America*, as their token Brit presenter.

"My mother," I said, pausing to control myself, "abandoned me in much the same way you did, at much the same time, except she was minting it in and having the time of her life, not laying on a hospital gurney waiting to have her stomach pumped."

Barbara, obviously feeling the tension that had mounted in the room, stood up and made her way to the kitchen. In true Gran style, I heard the cups being moved and the kettle gently humming. My father stood by the window, his back to the room, and I thought back to that awful day when once before his back had been to me, the day he left. Was it such an awful thing? Certainly there were worst things he could have done. He'd never been aggressive to us, he'd never spent nights out drinking, he'd never killed anyone and yet he lost everything, his family, his home, his job and reputation.

His stature was very much as I remembered it, although his shoulders didn't seem quite as broad and his hair, not so dark. The clothes he was wearing were unisex, and unlike on running days, he had no wig on.

"It was the shoes that finally made me realise" I said, getting up to stand with him. He looked down at the *D&G* trainers, smiled slightly and looked back at the window. "I realised that you and Barbara had the same make trainers."

"Lots of people have these trainers," he said, without turning back.

"That's true," I said. "But how many women wear men's trainers?"

"Women who have big feet," he said, looking back and smiling again.

"That's true, and on its own I might never have seen it, but Barbara was wearing the same men's trainers as you and she has little feet, she didn't need to buy big ones."

"That's very perceptive of you Remi," said Barbara, coming back into the room with the tea-tray. I bought them so that Milt's didn't stand out in the crowd but I needn't have bothered, the girls are much smarter than that. They had it all figured out, told me as much the first day Mary joined us, said it didn't bother them in the least."

"Did they know about me?" I asked.

"It didn't take long for them to pick up on it; they knew Milt had a daughter and that we stayed in this area in the hope that he could see you."

"Then why didn't someone say something?"

"They did in their own ways," said Barbara, laughing, "but you were too wrapped up in your own problems to hear them."

We sat down and drank tea, as civilised nations had done for many years before us. Tea, the national panacea of all worries and woes, was now calming the troubled waters that had lain between us for many years. I realised, that for those interceding years I had thought that my father had been homosexual and that his clothes' fetish was just part of a need to be female and yet, looking at Barbara and my father, it was obviously not the case. A thought struck me.

"You work?" I knew that he did, of course, how else could he have had an affair with his secretary. Barbara looked carefully at me. She knew where this was heading and although her eyes willed me not to go there, I carried on – after all, her pain was my pain now.

"I have a small legal firm," he said, catching Barbara's look out the corner of his eye.

She turned away and I carried on: "With staff?" I pursued. He looked at me, then at Barbara. He sat himself down on the small chair that faced opposite me and took hold of one of my hands.

As I pulled it away, I remembered that night of Friday the thirteenth, another time when I had pulled away, another time when I had chosen not to listen. I sat and waited for him to talk.

"I know what you're getting at, Remington." It was the first time anyone had called me that since my father had left, "And you're right to be angry with me but at least let me explain." His eyes implored me too listen, just like the last time, and this time I knew I would.

"What I did to Barbara," he said, turning, as if to speak to her directly, "was the worst betrayal a man could ever do." Despite pinching the bridge of his nose, tears ran down his face and he pulled a handkerchief out of his pocket and wiped them away. "Something I'll never forgive myself for," he turned once more to speak to Barbara, "ever."

She rose from her seat and sat down next to him, taking hold of his hand. She went to say something but he patted her and she stopped. "When I left you, I lost everything, everything I cared for, everything I'd worked towards... It was all gone.

When Barb told me she had cancer, it was the same and I was frightened, more frightened than I've ever been in my life because I knew I might lose everything again. You see Barbara is everything." He squeezed her again and she fiddled with her ring. The strain on both their faces was painful to witness and I truly wished I'd left well alone. I tried to interrupt but my father would hear none of it. He needed to explain, not for the first time and, I suspected, not just to me.

"I would happily have lost my home and my business. None of them," he emphasised again, "none of them meant anything to me without Barb. She was there at my lowest point; she brought me back to life." He looked at her again. "In more ways than one. She gave me something to live for, she understands me, like no else has. Without her, I'm nothing. When she told me she had cancer, I panicked in a terrible, despicable way. I know that. The one person I needed wouldn't talk to me. Of course Barb was getting through the best way she could, trying to be brave in front of me, even though she didn't feel brave. She kept her feelings to herself, and I, and my egotism, felt she was pushing me away just when I needed reassurance."

"Dad, I'm sorry," I said, reaching out to add my hand to theirs. "I'm sorry I brought it up, it's nothing to do with me and Barbara has already told me that she understood and forgave you. Anyway, if anyone should understand self-centredness, it's got to be me." I went on to tell him and Barbara about my friends and their problems, about all the things I'd missed over the years.

"Well it seems we are more alike than I thought," said my father.

"Even the illnesses," put in Barbara. "You should see him when he has 'Man' flu."

"And we both dress in ladies clothing," my father said, sheepishly.

"And apparently we both have 'buddy' good taste." I said, pointing down to all our designer trainers.

We sat catching up for another hour until I explained I should go home and enlighten Gran as to why I left in such a hurry. I hugged my father so hard that I knew, like me, he would check for broken ribs by the time I got outside. Barbara hugged me and held my hands before letting me go with a promise that I would turn up for running at the park on Monday.

"I'd like to introduce you properly to Mary," she said, smiling.

"I'd like that," I replied, kissing her cheek once more. I felt on a complete high as I made my way to the door. Finally, I'd been reunited with my father after all these years and on top of that, I'd also gained a mother and a friend, something I'd never had.

"Oh Remington, I nearly forgot, someone rang my office a few days ago, looking for you."

Who Cares?

"Looking for me? Who would be looking for me?

"Apparently it was a man, said he'd been trying to track you down, wanted a home address or a telephone number to contact you on, and asked my secretary if I was related to you. She's a new secretary," he said, reddening slightly, "so she had no idea, asked him to ring back."

"Did he say why he was looking for me?"

"Something about going to school with you."

My heart skipped a beat, was it possible that Norman was back in England? "Did he have an accent?"

"No, definitely not, according to Margaret, he had a true blue, upper-class accent."

"Oh," I said, feeling my optimism deflate.

"I think she said his name was Anthony Cavanaugh or Cavendish, something like that."

"Don't know anyone of that name," I said, thinking through a very short list of friends and acquaintances.

"Oh my goodness, Tony, I know someone called Tony." Of course and that's where the school connection came from, Marianne, she knew my last name.

"What's wrong Remi, do you know him?"

"Tony is one of the *Mafia* people I told you about Barbara." My father looked shocked.

"What do you mean *Mafia*, Remi, what's this all about?"

"I'm not sure Dad, I think I may have overheard something I shouldn't or got hold of something I shouldn't have." I sat down again and ran through the events of the past few months and the occupants of Wisteria Cottage. My father looked both worried and intrigued, whereas Barbara remained her usual calm self.

"I'm sure this is all something and nothing Remi," she said, finally. "I really don't think the *Mafia* operates from tiny cottages in leafy, suburban London. There must be a good explanation for all of this and if, and when, this Tony rings back to talk to your father, he will most certainly, find out what it's all about."

Despite my father insistence that he should walk me home, I made the short journey myself, giving me the chance to reflect on the events of the day.

Who Cares?

Of all the things that had happened throughout the course of this very strange and heated twenty-four hours, one thing still bothered me the most. Now I know you'll think it strange, you may even question the workings of my mind, given the immensity of the day, but the thing that bothered me the most, was Gran going to church and fetching home the vicar!

There are very few things I know for sure...granted, but the one thing I do know is, Gran never does anything without a good reason. Yes, I can hear you saying, perhaps, it was a perfectly good reason. Penny has a drinking problem and Stephen, the vicar, runs a self-help group. Apparently a match made in heaven, excuse the pun. But surely someone suffering from a broken heart would be in as much need of a friendly, good looking, shoulder-to-cry on vicar.

Twenty-eight

The more I walked, the more determined I was to have it out with Gran as soon as I got home. Family first and all that. If there's a good looking, well dressed vicar going spare then, fair play, I should definitely have had first dibs.

By the time I got home my annoyance was at a peak and as I walked through the door I was prepared for battle. Unfortunately, Gran was prepared for something quite different; the 'peppermint' brigade was assembled in the living room and just about to sit down for a game of Bridge.

To be fair they didn't smell of peppermint at all, in fact, I was strangely drawn to one lady who smelt divine. I sat down next to her, ready to introduce myself.

"I'm sorry," I said, "but I have to ask, what's that lovely perfume you're wearing?"

"Hello Remi, I thought it was you, I didn't know you were related to Petunia." I looked at her for a moment; she did look vaguely familiar but... "It's Jenny, you came to my home once, helped me get ready for bed." Obviously, I still looked a bit vacant... She carried on. "You made me Horlicks. Buttercross Road?"

"Jenny, of course, I'm so sorry. I didn't recognise you straight away, you look so well."

"Well the old hip is still painful dear but not enough to stop me coming for a game of Bridge. I need a bit of help getting in and out of the car but once I'm in and settled I'm perfectly Okay and it all helps to top up the pension," she said, winking.

"Don't be taken in by that sweet smile, darling," said one of the men players, laughing. "She's a wily old duck, she took me for twenty pounds last week, how else do yer think she's buys all them fancy clothes and expensive perfumes?"

"Well I do have a bit of a penchant for nice things," she said, whispering, her face turned away from the others, "but then they are a bit green, in the old Bridge department, if you know what I mean?"

"How do you know Gran, Jenny?"

"Well she's a lot younger than me, of course, but we often ended up in the same stage productions with the Amateur Dramatics Society. Your gran's quite a turn, my dear, that great figure and those shapely legs, no wonder she was such a wow at the Windmill."

"Windmill, what windmill? I didn't even know she worked at a windmill," I said, querulously. One of the men laughed and nudged one of the others.

"Went there myself during the war once, Perc'…Quite an eye-opener, I can tell yer. Who'd a fought old Pet was up there shaking 'er stuff and jiggling it all about."

"Always nude, never rude, that were their slogan, weren't it Jack?" But before Jack could answer, a rolled up newspaper came winging its way across the room, hitting Jack on the back of the head and knocking his glasses off sideways.

"That's quite enough of that talk from you two, get some money out of those long pockets and start losing like gentlemen," said Gran, retrieving her newspaper and giving Jack one last, friendly tap with it.

"Were only joshing Pet," said Jack, holding his hands up in acquiescence. "Anyway what's with you keeping it all under your hat? Not like you to be shy about these things."

"I'm not shy about anything Jack Marshall, as you well know and I never kept this under my hat, or anything else for that matter," said Gran, getting slightly defensive.

"Well they're big enough hats Pet, I'm sure you could hide a lot of things under them old straw hats you're always wearing." Gran's face turned a subtle shade of puce and I could feel a storm brewing, I'd seen that look many times before.

"If my hats offend you so much Jack Marshall I suggest the next time I'm wearing one, which will be always, you should stay well away." I watched on in amazement as Jack jumped out of his chair and raced after my quickly retreating Gran.

Who Cares?

Somehow, something about this whole confrontation didn't sit right. It may be my overactive imagination but it had the resounding ring of a lovers tiff about it.

The room went quiet and small looks were passed back and forth. I looked at Jenny enquiringly but she just shrugged her shoulder and raised her eyebrows, obviously as bewildered as I was. Percy called Jenny up to the table for a game of Black Jack while they waited for the others to return.

"By the way, the perfume," she said, "it's *Bvlgari*. Light, delicate, erotic and expensive …just like me! Hard Seventeen, is it Percy?" she said, getting up out of the chair. Percy nodded his head and laughed.

"Candy from a baby," she said, winking at me. Tentatively I got up, grabbed a few peanuts and walked casually towards the kitchen. I could hear Gran whispering but Jack's voice sounded small and contrite.

"Pet I love your hats, you know that darlin', I was just trying to make light of it all."

"Light of it all," repeated Gran. "It couldn't have been any heavier if you'd hired a sumo wrestler with a megaphone and shouted it from the rooftops. I'm surprised at you, Jack; I thought you had more regard for me than that, but I guess I was wrong. You acted like a couple of silly schoolboys, the pair of you."

"I suppose you got me there Pet, I guess I'm seventy-eight years young and getting younger but I didn't mean no harm by it, you know that. Anyway how comes you never told me you were one of those nude dancers at the Windmill?"

A sudden intake of breath caused a peanut to lodge in my throat and a coughing fit pursued.

"For goodness sake Remi, don't stand out there choking, come in and get a glass of water." Tail between my legs I duly obeyed, skulking into the kitchen still coughing. Gran handed me a glass which I drank from, until the choking subsided.

"Didn't I teach you better than to eavesdrop on conversations, Remi?"

"You did Gran," I said, getting my composure back. "You also taught me to be honest at all times."

"Have I not always been honest with you?"

"Yes Gran but you also taught me that omitting the truth can also be a form of lying."

"Whoops, hoisted by your own petard, Pet," he said, laughing at his own alliteration. Gran didn't need to tell Jack to leave, her eyes said it all.

"Firstly, Remi, I have never lied to you and had you ever asked me about my past, I may have told you about my earlier years but, in truth, Remi, you don't concern yourself with things like that. I suspect you may even think I've always been old." There was a certain degree of truth in that, Gran hadn't changed in all the years I'd known her, which either made her eternally young or old from the beginning!

"Right," said Gran, in her matter of fact way. "This is not the time to be discussing such things. After Jenny and I have relieved the men of their pensions," she said loudly, knowing that Jack would hear, "you and I can talk."

True to her word, after sufficient monies had been won off the men and the group had disbanded, she sat me down on the sofa, with Barty, to elaborate on her past.

"I'm only telling you this Remi because I want to, not because I owe you an explanation. What I did before and, for that matter, *since* you were born, frankly, is none of your business and I owe no one an apology for what jobs or decisions I've made in my life." Her grumpy demeanour I suspected, had more to do with Jack than it did me, as she made reference to her hats once more under her breath, before she sat down.

"I was just seventeen," she said, fidgeting slightly, her hands in her lap, "and my friend, Margaret, who was a few years older than me, had just landed an audition at a theatre in the West End. I persuaded her to take me along. Well actually," she said, looking rather sheepish, "I blackmailed her into taking me."

"Gran," I laughed. "I can't believe you, of all people, would ever blackmail someone!"

"Well, I didn't *exactly* blackmail her," she said, the emphasis being on exactly. "I asked her if I could go with her and before she could say no, I happened to mention that the only other plan I had for that day was to go out with Peggy Fletcher." I looked at her enquiringly.

"Well how does that equate to blackmail, Gran?"

"Well," she said, looking at me coyly. "She knew that I had seen her kissing Charlie Blackwell the night before."

"And?"

"And Charlie Blackwell was going out with Peggy Fletcher and they were supposed to be getting married later in the year."

"So she took you with her?"

"No, not exactly. She wasn't happy about it but she did say I could tag along but then on the day she was unwell and said she couldn't go."

"So you didn't go?"

"Of course I went Remi, I went in her place. Unfortunately when I got there it was packed, they were queuing around the block. I waited in line for my turn, well, Margaret's turn but before I could get to the front they closed the doors and told everyone the places had been filled."

"So what did you do?"

"I decided to walk round some of the other theatres and see if anyone else was hiring. I tried a few with no success and then I happened upon the Windmill. As I stood outside trying to pluck up the courage to go inside, a man came out and started changing the photos on the outside displays. He seemed quite old but of course he was much younger than I am now.

He had a friendly face so I asked him if there were any jobs going inside. He looked me up and down and said he thought I was probably too young and definitely too small. I remember pulling myself up to my full height and telling him, in no uncertain terms, that I was as good a dancer as he'd ever see and if he didn't get me an audition, I'd make sure that when I was famous I'd let his boss know that he'd turned me away. The man took a puff of his huge cigar and started to laugh. Without saying a word he turned and started to walk back inside. Knowing it might've been my last chance, I called out to him. When he turned round, I kicked my leg as high as I could and fell down onto the ground in the splits."

"What did he say to that?"

"He just put out a hand to pull me up, shook his head,

laughed and walked off."

"Oh poor you," I said. "You must have felt awful"

"I was mortified Remi. I grabbed my bag, brushed myself down and decided, I'd had enough – it was time to go home, but as I went to walk away the door opened again and a younger man came running out. He handed me a ticket and told me Mr. Van Damm said he would like me to come and watch the show. If I liked what I saw then I was to seek him out. I asked who this Mr. Van Damm was, but the boy just looked at me quizzically. 'Don't you know nuffing?' he said. 'Mr. Van Damm owns the joint.' With that, he took me into the theatre and sat me down to one side.

It was an hour before the show started and the theatre was packed with men. When the lights went down the stage was filled with the most beautiful and glamorous women I'd ever seen, dressed in the most exotic costumes and outfits, with huge feathers and headdresses. I was transfixed all the way through and when the show finished all the men ran from the back of the theatre up to the stage to try and grab the girls."

"Really?" I said, mesmerised with my own visualisation of the scene conjured up by Gran's words and facial expressions.

"After the show I had to wait for all the men to leave and even though it was light-hearted and amicable, some were still, literally, thrown out by the seat of their pants. I made my way round the back, pushing my way through the girls, the boys and all the props on the floor. When I eventually found the door with Mr. Van Damm's name on it, I knocked and hearing no answer, I popped my head round the door to see if there was anyone there."

Gran's face went an involuntary shade of red as she relayed the story. "Mr. Van Damm was there but he was, how shall I say, otherwise engaged."

"What?" My hand flew to my mouth. "Really?"

Gran laughed and grabbed my hand. "It was so embarrassing; the young lady in question still had her feathered headdress on. He barked at me to get out and as I slammed the door behind me, I saw some of the other dancers laughing. Apparently it was no secret that Mr. Van Damm had an eye for the ladies!"

Who Cares?

"So what happened next?" I said, pulling up my legs to get as comfortable as possible.

"Well, I waited for a while and then one of the lads that worked there brought me over a cup of tea and started talking to me. He gave me an invaluable piece of advice. He told me to act as if I'd never seen anything. If Mr. Van Damm thought I was embarrassed, he'd assume I was too young to work there. So that's what I did. The girl left the room and about ten minutes later the door opened and he called me in. I averted my eyes from the couch and sat, bolt upright, in the chair opposite his desk. I had on my best poker face," she laughed. "The first thing he asked me was did I like what I saw?

Without a second's heartbeat, I told him I loved it. He puffed on his big old cigar and asked me what I enjoyed about it and I told him in detail. I didn't mention the ladies that stood posing without clothes on and when I finished he picked me up on it. He explained to me that the nude models were not allowed to move; if it moves, it's rude, that was the Lord Chamberlain's ruling on it. So they never moved. He flicked his ash into the ashtray and told me that it was nothing I'd ever have to worry about and I thought he was turning me down.

I was just about to jump in and tell him I would pose nude if I had to when he explained that I fidgeted far too much to be a model but he would take me on as a pony. I was outraged and told him so. I wasn't going to dress up as the backend of a horse for him or anyone else. He laughed and coughed so much, I thought he'd have a seizure right there and then. Apparently all the smaller dancers were called ponies. He took me on and I started the next week. I was there four years and it was four of the best years of my life and despite what the likes of Jack think; I *never* posed nude."

"I'm also assuming you didn't end up on the casting couch either, Gran."

"You think right, Remi. Vivian – Mr. Van Damm – was one of the nicest people I ever knew. It was like one big family there, of course, some were closer than others," she said, smiling. "But, nevertheless family. As you know my father died during the war and Vivian was like a second father to me. So much so when Gramps and I got together we named our first and, sadly, only child after him."

"Of course, my mum... Vivienne"; I saw the sadness in her face and knew that subject was taboo. It was not only me Vivienne Hall-Smyth had let down, it was Gran, and that was one thing I could never forgive her for.

"Ah Gran," I said, taking her hand, "there's just so much I don't know about you but one thing I do know, for sure." She looked at me for a moment and I kissed her hand. "I know that I love you more than anyone else in the world."

We talked on for a while longer and then I went on to tell her all about my evening, about finding Dad and his relationship with Barbara. It was late into the night before we finished. Barty was already snoring away when we washed up the last of the cups and said our goodnights.

"There was just one other thing, Gran."

"Ah yes, Remi, I was wondering when you'd mention it."

"What do you mean? You can't possibly know what I'm going to ask."

"You're going to ask why I didn't introduce you to Stephen," she said, matter of factly.

"How?" I said, taken aback. "How could you know that?" And it wasn't for the first time I wondered if she could read minds.

"Because I saw your face when he came in Remi and I know you well enough to know that you would have thought about it, dwelt on it and finally turned it round in your head as a personal insult."

"You couldn't be farther from the truth," I lied. "It just crossed my mind, this very minute." Gran looked up for a moment and then at me.

"The reason I didn't bring him home for you Remi, is easy. He's not the one. He's perfect for Penny and I do believe that they'll make a very handsome couple but he's not the right one for you."

"How do you know that, Gran?" I spluttered, tears starting to well up. "And if he's not, who is the right one for me? Will I ever find the right one?" Gran smiled her, 'I know everything,' smile and took my hand and led me up the stairs.

"I don't know who the right one is, Remi, but I know he's on the way, have patience."

"But Gran," I protested.

"Trust me Remi, I'm a pensioner...." and with that she started serenading me with Mister Sandman, in her own inimitable style. She instructed me to take over the boom, boom, booms in the chorus and by the time we hit the top stair and the last line, the knees were bent, the jazz hands were out and we were singing "Mister Sandman send me a dream", in perfect harmony.

Twenty-nine

At seven-thirty on the Friday morning I woke in a panic. In the peripherals of my mind I could hear a fire-alarm ringing, someone was shouting out my name and water was spraying onto my face. When, at last, I managed to detach my mind from its sleep-induced trance and haul it back into the real world, it still took me a good few minutes to realise that it was my alarm clock ringing and Gran calling me to come down for breakfast. As I turned my head the water splashing was also explained as I looked into the deep-brown, mournful eyes of Barty who, it appeared, was trying to save me time on ablutions by washing me himself. Unbeknown to me at the time, this maritime disaster theme was to pursue me for the whole weekend.

On the surface the weekend ahead seemed well organised, straightforward with no obvious problems looming on the horizon. Underneath, however, my heart raced at the thought of my rendezvous with Michael and everything else seemed like just a means to an end.

I double-checked my work schedule to make sure I knew what I was doing. Originally I'd been working teas and bed calls Friday evening but changed them to tea calls only, after arranging my date with Michael. Saturday, I wasn't working and had all day to get ready to accompany Henry to his charity event. Yes, on the surface everything was swimming along perfectly... So who could have foreseen the storm about to brew?

There was still a lot to get done before I could enjoy the fruits of the evening, so I packed up some lunch and made my way over to Lucy's, to pick up the van. I dashed out of the house narrowly avoiding Gran who would have wanted to know if we were having supper together later on. I felt bad that I'd side-stepped her, after our heart to heart and all, but what she didn't know wouldn't hurt her, but then again, what didn't Gran know?

As I pulled up to Wisteria Cottage I was relieved that, yet again, the blue car was not outside. I'd asked Lucy, earlier in the week, if I could stop coming to the house but she looked so disappointed I had no choice but to back down. She did promise me however, that by the time Marianne had moved to her new address, she would be able to carry on the calls herself.

I unlocked the door quietly and tip-toed up the hall to check that the place was indeed, empty. Not for the first time, I found I was wrong. There was a small crack in the door to the kitchen and I could just see the back of someone pacing up and down, the dark hair suggesting it was Tony and not James. He was on the phone and had no idea that I had entered, luckily neither had Precious who was still sleeping in her basket. This time I checked the window to make sure that I was not caught out again by my own reflection.

I decided the best course of action was just to leave and I'd try explaining it to Lucy later. Decision made, I turned and started making my way towards the door but was drawn back when I heard something very strange. Tony had just told someone on the other end of the phone that his name was James Brodie and that, I knew, was a big 'buddy' lie. I crept back again just as Tony started making his way up the stairs. I opened the door just a smidge and popped my head through. I couldn't make out the whole conversation just snippets.

"But I did explain about the dog, didn't I?" He must have moved off into a bedroom because I missed the next line but as he came back into earshot, I heard more. "Yes I know, Shwachman Diamond, I'm well aware of it. It could fetch a lot of money and I'm well up for it but first I must find the dog." I heard a door slam upstairs and knew it was now or never if I was to get hold of Precious. I made a quick dash picked her up and made for the door. I didn't relax again until I'd picked up Lord and set off on our walk.

In my head I replayed the phone conversation I'd overheard. It was obvious that Marianne had lied to me about Barty. Tony *had* been out in the park looking for him that time, but why would she lie? Well I suppose that was an easy one, she was a mean-spirited witch who liked getting her own way but why then did Tony lie and pretend to be James and what had this diamond got to do with it?

It would've been a quick walk had it not been for a rather worrying re-acquaintance with 'Tweedy' – the reluctant squirrel killer. She saw me from across the park and made her way over to chat and pet the dogs. She was flushed from her walk but there was something else.

"I thought it was you," she said, reaching down to pat Precious whilst keeping Jacky on a tight rein. "I haven't seen you here for ages, not since…" The last line was left unsaid but we both knew. I wondered just how much she knew, had she guessed that I was the phantom shouter. I felt a surge of bile hit my throat.

"Actually," she said, looking more than a little too pleased about the whole event. "That terrible event and that awful day turned out to be quite a turning point for me." Her face flushed once again with, what was obviously not just energised blood flow from power-walking. In fact as I took a closer look at 'Tweedy', I could see she'd lost weight, her hair had been re-cut and her clothes were …Well, no longer tweedy.

"When I left you and headed off home, I thought I heard someone call my name. I turned but no one was there. I walked back up to the road again but couldn't see anyone. I began to think I'd made it up, perhaps it was my conscience pricking. Then I noticed someone sitting alone looking really sad and, just as you helped me, I thought I should go and see if I could help him."

My mind was racing ahead already, the shoes and the haircut told me everything but I let her continue and I gasped and sighed in all the right places as she explained that it was someone she'd known at school. He'd broken up with his girlfriend and she'd taken the dog. Well it didn't take a psychology degree to work out the rest of this little scenario, did it? They got together, he loved her dogs, and they were going to get married. It was a happy ever after…

I wished her well and was just about to leave when she called after me. "I don't even know your name," she said.

"It's Remington, Remi for short," I replied.

"I never really thanked you properly on the day and, somehow, I feel I owe you so much more now, so thank you." Reluctantly I accepted her thanks, knowing that yet another girl would be making her way down the aisle thanks to my bad luck.

"Sorry," I said, "did you tell me your name?" She laughed at her absentmindedness and put out her hand in a formal handshake.

"It's Pricilla, Cilla for short." I laughed, despite myself, at the thought of Pricilla hearing her name when I threw the evil taunt out of the window to be distorted by the wind. A taunt that would lead her to true happiness... If life were that simple, why couldn't it happen to me?

I popped Precious in through the door and made a hasty retreat back to the van without detection. I walked the other dogs and took a few minutes to sit with Henry, who was unusually excited about the prospect of the next day and the charity event.

"You're going to be the most handsome man there," I said, looking at the clothes he was proposing to wear.

"I'll be the luckiest man there anyway," he replied, winking at me. "Cos I'll 'ave the prettiest gal on me arm."

"You're an old smooth talker, Henry," I said, pinching his cheek playfully and kissing him on the head. "I'll see you tomorrow." I made off to the park hoping for a quick walk with Barbara, Dad and the girls but was surprised to see that the girls were there but Barbara was alone.

"Where's Mary?" I said, looking round.

"She's not here today," said Barbara, grabbing hold of my arm and walking me away from the others. "Your dad's here."

"What do you mean?" I laughed. "I know that."

"No," she said, more seriously. "I mean your dad's here... as your *dad*." She pointed towards the little café and there sitting at one of the tables was indeed, my father, dressed in jeans and cashmere sweater, just his *D&G* trainers giving the game away to a more voracious observer.

"Hi, Dad. What's up?" I was perplexed to see the change in him.

Who Cares?

"I thought it was time that I started acting like a father Remi, perhaps then you'll listen to me."

"Listen to you, what do you mean?"

"I mean this Michael thing Remi, I've been checking him out and I don't think he's on the level."

"What?" I said, jumping up from my seat. "What do you mean you've been checking up on him? Why would you check up on him?" I felt the onset of hyperventilation and tried to calm myself, but to no avail. I grabbed a bag from my pocket which I always kept for emergencies and blew deeply into it. The return to easy breathing was quick and I folded the bag back and looked over into my father's worried face. "What gives you the right to think I would welcome your interfering? I've managed all these years without it."

I saw the hurt on his face and knew I'd been unfair. I knew too that Barbara would be watching, but I didn't care. I turned on my heels and left.

Tea calls held the usual ups and downs related to Equality Healthcare but even so, I welcomed them and the relief that I did not have to think about my own life and the things that were swilling around in my head.

The day before I'd been out on a call for a new client, Mrs. Merchant, who was unable to get herself up and needed to be hoisted from chair to commode and back again. This meant we had to work in pairs so we could work the hoist and manage the client without any hiccups. I'd been teamed with Sam, who had taken me out when I first started, and the visit held no problems.

However, after the call, Mrs. Merchant phoned the office and said that I'd been rude and abrupt. Sam backed me up by saying that I'd been neither, but the office advised me to use extreme caution and be extra polite next time.

With this in mind, I stopped off at the local newsagents and bought Mrs. Merchant a box of chocolates. You know the ones, where the man would leap over mountains and swim rivers just to deliver the lady her chocolates, not the most expensive but certainly not the cheapest ones. Armed with my gift I breezed confidently through the door and bestowed them upon the, ever so slightly, cantankerous Mrs. Merchant. The look of surprise was worth the price of a box of chocolates alone.

"Oh my dear, you shouldn't have," she spluttered. "It's so kind of you but totally unnecessary."

"I didn't like to think that I'd upset you yesterday. I'm really sorry if I was a little sharp, I certainly didn't mean to be."

"Oh my dear, think nothing of it. We all have our off days but what a lovely gesture."

I heard Sam come though the front door and winked at her as she looked over towards the chocolates on Mrs. Merchant's lap. She reciprocated the smile and between us we started to hoist Mrs. M up and place her on the commode. We sorted out the medication, started the tea and placed her back into her chair. She was no longer Mrs. Merchant, she was Mrs. 'Buddy' Delightful.

Thoughtful of my other calls and aware that I had to get on, I paid my fond goodbyes to Mrs. M and headed out towards the door, leaving it ajar so that Sam could follow me out shortly. As I reached for the car door handle I realised I'd left my clipboard with my worksheet on it, inside. As I ran back and entered the door I could hear Mrs. M shouting and Sam was trying to pacify her.

"Can you believe the damn cheek of the girl?" I heard her saying. "First she's rude to me and pushes me about as though I were some sort of rag doll and then she comes back with a cheap box of chocolates and shoves them straight in my face."

"I'm sure she meant no harm, Mrs. Merchant," I heard Sam say. "She's a very nice girl and a very good carer."

"Good carer, my foot," she retorted. "She knows I'm diabetic, she's trying to kill me." My hand shot up to my mouth in utter surprise, of all the two-faced... I heard Sam saying goodbye and took that opportunity to walk back into the room and pick up my clipboard. Sam looked slightly worried but Mrs. Merchant held nothing back. "Hello Dear, I was just saying how sweet it was of you to buy me such a considerate present. They look absolutely delicious." I smiled, grabbed my board and followed Sam out, where we both collapsed in tears of laughter.

"A lesson to us," laughed Sam. "You can't please them all."

Who Cares?

It was better news when I rounded the corner to the small complex where Fred lived. A removal van was outside and all the belongings of one of the occupants were being put in. Normally that might equate to someone having passed on but, on this occasion, I could tell by the smiles on some of the faces, Mavis' in particular, that this was not the case.

"She's gone," she said, happily, as I got out of the car and made my way to Fred's flat. The joy on her face was infectious and I couldn't help but be pleased for this small, genteel redhead.

"Does that mean you and Fred are…..." I didn't have to finish the question, her face said it all. She sidled past me and took hold of Fred's hand.

"We're going to see how it goes," she said, looking furtively towards the removal van once more.

I made Fred something to eat and drink and helped him to the toilet – where he confided that Beryl had been too much for him.

"It was never her, you know, it were always Mavis but Beryl wouldn't let it go. She hounded me until I couldn't say no." Remembering the day when I caught them in the act, I couldn't help but wonder how much resistance he'd put up on that day, but I kept my thoughts to myself.

My last and final call of the day was to Henry. I'd saved him 'til the end so that I could sit and chat with him for a while. I needed to talk to someone about Michael and although he hadn't been very receptive last time, I was desperate to give it another go. I told him how Michael had said his marriage was a mistake, that he didn't love her and that it was me he wanted to be with. I explained how I felt, although in truth, I wasn't altogether sure how that was. When I'd finished I looked at him, hoping that he would have just the right words to waylay my misgivings about the forthcoming date.

"Well Henry, don't you think everyone deserves a second chance, hasn't he proved that he still loves me?"

"If you want my opinion darlin," he said, "although I doubt that you do, I think you're just rearranging chairs on the Titanic."

"What?" I laughed, stunned by such an opaque answer.

Who Cares?

"What I mean darlin is, I admire you for trying and I wish I could make it right for yer but at the end of the day, no matter what you do, that ship's still gonna sink."

His words hung over me like a leaded weight as I picked out an outfit for my date. First the dream in the morning and now Henry's reference to the same thing, perhaps fate was trying to tell me something. I held up a little, Lipsy dress and wondered if it was too short but before I could make my mind up my mobile rang out with the theme from *Mission Impossible*. It was Michael.

"Hey gorgeous, how are you?"

"I'm fine," I purred, "all the better for hearing you." Okay I agree, it's terrible dialogue, like something out of a sixties, Jane Fonda movie but give me a break, I'd had a hard day.

"Looking forward to tomorrow?"

"Tomorrow, what's happening tomorrow?"

There was a slight delay before he answered. "Our date, have you forgotten?" Quickly I struggled with the day's events. The date on the newspaper, the reporter on the television, the date I'd written and signed a dozen times today for Equality Healthcare.

"Today's Friday,"

"Yes, darling. Today is Friday but our date is for Saturday, which is tomorrow. Remember?" The tone in which he delivered this information was only fractionally more annoying than the fact that he was insinuating that I'd got it wrong, when, clearly, the day had been etched into my brain and was probably the last thing I would forget, even if I were to go down with acute dementia from that moment on.

"You said Friday, I remember it perfectly."

"The first time, darling, yes. But then it got rearranged for the next day and I rang you and told you." The word rearranged hit me like a bullet, the very same word that Henry had used to outline the futility of our relationship.

"You didn't ring me, I thought it was tonight," I said, feeling tears of anger or pity – I wasn't sure what – welling up in my eyes.

"Are you sure? I was positive I'd rung to change the date."

"I'm sure," I said in clipped tones that expressed my

annoyance.

"Arghh," he said, "damn my busy schedule, please tell me you can still come, darling, it's really important you're there."

"Well actually I can't, I'm going out tomorrow." There was a heavy silence and I almost stepped in to bridge it, when he spoke again.

"Please Remi, I really want you there with me, I have something I want to ask you." My fickle heart skipped a beat; they were the words that girls dreamt about. What I'd dreamed about and knew, no matter what it meant, I could not pass them up.

"Okay. I think I might be able to get out of the other thing."

"Great," he said. "I'll pick you up at the flat at seven." Before I could reply, he was gone. I felt excited knowing, that the next day, I would be meeting a man I thought I loved and yet sad that on the same day, I could be letting down a man I cared for very much. I just hoped Henry would forgive me. I ended my day as it had begun, Gran was calling me down to dinner and I had the feeling of impending doom in the pit of my stomach.

Thirty

I didn't sleep that Friday night. The prospect of the next day scared away any good dreams and I was too frightened to close my eyes for fear of a bad one. I checked my phone that I'd put on silent and saw three missed calls from Dad. I wanted to speak to him but he'd made it quite clear, before as Mary and again as my father, that he did not like or trust Michael Hayes and that was a conversation I could live without.

I had all morning to pick out something to wear, so as Gran busied about downstairs, I pottered about upstairs, under the guise of cleaning my room. I picked up the black, Lipsy cocktail dress again and tried it on. Actually, it looked better than when I'd first bought it, what with the weight loss and the toning that came with the dog walking; it looked pretty darn hot. I decided to team it up with a pair of black, ankle boots and a beautiful silk, cashmere pashmina which Gran had bought me for Christmas two years ago.

Before I could decide on accessories, or how to wear my hair, I was interrupted by Gran calling me from downstairs. Her voice was a little fractured and I guessed straight away that something was wrong. Gran was sitting on the floor, one arm wrapped around Barty.

"I think he's poorly Remi, he's hardly eaten a thing today and he keeps making a whining noise, as if he's in pain." Barty lay flat out and stared at me, almost too pleased to be the centre of attention but he did indeed moan when I touched his stomach.

"Look Gran, he might've just eaten something that's upset him. It's probably best to wait and see what happens, but if he's no better in the morning, I'll take him to the vet." I felt bad that my decision to wait was partly because I knew a large vet bill would just about wipe out my bank account but also because it was time I didn't have to spare.

My day was filled with avoiding calls from Dad and Barbara, interspersed with sighs from Gran and whines from Barty. Eventually I could take the stress no more and bundled Barty into the back of my car. Gran phoned the vet whilst we made the journey and was told they would have to get the emergency on-call vet out, as it was a Saturday. I counted down the minutes as we sat in the, unusually empty, waiting room. Probably other people have pets that knew better than to get ill at the weekend but not us. Barty sat, placidly, on the floor by Gran's feet, lifting his head only when the vet walked in the door.

He tried to jump Barty up onto the table but the poorly Barty was having none of it. So then Gran and I tried to lift Barty up which only succeeded in lifting his enormous, fat bottom two inches off the floor, and having our faces smothered in kisses – from the dog that is, not the vet – although in truth, that would certainly have brightened up the day.

Eventually the vet listened to Barty's heart and his grumbly tummy and told us that he'd keep him overnight for observation and X-ray him, either the next day or Monday morning. All the way home in the car I worried, selfishly, about the money. A night at the vet's didn't come cheap. I wondered if the vet would accept something in kind, like his shirts ironed, a back scrub or a home visit from a domestic, home-care goddess in her uniform and rubber gloves.

Inadvertently I laughed out loud which obviously caught Gran's attention but also incurred her disapproval.

"How can you be laughing at a time like this, Remi?"

"I'm not laughing at that, Gran; give me a little credit for the seriousness of the situation."

"Well what were you laughing at then?" she said, turning to face me.

"It was a sort of ironic laugh, Gran."

"Well what was so ironic that you felt you had to laugh then?" What was it about people who felt they had the moral, upper-high ground? Why did they feel it necessary to whittle away until, the low ground people felt compelled to say something that would undoubtedly be their undoing.

"If you must know, Gran, I was thinking about the vet."

"Ah ha," said Gran, in her 'I knew it all along' tone. I decided, in my new found maturity, to let the conversation drop and not follow through on what ultimately would lead to yet another, Gran victory. In fact I waited a whole sixty seconds before saying.

"What do you mean by, 'ah ha'?"

"Just what I say, Remi. Ah ha."

"But what does that mean?" I said, hearing the whining frustration in my own voice.

"It means Remi, that while I was sitting there worrying about poor Barty, you were probably wondering how old the vet was, and whether he's available." Damn that old woman and her psychic ways. "It was as plain as the nose on your face that he's recently divorced."

"What, how could you possibly know that?"

"White mark round his ring finger," she said, rather too smugly. I conceded defeat. There was no reasoning with Gran when she had a bee in her bonnet, the worst of it was, she was nearly always right.

It felt strange at home without Barty. How one, hitherto, uninvited dog could be so integral to the well-being and happiness of both of us in such a short period of time, was hard to believe. Gran ambled about, plumping cushions that didn't need to be plumped, wiping down sides that didn't need to be wiped and checking the time every ten minutes. I knew how she felt and even the anticipation of the evening ahead had lost its lustre.

Eventually, when it came time to get ready my heart started skipping beats again. Arriving downstairs, Gran gave me the once over. She knew, of course, that I had arranged to accompany Henry to the charity event, what she didn't know about was Michael.

"That's a little overdone for a charity event, isn't it, Remi?"

"There's never anything overdone about a little, black dress Gran, everyone knows that." She pondered on that for a while and plumped yet another cushion.

Who Cares?

"I wonder if it's too late to get a ticket, I could do with taking my mind off poor Barty." Now for anyone who's ever studied body language, my reaction would have been akin to waving a big flag with the words, 'I'm lying' emblazoned on the front, whilst plugging myself into a lie-detector and watching the needle shoot off the page. A small flush came over me, beads of sweat formed on my brow, my shoulders stiffened and my eyes jumped right and left, as I tried desperately to think of a good excuse.

"They've been sold out for ages, apparently."

"Really? I thought I saw a leaflet up in the local shop only a week ago offering tickets." Who knew if that was true, she was such a wily old thing and if she thought I was up to something, she was easily clever enough to outmanoeuvre me.

"There's no time, Gran, I need to leave in a few minutes."

"It'll only take me a minute, a quick dress change, a hat and a spray of perfume and I'm done," she said, getting up out of her seat.

"Gran, I'm sorry, I can't take you." She fixed me with her most piercing stare as she asked me why not and, in that moment, I knew that she already knew.

I explained what had happened, how the dates had coincided. I explained I was going to take Henry to the dinner and then leave him to go out with Michael returning in time to take him home. Uncharacteristically for Gran, she said nothing. It was, without doubt, one of the worst things she'd *never* said to me. Her eyes and her demeanour said it all. She was disappointed in me and worst of all... so was I.

She was feigning sleep when I went out the door ten minutes later. I knew she was pretending and I felt a deep-pang of hurt. In my whole life I couldn't remember a time when Gran didn't say goodbye when I left the house. It was the norm, a constant, an absolute ...but not that night.

As I got into my car, my phone rang and I felt flushed with relief. I should have known she couldn't do it; she wouldn't let me walk out without saying goodbye and telling me to take care, but as I looked at the display, I was hugely disappointed to see it was Michael.

"Hello gorgeous, are you on your way?"

"I'm running a bit late, Michael but I'll be there in about half an hour."

"Half an hour," he said, his voice stiff

"I may be a bit quicker, I've just got to take someone somewhere and I'll come straight onto you."

"What do you mean? Take who, where?"

"One of my gentlemen, I was supposed to be accompanying him tonight before you changed your plans but now I'm just going to drop him off and come straight over."

"For goodness sake, Remi, why don't you just order the old boy a taxi?" My stomach turned at his description of Henry as an old boy. In my eyes, Henry was anything but old, he was ageless and he was my friend.

"I can't do that, it's a special night for him, he's been looking forward to it and it's bad enough that I'm not staying with him."

"I don't believe you, Remi, this is a special night for me too but you're happy to let me down."

"I'm not letting…" But before I could finish he cut in.

"I'll wait for twenty minutes and then I'm leaving." With that he put the phone down.

When I arrived at Henry's he called out to me from the bedroom to say he'd be a few moments. I sat on his wooden chair by the fire and talked to Humphrey, who apparently had nothing to say as he didn't even turn his head to acknowledge me. I looked at my watch and wondered how long it would take for me to get to the British Legion club and make my way over to the flat, where I was meeting Michael.

I remembered that he had something to ask me. Was it *the* question? What if it was, what would I say? How did I really feel about Michael? The frightening truth was, I didn't know. I hadn't thought about him for months until he rang in the middle of the night. Trying to think about it logically, in the clear honest way that Gran would, was I in love with Michael? Or had I just wanted to prove that I was better than Martha and that he'd made a big mistake. Was this all about revenge?

I was in such deep thought I didn't hear Henry come into the room. When I looked up I felt a huge lump come into my throat. Henry was in full, military uniform. His tie was knotted to perfection, his shoes shone, his hat sat perfectly on his head and the left side of his chest was covered in medals.

"Henry, you look amazing." He turned so I could see the whole effect and, even at his age, he held himself straight and proud.

"So many medals, what are they all for."

"Nuffing special, gel, just the usual campaign medals …just for being there"

"Well you look incredibly smart and very handsome Henry." He put his walking stick on the side of the table and put out his arm for me to take it.

"You're not leaving that behind, are you, Henry? It's too dangerous; you might fall and hurt yourself."

"Listen gel, I'm not walking into that room wiv a stick and that's the truth of it and if you'd a told me sixty years ago that the most dangerous fing I'd be doing tonight was walking wiv-out a stick, I'd a laughed at yer. Now come on, gel, you're the only support I need tonight."

"Me and your pride you mean, Henry." I took his arm and slowly but surely we walked towards the door. It took more time than I'd imagined, chivvying him along the path and into the car but, eventually, we made it. I leaned over and buckled him in and as I pulled away he took hold of my hand and kissed it.

"You're a good girl, Remi." I watched him for a moment as he took the tickets for the function out of his pocket and thought, not for the first time, of all the life, this man had seen and lived in the years since his birth. Two wars, five kings and queens, umpteen prime ministers, landing on the moon, motorways, mobile phones, supermarkets; the list was endless.

"Right," I said, "let's have a look at those." I took what I thought to be tickets off Henry, but was surprised to see they weren't tickets at all. They were invitations. Henry hadn't bought tickets to this function; he had been personally invited with a guest. I had further assumed that as the function was being run by the British Legion, it was to be held at their local club, but I was wrong again. This particular charity event was being held at one of London's top hotels. I looked down at the invitation again and back at Henry. His clear, blue eyes held mine for a few moments.

"Somefing wrong, gel?"

"No Henry, nothing's wrong." Not with you at least, I thought to myself.

When we arrived and got out of the car, a valet came and immediately took it away, which was great because I didn't have to worry about parking, but bad because it just confirmed what I already thought – fate was conspiring against me yet again. How on earth was I going to be able to leave Henry here alone and go to Michael?

The foyer was huge but someone came over straight away and offered Henry a seat whilst we waited to go through.

"Can't we just go through now?" I said, impatiently.

"I'm afraid not," said the sickly-sweet receptionist with her elegantly manicured hands, her trim, little figure, and her tailored suit. "We're still setting out the last of the seating arrangements. It won't take us long; I'll get you a coffee while you wait."

I sat down next to Henry and looked at my watch, it had already gone past the twenty minutes that Michael had given me and he had not rung back. As I checked my phone to make sure I hadn't pressed the silent button, it rang.

"Are you nearly here?" he shouted abruptly down the line. I told Michael the reception was poor and said I'd ring him back. I excused myself from Henry and ran to the other side of the magnificent, open plan vestibule. It reminded me of a larger, grander version of Hillside School for Girls – my first school.

I recalled that last day as I ran out of the school trying to head Gran off. The butterflies in my stomach warned me that this could be, yet another, Friday the thirteenth for me. Suddenly it dawned on me, that this time I held all the cards. I was not running away, I was deciding which course of action to take.

Should I again try and head Gran, or in this case Henry, off at the pass, just to hold face with my peers? Or (and this was the big or), should I stop and decide what I really wanted to do and more importantly what was the right thing to do? I dialled the number and waited for him to pick up.

"Well?" was all he said! I took a deep breath and one last look at Henry.

"I'm sorry Michael, I'm afraid I won't be able to come this evening."

"What…What do you mean you won't be able to come?"

"What I said Michael, I had a prior arrangement and I now realise I can't let him down." There was a cruel and mirthless laugh at the end of the phone.

"Let me get this right, Remi. You'd prefer to go to some old codger's 'do' with some old boy who probably won't make it through the evening and probably can't remember your name, than come out with me?"

I looked over once more at Henry and saw the receptionist trying to raise him up from his chair. He pointed over to me and winked, and the receptionist waved and left him there. I knew Henry was perfectly capable of getting himself out of any chair, but there was no way he was going in there without me – that was the true measure of the man.

"Yes, that's about it Michael. I'm sorry, I've got to go."

"I never thought of you being so callous, Remi. You let me down tonight and it's over between us and I mean that." His voice was dark and malicious, a side I'd never really seen or heard in him before but then were many sides of the multifaceted Michael Hayes that I'd never seen before and it was only now that I knew – I didn't want to.

"And to think I was going to ask you to go away with me for the weekend." He laughed, bitterly.

I gasped and stifled a laugh, I wanted to laugh so badly but all I could do was to impart my last words. "Go home to your wife Michael, have a great life and don't ever ring me again. Goodbye."

I snapped the phone shut and felt empowered for the first time in my life. I'd made a decision on how I felt and not how others would see me and I'd ended a relationship that I knew in my heart was going nowhere. I turned around and saw Henry waiting patiently and I knew, more than anything in my entire life, that for once I'd made the right decision.

"Come on Henry, let's go and find our place, although for the amount of people who've walked through this lobby in the last ten minutes, I reckon we'll be able to take our pick of where to sit. No wonder they were advertising tickets only a week ago."

"I thought it was invitation only, Remi."

"Not according to Gran, she said they were advertising in the local shop." Henry's face was puzzled for a moment but soon recovered when the receptionist, a lady of many talents apparently, came over to show us the way and open the door. Henry was a little stiff from sitting and walked slowly, heavily aided by myself but eventually we made it to the proffered door.

When the door was opened to the function room, I was shocked to see it was like the Black Hole of Calcutta in there.

"Excuse me," I said in my loudest, most authoritative, professional carer's voice. "Are you cutting back on light bulbs or something?"

Miss Efficiency was taken aback by my commanding voice which echoed loud and resoundingly throughout the auditorium we were about to enter. She went to say something but I had my second bout of empowerment.

"Do you know how dangerous it is for someone of an older age to walk though a badly lit area?" Oh yes, I was on a roll; the old Equality Healthcare training was all coming back to me now.

I took the weight of the door from her and asked her to close her eyes.

"I'm sorry, Miss?" she struggled to see the name on my name tag, the one she'd given me only ten minutes before.

"Remington Hall-Smyth," I said, unusually referring to my full name, which I knew could sound pompous but on this occasion I was going for intimidating. Henry smiled, politely, at the receptionist and shrugged his shoulders and, reluctantly, she gave in and closed her eyes.

"Right, now stand on one leg with your eyes still closed." I could see a grimace on her lips but she obeyed and immediately started to topple. "You see," I said, euphorically. "That's what it's like with impaired vision, now if you would kindly turn on the lights, I will escort this gentleman through."

Suddenly, without a movement from the receptionist, all the lights came on in the adjoining room, the band started up and we were suddenly aware of faces, lots of faces.

As we took another step forward, egged on by Miss E, it became apparent that the room was absolutely packed.

Everyone was on their feet. Music started playing and as Henry came into clear view so they started to clap. They clapped with their hands and they stamped with their feet and they saluted.

Henry recognised someone who jumped out of his seat to shake his hand. The room was strewn with flags and banners, men in uniform and ladies in long dresses. Lights were flashing and people ran in front of us, clearing away the crowds like the sweeper on a curling pitch.

Eventually, after numerous stops along the way to greet people, we arrived at the top table and Henry was escorted to his seat. Someone touched my arm and pointed to another seat on a table in the corner reserved for me.

As I made my way through the tight gangway between tables I heard a loud shout and turned to see people on the top table all moving down one place. Henry waved and beckoned me towards him and one of the waiters helped me to my newly appointed chair, right beside the guest of honour.

"Henry, you shouldn't have, I would have been perfectly alright over there."

"Maybe you would 'ave, darlin' but I came wiv you and I'm staying wiv you, you're the most important person 'ere to me." My jaw felt tight and I clenched my teeth hoping that the tears would stay away long enough for people to start eating their meal. "Anyway gel, you didn't leave me, did yer," he said, in his all knowing way and taking hold of my hand. The tears started to fall, with or without permission.

Once the meal got under way, I relaxed a little and began to look round the room. The average age of the congregation was about seventy to eighty, all veterans of the war, wearing their medals and regalia; it was a very impressive sight. There were also ladies in uniform, something I hadn't given a lot of thought

Who Cares?

to before but of course they served as well.

As my eyes became accustomed, I started to see individual faces. There, three tiers back, was a table with faces I recognised. It was Gwen and Dolly sporting beautiful gowns, their hair professionally put up with little tendrils hanging gently round their face. I remembered that they'd mentioned they were going to a charity event but, of course, I never asked where or what it was about. They saw me looking and waved profusely in my direction, their faces beaming with pleasure.

The last course was placed on the table in front of me, a beautiful gateau full of cherries and cream and laced with something alcoholic. It was so gorgeous that I shovelled a huge spoonful into my mouth and, as I savoured the taste, I saw someone staring at me, with a look of disapproval – a look I knew very well.

There was Gran looking, actually, quite gorgeous, in a beautiful sequin-studded gown and, of course, a hat. Not her big, Audrey Hepburn style hat but a more modest, pillbox hat with a small veil. It complemented the dress and her face perfectly. I wanted to shout out my approval but, given the way we'd parted, I thought it best to wait until I could get to speak to her personally.

After the meal someone got up and asked for quiet. There was praise and plaques given out to many of the ex-soldiers sitting in the audience, and stories of bravery were abundant.

The last recipient was Henry.

We were told of his bravery under fire and how he was on reconnaissance with another soldier and saw an enemy party making towards camp, and the sleeping soldiers. Single handedly, these two soldiers took out twelve men, using only knives and their own strength. The other soldier, sadly, had later been killed in action. They were both awarded the Victoria Cross for their bravery. In total Henry had served in five campaigns and had been awarded medals for each one.

As he was awarded a plaque the whole room got to its feet. All those in uniform saluted, the rest clapped. Standing there, I realised how important my decision had been to stay tonight. I looked over at Gran, who must have known but hadn't said

Who Cares?

anything. I knew, instinctively, that she knew that the decision had to be mine and mine alone and I thanked God, I'd made the right one. Tears streamed down my face as I looked at the only person in the room still sitting: Henry.

If ever there was a lesson to be learnt in life it was this; People are not born old. They have lived long lives, full of experience, heartbreak and joy. Everyone has something to learn from them. Why shouldn't Fred have a girlfriend and enjoy the years he has left? If June wants to be grumpy and cantankerous, then that's her prerogative, and if the sweet and beautiful Jenny wants to take the guys for all they have with her poker prowess, then good on her.

Henry had never mentioned the fact that he'd been a war hero, or been awarded the highest decoration, he was without a doubt a hero once again. Mine.

Thirty-one

The next morning when I rolled downstairs, Gran was making breakfast. We'd settled our differences the night before and the atmosphere in the kitchen was light and cheerful.

"Full English today, Remi, are you up for it?" I smiled as she busied herself with cracking eggs and frying bacon.

"I could eat a horse, I'm starving."

"Have you seen the paper, there's a picture of you and Henry on page four." I flicked the paper open and looked at the picture of Henry standing proud and tall in his highly decorated uniform. Beside him was a woman with tussled, unruly hair, her mouth open and a look of a scared rabbit caught in headlights.

"I think that must have been taken when you first entered the room, just after you'd made the receptionist stand on one leg and close her eyes," said Gran, laughing merrily.

"Oh that's great, did everyone hear that?"

"Of course, you could have heard a pin drop, I thought shouting out your name in full, was inspired." I buried my head in my hands and groaned.

"Why do you always see the half-empty view of life, Remi? You were doing your job; you were concerned about the welfare of Henry. It was absolutely the right thing to do, I was proud of you."

"You were?"

"Of course, I'm always proud of you, Remi but yesterday…more than ever." I studied the picture again and read the whole article; it went on to list even more things that Henry had done during the war and stated that he was one of the most highly decorated war heroes of World War Two.

"Well who'd have known?" I said out loud.

"Only if we take the time to ask," said Gran, placing

breakfast down in front of me. "Does this mean we won't all be lumped under the title of 'Peppermint Brigade', from now on?" I stood up and gave her a cuddle.

"You've never been that Gran and just for the record, you've always been my hero."

We settled down to our lovely fry up and I started to peruse the rest of the paper. Naturally the headlines were all about some film star who was having an affair with her leading man, how could we survive without such relevant information? A big firm had closed down and hundreds had been laid off work, even the numerous and bloody wars had been relegated to page two. I was just about to close the paper in disgust when something caught my eye.

It was an article about a large shipment of diamonds that had been seized at Heathrow Airport. A large quantity had come into the country in packing cases containing animals that were destined for a small, out of city, zoo. It was not yet determined if the zoo had anything to do with it or whether the diamonds were to be extracted from the casing before they reached their destination. The haul was one of the largest they'd recovered and although their initial origins were more than likely to be South America, this particular batch had come in via North America.

"Eat up, Remi, it's getting cold." I took a mouthful of food and thought about the article. Where had I heard about diamonds recently? Not long ago, only in the past week, someone was talking about diamonds and their value. I put down my fork and looked at Gran.

"Oh my goodness, it was Tony, the *Mafia* guy," I said, not realising that this was not my inner-voice speaking.

"What was Tony and who's the *Mafia* guy? Gran asked, bemused.

"Look," I said, dragging the paper over to where she sat and tapping my fingers on the article about the diamond haul.

"Okay, I can see it, but what about it?"

"Gran, Gran, Gran, don't you understand. The other day when I was at Precious' house I heard the American guy called

Who Cares?

Tony, talking to someone on the phone. He was talking about diamonds and the huge value of them. He's got to be part of this smuggling gang, it all makes sense."

"No, Remi, it doesn't make any sense. You're putting two and two together and coming up with ten. Stop and think about what you're saying."

"I don't need to think, Gran, it's obvious. He comes from America, the diamonds come from America and he's had deliveries that he's had to pick up from Heathrow, and the other day I overheard him talking about diamonds."

"Remi," said Gran, getting agitated. "Tell me what he said about the diamonds; perhaps it will make more sense if you think it through again." I sat down and tried to calmly recall what I'd heard.

"He said that he knew about the diamonds and how valuable they were but first he had to find the dog. Oh, Gran, that's it," I said. "It's Barty! That's why he's in so much pain, they've smuggled diamonds inside of him. No wonder they were so upset at losing him and chased me across the park."

"Who chased you across the park, Remi and what has this all got to do with Barty?" I jumped out of my seat and grabbed the phone but who to ring first, the police or the vets? "Please, Remi, Calm down, you must have this all wrong, let's talk about it first."

"I can't Gran, Barty's life could be at risk. Don't you see…? They're diamond smugglers. That's why Barty's not been eating very well and why his stomach hurts. We need to get the vet to X-ray him today, now…"

Gran still looked confused but sometimes she does, all part of getting older probably. I knew I had to take control of this and deal with it myself. I phoned the vets but it went straight to answer phone, however it did impart a number to call in emergencies. I scribbled the number down and rang it immediately. Luckily, it was the same vet that had treated Barty when we took him in, his name was Martin Price.

"Martin this is Remington Hall-Smyth, we brought Barty, the Newfoundland, into you yesterday."

"Oh hi," he said, tentatively and I wondered fleetingly if he mistook my heavy breathing and our last encounter with a bit of a 'bunny boiler' situation!

"Have you X-rayed Barty yet?" I said, urgently.

"Erm… no, I looked in on him this morning and he didn't seem to be any worse, so I'm going to do it tomorrow."

"You have to do it today," I screamed, impatiently. "It's really important; I think he's been used in a smuggling ring."

"Excuse me,"

"Please Doctor, it's important that you X-ray him today, I'll explain everything when I see you and I'll probably be bringing the police with me."

"It'll take me half an hour to get there."

"Great, we'll see you there."

"See Gran, he took it seriously, he's going to X-ray him straight away. You get your hat and shoes on while I ring the police."

Okay, Gran didn't look overly convinced but nobody should step in the way of a runaway train and this time I knew I wasn't off the rails. I phoned the police and after giving them my details, which was infuriatingly time wasting, I explained the situation. They asked about Barty, his name, his breed, when had he come into the country. I looked at my watch and realised that fifteen minutes had already passed.

"I haven't got time to go through all this now; don't you see how big this is? This is a *Mafia* heist and you can get them." I gave them the address of the vets where Barty was being kept and with that I put down the phone, grabbed a pair of shoes and made my way out the door.

"Remi, you've still got pyjamas on, aren't you going to get dressed?" I looked down at my pink, spotted P.Js with dismay. I'd completely forgotten that I hadn't yet dressed.

"No time, Gran, I'll just pop a coat over the top." I looked around for shoes but none were to hand. I didn't have time to go upstairs and look for some so I put on the nearest things, which were a pair of pink, fluffy slippers. Oh well, all would be forgotten when I cracked the case of the biggest diamond haul and handed over London's branch of the *Mafia*.

We arrived at the veterinary surgery just as Martin Price was opening up and he didn't look best pleased. He looked worse still when he spied my pink slippers poking out from underneath my coat. We followed him in and were told to sit in the waiting-room while he went in to check on Barty and warm up the equipment. The silence was palpable. After all the excitement and intensity of the morning, the quiet and stillness was hard to bear. I got up and paced the room whilst trying discreetly to listen at the door.

The phone rang and I heard Martin pick up. I couldn't hear what was being said but I did gather it was the police. Good, at least they were taking this seriously. Before I could relay all this to Gran, the front door opened and two policemen walked in, at the same time the other door opened and Martin Price came out.

"If you could step this way gentlemen," Martin said, holding open the door. The two policemen gave a curt nod to Gran and me and went inside without saying a blooming word.

"Well, of all the cheek," I whispered to Gran. "That Price guy is trying to take all the credit for this, he didn't even introduce me. I should've gone straight to the papers."

"I hope poor Barty's okay Remi. What if they have to cut him open?" We waited for a few minutes more before I started pacing again. The door had a frosted pane but I squeezed my face up as close as I could. Suddenly the door opened and I fell slightly towards the policeman who'd opened it.

"Are you Miss Hall-Smyth?" he said, folding up a little notebook and placing it in a breast pocket.

"I am, Officer," I said, proudly.

"I wonder if we could ask you to come with us to the police station, there are a few questions we need to ask."

"Certainly," I said, picking up my handbag and giving Gran my, 'see I was right all along', look.

"Shall I come too? I'm her grandmother," she said, reverting to her full title.

"If you could stay here for a while, Mam and assist the vet with a few questions, I'll send another car to pick you up and bring you along later." Gran sat back down and looked towards the vet's door and then again at me.

"Will you be alright, Remi?"

Who Cares?

"Of course Gran, the officers here will make sure I'm given the protection I need, won't you, Officers?" There was no emotion in their eyes as they spoke.

"If you could just come this way, Miss..."

The journey to the station was short and relatively quiet. They asked a few questions about Barty, like what breed he was. It was polite conversation because I knew that they wanted to save the big questions for the Interview room and get it all on tape – all fresh and unrehearsed.

They helped me out of the car and guided me along the many corridors that made up the busy London police station. They took me through to a small room and kindly offered me a cup of coffee, proof, if ever I needed it, that I was a bit of a celeb.

Eventually everything was set up, the tape recorder was primed, two officers in attendance, one male and one female. After stating their names, the date and time, they started.

"For the record can you state your name?"

"I can indeed Officer; it's Remington Hall-Smyth." This continued with my address and date of birth.

"Can you explain how you came to be in possession of the Newfoundland dog that was taken to the veterinary surgeon yesterday?"

"Well if you've got enough time," I laughed. "It's a hell of a story."

"We've got time," they replied, their faces deadpan.

"To be honest Officer, how I got him isn't the point, it's what's inside him that matters."

"Ah yes," he looked down at his notes. "Precious diamonds, is that correct?"

"Yes, yes, that's right, so you've found them, I knew it."

"Actually no." said the female officer.

"What, you mean you've seen them on the X-ray, but haven't got them out yet?"

"No, we mean there are no diamonds in the Newfoundland."

"No diamonds? What about the pains in his stomach? He couldn't eat!"

"This particular Newfoundland has a sensitive dietary tract, not helped by the fact that he'd swallowed a sock."

"A sock, what sort of a sock? Did you check to see if there were diamonds in the sock?"

"Yes Miss. The Newfoundland passed the sock in the early hours of this morning. It was a pink sock with a little Scottie dog on it, but there were no diamonds inside."

Okay that was a little embarrassing... I'd been looking for that sock for days, it was one of a pair I wore to bed, but no diamonds, how could that be? I was so certain.

"Let's cut to the chase here," said one of the officers, getting agitated. "The story about the diamonds was a ruse to distract from the fact that this is a stolen dog which had to be taken to the vets. By telephoning us, it would look like you were the innocent party."

"But I am the innocent party," I shouted.

"Then tell us how you came to be in possession of the dog." I explained how I'd got Barty. I even explained the bit about how they were stuck together, which was very embarrassing.

"You say you're working for the owner of Precious but a Mr. James Brodie, who is the owner of Wisteria Cottage, and also the owner of Barty, the Newfoundland, says he is reliably informed that the lady who walks the dogs is called Analias."

"Yes, yes, that's right. That's me; I told James that my name was Analias."

"And why would you tell him that was your name when you've already stated that your name is Remington Hall-Smyth?"

"Because I overheard James talking about killing someone and burying them in the garden, I wasn't sure if he knew I'd heard him and I didn't want to give away my real name."

"Well this just gets stranger and stranger, doesn't it?" said the female officer again.

"Yes, it does," I said. "They're a really rum bunch in that house, I can tell you."

"No, Miss Hall-Smyth, I mean that you state you gave your name as Analias to Mr. James Brodie and yet he says he's never met or spoken to you."

"WHAT! Well then he's lying, not only has he spoken to me

on many occasions, he also asked me out, which I felt really bad about because he was going out with Marianne at the time but dropped her after he fell for me." The eyes of the female officer seemed to be wide open in amazement.

"Mr. James Brodie, perhaps you could describe him to us, seeing as you know him so well."

"Well, he's quite tall, blonde hair, wears expensive clothes and Calvin Klein pants." They both raised an eyebrow...

"Any accent?"

"Yes, he spoke with a very upper-class British accent, very well educated, I wouldn't wonder."

The male police officer shook his head and whispered something to the female, the only part of which I caught, was pathological liar.

"I'm not a liar," I shouted. "Everything I've told you is the truth; I've never stolen anything in my life." I jumped out of my seat and started making a dash for the door. I could hear Gran calling to me from outside somewhere. My breathing started to accelerate and I knew I was starting to hyperventilate again. Suddenly the room started to spin and I felt a cloud of darkness descend.

In the distance, I thought I heard someone call the duty-doctor and then someone rushed into the room claiming to be a doctor. I felt my head being lifted onto something warm and a hand brushing my face.

"Remi, it's okay." I opened my eyes a fraction and looked into a deep, dark-brown pair of eyes.

"Barty is that you?"

"Remi, it's okay, you're safe." For the third time in my life, I passed out completely. When I came round I was lying on a bed in a small, drab-painted room. Gran was sitting there holding my hand and as my eyes focused I could see she was smiling.

"I don't know how you do it, Remi. You're the only person I know that can see murder and intrigue around every corner and still end up taking home the honey and in this case, Sweetie, he's quite a honey!"

"Gran, what're you talking about, what's happening?" I

closed my eyes for a few minutes and drifted off. My head was spinning. No diamonds in Barty, and the police wanted to arrest me. Nobody seemed to believe me about Wisteria Cottage or the people who lived there. Strange hallucinatory images of different people all wrapped up together.

"Hey, Remi. How you feeling?" I opened my eyes and stared once more onto the deep-brown eyes that I'd woken up to before and my heart started to race.

"Norman?"

"That's me," he said, hands splayed.

"I don't believe it."

"Believe it, Remi. It's really me."

"How?"

"I've been back a year."

"A year," I gasped. "A year and this is the first time I've seen you."

"I'll tell you all about it later; let's get you out of here first."

"They think I've stolen a dog, Norman. I think they're going to arrest me."

"It'll be alright, Remi, I'll speak to them."

"NO," I shouted, jumping up. "Don't speak to them. There's *Mafia* involved Norman, you don't understand, it's dangerous. I think it could involve diamond smuggling."

"With these people who live at Wisteria Cottage?" he questioned.

"Yes. Tony, he's American, not that there's anything wrong with Americans of course," I spluttered.

"Of course." Norman rubbed his chin, but the small smile I thought I detected, shrank away.

"I heard him talking about some diamonds and that he knew how valuable they were but he had to find his dog first." I stopped for a moment allowing him time to take it all in. There was a muscle pulsating in his cheek.

"This diamond," he paused as if trying to recall something, "it wouldn't have been the Shwachman diamond, would it?"

"That's it," I said, touching my finger to my nose and pointing at him with the other hand, in true, *Give us a Clue* style. "That's the name, have you seen it in the paper, has it gone missing? I bet it's worth a fortune." He shook his head and a smile broke out all over his face.

"Remi, you're priceless, you haven't changed one bit. Stay here and let me talk to the police and then I'll take you home." Finally, after all the paperwork was completed, I was told I could leave and that all charges of theft had been dropped.

Gran was waiting for me and I looked anxiously around for Norman. "He's had to go somewhere, but he promised he'd come by tonight and explain everything."

The hours dragged as I waited for Norman to turn up but, worse than that, I had the strange feeling that Gran knew far more than she was letting on, as she kept singing, *'I Could Have Danced all Night'*, which was the song she always sang when she was in a *really* good mood. Gran phoned Penny and asked her to come over, then I phoned Juliet but despite trying not to tell her what it was all about, she weaned it out of me, like she always did.

"Oh wow, oh wow, I don't believe it. We're definitely coming, aren't we Becky?" Becky presumably had no idea where she was going or why but I knew she would be by Juliet's side.

By eight o'clock Juliet and Becky had been there an hour and Penny and Stephen walked in the door. Gran doled out the teas and coffees and I noticed that her pretty, little cups were out on display. Within a few minutes the doorbell rang and Gran jumped up to answer it. I looked round the room at my friends. Juliet was like a cat on a hot, tin roof; her excitement was palpable, she fiddled with her fingers and, occasionally, bit down the quick of one of them, Becky meanwhile, sat there not understanding what all the fuss was about.

Penny sat, relatively calmly, talking quietly to Stephen, only once or twice looking over in the direction of Juliet. I myself, well I tried hard not to think about anything. Of course I was excited to see Norman again but slightly angry that we'd lost touch in the first place and confused as to how he'd turned up at the police station.

As he walked in, Juliet immediately jumped out of her seat to embrace him and he reciprocated her affection in a fashion he had never done when we were younger. This was obviously a very good time to introduce Becky, I thought, feeling a little jealous. But before I could Juliet had returned to her seat and Norman had outstretched his hand.

"You must be Juliet's friend," he said, his broad smile showing acres of good dentistry. Becky, amazingly, blushed as she took Norman's hand. What a darn cheek. You're either gay or you're not, Missy...!

Even though I was sitting nearest to Juliet, Norman bypassed me and headed in the direction of Penny.

"Oh my goodness," I shouted. "There's something I have to tell you, Norman." I jumped up and stood between Norman and his, once old, nemesis, Penny. I had completely forgotten he would not know that we'd all become friends. I felt Penny stand up behind me and Norman placed his hands on my shoulders.

"It's okay Remi; your Gran told me all about Penny. Oh, and by the way, Remi, I think this is yours." He proffered a clear, plastic bag with something really gross inside. "Your sock, I believe!" I took the bag and sat back down in my seat. Norman looked at Penny for only a moment before putting out his hand.

"No hard feelings?" he said.

"Either way," she said, and after a short delay, they both laughed. Juliet and I both looked at each other. Penny had never let on that she knew about that last day at school. As she hugged Norman she looked over her shoulder at the pair of us and winked and we laughed. Still Norman didn't address me; instead he went on to chat to Stephen, which gave me a few moments to look at him properly.

His eyes were exactly the same, deep, honest, chocolate-brown with the slightest of gold flecks. He seemed taller somehow but not wiry; in fact he looked very fit with an athlete's proportion. He wore a beautifully tailored, cashmere jumper in a beautiful hue of baby pink and although it ran fleetingly through my mind that perhaps he, also, was gay, my pheromones were screaming differently, he oozed sex appeal. His *Diesel* jeans were well-fitted, and I do mean, *well-fitted,* and curved gloriously across his small, taught derriere, his long legs only accentuating his bottom even more.

Who Cares?

A small cough from Stephen's direction alerted me that everyone was staring at me, watching Norman. Hurriedly, I put out my hand and grabbed my cup and started drinking. Unfortunately, the cup was empty so I had to pretend to drink from the cup with exaggerated movements and loud swallows. Without saying a word to me, Norman stepped back and addressed everyone at the same time.

"I have a few things that I need to tell everyone, some of which, I should've told some people a very long time ago," he said, looking directly at Juliet and me. "Firstly though, I need to clear some things up for Remi. Before I left the police station today, I talked to the police and I can confirm that all charges of theft have been dropped." Juliet and Becky both looked in my direction and I mouthed that I'd tell them later. "Also they have looked into the people who are living at Wisteria Cottage and I'm sorry Remi, but they all check out."

"That's not possible," I said. "I've heard them talking about murder. One said he would take a knife to someone and then they said about bodies in the garden, and only the other day, about diamonds being smuggled."

"Remi, you've got this wrong. The house belonged originally to a business man who rented it out. He gave the house to his son, a Doctor James Brodie, who works at Great Ormond Street Hospital. When the son came to move in, there was already a sitting tenant there, Marianne, and she refused to move out. It was her dog that you used to walk, Remi."

"What about this guy called Tony?"

"Tony was just a friend of James and had been helping him search for something. He didn't live there and, since then, Marianne has moved in with him."

"Tony, wasn't he the American guy who chased you through the park, Remi?" Juliet asked, edging forward on her seat

"That's right," I said.

"No, that's wrong," said Norman. "James is the American guy and Tony is his friend. The blonde guy that you've been speaking to is Tony." I got out of my seat and paced the floor.

"Norman, you're a lovely guy and I'm really pleased to have you back, really pleased," I said, blushing slightly, "but the police have not done their homework on this. The blonde one is James, the dark one is Tony and Marianne has gone to live with Tony." I could tell he wanted to interrupt but I kept on going. "Who is the dark-haired, American guy?" I said, rushing it out quickly before he could say anything else.

"Remi, could you be wrong?" said Juliet. "I don't mean to be rude, you know that I love you, but sometimes when you hear something it seems to get distorted a little. Like that time when we were in Petticoat Lane and you overheard one of the market traders telling some little children that he had some chickens going cheap and you laid into him for selling chickens to children."

"That was a genuine mistake, nothing like this at all."

"It was exactly like this, Remi." She turned to look at the others. "He had some video footage of some baby chicks cheeping, that he was showing them."

"That is true, Remi. Unfortunately, sometimes you see something and without running it past your brain, you react with your mouth."

"*Et tu*, Gran," I said, feeling the knives coming out from all directions.

"Okay this is getting us nowhere, there's no need to apportion blame," said Norman. "Mistakes have been made and all that needs to be done now is sort them all out. I promised the police that I would make sure that Barty was returned to his rightful owner and that's the first thing I'm going to do." With that Gran got up from her seat and slowly went out into the kitchen to fetch him. I hadn't given a thought to old Barty and now he was going to be taken away from us. Worse still, I knew how much this was going to upset Gran and it was all my fault.

As Gran walked in the door, Barty went absolutely ballistic, jumping about all over the place, kissing Gran, jumping up at Norman, back to Gran, a quick lick for me and back again to the only person standing, which was Norman. He gave the dog a quick cuddle and taking hold of the collar, took him over to Gran and sat him down next to her. Barty snuggled his head into her lap and with tears in her eyes, she tucked her hands into his thick head of fur and kissed him. Norman leaned down and took

Gran's hand.

"The owner would like you to keep Barty; he thinks you've done a wonderful job with him and that he'd be far happier with you." Gran looked up, her eyes sparkling with unshed tears that suddenly gushed down her face. She grabbed hold of Norman's hands, pulled herself up and cuddled him tight.

"He's probably got no need of him, now the diamonds are gone," I said, whispering under my breath to no one in particular. Norman came and sat down on the arm of the chair I was sitting on and affectionately rubbed my back.

"There never were any diamonds, Remi, you just misunderstood but it's all been cleared up now."

"I'm sure it is, give Barty to Gran, tell the police I'm a fruitcake and everything is suddenly cleared up but I know the truth Norman, I heard him talking about the Schwarz diamond, or some such diamond, you told me yourself you'd heard of it."

"I have Remi and the police know all about it. Shwachman Diamond Syndrome is a rare genetic disorder affecting the pancreas, bone marrow and skeleton, it's a terrible illness that hasn't had the recognition it needs. Great Ormond Street is hosting a charity ball to raise awareness and funds for its research and it hopes to collect a lot of money. So you see, what you heard was perfectly innocent."

Reluctantly, I was forced to admit that probably, Dr. Brodie wasn't a *Mafia* godfather after all and, perhaps, I'd made a mistake with Tony as well, but then a thought occurred to me. I tried quickly to pass it round my brain but nothing came from it so I just spat it out.

"Okay a lot of this makes sense but why then did Tony ring my dad and say he was looking for me?"

"Perhaps, because he knew you had Barty and wanted him back," Gran said, still patting Barty's head. I got up from my seat and started pacing the floor with my hands behind my back in true *Miss Marple* style.

"If they knew I had Barty, then they would have known that I was the dog walker, so why didn't they just contact Lucy and she would have told them where to find me?"

"That's true," said Juliet to Penny. "There were easier ways to find her."

"No, it all leads back to the same thing, I overheard something I shouldn't have and they needed to eliminate me."

Norman burst out laughing again and the others followed suit. "Eliminate, Remi. That's a bit drastic isn't it?" said Norman, reaching into his pocket. "I guessed it would come as a bit of a shock to realise that you were totally and utterly wrong, Remi but I have Dr. Brodie's hospital I.D here which shows quite clearly that he is a doctor, actually he's a surgeon at Great Ormond Street Hospital and I'm sure they must vet all their doctors to make sure they have no *Mafia* links before employing them"

"You'd think so. Well I don't believe there's anything on that card that could ever make me believe differently. Whether you believe me or not, I know what I know."

"Let me see it," said Stephen. "I've had some dealings with the hospital and even more with forgeries." He took the identification and looked at it, then looked at it again. "Well I'd say this is pretty conclusive, this guy definitely looks dodgy."

"There you see," I shouted, jumping out of my seat and grabbing the I.D from Stephen. "At last, somebody can see it." I turned the I.D over and looked at it. It said Dr. James Brodie, with lots of letters after his name, Great Ormond Street Hospital, Children's ward. That part was perfectly correct; it was the photo that was unsettling. "This is you." I said to Norman.

"That's right," he said, looking very sheepish.

"Are you a spy, working undercover, trying to trap *Mafia* Tony?" He shook his head.

"Then what? I don't understand."

"Sit down, Remi, there's something I need to tell you. When I first started at Queen Mary's House, I had no friends at all. I wasn't in your class or even your year. So you never heard the register being called. If you had, you would've realised that my name was, and still is, James Norman Brodie."

"But everyone called you Norman."

"Everyone in my class called me 'Norman-no-friends', Remi. They called me it so often, it stuck and everyone in the school starting calling me it. When we started being friends, I was just so pleased to have someone to talk to; I didn't care what you called me. After that, it was too embarrassing to tell you."

"But we phoned your house and asked for you," chipped in Juliet.

"I told my stepmother what had happened so she knew who you meant when you called, my father was rarely there. Unfortunately when you telephoned me in America, my father answered and when you asked for Norman, he thought it was a crank call. It was years later that I found out that you'd called. When I tried to ring you, you weren't at the same address and you must have changed your phone. When eventually I qualified, I applied for a place at Great Ormond Street and took over one of my father's properties, which was Wisteria Cottage. I tried to find you, even roping Tony in to help. I had no idea that you were in my house and right under my nose all the time. Neither did Tony, after you told him your name was Analias"

We spent the evening reminiscing and catching up on all the things that had happened since we left school. Penny's story was, of course, the most remarkable. Norman – I mean James, wasn't the least bit surprised about Juliet and said he'd guessed it all along.

Eventually everyone started saying their goodbyes. Juliet and Becky promised to come back as soon as possible. Penny and Stephen invited us all over to dinner at Stephen's house, which was a real revelation. Gran winked at me and then said goodnight and kissed James fondly, thanking him again for Barty.

I walked James to the door but he turned before we got there. He kept one arm on the door frame and the other he encircled me with.

"I thought I'd lost you, Remi or I thought by the time I found you again, you would've been snapped up by someone else." His closeness and the intimacy of his words felt completely comfortable, even though we hadn't seen each other for so long. As I went to speak something caught my eye. On his arm was the watch I'd bought him all those years ago.

"You still have the watch?" He looked at it and then took it off and turned it over.

Who Cares?

"It says, 'all my love, Remi', it's the most precious thing I have." With that he leaned over and kissed me. It was like no other kiss I'd ever had. It was soft yet forceful, its passion held me and its tenderness expelled all the years that had gone before. I thought of Gran and her prophecy when I'd moaned about Stephen. She'd said that love was on the way; she said I'd know when it was the right one and as always, Gran was right.

Thirty-two

So there you have it. Twice fate dealt me what I believed to be a dirty hand, yet without those random acts of fate; my life would not have been so truly blessed. As Gran is often heard to say, life is like a rich tapestry but it takes a lot of stitches before we get to see the real picture.

Finding James again turned out to be one of my greatest blessings. The years had matured him into a far more confident and assertive person than he'd ever been at school, yet he still remained kind and thoughtful, surprising me with little notes, boxes of chocolates and little posies of flowers, all declaring his everlasting love. For my part, just seeing his dark, curly hair and those big, brown eyes made my toes curl up and when he kissed me, nothing else in the world mattered. Good looking, passionate, in love with me and a doctor, it was hard to believe that everything had turned out so well.

Wisteria Cottage became a second home, not only to me, but also to Gran who, like I'd predicted, fell in love with the gardens and made it her life-plan to sort them out and bring order to this little sanctuary within the suburbs. She, of course, was ably assisted by Barty, who knew quite a lot about digging and eating straw hats, apparently. Jack Marshall was also a frequent visitor to both Wisteria Cottage and Gran's house and I had the distinct feeling that she'd held him at arms length for many years because of me, which made it doubly-rewarding to see her so happy now.

James, as I now called him, although there were a few slip ups at first, was loved by everyone. Juliet and Becky were constantly on the phone and came over as often as their work would allow. We went on double-dates with Penny and Stephen and James added his expertise to help out with some of the many projects that Stephen managed. I was unsure how James would take to my father, given that he knew all about his chequered past but not only did they get on well when we met up together but they also got on famously when we ran with Barbara, Mary and the ladies.

I couldn't introduce James to all my Equality Healthcare clients as it would've been totally unethical to take anyone else into their homes. However there were two people that this did not apply to and they were Jenny and Henry. Jenny often played Poker and Bridge with Gran and the gang and even though I warned James not to be taken in by the quiet voice, beautiful face and snow white hair, he insisted that much of his university days had been misspent in playing Poker and set out to take them on, losing only a small fortune to both Jenny and Gran. Gran did, however, promise to buy bulbs and shrubs for his garden.

Strangely, I was more worried about James meeting Henry than anyone else, because in my heart I knew I wouldn't be able to bear it if they didn't get on but, luckily, my fears were unfounded. Still, it's strange how things work out, how fate twists the weave as it goes.

When I first met Henry, I thought he was going to die and yet here we were, as close as any two people could be. He had stepped in like a father and had mentored me in the important things in life. As in the war, Henry led by example. His honesty, bravery and straightforward talking earned him everyone's respect, not least of all, my newest love, James.

He did, of course, explain to James, that I was as nutty as a fruitcake and anyone taking me on would need extra insurance cover, but on the whole he conceded I was okay.

Life was perfect.

For the first time in my life everything was perfect, which naturally got me worrying.

Was this all too perfect, where could we go from here? What was going to happen to change it all?

You see, even though my brushes with fate had ultimately, with hindsight, turned out for the better, it didn't make it any easier to see the good side of a bad situation. Therefore when a gypsy came to the door selling pegs, I didn't hesitate. I grabbed my purse and paid over the top for a few wooden, dolly pegs.

And there it was… my big mistake. So thrilled was she with my bountiful contribution, totally uninvited, she offered me some foresight into my future. Now why would anybody do that?

More to the point why would anyone do that to someone who questions everything a hundred times over? Let's face it, if someone said I had a big heart, I'd be booking an appointment with the doctor straight away, just in case they had some divine intuition and knew that I had an enlarged heart that could give way at any moment.

I tried to stop her, I told her there was no need, and I even tried to shut the door saying I could hear the bath overflowing. Unfortunately nothing was going to stop her; it was like a scene from *The Shining* …here's Johnny!

As she put one foot in the doorway and grabbed my hand. "I see you saying goodbye to an elderly lady in a church," she looked up at me and then back down at my hands. I could see she didn't want to carry on, she made to pull away but I grabbed her and pulled her back to look at it hand again.

"What else?" I said.

"I'm sorry, my dear," she said, suddenly sympathetic. "It's Christmas and you're crying."

"The elderly lady, what does she look like?" She looked deep again into the hand.

"I can't see her face; she's wearing a big hat."

Before I could ask anymore, she took off with her ill-gotten gains to wreak havoc on the next householder. As I turned back inside I looked into the little sitting-room and saw Gran asleep in the chair, Barty by her side. This would be the cruellest trick of all, to have everything I wanted and yet lose something I loved so much.

There were still four months until Christmas and I tried desperately to put it out of my mind but I couldn't. Every time someone mentioned Christmas, a cold chill crept over me. The Christmas availability rota for work came through the door and I sent it back refusing to work over Christmas, just in case.

Who Cares?

As always Gran made plans for Christmas months in advance. She started singing Christmas songs in October and had wrapping paper and badly disguised shopping bags all over the house.

As I watched her, I wondered if this would be the last Christmas we would be sharing together. I knew that if it was I would always regret not getting involved and not making this the best ever Christmas for Gran. So I carried on worrying but I joined in the Christmas songs and in November I started putting up decorations. Even Gran was surprised that they were going up so early but I just didn't know how long she was going to have and I wanted to make the most of it.

One night, in the middle of November, I came home to find Gran speaking quietly on the phone. Her face looked a little concerned and as soon as she realised I was there she moved to another room. When she came back she was as bright as ever – in fact if anything, she was a little too happy. James came over later that night and when she went out to make some tea I quizzed him.

"Do you think Gran looks okay?" I asked. He looked at me strangely.

"I think she looks lovely, that colour suits her."

"No, not what she's wearing," I whispered. "Her health, does she look well to you or do you think she looks a bit peaky?"

He grabbed hold of the remote control ready to browse the channels but caught sight of the seriousness of my face.

"She looks perfectly healthy," he said, turning his face back towards the television screen.

"JAMES," I shouted, as quietly as I could. He dropped the remote and looked at me. "Go and have a better look at her, I don't think she's well." James leaned over, kissed my mouth and then got up and went into the kitchen.

He was in there quite a while and I could feel my heart starting to quicken. He came back and sat by my side.

"Now that you mention it, she does look a bit pale."

"Really... you thought she looked pale, but what does that mean?"

He held my hand and kissed it just as Gran came back.

Who Cares?

She placed the tea things down on the little table in front of me and as she looked up, she laughed. There was flour all over her face.

"What's wrong with you Remi? I'm perfectly alright. I'm not in the least bit ill; in fact I'm on top of the world." Naturally at that point she started singing *The Carpenters* song… the worst thing was James joined in and although he's brilliant at most things, a singer… he's not.

Despite both James and Gran's assurance that everything was fine, I still got the feeling that Gran wasn't telling me everything. She went out for whole days and didn't say where she was going.

One day I saw her speaking quietly to Stephen out in the kitchen and I got the instinctive feeling that Penny was trying to keep me talking so that I wouldn't interrupt them. When I mentioned it to Gran, she just laughed and said I was imagining it all.

The thing is… the thing that was really hard to get away from, was that I knew Gran. If she did have something wrong with her and she knew she was going to die, it would be just like her to arrange everything to save me doing it.

It was this fact that kept me worrying right through November and into December.

As we hit December and Gran's health didn't seem to be deteriorating I began to think on a slightly different track. The old gypsy didn't say which Christmas after all: perhaps it was next Christmas or even years from now.

Anyway, the Christmas spirit is very hard to get away from once it's in full flow. I had invitations to parties, drinks with the ladies, the theatre and, because I'd turned down work at Christmas, I had to work longer hours beforehand to make up for it.

It's fair to say that December went in a blink of an eye and I'm ashamed to say that I forgot all about the possibility of losing Gran, until, that is, Christmas Eve.

All our shopping had been bought. All our presents had been wrapped and we were sitting snuggled up on the couch together, the lights on the Christmas tree twinkling and Christmas songs playing quietly in the background.

James had other arrangements for the evening, so it was just to be us, Gran and myself.

Gran took my hand and patted it. "Do you know what, Remi? I'm really proud of you and the woman you've become."

"Oh Gran, have you been on the sherry again?" I asked, rubbing the back of her hand.

"No, Remi," she said, indignantly. "Well actually I did have a little one earlier with Jenny and Jack but that was ages ago and that's not why I'm saying this. I just wanted to take this time while we're on our own to tell you how much I love you and I wouldn't change anything about you."

I turned to look at her, there were tears glistening in her eyes and I took a tissue out of the box and wiped them away. As I did so, I could feel my own throat tightening and my own tears spilling down my face.

"Now see what you've done." I laughed, wiping them away.

"You know, I don't know how you've put up with me all these years," I said, looking down at the floor, unable to look her straight in the face.

"After Mum and Dad split up it couldn't have been easy for you, trying to take everyone's place, trying to keep me sane, always making me smile. I know I'm not the easiest of people to live with and I don't always do the right thing or say the right thing, but I do love you... more than anything, more than anyone in the world."

She kissed me lightly on the cheek and we hugged each other.

"Do you remember when I was little Gran, before the split, before everything? Do you remember when you and Gramps used to take me out and we used to dance along the streets and sing as loud as we could in the park and everyone would stand and stare at us, as though we were mad?" Gran nodded her head, tears once more rolling down her cheeks.

"Do you remember that thing we used to do?"

Gran looked up and smiled, the tears shining as the lights from the tree hit them. She remembered and nodded.

"Are you ready?" I said, holding up two, clenched fists

straight out in front of me. She nodded again and lifted her own hands. Together we touched fists together and shouted... "Best friends!" More tears came and we hugged each other tightly. At last Gran got up and made tea and, once the tears had subsided and the tea had done its job, we started laughing about some of the sillier times we'd spent together.

Our reverie was interrupted by the phone ringing and Gran jumped up to answer it.

"Oh that would be great, we'd love that. Pick us up in half an hour, and we'll be ready." I looked at her, confusion etched all over my face. Gran clapped her hands and danced her way round the room.

"It's Penny and Stephen, they've asked us to come to a Christmas service at the church. Wouldn't that be lovely?"

"Yes," I said, gingerly, although suddenly I was reminded of the Gypsy warning. Gran ran round the house getting ready and insisted that I make an effort.

"It's a church, Remi, you can't go in jeans and trainers, I'll find you something to wear. We're going to be the two best-dressed people in there." With that she skipped away again, insisting that I went and washed up.

After a quick wash I went back into the bedroom and there laid out on the bed was a beautiful dress that I'd never seen before. On the floor were shoes to match, and hanging on the wardrobe door was a beautiful pashmina in the exact colour of the dress. I looked over at Gran who, once more, had tears in her eyes but this time there was a huge smile on her face.

"I bought them for you for Christmas, Remi, but I'd love you to wear them to church today, I know they'd look lovely on you."

"Gran," I said, picking up the dress. "This is *Escada*, it must have cost a fortune; you can't afford this."

"I've already bought It, Remi and it's not about affording it, I wanted to buy you something special. Penny helped me find it and then helped me match up the shoes, do you like it?"

I picked it up and looked at it against myself in the mirror, it was gorgeous.

"Gran, I love it, I absolutely love it."

Who Cares?

"Then pop it on and I'll wait for you downstairs." As I turned I could see yet more tears on the brink. "I'd better go and have another cup of tea," she said, turning abruptly to go downstairs. "At this rate I'll be totally dehydrated."

Slowly, I put on the dress and shoes and looked at my image in the mirror. The dress was quite the most wonderful thing I'd ever worn. The body was in a soft-brown, floaty material with a fitted, Empire line. It was short with a jewelled under-bust embellishment and two rings with diamonds on the shoulders. The back had a deep V cut into it just before it flared out and the shoes matched beautifully. I pulled my hair back and let little tendrils fall gently around my face and down my neck. From my jewellery box I pulled out a single-stone necklace on a long chain and placed it the wrong way round my neck, so it lay perfectly in the V at the back.

Lastly I placed the soft pashmina round my neck and dropped it off my shoulders. The effect was quite staggering, I looked older somehow, matured, even intelligent looking. Now if I could just make it down the stairs without tripping over.

Gran stood back and whistled as I entered and, after curtseying, I did a little twirl.

"Wow, you look amazing," said Gran.

"Shame it'll be wasted on a few pensioners at the Christmas service," I said.

"No, Remi, it'll be packed, the Christmas service always is."

There was a beep outside and we both picked up handbags and hurried towards the door. As we reached it at the same time, I stood back to let Gran go through. Catching her arm as she went, I kissed her lightly on the cheek.

"Thank you," I said.

"Don't start me off," she said, waving her hand in front of her face. "Come on let's go and sing our hearts out." I laughed to myself. As if Gran ever needed an excuse to do that.

"Oops, my hat," she said, turning back to grab it from the hall. I felt my heart lurch at the thought of the Gypsy's prophesy coming true but Gran was down the path before I could talk to her.

The church was lit up beautifully on the outside, with

garlands of lights wrapped around some of the oldest trees and little, flickering candles in the porch way. By the open door, Stephen stood waiting to greet everyone in his full, clergy regalia, including dog collar. As each person reached for his hand he welcomed them by name and wished them a Merry Christmas. As Gran and I approached he leaned over and kissed us both.

"I'm so pleased to see you. This is such a special Christmas; it's nice to be able share it with friends." As he spoke he looked over our shoulder.

"She's just parking the car, she'll be here any moment," said Gran.

There seemed to be a moment's relief on his face and then, before greeting the next arrivals, he whispered, "Could I have a quick word with you both after the service, it won't take long but I could do with some advice." Gran agreed for the both of us and we headed on into the church.

As Gran rightly said, it was packed and as I scoured the lines as we passed, I was surprised to see it wasn't just pensioners, there were whole families rejoicing in the birth of Christ. Penny had told us there was a place reserved at the top in the first pew, so we made our way to the front.

The congregation was made up of complete strangers and yet many nodded and smiled as we wove our way along.

The service was lovely. There was a re-enactment of the baby Jesus being born and all the children were involved.

We sang well known hymns and at the end Stephen wished everyone a very merry Christmas. As the congregation started moving out towards the back of the church we moved against the tide and headed to the front.

The noise of everyone chattering and wishing each other well was quite deafening. So when Stephen suggested we move into the vestry, I was quite relieved. Soon Penny joined us with a tray of steaming, hot chocolate and some mince pies and we sat down on some little seats whilst Stephen disrobed.

Stephen explained that he wanted to start a new project in January, where he could go out into the community to bring comfort to the older members of the parish and perhaps persuade them to come into the church and join in all the activities.

Gran, naturally, was full of enthusiasm and volunteered to take him around to all the older people she knew. I also promised to contact work and ask if Stephen could be allowed to contact those that wanted to take part. We must have sat for twenty minutes or more chatting about their plans for the future and when I looked at Penny her face was radiant. Gran had certainly been right about the pair of them.

Eventually, Penny stood up and we took it as a sign that they needed to get on.

The cacophony of noise that had filled the church fifteen minutes ago had now subsided leaving an ethereal hush, as if God alone was worshipping there.

As we made our way out of the vestry, I was surprised to see that someone had already closed up.

All the main lights had been turned off leaving hundreds of little twinkling lights from around the pulpit and along the aisle.

As my eyes grew accustomed to the lighting, I started to make out movement. It was deathly quiet and yet I thought I could see faces as I looked out. I crept back a few steps and grabbed Stephen.

"I think there's another service about to start," I whispered.

"It's okay," he whispered back, "these things don't normally start without me." He laughed and pointed towards an opening near the lighted pulpit and, gingerly, we made our way over there. There were two steps going down from the raised area of the pulpit and as I put my foot out to step down, so someone took my hand as I nearly slipped.

"Whoops," I whispered. "Thank you so much."

"That's okay. I'll always be there to catch you." On hearing his voice, I looked up immediately into a pair of big, brown eyes.

"James…What the..?" I heard laughter and looked up. The nave of the church was filled and as I struggled to focus, each and every one of them lifted a candle into the air.

I caught sight of the first row and realised I knew them, Juliet, Becky, Penny, Gran, Jack and Percy. On the second row was Barbara, Hilda, Dolly and Gwen, all in beautiful dresses and matching hats.

Behind them I could see Jenny, June and Fred with Mavis. There were more pews behind and I knew everyone.

I looked back at James; his eyes were like that of a baby deer, kind, gentle and full of tears. To his side I saw my father and to his side I could see Henry.

Tears started to spill down my face and I could hear Gran crying from the other side. I turned to look at her and she blew me a kiss. James took my hands and held them close against his face.

"Remi, will you marry me?" My mouth was so dry I wasn't sure if the words I was forming would actually come out.

"What here, now?"

He laughed and took my fingers to his mouth and kissed them. "Right here, right now."

"But what about the white dress?" I said.

He laughed. "This is going to be a blessing in front of all your friends and family and then I'm going to take you away tonight, where we will be married on the beach and you will be wearing a white dress, I promise."

I heard a small cough from behind me and Stephen was there. "Are we ready?"

James looked deep into my eyes and said, "Well, are we?" I turned and stood shoulder to shoulder with James and kissed him deeply on the mouth.

"We are," I said.

The service was beautiful with quite the most romantic words I'd ever heard. The little tea lights flickered continuously and in the background I could hear the instrumental sounds of *Cavatina*. It was one of my favourite songs and I knew that Gran had chosen it specially.

As we stood, James pulled me close and kissed me and I could taste his tears in my mouth.

All our guests got up and clapped. Juliet raced to hug me and I could see Gran and Penny crying on each other's shoulders.

Outside everyone wished us well and I turned back to see Gran standing in the doorway alone. Gently I removed my arm from James who was about to object but, thankfully, was sidelined by Stephen.

"You knew all along?" Gran just nodded.

"I suppose nobody trusted me to know," I laughed, tears spilling yet again down my face.

"It was lovely this way," said Gran, dabbing at her face. I ran and threw my arms around her and we both cried together for a few moments. She stepped away and then took my face in both her hands. "God bless you, Remi."

I kissed her fingers and then took them down. I looked out at James and all my wonderful friends and then back at Gran. "He already has Gran, he already has."

DON'T FORGET TO JOIN DREW ON FACEBOOK

Acknowledgements

Thank you to Ray – for keeping the faith – when my own was wavering.

Ann (Kathy) – for rekindling the fire.

Laura – for playing the part of the beautiful Police woman!

Joan and Val – for their insightful appraisal and corrections.

To my mum – who *Else…* could Gran be?

Gaile – for believing in me and the book.

Everyone at UP Publications – who took on the mammoth task of editing it!

And finally
To the multitude of dedicated, domiciliary care workers that work tirelessly, everyday of the year, all hours of the day and night - to enable people to live out their lives in their own homes, independently and with dignity.

Who cares? – They do!

To follow Drew please visit
www.kinayle.com

Lightning Source UK Ltd.
Milton Keynes UK
UKOW040717210612

194756UK00003B/3/P